Dear Diary,

What was I thinking? ~~~~ a background in entertainment sim~~~~
I should have known that friends and family
and people who've worked with me within the
entertainment industry would read *All About Evie*.
I should have been prepared for the comparisons.
"Obviously Evie is your alter ego," said my husband.
"Do you really feel like that?" said my sister. *"I see
so much of you in Evie,"* said friends. And... *"I had
an audition that went down almost exactly like that.
Was that about me?"*

There are three answers to all of those questions.
Yes. Sort of. And no.

Didn't they read my Dear Reader letter?

*I admit, some of Evie's adventures and tribulations
are loosely based on my own experiences within the
entertainment industry. However, she and all of the
featured characters are purely fictional.*

I'm thinking I should make that my official
disclaimer. I'm thinking I should send a mass
e-mail to friends and family in preparation for
Evie's second adventure, because—*what was I
thinking?*—in this book Evie, Arch and Milo visit
Evie's native state (which happens to be *my* native
state) to bail her mom out of a scam. I'm thinking
I should call my mom. *"What you're about to read
is purely fictional! I didn't really do 'that' or 'that'
and I'm not going to do 'that,' although maybe I did
fantasize about 'that' one thing."*

Luckily, my friends and family have a sense of humor and actually adored Evie. As did multitudes of readers I have never met. Speaking of readers, I need to write a new Dear Reader letter for *Everybody Loves Evie*. I'm thinking of something along these lines...

To the readers who wrote and asked if I really have those costumes hanging in my closet... Yes. To the readers who wrote saying I'd have to fight them for Arch Duvall...you'll have to duke it out with Evie, because she's got a real thing for that bad-boy con artist. To those who wrote wondering about Evie and Arch's future, Arch and Milo's past, Milo's interest in Evie and Evie's new career with Chameleon—this one's for you. To those of you entering Evie's world for the first time, here's disclaimer #2: Although I extensively researched con artists and scams, Chameleon and A.I.A. are figments of my overactive imagination. Welcome to my world.

What do you think, Diary? What...oh, rats. My pen's running dry. Unlike my imagination. Heh. I'll be back.

Beth

Everybody Loves Evie

Beth Ciotta

HQN™

ISBN-13: 978-0-373-77298-8
ISBN-10:   0-373-77298-X

EVERYBODY LOVES EVIE

Copyright © 2008 by Beth Ciotta

This book is dedicated to my husband, Steve.
Your support and creative input stoked my
imagination and warmed my heart. I'm still flying.
All my love, always.

ACKNOWLEDGMENTS

To Cynthia Valero with affection and admiration. You went above and beyond, my friend. Here's to fanciful and satisfying storytelling.

To my editor, Keyren Gerlach (a dynamo and fellow animal lover)—thank you for embracing my characters and helping me to make their story shine! To *everyone* at HQN Books—my eternal gratitude for your tireless and wondrous efforts. To my agent, Amy Moore-Benson—your expertise and enthusiasm is priceless. How fortunate I am to be on this motivated and creative team.

Sincere appreciation to all of the readers, booksellers and librarians who recommend my stories to friends and patrons. Thank you for spreading the joy!

Special thanks to those who cheer me on and keep me going... Pom-pom shakers and friends extraordinaire Heather Graham, Mary Stella and Julia Templeton. The world's sweetest stalker-fan, Laurie, and her effervescent sister, Elsie. The always smiling JoAnn Schailey. My friends and coworkers at the Brigantine Branch of the Atlantic County Library—Sue, Alicia, Lesa, Denise, Beth, Doris, Jean Marie and Taylor. And to my wondrous family and diverse circle of friends. I am blessed!

Also available from Beth Ciotta

All About Evie
Seduced
Charmed
Jinxed
Lasso the Moon

**And look for Evie's next
Chameleon Chronicles adventure,
coming soon!**

Everybody Loves Evie

CHAPTER ONE

London, England
Trafalgar Square

CRIME DOESN'T PAY. Unless you're a professional grifter who's never been caught. Then, yeah, boy, *ka-ching!* Especially if you're playing the long cons. Time-intensive scams such as bank-examiner schemes, pigeon drops and investment swindles garner thousands, sometimes millions of dollars. Short cons, hit-and-run hustles, can be nearly as lucrative, depending on the grifter's charm and the mark's greed. Not that I understand the mechanics of all of these swindles. But, thanks to the man I'm sleeping with, I'm learning.

My name is Evie Parish and I'm a professional performer. At least that's how I used to make my living, singing, dancing and acting on the stages of the not-so-glitzy Atlantic City casinos. Unfortunately the entertainment industry has a bugaboo about mature women. My career, like my fifteen-year marriage, recently hit the skids. Not that I'm bitter. Okay, that's a lie. But I'm learning to let go. Over forty does not equal over the hill. In fact, I've never felt more alive. Creative sex and a challenging new career do wonders for the spirit. Just now, my thoughts were on the latter.

Both guilt and exhilaration rushed through me as I pocketed twenty British pounds and exited a touristy pub. My eyes registered the boxy black cabs and red double-decker buses navigating Trafalgar Square's congested streets, but instead of revved engines and squealing brakes, all I heard was the funky, eclectic soundtrack from the *Ocean's Eleven* remake. The caper music, though solely in my head, fueled my getaway and fantasy mind-set. I'd had to channel a female version of Brad Pitt's "Rusty" in order to pull off that shenanigan. I had a conscience. Rusty, the crooked card magician, did not.

Walk, don't run, I told myself. *Blend. Be a chameleon.* A no-brainer for an actress who's been everything from a premenstrual pumpkin to a roller-skating cowgirl, right? Right. Considering the heavy pedestrian traffic and considering that I'd dressed in black (London's denim), it was easy to lose myself in the crowd. I buttoned my peacoat against the brisk evening breeze. Even though I was wired tight, my stride was loose, my expression calm. My brain replayed my mentor's advice should the bartender come sprinting after me.

If the mark seems confused, go on the offense. If the mark seems suspicious or agitated, run.

But no one chased me down. No one yelled "Thief!" When I reached the corner of Northumberland and White-hall, I pumped my fist in the air and performed my signature victory dance. "I did it!"

"Bloody hell, Sunshine. *Dinnae* announce it to the world." Arch Duvall, a reformed con artist with a hot body and a sexy accent, clasped my arm and guided me across the bustling intersection.

I still couldn't believe I was with this guy. As in, having a pulse-tripping fling with this guy. Me, a contemporary Doris Day. Perky, blond (this month anyway), a renowned Goody Two-shoes. Meanwhile, *he* reminded me of the hunky leather-clad Scot in that *Tomb Raider* movie. Droolworthy physique, dark cropped hair and a perpetual five-o'clock shadow, hypnotic gray-green eyes and a devastating smile. Before you label me a shallow horn-dog, let me tell you his appeal runs much deeper than his rebel good looks. He isn't merely a fascinating confidence man, he's a performance artist. A kindred soul.

"It worked exactly like you said," I blurted. "I paid for my ale, played the dumb American when the bartender gave me all those weird coins in change. *Too confusing,* I told him. *Let me trade in ten one-pound coins for a ten-pound note, please.* He handed me the ten-pound note and I passed him the coins, only—"

"He told you you were one pound short."

"I pretended to be flustered. *Really? Are you sure? Maybe you dropped one. Oh, forget it. Just give me back the coins and—*"

"Then you really confused the *shite oot* of him. I was there. I saw." He shushed me and hurried me along.

"I just can't believe it," I said in a rapid-fire replay. "Because I distracted him by talking a blue streak and changing my mind about what I did and didn't want, I walked out of there ten pounds ahead of the game!"

"I know the scam, love. I taught it to you, yeah?"

Yeah. "Change raising," he called it. A short con. But if you scammed ten to fifteen cashiers in a day, you could make a decent score. It was one of a few grifts Arch had taught me this past week. The first I'd tried out on anyone but him.

Reality blindsided me like a ruthless heckler. Said

heckler being my conscience, and it screamed, *Crook!* I couldn't tune out or ignore the taunt, as it was—*gulp*—true. "We have to go back." I spun on the rubber heel of my high-top sneakers.

Arch caught my elbow and swung me back around.

"I know, I know. Returning to the scene of the crime is risky."

"There was no crime, love. He *gave* you too much change because he *allowed* himself to be distracted, yeah?"

"But his drawer will come up short tonight. He'll get in trouble, maybe even be accused of stealing." Deceiving the guy was one thing. Getting him fired—or worse—was unacceptable. Plus, the money in my pocket wasn't mine. Unlike Arch, I didn't see the difference between stealing someone's money and persuading them to *give* it to you.

"It's taken care of."

"What?"

"I know the owner. I also know you." He smiled down at me, a devilish grin that accelerated my already zipping pulse. "I only want you losing sleep over one thing, yeah?"

Nudge, nudge. Wink, wink. Sexy thoughts superseded guilt but then gave way to confusion. "Wait a minute. You mean. I didn't con the bartender for real?" For me, it wasn't about the score but the scam itself. Proving to myself—and Arch—that I had the chops.

"You conned him, love." His mesmerizing eyes twinkled with pride and…

Uh-oh. *Zing. Zap.* I knew that look. Not that we needed a reason other than that we were hot for one another, but anytime I went against my uptight Midwestern upbringing and deviated from the straight and narrow, Arch got turned on. Did I mention the creative sex? My hoo-ha ached in anticipation. His flat, newly inherited from his grandfather, was in Bloomsbury. A good thirty-minute walk, and that's if we hustled. Knowing us, we'd never make it that far. We'd end up in a coat closet or a darkened alley, making out like two hormonal teenagers. In the short time I'd known the man, we'd groped and shagged, as Arch called it, in some very unusual places. Mostly because I was opposed to doing it in bed missionary-style. Too intimate. Losing my heart to a born manipulator would be a mistake. Because of a cheating ex-husband, my emotions were already fragile. *Don't think about Michael. Don't think about how he's having a baby with his twentysomething girlfriend.*

Don't think. Live. I cupped the back of Arch's head and pulled him down for a kiss. Quick but deep. Lots of tongue. *Zap.* There it was. That white-hot connection that consistently melted my bones. Even as I eased away, something I dared not name sparked between us.

"Bollocks."

I smiled because that was his signature term for *I'm toast.* Leaning in, I felt John Thomas—a heck of a big guy—straining against his trousers. "Maybe we should get a cab."

He eyed the heavy traffic. "We can walk it faster, yeah?" He nabbed my hand and set a brisk pace, guiding me through hordes of international tourists and locals. I noted the Mall, a central square featuring fountains, bronze lions and a massive phallic monument to Admiral Nelson, on my left. Up ahead on my right, St. Martin-in-the-Fields, an eerie-looking church that dated back to the 1700s. Yes, I'd had my nose in a guidebook. Plus, Arch had toured me around, happy to show me the city he considered his second home. Everything about London, from the historical landmarks to the Beefeaters and bobbies to the apple-red telephone booths, was of curious interest to me.

Kind of like my companion. My mentor, my lover. A sexy bad boy with a sensitive heart and a James Bond aura. Okay, instead of a license to kill, he had a license to shill, but the man was still double-oh-seven *hot.* Sean Connery-esque accent. Pierce Brosnan wit. Daniel Craig intensity. Plus, like Bond, he worked for a government agency. Not a U.K.-based operation—go figure—but the covert branch of a U.S. agency. I'd never heard of the AIA—Artful Intelligence Agency—and I didn't know what they did exactly, but the specialty branch Chameleon busted up nefarious scams. Special Agent Milo Beckett, who'd founded the team, relied heavily on Arch's grifter expertise. Two weeks ago Arch had acted solo, hiring a civilian actress—me—to portray his wife on a couples' cruise. His goal: to take down the ruthless, unscrupulous *scum* artist who'd murdered his grandfather and who'd cheated countless seniors out of their savings.

I'd landed what I'd thought was a legit acting gig through a quirk of fate at a time when my life was falling apart. Turned out we were both in the midst of a personal crisis and proved balm for each other's emotional wounds. Just now, we were both on the mend. Not that sex was a cure-all, but it certainly didn't hurt.

Since Arch kept a tight rein on his emotions and personal history, I didn't know him well. But I liked him. Call me bewitched. The man was complicated and intriguing. A master of disguises. Charismatic and dangerous. He could charm the devil into trading his pitchfork for a halo. By his own admission, he could not be trusted. I didn't wholly believe that, although I was stymied by his absolute lack of guilt pertaining to his past grifts. *There are scam artists and scum artists,* he'd once told me. Dinnae *confuse the two.* Did I mention he was slick? Just like my ex-husband, a silver-tongued, double-talking entertainment agent. *S-L-I-C-K.* Arch couldn't be more wrong for me, and yet he felt like the perfect fit.

Lost in my thoughts, I heaved a dramatic sigh. "I'm screwed."

"Not yet, lass. But soon."

That promise sizzled through my skin and ignited a fire down below. My brain and body burned with immediacy. This was my last night in London. My last night to enjoy whatever it was Arch and I had going, because once we were both back in the States, whatever *this* was had to end. He didn't know that yet. He also didn't know that I'd talked Beckett into hiring me as a full-time member of Chameleon. I'd been waiting for the right time to tell him, like maybe three minutes before I got on the plane. I didn't want to break off with Arch, but I didn't want to compromise my new job, either. Beckett had a no-hanky-panky-between-team-members policy. This was my shot at being a real-life Charlie's Angel. A kick-butt crime fighter. The casinos didn't want me, but my country did. Powerful motivation for sacrificing a fling. Clichéd as it was, I hoped we could still be friends.

The thought of possibly severing our unique connection made me sad and reckless. I squeezed his hand and jerked him toward a small, chic restaurant. "There's gotta be a coat closet in there."

He tugged me in the opposite direction, hustled me through the doors of the National Portrait Gallery.

"You're kidding."

The sizzle in his smile said otherwise. He guided me up the stairs into a main concourse, a chaotic room brimming with museum visitors.

My skin prickled with two parts excitement, one part dread. A darkened alley would've been preferable. Seedy but less crowded. Then suddenly we were in a deserted hallway. We passed two doors. The third was ajar. Arch tugged me over the threshold. Not a coat closet but a janitor's storage room. Close enough.

I jumped his bones.

The unexpected impact knocked him against the wall of shelves. A metal bucket fell and clipped his shoulder— "Dammit!"—then clanged to the floor.

"Sorry. Let me kiss it and make it better." I shoved his leather blazer off his shoulders. What I really wanted was to rip off his shirt and lick the Celtic tattoo banded around his bicep. That tattoo drove me wild. Only I couldn't get to the tattoo because his jacket snagged at his elbows. "I guess I should've waited until we stripped and then jumped you."

"Do you really want to get naked in a room full of cleaning products, Sunshine?"

"Good point." My luck, I'd topple into a bin of toxic rags and break out in hives. I wiggled against his arousal. "Maybe just *half*-naked."

"You're killing me, yeah?" He whirled and pinned me against the wall, kissing me into a stupor. He was good at that—kissing me stupid. I willed my knees not to buckle as he worked the buttons of my peacoat. I fumbled with his belt buckle. His fingers skimmed beneath my long-sleeved T-shirt and expertly unclasped my lacy bra. I moaned my approval even as my mom chastised from afar, *Are you crazy?*

Mom and I didn't see eye to eye on a lot, but I had to agree. Fooling around in a popular museum wasn't the brightest idea. Then again, I was in idiot mode. I reached into Arch's briefs and palmed JT—big, hard and ready to rock...*me.*

Arch caressed my breasts and whispered sexy expletives in my ear as I stroked his admirable length. Scottish accent plus dirty talk equals me squirming and begging. "Touch me." Crazy talk. What if someone walked in? Even as that thought crossed my lust-soaked brain, I shoved his pants down over his hips, gasping as he sucked my earlobe and unzipped my pants. I almost came undone the moment his fingers dipped into my panties. I groaned, anxious and disappointed when his hand stilled—climax interruptus. "Why—"

"We've got company, love."

CHAPTER TWO

YOU KNOW THOSE PEOPLE who constantly break rules and never get caught? I'm not one of them.

Escaping that pub after pulling that short con had to be a fluke. The one time I played hooky in high school… busted. The one time I ignored the no-right-turn-on-red sign…busted. So, naturally, the one time I attempted to have sex in a museum's broom closet had to end badly. Naturally, the door creaked open.

Busted.

Heat flooded my cheeks, leaving the rest of my formally hot-to-trot body cold. Could've been worse, I rationalized in a fluster. We could have been full monty. We could have been boinking like bunnies. This was just embarrassing, especially for Arch. Even though my shirt was askew, he'd been caught with his pants down. Luckily for him—and the wide-eyed cleaning man—his three-quarter-length leather jacket covered his spectacular butt.

"What the—"

"Dammit, honey," Arch said in an American accent, "I knew this was a bad idea." He winked at me while subtly removing his hand from my private region. Thank goodness his six-foot body shielded my much shorter self. "The wife and I are on our honeymoon," he said, turning slowly to face our intruder. "Can't blame us for… Marvin?"

"Ace?" The janitor cleared his throat, closed the door with a firm thud. "Do me a favor and pull up your trousers. Don't fancy seeing your naughty bits, eh? Blimey."

Marvin chuckled in an easy manner that intimated he and Arch were friends, or at least on friendly terms. Curiosity almost bested my mortification. Almost. Cheeks flaming and bra willy-nilly, I pulled down my shirt and zipped up my pants.

"Guess there's not a lock you can't crack," Marvin said.

"The door was open," said Arch.

"The new kid must've been in here. He's always forgetting something—scrubbing the toilets, polishing the banisters, locking the supply closet. A good bloke but easily distracted. Spend half my days cleaning up after him." He snorted and chuckled. "Get it?"

Arch whispered in my ear. "As often as I can." Eyes twinkling, he angled away, and Marvin and I got our first clear look at each other.

"Who's the bird?"

"Evie," Arch said while tucking in his shirttails.

"Pretty bit of stuff."

"Thanks," I said, hoping that was a compliment. I didn't *feel* pretty. I felt self-conscious. Marvin, who looked to be in his sixties, wasn't leering exactly, but he was definitely checking me out. I smoothed my passion-mussed hair from my face and hoped my long-lasting lipstick hadn't smeared.

"Known this boy since he was in short pants," he told me while pushing his electric floor buffer thingy into the corner. "Started hanging around the museum when he was a kid. Inherited an appreciation for art from Bernard—along with his fine eye for women." He clucked his tongue in wonder. "Ace always gets the pretty birds."

"Marvin was a good friend of my grandfather's," Arch said, clearing up one relationship while I pondered countless others. Exactly how many *birds* were we talking? Was he currently involved with any of these other women? Why hadn't I asked? Why had I just assumed that I was special and that we were exclusive? Talk about naive. Or stupid. Just because we'd worked one sting together. Just because he'd bought me a plane ticket and said he wanted my company while he tended to his grandfather's estate. That didn't make me the girl of his dreams, just the girl of the moment.

Marvin's keen blue eyes ping-ponged from Arch to me and back. "You didn't really get married, did you?"

"Hell, no." Arch glanced over his shoulder. "No offense, love."

"As if I'd shackle myself to you. No offense, *Ace.*"

Marvin cackled.

Arch grinned.

I wanted to smack them both.

"Can we talk?" the older man asked Arch.

"Sure."

"In front of her?"

"Aye."

That would have earned him points except they inched away and lowered their voices. I took the opportunity to reach up the back of my shirt to fasten my bra. I pretended not to listen.

"Guess you came back to look after Bernard's interests," Marvin said.

"Aye. He willed me his flat and everything inside. Spent the last week going through his belongings, yeah?" He glanced my way, his mesmerizing eyes warm with affection. "Evie's been a big help and a pleasant distraction."

My heart performed gymnastics.

"Distraction, eh?" Marvin shook his head. "I'm all for a bit of spontaneous slap and tickle, but a tumble in the museum? What if you'd been rousted by someone other than me? The last thing you need is a run-in with Scotland Yard."

"*Dinnae* think it would've come to that, mate."

"Don't be so sure. These are tense times. Bloody terrorists. What's this world coming to? Violence everywhere, even in our own circle. Look what happened to Bernard—God rest his soul."

Arch shifted his weight and looked away.

"Didn't see you at the funeral, son."

"I mourned in my own way."

The older man nodded. "There's a rumor circulating about Simon the Fish."

"If it has anything to do with him being dead," Arch said, "it's fact."

Marvin's nose whistled with a sigh of relief. He moved forward and clapped an arm about Arch's shoulders. "We knew you'd see justice done. I'll pass on the good news."

His words sent a chill down my spine. Even though I'd been excluded from the conversation, I knew they were talking about Arch's grandfather, a career art forger who'd been lured out of retirement and ultimately double-crossed. I'd helped Arch perpetrate a ruse that was supposed to end with this Simon-the-murdering-Fish behind bars. Instead he'd ended up dead. Up until now,

I'd blamed myself since I'd unwittingly botched the sting. If not for me, Simon wouldn't have pulled a revolver. There wouldn't have been a struggle that resulted in Simon being shot and Arch holding the smoking gun.

I hadn't witnessed the actual shooting because I'd been disoriented, then knocked out, but Arch had claimed self-defense. I believed him. Beckett believed him. Then again, the agent had advised Arch to disappear and lie low while he smoothed things over with the AIA.

I'd assumed the smoothing over had more to do with Arch and Beckett acting outside of agency jurisdiction than with the actual shooting. After all, it had been, as they say in the movies, a clean kill.

So I'd been told.

Ugly thoughts riddled my brain, causing my neck to prickle with a nervous rash. "I can see you two have some catching up to do. Besides, I need to use the ladies' room. Excuse me." I stepped into the hall, desperate to purge my escalating suspicions.

"Think she's embarrassed, son," I heard Marvin say behind me. "Can't blame her. What are you now? Thirty-four?"

"Thirty-five."

"A bit old to be snogging in a closet. If you didn't want to take her to Bernard's place, you could've…"

The door clicked shut. Even though I could no longer hear them, the conversation clanged in my head, especially that part about Arch's age. "Bastard."

Anger propelled me down the hall. I made it halfway up a set of stairs before Arch snagged my arm. "The privy's in the opposite direction, yeah?"

"I'm not going to the privy."

"Where are you going?"

"Out."

"That's not *oot*. That's up."

"Then I'm going up. Please let go." I slipped his grasp and continued on.

"You're pissed."

"You lied to me."

"Aboot?"

"About your age."

"For fuck sake, Sunshine."

I hit a landing and pushed through a door. I really wanted to hit and push Arch, but I wasn't the violent type and I'd just walked into a populated gallery. Good girls don't cause scenes. And neither do Chameleons in training. *Blend, Evie, blend.* I pretended interest in a painting. I pretended to be calm. "You told me you were thirtynine."

"I told you what you wanted to hear."

"I wouldn't have slept with you if I'd known you were six years younger than me."

"Aye, you would have," he said with damnable confidence. "You just would have obsessed on it afterward."

We'd had this conversation before. It was part of my personal crisis. He didn't understand my preoccupation with my age. Then again, he wasn't an over-forty female trying to survive in a youth-obsessed industry. These days when auditioning performers, ninety-eight percent of the entertainment executives focused on youth and beauty. Talent wasn't a requisite as much as a bonus. Michael, my ex, had told me that himself, and, as an agent who booked performers for buyers, he would know. To add injury to insult, after fifteen years of blissful—okay, *amiable*—marriage, he'd dumped me for a twentysomething lingerie model. So, yeah, I had a big flipping chip on my shoulder regarding age.

I hadn't given that obsession much thought over the past two weeks. Not being in Atlantic City and losing gigs to girls half my age and with a quarter of my experience helped. Not being around Michael and his young squeeze helped. Having sex with a charismatic hunk and learning the ins and outs of an exciting new career worked miracles.

Now the anxiety that had ruled my life pre-Arch was back. My jaw ached—remnants of TMJ. My skin itched—a nervous rash. Rejection had one-two punched my self-esteem. "I don't want to go back." I turned away from the paintings, pinpointed the nearest exit sign.

"I said goodbye to Marvin."

"I'm not talking about the closet." And I didn't want to talk about Marvin. I didn't want to know the connection between an art-museum janitor and an art forger. I didn't want to know who the collective "we" was and how they'd known Arch would seek justice. Mostly because Marvin made justice sound like revenge. I didn't want to know why Arch should be leery of Scotland Yard. Although, given his shady past, there were probably dozens of reasons. I didn't want to know about any of that because I feared the truth was more than my squeaky-clean morals could handle.

Bottom line—I wasn't okay with what Arch and his grandfather used to do. I wasn't okay with his past, because his past was full of deceit. I'd fallen for the new Arch. The man who used his intelligence and experience to bring down the bad guys. After meeting Marvin, I wasn't sure that Arch had forfeited his old lifestyle. Obviously he hadn't cut ties with old cronies. Not that I intended to kiss off my entertainment friends when I started with Chameleon. I couldn't imagine life without my best buds. Then again, Nicole and Jayne weren't criminals.

"Keep clenching your teeth like that," Arch said, "and your jaw's going to lock."

I hoped not, but it was possible. It had happened before, and he'd witnessed an episode firsthand. TMJ was stress-related. I needed to relax. "I'm fine," I said, even as I felt a twinge of pain. *Chill, Evie, chill.*

"You said you didn't want to go back," he said as we breached the main doors. "Back where?"

"To where I was. What I was."

He lit a cigarette—amazing how he made a nasty habit look sexy—and walked beside me in silence as I headed toward Leicester Square. Probably trying to get a bead on my mind-set. Welcome to the club.

Though it was early spring, there was a blustery nip in the air. At least it wasn't raining. Although it was damp and gray. All I needed to augment my dismal mood was a blanket of London's famous fog. Hands stuffed in my coat pockets, I breezed past the discount ticket booth and cut through the heart of the theater district. I saw the play and movie marquees, heard music from a nearby dance club. I imagined countless singers, musicians, actors and dancers warming up for a night's performance. My old life. My stomach spasmed just thinking about my washed-up career. "I have to move on."

"You need to slow down and talk plainly, yeah?" He nabbed my elbow and pulled me onto a park bench.

I didn't look at him. I couldn't. "This isn't going to work."

"What?"

"Us."

He blew out a stream of smoke. "Because I'm a few years younger than you?"

"Six years younger. And, no, that's not the reason, though it doesn't help."

"Because I lied *aboot* my age?"

"No."

"Then what?"

"I could name a million reasons."

He crushed out the cigarette. "Name one."

"Milo Beckett hired me."

No reaction.

"I'm going to work full-time for Chameleon."

He looked at me, expressionless.

He was good at that, not telegraphing his thoughts and emotions. Still… "I know what you're thinking."

"Yeah?"

"You think I'm not cut out for it. That I'm too nice."

"There is that."

"I'm capable of fighting my nature. I'm capable of change. I *have* changed."

"You'd never survive in my world, Evie. You feel too deeply."

"What world are we talking about, *Ace?* Your old world or your new world?"

"One and the same, yeah?"

"No. Smoke and mirrors. Confidence games. I get that similarity. What I don't get is your inability to differentiate between conning innocent people and conning people who prey on the innocent. Your past grifts were for personal gain at someone else's expense. Chameleon grifts are for the greater good."

"You can't cheat an honest man, and I never conned anyone who couldn't afford the loss."

He didn't sound or look angry, but my internal radar blipped. I'm pretty sure I'd just insulted him. There was always a calm before Arch's storm. "The difference between a scam artist and a scum artist, huh?"

"Aye."

Night and day to him. Bad versus evil to me. He was right. I'd never cut it as an honest-to-gosh grifter. Guilt would eat me alive or land me in jail. But those same morals, coupled with my artistic nature, told me I was a born Chameleon. They conned cons. Entrapped sociopaths through elaborate and sometimes not-so-elaborate schemes. Smoke and mirrors. Deceiving for the greater good. I wouldn't feel guilty about duping scum artists. I'd feel like a superhero.

"After a devastating divorce and a year of celibacy, I've rediscovered passion, thanks to you. Now I need purpose. A new goal—because I'm not going to invest in plastic surgery, BOTOX injections and a lifetime supply of diet pills just so I can perform in the casinos."

"Glad to hear it."

"I'm a decent singer and dancer and a damn good actress."

"Absolutely."

"Those acting skills, along with my excellent memory and a talent for sleight of hand make me perfect for Chameleon. I can tap dance with the best of them. All I need is to learn the steps. You've been teaching me the basics. You've seen me in action. You know I can do this."

Looking up at the darkening sky, he dragged both hands over his head and laughed low. "Bloody hell."

"What?"

"All this week I thought I was educating you so that you *wouldnae* fall prey to another scam."

This wasn't news to me. While sightseeing on St. Thomas, I'd fallen for a street hustle. As a result, Arch had designated himself my mentor. In a world where a sucker is born every minute, he'd declared me a grifter's dream. Gullible and trusting. Easily persuaded and deceived. If I learned how the grifts work, I'd spot them coming a mile away.

"In truth, I gave you a crash course so that you could impress Beckett when you reported for your first day." He angled and regarded me with an amused expression. "You snowed me, Sunshine."

"You think I manipulated you?"

"Didn't you?"

My stomach clenched.

"When did Beckett hire you?"

"The day I woke up in the hospital."

"Ten days ago. Yet I'm just hearing *aboot* it."

I wet my lips, scratched my neck. "I tried to tell you at the airport, before we all flew out of La Romana. You cut me off and…" I blew out a breath. "I was going to tell you first thing when you picked me up at Heathrow, but you distracted me and…"

"Yeah?"

"Well, the days just sort of whizzed by and the right moment never…"

"Uh-huh. You *didnae* tell me Beckett hired you because you were afraid I *wouldnae* approve. You worried I'd stop teaching you the basics, yeah?"

"No."

He stilled my nervous scratching.

"Maybe." My brain acknowledged the ugly truth. "Oh, God, Arch. I used you."

"*Dinnae* look so stricken, love. I'm impressed."

"I *manipulated* you."

"I *didnae* feel a thing. Either I'm slipping or you're

gifted. A bit of both, I imagine." He clasped my hand and skimmed his thumb over my knuckles. "Beckett has a brilliant eye for talent. He's also obsessed with his work. If he hired you, it's because he believes you're a valuable asset to the team."

My heart pounded. I wasn't sure if it was because of Arch's touch or Beckett's belief. Probably both. "What do you think?"

His mouth quirked. "I think you've changed."

I took that as a compliment. Three weeks ago, my self-esteem had been at an all time low, but instead of sticking my head in the sand, I'd taken a walk on the wild side. For the first time in years I felt genuinely motivated and happy. Well, except for now. Just now I felt ill. "I hope you don't think I slept with you just to learn your secrets."

"You slept with me because you wanted me, yeah?"

I rolled my eyes, but it was true. "Please don't make me say it out loud. Your ego is scary big enough."

He smiled, that ornery smile that made the back of my knees sweat. *Great.* "You once said that mixing business with pleasure is messy."

"Aye."

"Beckett said the same thing."

"He would." The grin broadened. "So you're breaking off with me, yeah?"

"We'd have to be in a relationship to break up. You don't do relationships, remember?"

"That bang-on memory of yours is going to bite me in the *arse* one day."

I forced a smile of my own. "Maybe it'll save your ass."

He laughed. "Maybe."

I marveled at my sudden calm. Another talent of

Arch's: obliterating my frustrations. "So you're okay with me working for Chameleon?"

"Not my call, Sunshine."

I frowned. "You're not okay with it."

"I'm okay with you."

The man talked in circles, but I was used to it. So had my ex. "What about the not-having-sex part?"

"Are you sure you're not breaking off with me? That sounded a wee bit like the 'can we still be friends' speech, yeah?" He squeezed my hand and smiled. "We don't have to shag to get on."

I scrunched my brow. "The least you could do is sound disappointed."

"*Didnae* say I *wouldnae* miss it." He kissed me then. Slow. Deep.

Heat spiraled through my system. I dug to the center of my soul not to feel anything other than lust. Lust I could manage. Anything deeper was dangerous. Loving a man like Arch was insane. First, he was too young for me. Second, what if he'd plotted to kill Simon the Fish from the get-go? Third, he'd once told me I couldn't believe anything he said. One way or another, the man would mangle my heart.

He eased away, and my heart thump-thumped at the teasing sparkle in his eye. "So how do you want to spend your last night in London, friend?"

Sweaty-kneed, I gave him a come-hither grin. "I haven't officially started with Chameleon."

He nipped my earlobe. "I'll race you back to the flat. First one to get naked gets to be on top."

CHAPTER THREE

Atlantic City, New Jersey

SHE LOOKED LIKE MEG Ryan, *only shorter and softer. Blue eyes, full lips and pair of killer legs. She ran toward him singing a Joni Mitchell classic. "Help me! I think I'm falling..."*

Her voice jumped an octave, a feminine squeal, as she tripped and plowed into his open arms. They landed on the beach, rolled around in the sand and surf. "From Here to Eternity," she said in her little-girl voice. She was obsessed with Hollywood. A real fruitcake. Twinkie, he called her, because she was so damn sweet. He shouldn't do sweet, but he wanted to do her.

"Help me," she sang in his ear.

"I'll save you," he said.

"My hero." She flashed her dazzling smile and breasts.

He reached for those perfect 32Bs, but an alarm stopped him cold. No, not an alarm. A phone. What was a phone doing on the beach? "If this is a dream, please don't let me..."

Milo Beckett woke up reaching for thin air. "Dammit." He squinted at the digital clock, cursed again. Not bothering to turn on a light, he palmed his cell phone and fell back against his pillows. "Beckett here. What's up?"

"Are you mental?"

"I'm sleep-deprived. It's 3:00 a.m., Arch. This better be good."

"She's not like us."

"Who?"

"You know who."

"Ah." Evie Parish. The woman of his fractured fantasy.

"Why *didnae* you tell me you hired her?"

"Figured you had enough on your mind. The shooting. Dodging Scotland Yard."

"Haven't given the shooting a second thought, mate."

"That because it was a straight-up accident? Or because he deserved to die?"

"Let's just say the world's better off, yeah?"

"Skirting the issue."

"Speaking of skirts, what's the deal with Evie?"

Milo reflected on the half-pint fireball awakening in the island hospital. How she'd asked after everyone's welfare, never complaining about her own injury. He remembered her passionate argument regarding her qualifications and the spark of desperation in her deep blue eyes. He remembered how she made him feel every time they were in the same room—alive, amused and, dammit, randy. "She wanted to work for Chameleon," he said. "I agreed to give her a shot. I didn't specify the job." Arch didn't comment, but Milo heard relief in the significant pause. "Unlike you," he continued, "I wouldn't put an untrained civilian in the field."

"Aye, except she's not a novice anymore."

"One sting does not make—"

"I taught her a few short cons, yeah?"

Milo pressed a thumb and forefinger to his closed lids. The throbbing behind his eyeballs promised to intensify within the next thirty seconds or however long it took his partner to explain his asinine actions. "Why?"

"Because she's gullible and someone needed to open her eyes to the real world."

"Huh."

"Stop projecting, Jazzman."

"Who's projecting? One minute she's anxious to start her new job, the next she remembers she booked a vacation. To England, no less. I assumed it was your doing, but I didn't pry. Figured you had unfinished business."

"Figured I owed her after dragging her into that land-investment mess. So I treated her to a holiday. So what?"

"So is it finished?"

"Aye."

"Good. Because mixing business with pleasure—"

"Messy. I know."

"Look what happened with Gina," Milo said. An ex-cop, Gina Valente was a valuable member of the team, and they'd almost lost her because of Arch's fickle dick. Thwarting company policy, they'd had a short fling. Shorter than what Gina would've liked.

"She still pissed?"

"I think her exact words were *I'm over that amoral prick.*"

"All's well that ends wonky. Nice to know."

Milo rolled to his side and felt his nightstand for the ever-present bottle of pain relievers. "When are you coming back?"

"Depends. We clear with the Agency?"

"Yes and no."

"Meaning?"

"Chameleon's on sabbatical until the new director re-evaluates our purpose."

"You've got a new boss?"

"*We've* got a new boss. Vincent Crowe. Company man."

"Hard-ass?"

"You got it." He popped two aspirin and swallowed them dry.

"You *dinnae* sound happy, mate."

Try miserable. Even before Crowe had been appointed, the Agency had started mangling Milo's vision for Chameleon by inundating the team with cases pertaining to high-profile scams. Scams that target the select upper crust, as opposed to those that ruin lives of the blue-collar majority. Given his dealings with the new director thus far, he feared his vision was one step closer to history. "Maybe Evie could sing me a song. Cheer me up. Where is she, anyway?"

"Just put her on a plane. She's on her way home. Be warned, she's over the moon *aboot* her job with Chameleon. Has illusions *aboot* saving the world. Reminds me of you, yeah?"

"I don't want to save the world, Arch. Just a naive few."

"People like Evie."

Milo didn't comment.

"I've seen the way you look at her, mate. Remember what you told me *aboot* mixing business with pleasure."

"That a warning?"

"Just an observation."

The exchange reignited Milo's previous suspicions that Arch had fallen in love. Dangerous territory for a man who valued emotional detachment. *Never attach yourself to anyone you can't walk away from in a split second.* "You sound jealous. Just an observation."

"Bugger off."

"Fuck you."

"Beckett?"

"Yeah?"

"Try a glass of warm milk. And *dinnae* worry *aboot* Crowe."

"Thanks." Milo disconnected and fell back against his pillows. His relationship with Arch was complicated. Onetime rivals, they now danced the same dance. Partners in anticrime. Arch occasionally slipped into old routines, solo. His last performance had earned Milo an ass chewing from Crowe. It had also pulled Evie Parish, a sexy variety performer, into their lives. As if he needed another complication coming between him and his professional goals.

He massaged his temples, dreaded another bout of insomnia. He swung out of bed and headed for the kitchen, contemplating this new and constant restlessness. He needed to take charge.

First order of business: tackling insomnia. Which meant two things: addressing his discontent with the Agency and getting a grip on his infatuation with Twinkie. In a warped, adversarial way, he considered Arch Duvall a friend. But it was his obsession to learn everything the crafty genius knew about grifting that motivated Milo to keep him close. If he pursued this attraction to Evie, he risked driving a wedge between him and the Scot. Just because Arch claimed the affair was over didn't mean he was over Evie.

Face it, Beckett. Hiring Twinkie was a mistake. "That's what you get for thinking with your dick." He opened the fridge, nabbed the milk. "Just an observation."

CHAPTER FOUR

JET LAG. THE AWFUL zombielike sensation rivaled motion sickness, and I suffered from both.

Queasy and fog-brained, I dragged my suitcase into my apartment, a one-bedroom rental with minimal furnishings and three weeks of dust. I added depressed to the list. It didn't just *feel* empty, it *was* empty. I wish I could say someone robbed me while I was away. But, no, this was my doing. I'd moved in after the divorce, but I'd never really *lived* here. I'd purchased essentials—a couch, a television, a bed—and hadn't bothered decorating. I was too busy wallowing in my postdivorce funk and pitiful work schedule to give two figs about curtains, wall hangings and knickknacks.

Bleary-eyed, I scanned the living room—strike that—sterile room, wondering how I'd been immune to the starkness for so long. Maybe I was just hypersensitive since I'd spent the past week in Arch's grandfather's apartment. The Bloomsbury flat was twice this size, but you could barely move what with all the clutter. In addition to the late resident's own artistic creations, the flat had exploded with eclectic collections of paintings, sculptures and ceramic figurines. Not to mention art-history books, mystery novels, videotapes and impressive antique furnishings. Helping Arch sort through and decide what to sell off or give away had been difficult because, to me, everything was worth keeping. Bernard Duvall had surrounded himself with a lifetime of charming treasures.

I'd created a shrine to midlife crisis.

Mental note: tomorrow buy something cheery and useless. Even toss pillows would be an improvement.

Pillows made me think of bed, which made me think of sleep. But first I needed to make a few calls. I kicked off my cushy suede clogs and plopped down on my sofa—a boring contemporary piece that I'd picked up on sale. At the time I hadn't cared that it was monochromatic gray. Mental note: opt for colorful, *whimsical* toss pillows.

I reached into my *I Love Lucy* travel tote for my cell phone. My fingers connected with my journal—the keeper of my innermost thoughts.

Although I had little trouble expressing myself to Arch, in general I internalize. It stemmed from a suppressed childhood. My mom, a conservative high-school math teacher, didn't understand my liberal artistic temperament. My brother was as uptight as Mom. My dad, though a right-brained workaholic, seemed to get me more than they did. Knowing I bottled my emotions, he gave me a diary when I was a kid, telling me when my heart and mind got jammed to pour my feelings onto the page. I've since filled a hundred diaries. Okay, that's an exaggeration. But you see my point. Diaries were a staple in my life. I pulled out the newest—a gift from Arch— and placed it in my lap. A bright yellow journal featuring a photo of tropical skies and a brilliant ball of fire. *Sunshine.* Aware of my nightly habit, he'd bought the thoughtful memento in the islands.

I opened the book and smiled at the chicken scrawl on the inside cover. *For private stuff. Arch*

I basked in his kindness while turning to the next page and my own purple-penned scribbles. I'd titled the first page The Chameleon Chronicles. I'd already filled a good twenty pages with my adventures in London. I'd also penned a few hopes and fears and some personal stuff about Arch. Private stuff. Stuff I didn't intend for him to ever know. Especially since we were now absolutely, officially, *just friends.*

Frowning, I set aside the journal and snagged my cell. I immediately checked the battery. Sometimes I forgot to recharge it. Okay, a lot of times. According to the bars, I had full power. At least one of us had juice.

Falling back against the blah-boring sofa, I checked my messages, imagining fifty calls from Arch begging me to return to London. *I* cannae *live* withoot *you, yeah?*

But instead of a Scottish accent, I heard the nasal twang of a high-school rival. *"Evie? Monica Rhodes here. Since you're too busy to attend the Greenville Civic Theater's upcoming benefit, I wondered if you'd solicit one of the casinos for a donation. Surely you know people. A weekend stay would bring a tidy sum at the auction. I would have e-mailed, but you don't respond in a timely manner and I'm in a hurry to wrap things up. I asked your mom for your number. Hope you don't mind."*

"Actually, I do," I said, even though I was talking to a recording. Monica Rhodes had been the president of my high-school drama club. Later she'd snagged the role as director of our hometown's civic theater. She was and still is a bossy, competitive witch. I'd responded to her e-vite three days after receiving it. For me—someone who's not glued to the Internet—that *was* timely. *Unable to attend due to work,* I'd written. A big, fat lie, but I had my reasons. I'd listed them at length in my diary.

"As you know, Mrs. Grable is moving to Florida to enjoy her golden years. Several of her past students are reuniting for a special benefit performance and going-away party. As one of her pet pupils, I thought you'd want to contribute—"

I cut Monica off midsentence, something I'd never do in person. Nice girls don't interrupt. Except I wasn't so nice anymore. I'd tarnished my conservative, respectable crown when I'd taken up with Arch. I was learning to speak my mind, stand my ground. I was...evolving. Even though I had fond memories of my high-school drama teacher, I wasn't eager to be reminded of who Mrs. Grable thought I'd been destined to become. A big-time star. I wasn't thrilled about attending a party and having to meet my thespian classmates' spouses. I could hear it now.

Where are you performing, Evie?

I'm between bookings.

When's your next engagement?

I'm considering my options.

Where's your husband?

Boinking a lingerie model.

Kids?

Me? No. But there's a bun in the model's oven.

You can understand my reluctance to commit. I made a mental note to send Monica an e-mail—no way did I want to actually speak to the petty woman—explaining the improbability of obtaining a donation from an Atlantic City casino for a civic theater in Greenville, Indiana. Instead I'd offer a personal monetary donation for the cause. For now, I wiped Monica from my mind, punched auto-dial and focused on a true friend.

Nicole answered on the second ring. "Please tell me you're home."

Her husky smoker's voice was music to my ears. I'd been so consumed with Arch these past days I hadn't realized how much I'd missed my best buds. Nicole Sparks, a tall, lithe beauty with mocha skin, green eyes and a no-nonsense demeanor, and Jayne Robinson, a not-so-tall kewpie doll with big brown eyes, vibrant red curls and a fascination with the supernatural. Both closing in on forty. Both seasoned performers. Both hurting for work.

"I'm home." Such as it was.

"For how long?"

Nic was nothing if not blunt. I steeled myself before asking, "What do you mean?"

"First you split for the Caribbean for several days—"

"A last-minute booking."

"So you said, although you never filled us in on the particulars. You returned home ahead of schedule with a bandaged head and flew out again the next day. Said you were meeting a friend in London. Only after significant badgering did you admit said friend was the hunk you lusted after on the elusive cruise-ship gig." She paused, and I knew without seeing her that she'd just lit a cigarette. Nic had a few vices, but smoking, as far as I was concerned, was the worst. "We're thrilled that you're getting some nooky, Evie. God knows Jayne and I have been trying to hook you up for months. But why all the secrecy?"

"He's not married, if that's what you're worried about." I wasn't sure about a lot where Arch was concerned, but I was one hundred—okay, ninety-nine percent—sure that he was single.

"We're worried about you," she said. "When I called

with the news that Michael had gotten Sasha pregnant, you said you didn't care."

I palmed my upset stomach. Motion, not morning, sickness mixed with suppressed bitterness. "I *don't* care."

"Bullshit. The only reason you never had a baby was because Michael said he didn't want children. And now—"

"Now he's with someone else and I've moved on."

"That simple?"

"Yes." Not really, but I refused to give the matter deep thought. If I went there, I worried I'd mourn my time for having kids had come and gone. I worried I'd feel sorry for myself. I'd wallowed in self-pity for more than a year and it's not a place I wanted to revisit.

"So have you talked to him?"

"Michael? Not since before I left for the cruise. We didn't part on the best terms. He probably figures you told me about the pregnancy. I'm guessing he's waiting for me to call him first. I'm thinking I don't feel like it."

"Have you called his office, talked to Violet about auditions or outstanding checks or…anything?"

Violet was Michael's secretary, and though we'd always been friendly, we'd never been friends. "After the flashing fiasco, I don't expect Michael Stone Entertainment Inc. will be sending me on any immediate auditions. The agency doesn't owe me any money and Violet and I aren't chatty." I narrowed my eyes. "What's up?"

"I'd rather tell you in person."

"Has he decided to drop me as a client?"

Silence.

"I'll take that as a yes." I wondered if Sasha had pressed him to do so or if he'd decided I was, as I suspected, washed up in this town. Not that it mattered. Deep in my heart, I knew it was time to break clean with my ex, but that didn't mean I'd make it easy for him. My days of rolling over were, well, over. "If he wants to release me as a client, he'll have to track me down, because I'm not going to make first contact or open any of his e-mails. The least he can do is tell me in person."

"Evie—"

"Listen, Nic. I know I haven't been myself lately, but that's a good thing, trust me." A headache needled behind my eyes. "Just now I'm exhausted. How about you and Jayne come over tomorrow night? We'll have drinks and catch up."

"We'll bring the margaritas."

"Swell."

"I'll let Jayne know you're home safe. You get some rest."

"Thanks, Nic. Thanks for caring."

"That's what friends do."

She signed off without any smooches or sappy good-byes. I wasn't insulted. Nic wasn't the sappy sort. Jayne was another specimen altogether. If I called her now, she'd keep me on the phone for an hour, fussing and spouting New Age gibberish regarding fate and destiny. Nic, bless her soul, was saving me from a woo-woo lecture. At least for now.

I massaged my temples and contemplated calling my dad. It had been a while since we'd spoken. Not that that was unusual. The Parishes were minimalists when it came to communication. I'm pretty sure we're listed in the dictionary under *dysfunctional*.

Still, I couldn't get over the fact that, after twenty years as a bank president, Dad had snubbed retirement *and* Mom and bought a tavern. He'd never been a barfly.

Although he enjoyed the occasional beer, the man could nurse a can of Bud for an hour. It had to be a life crisis. I could sympathize. I *wanted* to sympathize. But if I called him, I'd have to call Mom. Otherwise, she'd hear about it and accuse me of taking sides.

My parents had split up just before my cruise, for reasons I still didn't understand. Neither of them wanted to talk about it, which was normal since it was a private matter and they never talked about emotional issues. My brother, Christopher, who lived near our parents, assured me he'd "fix it."

I decided to wait until tomorrow, until I had more energy, before touching base on the home front. If something were terribly wrong, one of them would have called. Maybe.

I pushed my ex and my family from my mind and concentrated on my new job. Sitting straighter, I dialed the number given to me by Special Agent Beckett, who I still thought of as Tex Aloha—don't ask.

"The Chameleon Club," a deep voice answered.

Suddenly jazzed, I stood and paced. "Is Milo Beckett there?"

"Sorry."

Beckett had asked me not to refer to him by his official title, which only heightened the intrigue. He'd also asked me to call him Milo, but I wasn't comfortable with that. He was, after all, my boss—and a government agent, to boot. I wasn't sure if I should leave a message, only he *had* given me this number—oh, and a name. "Are you, by chance, Samuel Vine?"

"I am."

"Then I'd like to leave a message. My name is Evie Parish and Mr. Beckett—"

"Hired you."

"He told you about me?"

"He did."

I detected a smile in his voice. A smile at my expense. My heart pounded, and it wasn't from pacing. Had Beckett told this man I'd tackled him? Had he told him about my lockjaw incident? Or how I'd ended up topless in St. Thomas? The government agent had witnessed more than a few embarrassing bobbles on that cruise, and it burned my buns that he'd shared them with Mr. Vine, whoever Mr. Vine was.

"Are you coming in?"

I blinked. "When? Now? No. I just got… I was in…"

"England."

"How did you… Oh, right. I guess Mr. Beckett told you about my vacation."

"He did."

Mr. Vine was a man of few words. If he *was* privy to my Caribbean misfortunes, perhaps he'd keep my antics secret. One could hope. "Would it be all right if I came in tomorrow? Do you think you could ask him—"

"Tomorrow is fine."

"Don't you think you should ask—"

"We'll expect you at noon." He gave me an address, then said something about getting back to work—him, not me. Then he said, "'Bye, Twinkie," and hung up.

I gaped at my phone. Before I'd known Beckett for who he really was, I'd known him as a Texas oil baron. He'd been undercover and his disguise had been a hideous combination of the Duke meets Don Ho. Hence my thinking of him as Tex Aloha. He'd repeatedly referred to me as Twinkie, and although I'd been disguised as a bubble-headed bimbo, I totally resented that name. "I can't believe he told his associate to call me…" I couldn't say it.

I didn't even want to think it. Did he tell the rest of the team, too? "Great."

The needling behind my eyeballs graduated to stabs. I stalked to the bathroom in search of Tylenol. I told myself to calm down. Milo Beckett was now my boss, and though I'd only gotten to know the real him over a sporadic two days, he seemed pretty decent. Tomorrow I'd tell him—nicely—that I didn't appreciate the nickname. Evie is fine, thank you very much. I washed down two capsules with a paper cup of lukewarm water, then schlepped into the next room and collapsed on the bed.

Almost time for blissful oblivion. One more call, and I'd saved the best for last. His was the voice I wanted in my ears when I fell asleep. I took a deep breath and willed my heart not to flutter. I reminded myself that we were just friends now. Parting at the airport had been easier than I'd anticipated. No bittersweet *Casablanca* ending. Mostly because Arch still flirted, and when the time came to board, the kiss we shared didn't feel like goodbye. It felt like maybe later.

Smiling, I dialed the number he'd given me. He'd told me to check in when I settled in my apartment. I assumed he'd be waiting on pins and needles, wondering if I'd arrived safely. I assumed he'd answer on the first ring. Three rings in, I heard an automated greeting. Taken aback, my brain glitched. "Hi, I…it's me. Evie. I…well, I'm home and I'm okay and I'm…here. Right. I said that. Okay. Call. You know… If you feel like it." I signed off before I made an idiot—strike that—*more* of an idiot of myself.

I placed the phone on my nightstand, within reach. I told myself not to obsess about where he was and why he hadn't answered. It was probably the middle of the night there, only I was too tired to do the math. I told my-self to journal my frustrations, only I was too tired to hold a pen.

"Just friends," I mumbled. "Coworkers." I repeated those words like a mantra over and over until I started to drift.

Just. Friends.

It triggered a tender memory: spooning with Arch and quoting lines from *Titanic*.

I don't know this dance.

Just go with it.

Right.

CHAPTER FIVE

I WOKE WITH A START. I'd been dreaming about Arch. About pulling a con, only I screwed up—or, as Arch put it, cracked out of turn. *You're not up to this,* he said, only he'd morphed into Michael, who had his arm around a young girl with a swelled tummy, and when he spoke again he said, *You're too old for this.*

It was a crummy, awful dream.

Fuzzy-headed, I lay there for a second, willing away a sense of failure and loss. I rolled to my side, wanting to snuggle with my Scottish lover, only he wasn't there. Right. *He's in London. I'm at home. And Michael and Sasha are shacked up and celebrating future parenthood.* Not that I cared. Okay, that's a lie. But obsessing would only agitate my TMJ.

I massaged my tight jaw and squinted at the alarm clock. Eleven-thirty in the morning.

It took a minute to register.

Eleven thirty-one.

Head thunk. The next morning!

I kicked off my duvet, collected my wits. I'd fallen asleep around this time yesterday, woken up in the middle of the night, unpacked, showered and journaled in my diary. Wide-awake, I'd booted up my laptop, thinking maybe Arch had e-mailed—he hadn't—and ended up clicking on Amazon.com and ordering books about con artists and scams. Eyes and heart heavy, I'd snuggled under my cover, waited for Arch to call—he didn't—and at some point fallen back to sleep.

I shoved my tangled hair out of my bleary eyes. "I'm supposed to be somewhere," I rasped.

The Chameleon Club.

"Crap!" The curse came out a garbled croak. Clasping my throat, I flew into the bathroom. I was hoarse. My throat hurt and my nose was stuffed. I blamed it on a screwed-up body clock. On three weeks of travel. On the drastic changes in climate—balmy Caribbean to chilly London to windy and damp Brigantine. I sneezed, then coughed. "Great." My first day on a new job and I was sick. If I lingered too long over my appearance, I'd be late. "Damn!"

I primped and dressed in record time. Minimal make-up, ponytail and as close to a conventional men-in-black suit as my funky wardrobe would allow. Medicated on Robitussin and herbal cold caplets, I grabbed my purse and sailed out the door. Barring a flat tire, speeding ticket or head-on collision, I'd arrive at the Chameleon Club five minutes ahead of schedule.

I didn't factor in the possibility of torrential rains.

On the short drive to the Atlantic City Inlet, the dark, fat clouds that seemed to be hovering exclusively over *my* car exploded. I'm not the world's greatest driver on a clear, sunny day. I know this. If I hydroplaned, I was screwed. So I slowed to a crawl. Death grip on the steering wheel, I swiped off my MIB shades, leaned forward and squinted through my blurry windshield. The wipers weren't wiping as much as streaking. Or maybe I needed glasses. I was over forty, after all.

"You're too old for this."

The need to meet with Beckett and to start this new and exciting phase of my life intensified with each sluggish mile. I'd purposely taken the back route so I wouldn't have to navigate Atlantic or Pacific Avenue, the city's main drags, the streets that paralleled the boardwalk casinos. I no longer felt welcome or wanted within the gambling venues that had once provided the bulk of my work. My last audition had been disastrous, and as it had transpired only a few weeks before, the wound resulting from the insensitive behavior of the baby-faced execs was still fresh.

As a professional, Ms. Parish, I'm sure you understand that we're looking to please our demographic.

Meaning they wanted someone younger. There was a time when you paid your dues in roadside bars or summer stock, when you *earned* a booking in a casino venue. Those days were gone. These days the number-one priority wasn't experience, but sex appeal. In demand? Young, slender females, willing to dress provocatively. Perky boobs were a plus. Since I was perfect for that job, and since those execs had managed to uncork my bottled angst, my response had been less than gracious. Wanting to prove I met their physical requirements, I'd flashed a thousand-watt smile in tandem with my perky 32Bs. They'd responded by having me escorted off property by security. No Hollywood ending for me. Typical.

My jaw ached like the devil. *Stop clenching, Parish. The last thing you need is another lockjaw episode. Go to your happy place.*

Unfortunately, my happy place was in London, with Arch. Arch, who hadn't returned my call.

I sneezed into a handful of tissues. "It's only been a day

and a half," I rasped. "He's not your husband. He's not your significant other, lover, crush or whatever it is they're calling it these days. He's your friend. *F-R-I-E-N-D.* Friend."

The self-directed lecture helped a little. Anything to keep me grounded. Lord knows I didn't need another worry. I was stressed enough. Stressed because of the blinding rain. Stressed because I was running late. Stressed because I was obsessing on my washed-up career. "I don't want to go back. I want to zoom forward."

I turned onto North Maine Avenue and focused on the Chameleon Club a few blocks ahead. No more auditioning. No more rejections. The enormity of my relief took me by surprise. There was a time when I believed I'd been born to entertain, period. But after my boneheaded behavior at that botched audition, I'd been certain I'd never work in this town again. A traditional nine-to-five had loomed in my future, and given my specific skills, prospects were limited and frightening. I'd dreaded a normal life. I'd dreaded never again hearing the sound of applause.

Today, this moment, I didn't care if I stepped foot on another Atlantic City stage. Ever.

The world is our stage, Arch had told me when we'd first met. As a con man's shill, I'd still be acting, but on a grander, more important scale. Evie Parish: Crime Fighter. I'd always felt that I was meant for something bigger. *This,* I thought as I sniffled and steered into a puddle-ridden parking lot, *is it.*

The rain poured. The wind howled. The herbal medicine sucked. It had yet to curb my sneezing or clear my sinuses. All I felt was sluggish. Damn jet lag.

I reached beneath the front seat and yanked out a

compact umbrella. The club was only a few feet away. Nothing was going to keep me from this appointment. Not rain nor snow nor shoe-sucking mud. I rolled back my shoulders, forced open my door and braved the elements.

Holding on tight to my flimsy umbrella, I sloshed across the parking lot, frowning when I read the sign: Please Use Boardwalk Entrance. The famous Atlantic City boardwalk stretched the length of town along the ocean and curved around to the lesser-known, more secluded Inlet. No casinos here. Gardiner's Basin, a historic region hugging the bay, offered an aquarium, a small maritime museum and old-fashioned fun. Unfortunately, I was navigating the wasteland smack between the Basin and downtown AC. Run-down buildings and vacant lots. No fun to be had here unless you got a thrill out of the possibility of being mugged.

I scaled the steps leading up to the boardwalk and squealed as the gusting wind blew the rain at a hard angle. Umbrella or no, I'd be soaked by the time I reached Beckett. I barely cared. At this point I just wanted to get inside.

Fate had other ideas.

My heel was just narrow enough to wedge into a large gap between two soggy wooden boards. As I struggled to free myself, the wind blew my umbrella inside out. "Dammit!"

"Can I help you, ma'am?"

I peered up through the pelting rain to find a scruffy-bearded young man with his hands stuffed in the pockets of a ratty trench coat. He could be a drunk, a pickpocket or a panhandling con artist. Arch had made me leery of, well, everyone. Even if he was an upright guy, he reeked of some god-awful cologne and he'd just called me ma'am. Two reasons to make me grimace.

"Looks like your heel is stuck," he yelled over the wind.

Well, duh.

"And your umbrella—"

"Yes, I know," I yelled back. "I'm fine. Thank you." I imagined him getting close enough to help, then snagging my bag. Jayne had been mugged last summer on her way from a casino to the self-parking lot. Busy season, busy area, broad daylight. And here I was, alone on a stormy day in the flipping Inlet. Maybe it was the adrenaline, but I jerked again, and this time my heel popped free. I staggered, but when the bearded stranger reached out, I slapped his hand. "Don't touch me!"

"Listen, ma'am—"

"Beat it, kid, or I'll stab you with my umbrella. I warn you—I'm trained in the art of peculiar weaponry." Whatever that meant. But it sounded ominous to me.

I guess it sounded scary to him, too. "All right. All right. Jeez." He backed away, shoved his sodden hair out of his face.

Yup. His expression told all. He thought I was dangerous. Or crazy.

Good.

The wind tore the umbrella out of my hand, and though it was mangled, I gave chase. My luck, if I abandoned it, a cop would magically appear and ticket me for littering the beach. I nabbed the useless thing and turned back toward the club. I didn't see or smell Bearded Boy. Things were looking up. I race-walked, putting my weight on my toes in hopes of avoiding another stuck-heel episode. *Please, don't let me slip.*

I was wind-ravaged and soaked by the time I breached the front door of the Chameleon Club. I shook like a wet dog, then leaned against a cigarette machine, composing myself and allowing my eyes to adjust to the dim light.

I'd expected a professional reception area, something representative of a government agency. And a secretary. You know, a pristine-suited Moneypenny type who'd lead me to the high-tech, supersecret office of Special Agent Milo Beckett. I'd expected to step in to spy world.

The Chameleon Club was a dive bar.

The interior looked as if it dated back to the late '50s. Not a trendy retro look but a never-been-refurbished look. The tables and chairs, the painted walls, the linoleum floor. Faded, chipped, cracked, warped. At least it was tidy and didn't stink.

So…what? Beckett and his team squeezed into a cracked vinyl booth and devised stings over pretzels and beer? I refused to believe it. There must be a back room, a secret room. Maybe they met in the basement or on the second floor. There had to be more to this place than met the eye. *Smoke and mirrors.* I checked my watch. Twelve-ten. Surely Beckett would forgive my tardiness once I explained the circumstances. All he had to do was look at me.

So much for dressing to impress.

I looked around but didn't see my new boss. Maybe he was running late, too. Maybe I could slip into the bathroom and check to make sure mascara wasn't running down my face. It was waterproof, but the label said nothing about monsoons. Then again, maybe Beckett was in the secret office, waiting.

I stifled a sneeze and squinted at the bar on the opposite wall. A dark-skinned elderly man wearing a white shirt, black vest, skinny tie and a porkpie hat stood behind it, polishing glasses while talking with a couple of early-bird patrons. Probably he knew where Beckett was. Definitely he could point me to the ladies' room. Even though I looked like a drenched ragamuffin, I approached with the confidence of a pageant queen. He saw me coming and moved away from his patrons, nabbing a shot glass and a bottle of whiskey along the way.

"Twinkie?" he said when I reached the bar.

I'd know that deep voice anywhere. "Samuel Vine."

"They call me Pops."

I grasped the warm palm he offered and shook. "They call me Evie."

I'm thinking he got the hint that I wasn't keen on the cream-puff nickname. He grinned, a flash of crooked white teeth. "Welcome."

"Thank you."

He poured a shot of whiskey. "For the chill."

I patted my face dry with a cocktail napkin and tucked my drenched hair behind my ears. The black scrunchie ponytail holder was out there somewhere, blowing in the wind. "No, thank you. Too early for me."

"Soaked like that, you're primed to catch cold. Already sounds like one settled in your throat."

"I'm fine. Just…wet."

He nudged the glass closer.

It felt rude to refuse his hospitality. Plus, he was an elder, late sixties at least. Snubbing his kindness didn't sit right with me. Call me old-fashioned. I resisted the urge to hold my nose but held my breath and threw back the whiskey in one shot, determined not to taste it.

I choked and coughed while it burned my throat and singed my stomach. In between the hacking, I managed to thank Pops.

He stroked his wiry silver moustache, a polite but poor attempt to hide a smile. "You okay?"

"Fine." I wiped tears from my eyes, brightened when I noticed no black smudges on my fingers. Tear- *and* monsoon-proof. Points for Maybelline. "If you could just direct me to Mr. Beckett…"

"He isn't available."

"We have an appointment."

"He had a conflict. He asked me to get you started. He'll be down later."

So the offices *were* upstairs.

Pops waved over one of the barflies, an Antonio Banderas look-alike sporting a slicked-back ponytail and a thousand-watt smile. "This is Tabasco. He'll be accompanying you."

"Accompanying me where?"

On the flight home from the islands, Beckett had mentioned key members of Chameleon, describing Jimmy Tabasco as a transportation specialist, so I was surprised when Zorro dude grinned and replied, "On the guitar."

"Sorry?"

"I'm not a professional like you, but I have a good ear and can read chord charts."

"We don't have a stage," Pops said. "But we made space over there beside the jukebox. Tabasco appropriated a small speaker system and a microphone."

Appropriated?

"I set up a Shure 58 for you, hon, but if you prefer to use your own mic—"

"Evie," I said. What was it with these guys and sweetie-pie nicknames? "And I'm sorry, but…why do I need a microphone?"

"You want to sing acoustically?" He scratched his jaw, shrugged. "Twinkie and Tabasco Unplugged. Works for me. How about you Pops?"

"Fine."

"Not fine," I croaked, a hint of hysteria in my voice. "There's been a misunderstanding. Beckett didn't hire me to sing."

"He did," Pops said. "Wednesdays through Sundays."

"That gives us two days to rehearse," Tabasco said. "Although maybe we should skip today. You don't sound so good."

"I'm fine." I sneezed into a cocktail napkin. "Just confused. Beckett hired me to… He said I could…"

Both men raised their eyebrows, waiting for me to elaborate. Only I realized Milo Beckett had never specifically stated my job responsibilities.

No, no, no. My luck couldn't be *this* bad. Today was supposed to be the first day of my new life. A step forward, not back. I wanted to be Evie the Chameleon, not Evie the lounge lizard!

Tabasco glanced at Pops, then back at me. "I brought along *The Real Book,* in case you didn't bring your own charts. Do you know your keys?"

My heart roared in my ears. Maybe I was still asleep, still dreaming. Maybe this was a result of mind-bending jet lag. "I'm a chick singer," I said deadpan. "Of course I don't know my own keys."

Tabasco chuckled at the inside joke.

"Besides, *The Real Book* is useless since I don't sing standards."

"Only kind of music Jazzman allows," Pops said.

I palmed my damp, pounding forehead. "Who's Jazzman?"

"Milo Beckett." Tabasco motioned to Pops to pour me another drink. "Maybe you should have another shot, hon. You look pale."

"Maybe I should." Jayne had bought me that herbal medicine, and, like a cosmic ring she'd once given me, it was a clunker. Maybe I could kill the germs with alcohol and at the same time bolster myself for a confrontation with Beckett. I threw back the whiskey and only choked and hacked half as long the second time around. "How do I get upstairs?"

Tabasco shook his head. "I don't think—"

"Let her go," Pops said. He pointed to a door marked Private. "Through there and up the stairs. When you reach the end of the line, knock."

"You might want to button your jacket, babe."

I ignored Tabasco's advice and strode toward the marked door. I'd be damned if I'd gussy up for Beckett. He'd tricked me, conned me. What I wanted to know was why.

CHAPTER SIX

BY THE TIME I HIT THE top landing I was primed for a fight. Whatever truce Beckett and I had silently agreed to in the islands had shattered along with my *Charlie's Angel* fantasy. An image of that cocky SOB Tex Aloha exploded in my brain along with every other man who'd ever tripped up my dreams. If he thought I was going to roll over and take this news like good ole roll-with-the punches Evie Parish, he was wrong with a capital *W.*

"I've changed with a capital *C!*"

Hopped up on righteousness, I banged on the door with my umbrella, then charged ahead expecting a spacious loft. Stark white walls. Stainless steel desks. Men in black tinkering with superspy gadgets. Instead I stepped into a compact living area reminiscent of Sam Spade's apartment in *The Maltese Falcon.* My gaze skimmed over the padded rocking chair, leather sofa, wooden bookcase and spindle-legged desk—all circa 1940—and landed on the scarred wood molding framing the nearest window. Was that a bullet hole?

"Can I help you?"

I whirled, envisioning a hard-boiled dick in a dark suit brandishing a revolver, and slammed into a hardheaded dick in a towel holding a bottle of aftershave.

I bounced off Milo Beckett's bare chest with an *oomph.*

"Damn, Twinkie, you're soaked."

"Yes, well, that's what happens when you get caught in a rainstorm with a cheap-ass umbrella!" The flutter of embarrassment I'd felt interrupting his postshower primping evaporated with that cream-puff innuendo. I didn't give two figs that he was half-naked, nor did I allow my female appreciation of his very male essence to distract me from my mission. "I have a bone to pick with you!"

"Could it wait until I'm dressed?"

"No. First of all, my name is Evie. Twinkie is… degrading."

"Barging into my apartment without invitation is rude."

"I knocked."

"You pounded."

"*You* lied." Maybe not the best thing to say to your new boss on the first day, but I was steamed and fueled by two shots of whiskey.

"If this is about your position with Chameleon, you might want to rephrase that last statement."

He was right. I knew it and he knew it. Damn. Rattled, I drew on the film-noir atmosphere and channeled Sam Spade. "People lose teeth talking like that," I drawled in my best Bogie impersonation. "If you want to hang around, you'll be polite."

He looked at me as if I'd grown a second nose. If he were Arch, he would've come back with, *"The Maltese Falcon. 1941."* The sexy Scot could quote as many movies as me, maybe more.

Beckett leaned forward and sniffed. "You've been drinking."

"Pops said whiskey would take off the chill." Yeah, boy, ain't that the truth. I was burning up.

"I'll fix you some coffee."

"I'm not drunk, Beckett. I'm mad. At you."

"Got that when you barged in, *Twinkie*." He tossed the capped aftershave onto a worn leather ottoman and readjusted the towel that rode dangerously low on his hips.

I dropped my umbrella and purse on the hardwood floor, peeled off my cold, wet jacket and chucked that, too.

We stared each other down for what felt like an hour and probably amounted to three seconds. Absurdly, it felt like a game of chicken. I refused to buckle first, but when his gaze slid down my body, lingering on my chest, I panicked. Was he thinking about the time he'd seen me topless? "You misled me," I said, inwardly cursing him a pig. At the same time, my own traitorous gaze raked over his lean, mean form. What was it about a man in a towel and the smell of deodorant soap and woodsy cologne?

"I didn't do anything except agree to a trial run."

Startled, I glanced back up and found him watching me with a knowing smirk. He thought I was checking him out, which I sort of was. *Busted.* Could this day get any worse? "But you knew what I was thinking. I mean, that day, when I asked you for a job."

"I did."

"So?"

"You thought wrong."

I stamped my foot in frustration. He talked in circles, just like…

Oh, no. "Arch put you up to this, didn't he?" I whirled and paced, my mind tripping over rapid-fire thoughts. "I knew he wasn't happy about me grifting for you, with him, but I didn't think he'd go behind my back and…" I sneezed.

"Bless you."

"Thank you. I didn't think he'd sabotage my future," I ranted without missing a beat. "He knew how important this was to me. I've been studying and practicing and…I even stole, I mean distracted…*dammit!*" I stopped in my tracks, tongue-tied with a zillion curses. All of them directed at Arch Duvall. "No wonder he didn't call me back. He's avoiding me. He…" I faltered, realizing I'd just shot myself in the foot.

"Looks like you weren't the only one who was misled."

I could feel myself blushing from bleached hair follicles to painted pink toenails. My skin actually sizzled. "Okay. I might have been a little less than truthful back on the island when I intimated there was nothing between Arch and me other than friendship."

Beckett raised a brow. "Really?"

His sarcasm grated big-time. I planted my hands on my hips, straightened my spine. If I could stand up to several marketing and entertainment executives, I could handle one arrogant Fed. "I slept with Arch. We had a fling. There. I admitted it. Are you happy now?"

"Did you get him out of your system?"

My skin prickled with a nervous rash. But I didn't scratch. That would be what Arch called a "tell." I nodded and delivered a firm, "Yes."

"Until you get better at lying, I'm not putting you in the field."

How did he know? I didn't *scratch!* Furious, I stalked closer. "Now, just a minute. I—"

"Watch out, sir! She's dangerous!"

I turned at the familiar voice. Smelly Bearded Boy, but without the ratty trench coat. He stood on the threshold of another door, holding a stack of manila envelopes. What the…?

"I tried to help her and she threatened me. She… she…" He stammered and stared. At my *chest!*

"You," Beckett said, pointing a finger at Bearded Boy, "go and fetch Evie something to wear from wardrobe."

The kid's eyes widened at the sound of my name. "She's—"

"If you call me Twinkie, so help me—"

"Go," Beckett ordered.

Bearded Boy, who I guess worked for the club, scrammed down a back set of stairs. I'm not sure who he feared more, me or Beckett.

"You," he said, grasping my shoulders and steering me into his bathroom, "get out of those wet clothes and into a hot shower. You're hoarse. You're sneezing. I'll be damned if I'll have a team member keel over from pneumonia." He gave me a shove and shut me in. "I'll get dressed and make you some tea and honey," he said through the door. "When you come out, we'll discuss this rationally."

I stood, stunned, listening as another door slammed. He'd just called me a team member. Maybe I'd misunderstood. Maybe the singing gig was a cover. Or just temporary.

Until you get better at lying, I'm not putting you in the field.

There was hope. I performed a happy jig. At the same time I caught a glimpse of my reflection in the vanity mirror and froze. My thin white blouse was drenched and transparent. So was my sheer bra. Unbelievable.

In addition to Beckett, now Pops, Tabasco and Bearded Boy had all gotten a primo look at my boobs.

CHAPTER SEVEN

MILO JAMMED HIS LEGS into a pair of jeans and pulled on a clean T-shirt. He raided his top drawer. "Why is it I can never find a damn pair of matching socks?" He pulled on one blue, one black, and shoved his feet into a pair of brown Skechers.

A day that had started off bad just tanked. If Vincent Crowe hadn't phoned at six-fricking-o'clock this morning, ordering him to the Philadelphia office for a rundown on a fricking politician's *personal* crisis, he wouldn't have been racing to get back to the club for his meeting with Evie. He wouldn't have blown out a tire and gotten caught in a downpour changing that flat and chasing a fricking renegade lug nut down the muddy embankment. He wouldn't have had to shower and change, ultimately getting caught with his pants down, not to mention his guard.

A drenched and tipsy Evie stoked dangerous feelings, making Milo edgy. Make that edgi*er*.

His muscles bunched as he tied his shoelaces and waited for the sound of groaning pipes, the rhythmic blast of his shower massage. He imagined Twinkie naked. Standing in his claw-footed tub, hot water racing over her hot curves. Strategically aimed shower pulsations urging her to let go.

"Christ." Managing his fascination had been easier when she wasn't around.

He straightened and adjusted himself. He conjured thoughts of Sister Rosa, his fifth-grade Catholic school-teacher with the pop-bottle glasses and hooked nose. After a two-second appearance, the finger-wagging nun morphed into a gyrating babe. Not his fault. He'd been treated to a personalized version of a wet T-shirt contest. Another vision to haunt his dreams. Evie in a clingy, see-through shirt. Instead of alerting her to her sexy state, he'd tried his damnedest to ignore it. He didn't want to embarrass her on top of pissing her off. Between the pacing and her heated mood, the thin blouse would quickly dry. She'd be none the wiser.

Enter Woody.

He couldn't blame the kid for staring. Before making a concerted effort to avert his own gaze, Milo had copped a look, too. What hetero man wouldn't? But Woody had been two seconds from outing Evie's visible nipples. Hence plan B: getting her out of the room and out of those clothes.

The only thing better would be getting her into his bed. But that wasn't going to happen. Even if he ignored his own policy against mixing business and pleasure, even if he acted out of character, poured on the charm and se-duced a friend and associate's woman, nothing would come of it. Twinkie was a good girl. Until she got over her infatuation with Arch, she'd be true to the man, even though that man would never commit to a long-term re-lationship.

Better to practice restraint. One of three things would happen: either his infatuation with Evie would fizzle or Evie's infatuation with Arch would fizzle or Arch would expose himself as amoral, scaring Evie off and into the arms of the better man. And Milo believed wholeheartedly and without arrogance that he was, in this instance, the better man.

"I can't believe I'm having these thoughts."

Evie's mentality closely resembled that of his ex-wife's. The dreamer and the realist, a recipe for disaster. A smart man would learn from his mistakes. Unfortunately, every time Evie entered his personal space, Milo's IQ dropped.

He heard sneezing and mumbling through the paper-thin walls. He imagined his new employee peeling off layers—damn—and decided to dump some grief on the man who'd dumped her into his life in the first place.

Arch answered on the second ring. "Navigating rush-hour traffic, mate."

"Navigating some prickly territory myself."

"Burst Evie's bubble, yeah?"

"Yeah."

"She wanted to tackle crooks and you've got her typing reports."

"No typing."

"Waiting tables?"

"Singing."

"What, like a singing bartender?"

"No. Like a lounge performer."

Arch whistled low. "No wonder she's pissed."

"I hired her to do what she does, what she's good at."

"She doesn't want to go back."

"What does that mean?"

"Means she wants to break with the past. Offering her a job as a singer in a low-class pub sets her back *aboot* twenty years, yeah?"

Milo knew about the need to move on. Like Evie, he'd recently survived a divorce. He'd also suffered his share of professional growing pains. This morning's confrontation with Crowe had elevated his craving to cut ties with the Agency. He'd gotten into this line of work to help the common masses, not the privileged few.

Prevented from doing what you're compelled to do by the man who signs the checks. Milo could imagine Evie's misery and he empathized. But not enough to put her in the field when she lacked the fortitude and training.

"She thinks you asked me to pull her out of the game," Milo said. "Thinks you didn't approve of her being an active player."

"I *dinnae*," Arch said.

"But the singing position was my idea."

The Scot held silent for a moment. Milo heard an eighties dance tune in the background—Culture Club?— and the blaring horn of an irate driver. "*Dinnae* correct her misassumption," Arch finally said.

"You *want* her to be mad at you?"

"It would be better if she thought less of me, aye."

"Hell," Milo said with a short laugh, "all she had to do was ask for a copy of your personnel file." Not that he would have turned it over. He had strict views on confidentiality. Still, he wasn't above taunting the man who'd made his life hell when they'd been on opposite sides of the law. "Did you come clean and tell her you had an affair with Gina?"

"Why bring up a dead issue?"

"Because if you're looking to cool Evie's jets, that would do it." Someone pounded on the door. "Hold on." Milo opened up expecting Woody with an armful of dry clothes. Instead Evie stood on the threshold, a dry towel wrapped around her upper body. Which would have been sexy had she taken off her clothes first.

"Here's the thing," she said, "I can't get naked in your apartment."

"Bloody hell," Arch said in Milo's ear. "What the—"

"I'll call you back." He disconnected, shoved the phone in his back pocket. "If you're worried about someone walking in on you, lock the door."

"It's not that."

"Then what?"

"I don't know you well enough."

"You didn't know Arch at all and you used his shower. Hell, you slept in his suite."

"That was different. I was working for him."

"You're working for me now."

"We were posing as a married couple." She sneezed into a wad of toilet paper and leaned into the doorjamb for support.

"You'll be posing as a hospital patient if you don't get into dry clothes."

Just then, Woody blew in, two hangers dangling from his fingertips. A nurse's uniform and a nun's habit.

Milo's ass vibrated. He ignored the incoming call, frowned at Woody. "You're joking."

"All of the women's clothes are in Hot Legs's size," he said.

"Who's Hot Legs?" asked Evie.

"Gina," Milo said. His primary female operator. Arch's previous conquest. The woman who'd put Evie through the wringer on that cruise. Those two had clashed like a pit bull and a poodle. Hell would freeze over before Twinkie would wear anything worn by Gina "Hot Legs" Valente.

"She's taller and thinner than you," Woody said, "so I figured anything with pants was out. These are sort of shapeless, so—"

"I'll risk pneumonia," Evie said with a tight smile. "Thanks all the same."

Woody looked clueless and Milo had to bite his tongue. *No wonder your girlfriend left you.* He may as well have called Evie short and dumpy. From her pinched expression, that's exactly what she'd heard. Women had an uncanny way of twisting a man's words when it came to their appearance. He'd learned long ago that when a lady friend asks, *Does this make my ass look big?* the safest answer is a simple no.

"You don't look so good, ma'am," Woody said, digging a deeper hole. But he was right. She was flushed, perspiring and shaky on her feet.

"Yeah, well, you don't smell so good."

Woody, who'd been trying to win back his girlfriend by changing everything from his wardrobe to his brand of toothpaste, looked crushed. "You don't like my cologne?"

"How to put this kindly?" she said with a notable slur. "No."

Milo studied her hard. "How many shots did Pops give you?"

"One," she said, holding up two fingers.

Woody whistled. "Oh, man. She's—"

Milo cut him off before he could say *crocked.* Knowing his caretaker/bartender he wouldn't have knowingly poured more than this half-pint could handle. Obviously she had no tolerance. "Nix the clothes," he said to Woody. "Tell Tabasco rehearsal's canceled. Our star's under the weather."

"Don't tell him that!" she cried. "It makes me sound like a diva. As long as I have a voice, I can sing."

"But you're hoarse," said Milo. And looped.

"So I'll sound like Janis Joplin."

"Did Joplin sing jazz?" Woody asked.

"No, and neither do I."

"Actually," Milo said, "she recorded a rendition of 'Summertime.'"

"Oh, right. Joplin did do Gershwin." She snorted. "Not literally, of course. Regardless, jazz is not in my repertoire."

"Only kind of music Agent Beckett allows," Woody said.

She crinkled her nose and Milo smiled. "My club. My rules."

"Dictating the artist's song list," she grumbled, then sneezed. "I already feel at home."

Bitterness laced her tone and stabbed at Milo's conscience. Again the phone vibrated, and he thought about what Arch had said about her wanting to ditch her old life. Thing was, he'd seen her perform—singing, dancing, acting. She possessed charisma and talent. *What's pushing you to abandon your God-given gifts, Evie?* He hated that he cared. "So you're willing to work as the club's house singer?"

"As long as I don't have to sign a contract. I'm agent-free—or is that a free agent? Whatever. I'm acting on my own behalf and I am a man of my word."

Milo bit back a smile, thinking she was cute when loopy. "Fine by me." He'd utilized Michael Stone's services once. After meeting Evie and learning how he'd screwed her over, he liked the smooth-talking bastard even less.

"What should I tell Tabasco?" Woody asked, eyeing Evie, then Milo.

Evie spoke first. "Do you have a clothes dryer in this joint?"

Woody nodded. "In the basement."

"Tell him I'll be down in twenty minutes."

Milo guesstimated she'd be down for the count in ten, but he jumped on the chance to get her out of those wet clothes. "I can loan you some jogging pants and a sweatshirt while you wait."

She nabbed the nurse's uniform from Woody. "This will do. Thanks." She weaved into the bathroom.

Woody escaped down the stairs.

Two doors slammed shut and Milo's ass vibrated. "What?" he barked into the cell.

"*Dinnae* bite my head off. You're the one who hung up on me, yeah?"

Arch sounded calm—but then, he always sounded calm. Milo knew him well enough to know he was agitated. He pushed, hoping to confirm or negate suspicions that Arch had fallen head over heels. "Something came up."

"That why you're trying to get Evie *oot* of her knickers?"

"Jealous?"

"Concerned."

"Not much of a difference."

"Enough of a difference."

Just then, the topic of discussion stepped out of the bathroom looking like Nurse Goodbody. Milo's mouth went dry.

"Still there, mate?"

"Uh-huh."

Not looking at him, she tugged up the plunging neckline. "Where'd you get this nurse's uniform anyway?" she slurred. "Frederick's of Hollywood? Maybe I should have opted for your shirt, Beckett. It would've covered more."

"What the—"

"Call you back." Milo snapped the phone shut. He imagined Arch scrambling to book the next flight back to the States. Wasn't sure how he felt about that. Yesterday he'd been bent on guarding their partnership. Today he considered the possibility that he'd learned all that he could from the grifter. Maybe it was time to break off with Arch *and* the Agency, strike out on his own. It would certainly make life simpler.

Growing pains.

He studied Nurse Evie Goodbody, registered another kind of ache. Christ.

She palmed her forehead, groaned. "Something's wrong." The color drained from her face. "Help me," she said, just like in his dream. And toppled into his arms, just like in his dream.

Only there was nothing sexy about this moment. She was feverish and semiconscious. Milo swooped her up and placed her on the sofa.

"Must be allergic," she said.

"To whiskey?"

"Echi-something." Her eyes closed. Her limp hand pointed. "Purse."

Milo found a black purse under her soaked suit jacket. He rooted through the contents, marveled at how much junk a woman could cram into a small space. He palmed her ringing cell, glanced at the caller ID. Nic. Man? Woman? Friend? Family? Someone who'd be aware of Evie's medical history? He allowed the call to roll over to voice mail, dug deeper and nabbed a small plastic bottle. *Echinacea.* An herbal remedy for colds.

Milo uncapped the bottle, tapped out a few capsules and read the inscription. "Hell."

CHAPTER EIGHT

"Midol?" Nicole, my chain-smoking, designer-chic friend, spread a coverlet on top of my duvet—as if I wasn't warm enough—and settled on the end of my bed.

"Yup," I croaked, feeling as foolish now as I had several hours earlier when Beckett had informed me of the mix-up. "It's Coco's fault," I said for the second time today. "My neighbor's poodle. A while back I agreed to dog-sit, not knowing Coco was cuckoo. He chewed up two paperback novels and destroyed the cardboard box containing the pain relievers. Needing a container, I swapped out the herbal capsules to salvage the Midol. At the time, the cramp stuff was more important than the cold stuff. Only I forgot about the swap."

"Only you," Nic said with a grin.

Beckett had said the same thing.

I'd have to commit the mortifying scene to my diary. Someday it would strike me as funny. Maybe.

Doped up on Robitussin, Midol and whiskey, I'd suffered slurred speech, noodly limbs and severe fatigue. But I didn't pass out. Partly because I was too stubborn and embarrassed. Partly because Beckett had plied me with hot tea and questions. He must've been desperate to keep me alert and talking. Surely he wasn't *that* interested in my entertainment background. After a couple of hours, the storm had subsided and he finally agreed to drive me home. But only if I called someone to check in on me. Like I couldn't take care of myself. Okay, I screwed up my medication, but that was a freak accident. Swear. "That's what I get for not looking at what I put in my mouth."

"I could comment on that," Nic said. "But I won't."

Jayne's angelic face heated to a shade that nearly matched her fiery ringlets. "Madame Helene warned me that a loved one was at risk."

"Madame Helene's a nut," Nic said, not for the first time.

Ah, yes. My two best friends: Yin and Yang. Where Nic was the realist, Jayne was the spiritualist. A bit flighty and a lot gullible. Nic and I loved the Bohemian whack-a-doodle but questioned her faith in a certain bangle-wearing whack job. The notorious Madame Helene.

"Loved ones are always at risk," I pointed out calmly. "Everyone's at risk. Every day. Not just physically but emotionally. Intellectually."

"Deep," Nic teased.

I blew my nose into a tissue. "Just saying there are people out there who will take advantage."

"Cynical," Jayne said.

"Educated," I said, thinking about Arch and his sucker-born-every-minute mentality.

My fuzzy brain worked double-time trying to determine how much I could tell my friends about the Chameleon Club and the players I'd met thus far. I hated lying to them, but I didn't want to divulge any secrets that would get me kicked off the team. As it was, I'd been benched. "Did you say you brought chicken soup?"

"Along with crackers and ginger ale," Nic said. "When

you called to say you were sick, we figured we should pass on the chips and margaritas."

Jayne scrambled off the bed. "I'll heat up the soup. We can drag in a couple of TV trays, have supper together and, if you're feeling up to it, Evie, you can tell us about the cruise and jolly old England."

Nic smiled and squeezed my toes through the covers. "Mostly we want to hear about Arch."

The mention of the man who'd yet to return my call filled me with equal parts anger, sadness and anxiety. Had he been arrested by Scotland Yard? Run down by a double-decker bus? Or was he simply ignoring me?

"You all right?" Nic asked as she rose.

"Peachy," I croaked, then blew my nose. "Maybe you guys should go. I'm probably contagious."

"We haven't seen you in almost three weeks. We're not going anywhere." She squeezed my toes again, which was pretty affectionate for Nic. "I'll help Jayne with the sick-people supper. Call if you need us. Or maybe you should just bang on the wall. You haven't got much of a voice left." She smiled. "Good thing you don't have to sing tonight."

"Yeah. Good thing."

As soon as she left the room, I pushed myself into a sitting position and nabbed my cell off the nightstand. Three voice messages. Heart pounding, I connected and listened.

The first message was from my mom, mentioning the upcoming theater benefit. *"Connie Grable still asks after you, Evelyn,"* she said. *"I know you're busy, but the least you could do is attend her special night."* Then she hung up. Huh. Although they were teaching colleagues, it's not as if Mom and Mrs. Grable were best buds. Plus, Mom had never encouraged my artistic interests. I clearly recall her trying to talk me out of joining the drama club in the first place, thinking my time would be better spent boning up on algebra. Like any amount of studying was going to help me to understand quadratic equations. I'm lucky I can balance my checkbook.

I replayed her message, considered. Did she need me to help her to square things with Dad? Nope. That couldn't be it. She blamed me for the failure of my own marriage. I'm the last person she'd ask for matrimonial advice. What then? Did she miss me? The possibility made me all warm and fuzzy. Or maybe it was my chenille sweats and thick socks.

I saved the message and moved on to the next one.

Dad. Sweat beaded on my forehead as I listened to his succinct message. *"I'm thinking it's time we discussed your moving home, little one. Don't call me back on your dime, I'll call again tomorrow. 'Bye, now."*

Okay, something was definitely up. Did he want me to move in with my mom so she wouldn't be alone? Did he plan on making their separation permanent? Or, knowing I no longer had a husband to lean on, did he worry I'd fall flat on my face? I wasn't fond of any of those possibilities.

I skipped to the next message fully expecting to hear my brother's businesslike drone.

"Hey, Sunshine."

Oh, boy. Oh, boy. Not a John Boy twang but a Highlander lilt. Arch's voice flowed through me like heady dark ale.

"Got your message. Glad you're home safe. Dinnae let Beckett work you too hard, yeah? Take care, lass. Cheers."

"That's it?" I couldn't believe it. No invitation to call

him back. No clue as to when he'd be returning to the States. Could his message be any more impersonal? *Friends, just friends,* I told myself and tried not to feel depressed that Arch was honoring my wishes. A modicum of resistance would've been nice.

I tossed the phone into the nightstand drawer and slammed it shut.

Nic peeked in. "You rang?"

"No. I…no. Sorry."

"You look ticked." She carried in two TV trays and set them germ distance away on either side of the bed.

"I'm just bummed about this cold."

"I'm thinking you're bummed because you're here and Arch isn't."

"We're just friends."

"Since when?"

"Since always. We had a fling. Period. No emotional ties. No promises. Just great sex."

"Sounds perfect and totally unlike you."

"Yeah, well, I've changed."

"Don't go changing too much," Nic said with a quirked brow. "We're pretty fond of the old Evie."

"You'll like the new and improved Evie even better," I said. "No more moping over Michael. No more wasting my time trying to land casino gigs."

"I'm liking your attitude, girlfriend. But you do need a paycheck."

"As it happens, I have a new job."

Jayne bopped in carrying a bed tray loaded with a bowl of soup, a plate of saltines and a glass of ginger ale. She placed it over my lap. "What did I miss?"

"Evie got a new job," Nic told her while eyeing me with curiosity.

"A day job?"

As in a real job, aka a nine-to-five. Shudder. "No. A singing job."

"Sounds like your old job," said Jayne. "What casino?"

"Not a casino," I said. "A club. The Chameleon Club."

Nic narrowed her eyes. "Never heard of it. Where is it?"

I stated the address and got the anticipated groans. "I know it's not in the best area and it's not a casino lounge or an upscale dance club, but it's a steady gig—Wednesdays through Sundays. And the pay is decent." Although, come to think of it, I had no idea what the pay was. Maybe Beckett had mentioned it. I couldn't be sure. Half of our conversation was a blur…like the ride home.

"When do you start?" Nic asked

"As soon as I get rid of this cold."

"Did Michael book this gig?" Jayne asked.

"No. He won't be handling me anymore."

Nic snorted. "You can say that again."

Maybe I should. Saying it out loud, stating that we were over personally *and* professionally, worked better than medicine. "Strange," I said, hand over heart. "My chest feels lighter and I can breathe easier."

"That's because you're getting a nasty infection out of your system," Nic said. "That man's been plaguing you for months. Wait'll he learns you're finally and totally over him. His frickin' ego will be crushed."

"Too bad you couldn't rain on his parade before he left for Paris," Jayne said.

I cocked my head, unsure if I'd heard correctly. "Paris? As in France? As in the Eiffel Tower? The Louvre Museum? Champagne and decadent desserts?"

Jayne flushed.

Nic sighed. "I thought we agreed to wait until she was feeling better."

"It slipped out."

I sipped ginger ale to dissolve the lump in my throat. "Tell me."

"Michael and Sasha eloped," Nic said.

"They're honeymooning in Paris," Jayne added.

The city I'd dreamed of visiting since I was a little girl and first saw Gene Kelly and Leslie Caron dancing and singing in *An American in Paris:* The city of *amour.* The city Michael had promised he'd take me to someday. Instead he'd taken Sasha. *"C'est la vie,"* I said as blandly as possible, then spooned chicken soup and focused on not clenching my jaw.

Jayne screwed up her face. "I thought you'd be upset. Don't you care that he didn't tell you about the baby or the marriage, that he just whisked off the other woman to the city of your dreams?"

"Sasha's no longer the other woman," I said, careful not to choke on the words. "She's his wife. And, no, I don't care. I've moved on."

"The new and improved Evie," Nic said with a skeptical gleam in her eye.

"Oh," Jayne said, looking befuddled.

"Consider me enlightened," I said, speaking to her New Age sensibilities.

"But—"

"This soup is delicious," I said. "Aren't you having any?"

Jayne eyed Nic.

Nic eyed me. "Only if you tell us about the Scottish hunk you boinked and dumped."

Jayne blinked. "You dumped Arch?"

"Yeah, but first they had great sex," Nic said.

"Creative monkey sex," I said, knowing that I had to tell them something about the last two weeks. Since I couldn't talk about Chameleon, that left sex. Since I wouldn't be having it anymore, at least not with Arch, the least I could do was relive the best romps with my best buds. Arch wouldn't mind. In fact, I could envision his cocky smile.

"Interesting," Jayne said.

"I'll say." Nic strode for the door. "I'm going to get my soup and—be warned—I'll be eating slowly. I want details. Every position. Every location."

Jayne hovered in Nic's wake. "I meant, interesting how you have this fascination with monkeys. Remember when you e-mailed me from the ship asking what my dream books said about gorillas?"

I slurped some broth. "Uh-huh." I'd been plagued by dreams of me in a gorilla suit hawking used cars. The hairy demise of my entertainment career.

She crossed her arms over her gauzy peasant blouse. "Do you remember what I wrote back?"

"Word for word." I had this gift. Mostly, after reading something once, it was ingrained in my brain. Memorizing scripts had never been a problem. I'd retained a character profile Arch had given me after one reading. I remembered how impressed he'd been. That same night we'd shared our first atomic kiss.

I squeezed my thighs together and cursed some inappropriate tingling. Beckett had asked me if Arch was out of my system. Normally I'm a damn good actress. That I hadn't been able to disguise my infatuation was disconcerting. Either I was slipping or Beckett had a superior bullshit detector. I'm thinking the latter, which meant I needed to pull off a major deception to earn my Chameleon stripes...scales...whatever.

I broke some crackers into my soup and glanced at Jayne, who was still waiting for me to reiterate her summation. "You said that if I dreamed about apes, then beware of a mischief maker in my business or social circle. Unless the gorilla was docile. Then the dream was a forecasting of a new and unusual friend."

"I'm guessing since you dumped Arch, he was a mischief maker. At least you got great sex out of it," she said with a beaming smile. "And also proof that there is some stock in my metaphysical interests." She flounced out of the room, glanced over her shoulder. "Just so you know, I'll be eating as slowly as Nic."

In their absence, I thought about Jayne's dream interpretation. Arch was a mischief maker, to be sure, but I'd considered him that new and unusual friend. No matter our differences, there'd been that indefinable connection. It bothered me that he'd been able to sever it so easily. A friend would have returned my call right away. A friend wouldn't have left me a message with no invitation to call back.

"Ouch."

So much for the new and improved Evie who dumped gorgeous flings without a second thought. *No emotional ties. No promises. Just great sex.*

Right.

CHAPTER NINE

AMAZING WHAT SIXTEEN hours of sleep can do for a run-down body. By midday the next day I felt half human. Although I suffered the occasional sneeze and my voice was still ragged, I'd stopped coughing and I could breathe fairly well. Chicken soup and girl talk had worked miracles—and, okay, later I'd broken down and taken a slug of nighttime cold medicine. Desperate for relief, I didn't care about the groggy side effects. In fact, I counted on the greenish liquid to knock me out, which it did. No dreams about Arch winging through London with a flock of pretty birds or a certain honeymooning couple breezing around Paris.

I did, however, dream about my folks. First thing, I tried to call Mom, then Dad. I got their respective answering machines. My brother was unavailable, as well, tied up in back-to-back meetings, according to his secretary. I left messages. I wrestled my runaway imagination to the ground. *Don't borrow trouble,* I could hear Arch say.

"Don't think about Arch." He sure wasn't thinking of me. I told myself to stop pouting. I wanted a hot fling. I got it. I wanted to break off. We did. Possible his idea of friendship differed from mine. Possible things were hunky-dory between us and I was overreacting due to an overactive imagination. Yeah. That was it.

After a healthy breakfast and a reviving shower, I was ready to face a new Zip-a-Dee-Doo-Dah day. Beckett had barred me from the club until my cold was kaput, but that didn't mean I couldn't prepare. I'd spend the next day or two cramming. Bone up on jazz standards and common grifts. Somewhere I had the soundtrack from *Lady Sings the Blues*. I'd be hard-pressed to find a cheery song on that Billie Holliday tribute, but at least it was jazz. I could listen and absorb while reading up on classic cons. Since I'd paid for rush delivery, I expected the books I'd ordered today. The better I understood the mechanics and lingo, the better my chances of being taken seriously by Chameleon.

Shopping was also on today's itinerary. I had an apartment to decorate. Even Beckett's bachelor digs had more personality. I needed to get a life. I was pretty sure I could find one at Wal-Mart. That store had everything. I'd shop for CDs featuring jazz vocalists and DVDs featuring con artists—anything to immerse myself in the world of grifters and scams. Then I'd stroll the home-furnishing aisle looking for colorful curtains and toss pillows. Maybe a coordinating area rug and whimsical wall hangings.

Sipping my second cup of tea, I peeked through the blinds to check the weather and saw my car sitting in the parking lot. It made me think of Beckett. He could've poured me into a cab. Instead he'd insisted on seeing me home personally. He'd driven my car, asking Tabasco to follow so that he had a ride home. I thought about the way he'd blown off business to look after my welfare and blushed. He'd been a perfect gentleman. I'd been a pain in the neck.

I'd barged into his apartment and picked a fight…

while under multiple influences. My first day with Chameleon had been a mortifying disaster, yet instead of focusing on the negative, I contemplated Milo Beckett's caring manner. First in the hospital after the Simon the Fish shooting. Then yesterday. Granted, he hadn't given me the job I'd wanted, but his reasons had merit. He didn't think I was ready to tangle with professional grifters. The opportunity, however, was there. At least he was giving me a chance to prove myself. To think, I'd first pegged him as an obnoxious womanizer. Then again, I'd first met him as Tex Aloha.

Now I could only think of him as Beckett or Jazzman. Everyone at Chameleon had a nickname. Pops, Tabasco. Even Bearded Boy, whose real name, I'd learned, was Woody, answered to The Kid. Arch was Ace. Oh, and let's not forget Gina. Of course the boys would dub the brunette bombshell something sexy like Hot Legs. Me, I got stuck with Twinkie. Although it could've been worse. Nipples. Headlights. Hooters. Yeah, could have been worse.

I rinsed out my cup and headed for my bedroom. My phone chirped with an incoming call. My hopes soared. My heart raced. "Yeah?"

"What kind of way is that to answer the phone?"

Arch's way. "Sorry. Hi, Christopher." My brother.

"What's wrong with your voice?"

"I have a cold. No biggie. It's almost gone." God forbid he feel compelled to offer comfort. "Thanks for returning my call."

"I was going to call you today anyway."

"You were? Is everything okay?" Because my brother never called to chat. He was, after all, a Parish.

"No, everything is not okay."

I sat on the end of my bed. I struggled not to borrow trouble and failed. "Mom didn't file for divorce, did she?"

"No. But Dad might when he gets wind of her shenanigans."

"Shenanigans?" Our mom made June Cleaver look like a party girl. We're talking straight arrow. An apple-pie conservative. She did not engage in shenanigans.

"She's taking dance lessons."

"Dance lessons? Mom?"

"There's a new instructor in town. He's teaching over at the civic center. Line dancing. Ballroom. Rumor has it Mom's kicking up her heels."

"I can't believe it."

"That's the least of it."

I braced myself. Converting to Democrat? Drinking cosmopolitans?

"She cashed in two war bonds."

"What? Like savings bonds?"

"Exactly."

"I didn't know she owned bonds."

"Neither did I. Given the date of purchase, someone must have gifted them to her as a child."

"And she's just now cashing them in?"

"She showed up at the bank on my day off and withdrew the bonds from her safe-deposit box. I'm convinced she didn't want me to know about it. But it was a sizable amount. It was Mom. Naturally it came to my attention."

Naturally. He was, after all, the bank president. "Did you ask her about it?"

"She told me to mind my own beeswax."

My stomach clenched at an uncomfortable thought. "Are Mom and Dad hurting for money?"

"No. Between their savings and pensions, they're set. Even with the purchase of the tavern."

"That's a relief. So what did Mom need the money for?"

"That's what I'd like to know."

My brother, the man who never panicked, the man who considered himself a superior problem solver, sounded worried. My pulse galloped. "How much money are we talking?

"Six thousand."

"Wow." I nibbled my thumbnail, deep in thought. "Maybe she's buying a new fridge or converting my bedroom into a home office like she's been talking about forever. You know, treating herself to something special since Dad treated himself to the Corner Tavern."

"I haven't seen any workers at the house or a delivery truck in the driveway."

"Well, what do you—"

"You don't want to know what I think."

Shrieking would only aggravate my scratchy throat. "Just tell me."

"I think she has a boyfriend."

"What!" So much for staying cool. I bolted to my feet and paced to walk off anxious energy.

"Someone's put a spring in her step."

"Maybe it's the dance class."

"Or someone in that class. She's been spotted with that instructor—once at JCPenney, once at Pizza Hut."

"So what?"

"So they were together. As in shopping together. Eating together." Dramatic pause. "Like a date."

I rubbed a dull throbbing at my temple. "This is crazy talk, Christopher. Mom wouldn't…she couldn't…she's *married*."

"So was Michael."

Ouch. "Nice."

"Sorry," Christopher said, his tone as tight as his wallet. "It's been a rough few weeks."

I could envision my brother squeezing one of those squishy stress-reliever balls, whereas I clenched my jaw.

"This all started when Dad bought the Corner Tavern against Mom's wishes," he said.

"Why did he do that, anyway?"

"I'm pretty sure he did it for you."

I stopped in my tracks, sank to my knees. "What are you talking about?"

"Dad's been pretty closemouthed. All Mom and I got out of him was that retirement was for the birds. He needed to keep busy. Missed shooting the breeze with the town folk. But yesterday I stopped in there, and what do I see?"

"I'm scared to ask."

"A stage. Complete with a lighting and sound system. The bartender said Dad's been auditioning bands. Bands without a female singer and not opposed to adding one."

I'm thinking it's time we discussed your moving home, little one.

"Oh, no."

"Here's the thing—I thought this tiff between Mom and Dad would blow over. It didn't. I thought I could reason with them. I can't. Between my responsibilities at the bank and the time I've spent trying to mend parental bridges, I've been neglecting Sandy and the kids."

My brother's wife and stepkids were high-maintenance, his job high pressure. To relax, he played tennis and golf and worked out in a home gym. Although he was younger than me, he was probably a prime candidate for a heart attack or a stroke or some other god-awful ailment that plagued type A personalities.

"After telling me to butt out of her business," Christopher added in a low voice, "Mom threatened to never speak to me again if I mentioned the bonds to Dad. Whatever she's doing with that money she's doing behind his back. What if she's become addicted to the shopping network? What if she's plotting to run off to Mexico with her boy toy?"

"This is our sixty-three-year-old, never-been-on-a-plane mom we're talking about."

Only Christopher wasn't listening. He'd made up his mind and, if you asked him, he was never wrong. "Maybe I should confront Fancy Feet. Tell him to back off. If he thinks he's going to seduce her out of her savings…"

"Maybe he's sincerely attracted." I didn't want to believe anything tawdry was going on, but I felt compelled to stand up for Mom. She was tough, but she wasn't an ogre.

"Men aren't typically romantically attracted to women several years their senior, Evelyn."

Double ouch. I pressed a hand to my hot cheeks. *Some men are,* I wanted to say but didn't. "Don't confront the man, Christopher. If you're wrong, you'll embarrass Mom. And if you're right…" *What a mess.* "Just don't."

Meanwhile, his accusations rooted and blossomed. What if Mom had been suckered by some sort of swindle? I could envision Arch sitting across from me, lecturing me on a grifter's prime mark: the weak and gullible and, often, as with the investment scam we'd busted on the cruise, the retired.

Adrenaline surged, clearing my clogged sinuses and rocketing me to my feet. I was halfway to my closet when my brother said, "I could use some help here, sis."

This was a first. My brother crying uncle and reaching out. To *me,* of all people, the black sheep of my grounded, successful family. And he wasn't the only Parish acting out of character. Knowing work was sparse in Atlantic City, my suit-and-necktie Dad had bought a seedy redneck tavern to bolster my singing career. No-nonsense Mom was learning the Bus Stop and the mambo and spending a wad of dough on who knows what. Was she having a breakdown? Was her message about me coming home for the benefit a veiled cry for help?

"I'll be there day after tomorrow, latest."

Tears pricked my eyes as I dragged out Big Red—the monstrous suitcase I'd toted to the Caribbean and London—for the third time this month. My noncommunicative, wholly reliant family needed me.

CHAPTER TEN

THE SUN WAS SHINING as I peeled rubber through the Inlet and parked in the semimuddy lot of the Chameleon Club. My mood was black. I'd tried calling Arch three times while I'd packed. I needed his advice and all I got was his voice mail. Instead of leaving a message, I'd hung up, disconnected from the man in more ways than one.

My pulse and brain raced in tandem as I scaled the steps and power walked toward the boardwalk entrance. No umbrella. No spiky heels. No mishaps. I breezed inside and glanced at the bar. Pops was engrossed in conversation with two barflies, neither being Tabasco. I scanned the club for Beckett. Not seeing him, I strode for the door marked Private.

"Not there."

I forced a smile and faced the leathery bartender, dressed much as he'd been the day before, only his vest was red instead of black. "Is he around?" Again I thought of secret rooms for secret-agent plotting. "Somewhere?"

"He is."

I motioned Pops to the opposite end of the bar, away from his friends' big ears.

He approached me with wary eyes, palming that retro rolled-brim hat to the back of his silver head. He looked a little like Morgan Freeman, dressed a lot like Buster

Keaton and sounded exactly like Barry White. "Aren't you supposed to be home, recovering?"

I fidgeted under his stern expression. "I feel much better." I pinched my nose and suppressed a sneeze.

"Uh-huh."

I bucked up before he could offer me a shot of whiskey or fatherly advice. "I need to speak with Beckett. It's important." I could have called but felt better asking for a leave of absence in person. My stomach knotted thinking I could be ruining any chance of ever becoming a full-fledged Chameleon. Quite possibly the government agent would question my reliability, my dedication to the cause. Sure he was nice, but business was business.

"He's in a meeting," Pops said. "Also important."

I instinctively knew that, unlike yesterday, he was not going to steer me in the direction of the boss. The silver fox had shifted into guard dog. Any other time I'd be tempted to win him over. Just now, I was desperate to split town.

"Okay. Here's the deal." I braced my hands on the bar and leaned forward, delivering the spiel I'd intended for Beckett. "I need to take a leave of absence. Postpone my engagement. Whatever. I know this looks bad—I haven't even started—but this is an emergency. A family emergency."

"Should've said right off." Pops turned and made a phone call. His voice was low, the conversation brief. He hung up, telling Stan, one of the two old coots sipping beer, to mind the store. He grasped my elbow.

Thinking back on how I'd pulled one over on that bartender in the London pub, I leaned in to Pops and whispered, "Aren't you afraid Stan might steal from the register or liberate a beer from the fridge?"

"Nope."

A trusting con man? At least I *assumed* Pops was a former con man. Beckett had called him a vital part of the team. Someday, when I wasn't in a hurry and he was more talkative, I'd try to find out more about him. Just now, I followed silently as he guided me through the ill-arranged tables and chairs, past the jukebox and *appropriated* sound system. Tabasco sprang to mind.

From what I remembered of my Midol-fogged discussion with Beckett, in addition to being a transportation specialist, Tabasco also begged, bargained and borrowed props for stings. *Location scout* was the technical term. Apparently his many talents extended to the acoustic guitar. Whether he was a decent player remained to be heard.

I banged my hip on a chair, swallowed a yelp and focused on where I was going. For the first time I noticed a pronounced hitch in Pop's step. "What's wrong with your—"

"Old injury," he said, a *mind your own beeswax* lingering in the stale air.

He unlocked a door and guided me through a jam-packed storage room. I was rubbernecking at the eclectic collection of *stuff,* likening Beckett to Arch's pack-rat granddad, when I realized Pops had opened a second door, a door I hadn't noticed. A dangling yellow bulb cast minimal light on a cobwebbed stairwell. Pops and I descended the creaky wooden stairs into near darkness. Together we clung to the banister—me for nerves, him for support.

The basement, I assumed. Was Beckett doing laundry? But, wait. Pops had mentioned a meeting. Maybe the basement wasn't a basement at all but a high-tech hidey-hole for Chameleon HQ. The theme from the sixties sitcom *Get Smart* welled in my brain along with visions of Maxwell Smart and Chief behind closed doors plotting CONTROL's latest mission to obliterate KAOS.

The music died the moment we reached the bottom and Pops clicked on a light. Nothing high-tech about this low-ceilinged basement. Cluttered like the storage room with box upon cardboard box. The room felt damp and cool and smelled musty, although I did catch a whiff of fabric softener. My gaze followed my nose, zeroing in on a washer and dryer that, given the avocado finish, dated back to the seventies. The nearby freezer looked a decade newer, which still made it a dinosaur in appliance years. Next to that, shelves stacked with cans of assorted party snacks. I wondered how long *they'd* been there.

I did a visual sweep of the room. Crates of liquor and soda. A wall of tools and a carpenter's table. Weight bench and barbells. So that's how Beckett maintained his chiseled torso. Except he wasn't pumping iron now. Or pounding nails. Or washing clothes.

"Pops, I…" My impatience evaporated when I whirled and caught him swinging aside a wall clock to reveal a security pad.

"Turn away," he said.

"Why?"

"Heard you got total recall."

My chest bloomed with pride. So Beckett hadn't focused solely on my mishaps. He'd touted my talents, as well. This time my smile was genuine. "I don't know about total recall, but I do have an exceptional memory when it comes to—"

"Turn away."

"Right." I faced the opposite wall and soon heard voices, one louder than the others and not happy. My mouth dried with excitement and nerves as Pops tapped me on the shoulder and I saw the snack shelves had slid open. *A secret room.* I took in the blue carpet, acoustical-tile ceiling and soundproof walls. It reminded me of a posh recording studio complete with state-of-the-art audio and visual equipment, computers and a too-cool-for-your-shoes black leather sofa and chairs. Yowza.

Parked in the center of that cushy sofa was Tabasco. Standing over his shoulder, arms crossed and hands tucked under his pits, was the Kid, the technical brains of the outfit. Looming center stage in a face-off with Milo Beckett—Gina "Hot Legs" Valente. It was the first time I'd seen her since the Simon the Fish fiasco. To say we had unresolved issues was an understatement.

Focused on one another in an intense showdown, they'd yet to notice us. I stood, silent and mesmerized, as the Angelina Jolie clone knocked the back of her hand against the government agent's shoulder. "What are you smoking, Jazzman? Say no to the AIA director and you can say goodbye to your career."

Beckett, who reminded me a little of George Clooney, glowered. "I didn't sign on to act as a politician's personal avenger."

"No," she shot back. "But you did sign on to dupe swindlers who feed off poor, vulnerable saps."

"The senator's wife is not vulnerable, nor is she poor. She's a gambling addict. His problem. Not ours."

"Not true," Tabasco cut in. He planted his feet on the floor and braced his forearms on his knees. "The new boss—what's-his-name…"

"Special Director Vincent Crowe," said Woody.

"Crowe, whose shit list we're on at the moment, made it our problem when he asked you a favor," Tabasco said.

"Way I see it, we win back the senator's money, we win over two powerful men. Men who could make our lives heaven or hell. I vote for the easy life."

"Doesn't cost us anything but time," Gina said.

"Maybe, maybe not," Beckett said. "I have a bad feeling about this one."

"You're just bent because the victims are rich and influential," she said. "Stop focusing on the financial angle and consider the emotional damage. Guilt, shame, anxiety. I'm not ready to turn my back on a mark just because she's privileged."

Woody cleared his throat and pointed to me.

Gina glared. "You have *got* to be kidding." Pinch-mouthed, she angled away from Beckett and planted her knockout body next to Tabasco's.

She didn't say anything else. She didn't have to. I could read the disapproval in her kohl-lined eyes. She didn't like that I was in this room. Didn't like that, because of Beckett, I now circulated in her professional world. Basically, she didn't like me, although I had never understood why. Mostly everybody likes me. I'm a likable kind of girl.

Tabasco smiled at me in a way that probably caused most women to swoon. All I felt was the urge to roll my eyes. Gina elbowed him in the ribs.

Woody backed away when Pops nudged me deeper into the room. The Kid probably doubted my mental stability. Based on our interaction thus far, I couldn't blame him.

Beckett turned. "What's this about a family emergency?"

He didn't look any happier than Gina. My anxiety skyrocketed. I didn't want to blow my job with Chameleon. I loved this job that I hadn't even started. But I couldn't, wouldn't, ignore the troubles on the home front. Still, I didn't want to discuss my parents' behavior in front of the entire team. "I didn't mean to interrupt—my timing stinks," I blurted.

Gina grunted. "What else is new?"

Beckett shot her a look, then approached me. "Spill."

His tone was no-nonsense, but when he moved closer, I realized concern shone in his gaze. My gut said he'd understand. "Something's wrong with my mom."

"Is she sick?"

"She's…not herself."

"When are you leaving?"

"Right away," I said, grateful when he didn't press for details. "I don't have a flight yet, but—"

"Tabasco can fly you. He owns a plane."

"What kind of plane? One of those little propeller jobs?"

"Not so little," said the pilot. "Single-engine Cessna. Seats six to eight, depending on cargo."

"Propeller?" I pressed.

"Yes," the team answered as one.

"Thanks, but no, thanks."

"Motion sickness," Beckett explained, and though he probably thought he was being helpful, he'd made me look weak in the others' eyes.

Feeling defensive, I looked around his shoulder to Tabasco. "I appreciate the offer, but I wouldn't want to pull you away from the senator's case."

"About that," Beckett interrupted. "What's said between these walls—"

"Stays within these walls. Understood." I pantomimed zipping my lip and throwing away the key. Not that I even knew who they were speaking of specifically. Still, I could keep a secret. My diary was full of them.

There was an awkward silence. I'm accustomed to being the center of attention. I'd made a decent living in the spotlight for more than twenty-five years. But this was different. This was personal. I scratched my neck.

"Commercial flight will cost her a fortune," Pops said, "considering she's booking last-minute. Why don't you have the Kid work some of his magic?"

"Good idea," Beckett said.

I was stunned by Pops's lengthy sentences as much as his thoughtfulness. As he'd said, a last-minute ticket wouldn't be cheap. If Woody could help… "Is it illegal?"

Beckett's mouth curved. "We call it *creative*." He turned to Woody. "Round trip. Philadelphia to Indianapolis."

"Return date?" Woody asked.

Beckett looked at me and my insides churned. "I don't know. I…you see…" What the heck. I blurted a condensed version of my brother's story, bracing myself for snorts and scoffing when I summed up with, "I'm worried someone's swindling my mom."

"Sweetheart scam?" Tabasco said.

Gina shrugged. "Maybe she's just letting her hair down."

"Let's find out." Beckett looked at Woody. "Book two one-way flights, plus a rental car."

"I'll ready your suitcase," Pops said, and limped from the room.

Gina stood. "Hold up, Jazzman. What about the senator?"

Beckett rocked back on his heels, considered. "He lives just outside of Hammond. How far is that from your hometown, Twinkie?"

I blinked. "Hammond, Indiana? We're talking about a senator from my home state?"

"Yes and yes. How far?"

"Two, maybe two and a half hours."

He looked at his team. "I'll drive up and interview the senator's wife in person."

"So we're taking the case," Gina said. "Because if we don't, seems to me we're facing something more permanent than suspension."

Beckett didn't comment. Either he didn't care or he wasn't concerned.

His silence triggered hard stares and confrontational body language. I wasn't sure what I'd stepped into, but I hoped it worked itself out before I returned.

"You can't come with me, Beckett," I said. "How would I explain you to my family? Chameleon's covert and you're a Fed. What if I'm wrong? What if there's no swindle? What if my mom *is* having an affair?" I clamped my hand over my mouth as soon as the words flew out. Crazy talk.

"Didn't you say something about a high-school reunion?" Beckett asked.

"A civic theater benefit with high-school alumni. Yes, but—"

"Will the others bring their husbands?"

"Yes, but—"

"Do you have a boyfriend?" Pops asked.

I thought about Arch, looked at Beckett. I forced my fingers not to scratch. "No."

He smiled. "You do now."

CHAPTER ELEVEN

MILO STARED DOWN the rental-car representative—a pale, thin-lipped kid with slicked-over hair. Pee-wee Herman's younger brother. "What do you mean there are no available cars? I have a reservation."

"You *had* a reservation, sir. You canceled it."

"I didn't."

"You did." Pee-wee passed him a computer-generated form. "Says so right here."

"No one has luck this bad," Evie grumbled from behind. "Not even me."

Nonstop flights had been sold out, doubling travel time to four and a half hours. To aggravate matters, due to misinformation, they'd missed their connecting flight. Stranded at the Cleveland airport for what seemed like days. Now this. Milo glanced down at the sheet, glanced up at the representative. "My girlfriend and I have been traveling for—" he checked his temper and his watch "—ten hours. We're exhausted, we're frustrated and we're expected. I need a car. Stick. Automatic. Compact or luxury. Whatever you've got."

"But I don't have anything, sir. There are several conventions in town. Good for us, bad for you." He passed Milo back his credit card. "Sorry."

"Unbelievable," he said to himself as he turned to

Evie. Only she wasn't there. She was standing across the way, talking on her cell phone. He wondered if she was talking to Arch—or, rather, to his voice mail. The Scot had mentioned dodging her calls, hoping to cool any lingering heat. Although that had been before the whiskey/Midol incident.

After driving Evie home and seeing her settled, he'd called Arch to disabuse him of the notion that he'd made a pass. Allowing him to believe otherwise, using Evie to somehow manipulate him, didn't sit right. Granted, he'd considered it, but he couldn't do it. To Arch, yes. To Evie, no. "You know me better than that," he'd said.

"*Dinnae* mistake my concern for anything beyond friendship," had been Arch's reply.

They'd left it at that, and Milo decided, whether the Scot was in love or not, he was sticking to his personal code, distancing himself so, if the need arose, he could walk away from Evie without a second thought. It made Milo feel less uncomfortable about his own interest in the woman.

His mouth curved when she turned around and he got another look at her Mighty Mouse T-shirt. It didn't matter that she was over forty; like Goldie Hawn, she was perpetually cute. He wondered if she'd appreciate the observation. Probably not, given her dislike of her moniker. Twinkie. Not degrading, he thought, *fitting*.

She closed her eyes and massaged her jaw and he felt a stab of guilt. She was worried and tired, and here he stood admiring the curves even her cargo pants couldn't disguise. He wheeled over her beet-red suitcase along with his beat-up Samsonite just as she disconnected.

"I booked us a room at the Airport Ramada."

So she hadn't been talking to Arch. This day was

looking up. "Why? Your parents live ninety minutes north."

"Except we don't have a car."

"We'll try another agency."

"Even if we snag wheels," she rasped, "by the time we fill out the paperwork, load the luggage and get on the road, we won't hit Greenville until one in the morning." Between exhaustion and her lingering cold, she barely had a voice. "I'm fried, Beckett. I need a clear head to focus on our ruse. I need energy to deal with whatever's happening at home."

He could use some downtime himself. He'd volunteered for this unofficial mission on a whim. She'd walked in, Miss Damsel in Distress, and he'd jumped on his white charger.

I'll save you.

My hero.

But it was more than an opportunity to bring his fantasy to life that had prompted him to offer himself up as her boyfriend. He knew she'd been nervous about compromising her job with Chameleon by taking a leave of absence before she'd even started. That she'd set aside her own ambitions to race to her family's rescue stirred him. Yes, he was physically attracted to Evie, but he also felt genuine affection.

Mixing business with pleasure suddenly seemed like a kick-ass idea. This trip to Small Town, USA, provided him with a chance to get to know Evie away from Arch, away from Chameleon. Some quiet time to reevaluate his life. Even though he'd assured the team he'd look into Crowe's unofficial directive, that didn't mean he'd take on the job. He hadn't signed up with the Agency to bail rich politicians out of financial jams. He'd signed up to burn low-life grifters who scammed naive marks out of their life savings. Specifically the scum artists, as Arch called them, who targeted the needy, preyed on the vulnerable and naive. Everyday Joes like Mrs. Parish. Not that he was convinced the woman was being scammed.

Twinkie, on the other hand, was certain her mom had fallen victim to everything from a Sweetheart swindle to a Nigerian scam. While he'd tried to unsnarl the travel knot in Cleveland, she'd had her nose stuck in a research book she'd purchased online. The more she read, the greater her fears. Like a hypochondriac perusing a medical encyclopedia.

"All right," he said. "We'll call it a night. Want to call and give your mom an update?"

"The only one who knows I'm coming is my brother, and he's not expecting me until tomorrow or the day after."

On the flight, he'd asked her about her family. She'd confessed they weren't close, but she loved them and assumed they loved her, even though they'd never said the words out loud. Having grown up in a repressed environment, he marveled at her natural vitality and warmth, although she *had* called herself the black sheep of the family.

He was beginning to feel the same way about himself and the AIA.

"You okay?" she asked.

"Just tired," he said, fighting the urge to confess his career crisis. Even though he knew she'd empathize, she had enough on her mind. And, besides, he'd figure it out. He always did. "Good thinking. The room," he clarified while hauling their bags toward the signs marked Taxi Service.

"Luckily, there were some cancellations so I booked

two." She hurried alongside. "I know we're supposed to be sleeping together. I know we'll have to put on a show once we get there. But until then—"

"Got it, Twinkie."

"I wish you wouldn't call me that."

"I know." Smiling, he loaded their bags into a cab parked curbside, helped her into the backseat and gave the driver their destination. It was late. Dark. He couldn't see her expression, but he could feel the tension radiating from her compact body. "Whatever's wrong," he said, "we'll fix it."

"I appreciate this, Beckett."

"Milo. Starting tomorrow, we'll be a couple. Beckett won't cut it."

"Got it."

He frowned at her weary tone, instinctually wrapped his arm around her shoulders, offering comfort. She didn't pull away, but she didn't relax against him, either. "You all right with this, Twinkie? Sure you'll be able to convince your family and friends you're crazy about me?"

"Absolutely," she said with a smile in her voice that inspired hope for the better man. "I'm a damn good actress."

DEAR DIARY, I FELT another snap.

Hunched over the cheap desk of my standard, generic hotel room, I scribbled in my diary. Two pages of purple-penned rant.

The first snap had been three weeks ago. The audition from hell. That snap had been loud and proud, felt by me, witnessed by a dozen or so bystanders. This snap had happened tonight, when Beckett put his arm around me. A quiet but worrisome snap. And, because of my superb acting skills, no one knew about it but me. And my diary.

I like Beckett. A lot.

He didn't make my heart flutter, like Arch. He didn't summon my inner bad girl. I didn't want to jump his bones, but I did want to take comfort in his arms.

Would my heart flutter if he kissed me?

On the cruise ship, we'd engaged in a brief couple's dance. A slow dance. I remember he had good rhythm. I'd been impressed. I remember my skin tingled. I'd been unsettled. I'd told myself I wasn't actually attracted to him, but he was an attractive man and I was desperate for physical intimacy.

Only now I wasn't desperate. I'd just had two weeks of nonstop creative physical intimacy with Arch.

What's wrong with me?

I started making a list, but that seemed unproductive, so I started another list. Make that two.

Arch

Unpredictable
Smart
Dangerous
Sexy
Shady past
Kind
Skewed morals

Beckett

Stable
Smart
Safe
Sexy

> Commendable past
> Kind
> Solid morals

"Crap." Arch had more cons than pros, which made sense, I guess, considering he's a *con* artist. "Former con-artist," I reminded myself. Then I added to his list *Doesn't do relationships.*

If I recalled right—and I usually do—Arch had mentioned Beckett had been married for several years, before his wife left him, which prompted me to add to his list *Dumped like me.*

No doubt about it, Beckett was more my old-fashioned, good-girl speed.

But Arch was the one who made my spirit zoom.

I blinked down at my lists, noted that I'd doodled hearts and tried on both their last names for size. "How old am I—fourteen?"

I slammed the diary shut, thinking that was a bad question, because the correct answer was: forty-one. Old enough to know that someday, when the time was right, I wanted to commit to one man. Kind of hard to pledge your heart to someone who doesn't do relationships. "I'm not even sure if he can do friendship."

The shower came on in Beckett's room. I remembered finding him in his towel two days earlier. I tried not to think of the hard-muscled chest. It didn't help my confusion at all.

Brain buzzing, I reopened the diary.

This is all your fault, Ace.

And spent the next twenty minutes blasting Arch Duvall and the dark horse he rode in on.

CHAPTER TWELVE

MORNING CAME SOONER than I would have liked, given I'd slept like a kid hopped up on a six-pack of Red Bull.

Although we'd easily booked a car and were now zipping up the interstate, my mood was tense. Sure, I was worried about my parents and, yes, I was uncomfortable with this awareness of Beckett, but it was Arch who'd plagued my restless dreams. In la-la land I'd hit him with everything I'd written in my diary before I'd collapsed on that hotel bed. In la-la land, as in reality, he calmly listened to my rant, pointing out *I* was the one who ended the affair and, had I left him a message about my mom, *bloody hell, aye,* he would have been on the next plane. In la-la land, as in reality—or at least my old reality— we ended up rolling around on the floor making crazy, heated whoopee.

This morning I was more vexed with him than yesterday. I refused to analyze the tightness in my chest. "Bastard."

"Me or the driver who just cut me off?" Beckett asked.

Arch, I wanted to say but didn't. "He could have at least used his turn signal." A calculated guess, since I'd been zoning.

Hands steady on the steering wheel, Beckett just smiled. He'd insisted on driving, even though we were on my home turf. The man was a control freak—add that to the list—but I didn't mind. Not in this instance. Too much travel and anxiety in too few days, coupled with the tail end of a cold, made me grumpy. I slurped more Dunkin' Donuts java, gunning for a caffeine jolt.

"Maybe you should ease up. That's your third cup in two hours."

"I need all the bean juice I can chug. I didn't sleep well last night."

"Want to talk about it?"

"No."

"Nervous?"

"Anxious. Except for a quickie weekender last year when I attended my brother's wedding, I haven't been home in three years. How awful is that?"

He didn't comment.

"My track record wasn't much better before that. It used to be because of work. Either I was booked or, if I wasn't, I was afraid to leave for fear of a last-minute offer. In show biz, when it rains, it pours—you take it when you can get it."

"Unstable business. I'm sure they understand."

"Not really. Mom never approved of my performing for a living. She wanted me to go to college. Wanted me to have something solid to fall back on. Logically, she was right. I'd be flipping burgers right now if it weren't for Chameleon. It's just she wanted me to be something I'm not."

"And that would be?"

"Normal."

He laughed and the tension in my jaw eased. He wasn't laughing at me. He got why my mom's vision was absurd. He got *me*.

I ignored the warm fuzzies, sipped more coffee and studied my boss—make that *boyfriend*—over the rim of my foam cup. Beckett was certainly attractive, though in a quiet way. He didn't ooze charisma like Arch, but he oozed confidence. He was talented and nice—mostly—and smart. A flipping government agent, for crying out loud.

"Do I have doughnut crumbs on my face?" he asked.

"What? No. Why?"

"You're staring."

I blushed. "I was just…I was wondering…do you have a girlfriend?"

"Yeah. You."

"I mean, for real."

"No one steady." He cast me a sidelong glance. "Why?"

"Just wondering."

"So you said."

"It's just that I'd prefer not to kiss someone else's boyfriend."

Another glance. "You're going to kiss me?"

"When I have to."

He shook his head. "Good thing I don't have a fragile ego."

"I didn't mean it like that. I just meant it will be easier to pretend I'm hot for you if—"

"I know what you mean."

I pressed back in my seat, overwhelmed with a wave of déjà vu.

Arch and I had traded similar words the first day we met. I'd been hired to play his wife, only I'd thought it was a gig, not a mission. Pretending to be hot for the man had been cake since I wasn't pretending. With Beckett,

I'd definitely be acting. Although it wouldn't be a *huge* challenge since I wasn't exactly repulsed by the man. An understatement, and one I chose not to dwell on.

I swallowed. "So there's no one special."

He focused on the road. "I wish there was."

Okay, that was sweet. That was…dangerous. I focused on my coffee instead of his handsome profile. It would be weird to kiss Beckett. Not just because he was my boss but because he was Arch's friend. And because I had feelings for Arch, although I kept trying to squash them down. And—gads—what if Beckett's kiss tripped my heart the same as Arch's? Wouldn't *that* be a mess? Although it could be a blessing. Maybe I needed a distraction. Maybe the fling with Arch had merely been a warm-up for the real thing with…someone else.

Maybe you should forget about your love life and focus on your future as a Chameleon. Face it—mixing the two is a recipe for disaster. Beckett's said so himself more than once.

Right.

It's the reason you broke off with Arch to begin with, right?

Mostly.

So you better hope to hell Beckett doesn't make your heart flutter.

When, I wondered, had my life gotten so complicated? Although complicated beat depressing. Or boring.

My temples throbbed with a tension headache. "You wouldn't happen to have any aspirin, would you?"

He pulled a travel packet from his pants pocket and passed it to me. His lip twitched. "You don't get looped on Tylenol, do you?"

"No," I said, cursing my heated cheeks. I ripped open

the packet and swallowed two caplets, wondering what kind of a man carried aspirin in his pocket. Did Beckett suffer from chronic headaches? Migraines?

"Sure are a lot of cornfields around here," he said before I could ask.

"This *is* farm country."

"I can smell that."

I wrinkled my nose, smiled. "Pigs."

"Your family doesn't—"

"No. We live in town. Speaking of—make that next right." My adrenaline spiked as he veered off the highway and onto the narrow gravel road I'd traveled a bazillion times in my youth. The rental car's tires bumped in and out of potholes and crunched over rocks as we zipped past pastures, fields, barns and hundred-year-old farmhouses.

"I'm seeing lots of tomatoes—"

"Soybeans."

"—and towers—"

"Silos."

"But no town on the horizon," Beckett said. "Sure you remember the way? It's been three years, after all."

I rolled my eyes. "I'm taking you the back way."

"So is Greenville like Hooterville?" he asked, tongue in cheek.

"A *Green Acres* reference? I'm shocked. Can't imagine you watching hokey sitcoms. You seem more like a CNN kind of guy. Anyway, yes, Greenville's a speck on the map. Hope you weren't expecting signal for your cell or access to the Internet."

He frowned.

"Kidding," I said. "Well, about the splotchy Internet access anyway."

He flipped open his phone, noted the signal. Or absence thereof. "Shit."

I grinned. "Sorry you came?"

"No."

"Me, neither." God help me, I meant it.

AS ANXIOUS AND distracted as I'd been for the last twenty-four hours, the moment I saw the sign—Greenville, Population 10,200—I pulled it together. Call me calm and confident. Call me motivated. I fully intended to solve the mystery of my mom's peculiar behavior and to reunite my parents within a week's time, if not sooner. What's more, I intended to fool my family and my drama-club alumni into thinking that, though divorced, I was currently and blissfully involved with Milo Beckett, owner of a retro bar known as the Chameleon Club, where I'd recently landed a house gig. *The more we stick to the truth,* he'd said, *the more they'll buy it.* I'm thinking he also figured the less the chance I'd crack out of turn. All because he thought I was a terrible liar. Arch thought so, too. I'd show them—or at least Beckett—and I'd secure my place on the team. *Until you get better at lying, I'm not putting you in the field.* Yeah, boy, watch my smoke.

I directed Beckett to make a right onto Main Street. "Our house is four blocks down on the left. Two-story. Redbrick, green trim."

"You just described half of the houses on this street." He glanced around. "Quiet. Scenic. Nice. What are those, maple trees?"

"Mostly. A few oak. All ancient." They lined both sides of Main, along with an occasional gas lamp. Greenville was big on retaining certain historical aspects. Several properties had wrought iron fences, and the sidewalk—buckled and chipped—was constructed of brick. Hazardous but charming.

Like Arch.

Stop thinking about him.

"More Mayberry than Hooterville," Beckett said.

Another sixties sitcom reference. "Didn't realize you were a TV addict."

"I've been battling insomnia lately. Three words. Nick at Nite."

Fatigue headaches, was my first thought. That explained the Tylenol. Maybe. My second thought was that we had something in common aside from both being dumped by our spouses. A fondness for classic TV. It occurred to me that I knew even less about Beckett than I knew about Arch, and since I knew next to nothing about the sexy Scot, that was saying a lot. I massaged an ache in my chest.

Stop thinking about Arch. Right.

"What's up with the insomnia?" I asked.

"Restless."

Duh. "Want to talk about it?"

"No."

"Maybe you're lonely." Sleeping alone after sharing a bed with someone for umpteen years was a difficult adjustment. Been there, experienced that.

"Maybe we should get into character. This is your block. Which is your house?"

I pointed. "That one." Stage jitters attacked as he swung into the driveway and I prepared for a humdinger performance. I methodically abandoned the real me, the me who felt as though she was returning home a failure— no husband, no agent, no Oscar or Grammy—and channeled the me I wanted to be. A confident, adventurous woman pursuing a new career. "I can do this," I said to myself as Beckett rounded the car and helped me out.

"*We* can do this," he said with a reassuring smile.

I took the hand he offered, my concocted persona seeping into my bones as our fingers interlaced. I didn't feel a zing or a zap, but I did feel the support of a friend. Warm fuzzies. Fuzzy fur. *Unless the gorilla was docile,* Jayne chanted in my head. Then the dream was forecasting a new and unusual friend.

Then where did that leave Arch?

I choked back unexpected tears, assuring myself that the bizarre reaction was due to my conflicting emotions regarding my parents and their troubles and not because of the confusion regarding my feelings for Arch and Beckett.

Yeah. That was it.

We scaled the cement steps, my pulse racing as we crossed the porch and I prepared to knock. Even though I'd grown up here, I didn't feel comfortable just walking in. It's not as though Mom expected me. But then the front door swung in and there she stood. At least I think it was her. The judgmental blue eyes and pinched mouth were familiar. As for the rest—holy makeover! I'd never seen Mom in jeans, let alone with her shirttails hanging out. She'd knotted a navy-blue scarf at her neck and—color me shocked—after fifteen years of the same look, she'd allowed her stylist to dye and cut her hair. Goodbye dull gray bob, hello soft blond pixie. She looked at least ten years younger than her sixty-three, and my first thought was, *Oh, my God, Christopher's right. She's having an affair!* She cashed in those bonds to fund a new Marilyn Parish—new wardrobe, new lifestyle and, sweet lord, maybe that trip to Mexico.

"You could have prepared me, Evelyn," she said. "I raised you better than that."

Some things never change. My foot wasn't even in the door and I'd already disappointed her. I fumbled for an excuse. *I thought Christopher might have mentioned it* wouldn't wash since he'd called me on the sly. I settled for, "I wanted to surprise you."

"An impromptu visit from you is one thing," she said. "But to say nothing of your...friend."

"I'm sorry." It reminded me of the time I invited Mindy Klinger, my best friend in grade school, to sleep over without asking permission. Jeez, Louise, if I wanted to feel younger, all I had to do was come home. With each ticking second I regressed another ten years.

"And what's with this getup?" she asked, motioning to my clothes. "You're dressed like a twelve-year-old, for pity's sake."

At this rate, by dinnertime I'd be back in the womb.

I wanted to explain that my retro cartoon T-shirt was actually fashionable and acceptable for someone my age, but I was too mortified to speak.

Beckett seized the awkward moment, releasing my hand to shake Mom's. "Pleased to meet you, Mrs. Parish. I'm—"

"The baron's personal aide. Yes, I know. Please call me Marilyn, and welcome." She pumped his hand, then waved us inside. "Get off the porch, for goodness' sake. We don't want the neighbors to talk."

Talk about what? I wanted to ask but didn't. My mind was stuck on that other part. The baron part. But I didn't ask about that, either, because I couldn't get a word in.

"I'm beside myself, Evelyn. Nobility. Here in Greenville. In this house. Sitting on *my* sofa. If I'd known, I could have at least shopped for Earl Grey. The only tea I had to offer was Lipton. *Lipton,* for pity's sake."

Her rambling stupefied me, but then we stepped into the living room and it all made sense. Strike that. It made no sense at all.

Arch.

My heart pounded as I drank in the delicious sight of him. He'd shaved his cropped beard into a trimmed goatee, sophisticated yet roguish. Dressed in a tailored charcoal-gray suit, crisp white shirt and a striped black-and-gray tie, he looked like a cross between a Wall Street tycoon and a model for *GQ* magazine. I'd seen him in a suit before, but he'd been disguised as a geeky sixtysomething yachting snob—pot belly strapped under his oxford shirt, ascot knotted at his neck, gray hair, fake jowls. The man walking toward me was all Arch. All sexy, all charismatic, all hunki-fied.

Zowie.

He took me in his arms, enveloping me in his aura of potent machismo. *Zing. Zap.* My body pulsed with equal parts desire, confusion, relief and rage. I wanted to kiss him. I wanted to punch him.

"Hold that thought," he whispered in my ear as if reading my scrambled mind. "Feels like we've been apart three years instead of three days, lass," he said loud enough for all to hear, which made me think it was an act. He excelled at manipulating people, and just now, for whatever reason, he wanted my mom to believe he'd missed me. If I weren't savvy to his charms, I'd believe it myself. But he hadn't *missed me* enough to return my call or to be available when I needed his advice. Or to invite me to return his one miserably impersonal message so we could have a decent conversation.

It hit me then. Like a flipping pie in the face. Arch

wasn't the one having trouble with our new "friend" status. It was me. My overreaction to our lack of contact hadn't been one of a friend but a lover. *Crap.* I'd declared our fling over. Trouble was I wasn't *over* Arch.

Okay, this sucked.

He brushed his mouth across my lips, escalating suckdom to new heights. I was too gaga over that brief, body-tingling kiss to speak, although I did sigh. And I think my knees sagged. Beckett no doubt noticed. Not that he'd believed me when I'd said I'd gotten Arch out of my system. But this was just proof that I'd lied and that my bluffing skills needed work. *Double crap.*

Not only that, but this blew Beckett's initial plan sky-high. How could he be my boyfriend if Arch was my boyfriend? And why exactly had Arch stepped up to the boyfriend plate? And *what* was with the baron angle?

I glanced sideways and, though the agent's expression betrayed nothing, I knew he wondered the same thing. I found it hard to believe that he'd known Arch would be here. Nothing up to this point supported that theory. Nope. I suspected he was as surprised as me. We both held silent, waiting for the cagey Scot to show his cards.

Instead Mom, who was abnormally chatty, revealed her hand. "I can see you're uncomfortable, Evelyn. Don't be. Baron Duvall—or is it Baron Archibald—"

"Just Arch," he said.

"—explained the circumstances. Normally I don't approve of lying, but I understand his immediate need to keep your relationship secret. Scottish nobility and an American entertainer." She snorted in a knowing manner. "The press would have a field day. And considering his charity work, well…" She fluttered a hand, leaving off the rest of Arch's tale.

Okay. Never mind that she'd just suggested I was worthy of a scandal sheet simply because I'd chosen the stage over scholastics. But what the heck? Arch had passed himself off as a privileged noble and us an item? For what purpose? And how did he know we'd be here? I didn't know about Beckett, but my head hurt.

Arch graced my mom with one of his knee-buckling smiles—at least that's how they affected me. "Again, Marilyn, I appreciate your cooperation in this delicate matter. Your daughter and I aren't hiding our relationship, but we are keeping a low profile. I wanted to meet her family with*oot* the interference of the paparazzi. You know how intrusive they can be, yeah?"

"Monsters," she said with a scowl. "Look at how they hounded poor Princess Diana and Dodi, and we all know how *that* turned out."

I dipped my chin and massaged my temple when I really wanted to roll my eyes. Mom—logical, grounded Marilyn Parish—had fallen for Arch's cock-and-bull fairy tale like a gullible kid.

Beckett stood beside me, hands stuffed in the pockets of his Dockers, expressionless, silent. I imagine he was doing the same as me: trying to assess the situation. It was like walking in on the middle of a movie.

Eureka!

"The Prince and the Showgirl," I mouthed and Arch winked at me. Yeah, boy, he'd ripped this scenario out of the 1957 movie starring Laurence Olivier and Marilyn Monroe. Considering he'd fashioned our last aliases after characters from another Monroe classic, *Some Like it Hot,* he probably thought I'd get a kick out of it. An inside joke, except I didn't get it. Why the charade?

"A driver dropped me *aboot* twenty minutes ago. I

didnae expect to arrive ahead of you," he said, at last addressing his partner.

"Missed our connection in Cleveland," Beckett said, folding his arms over his maroon polo shirt. Unlike Arch, his attire was casual. Unlike Arch, he'd blend in here. "Tried to reach you on your cell," he continued. "Couldn't get through."

I didn't know if he was telling the truth or playing along. My patience thinned by the minute.

"Between our time in the air and spotty reception, I assumed as much." Arch wrapped an arm about my waist, kissed the top of my head. "If she were under anyone else's protection, I would've worried, yeah? *Dinnae* know what I'd do with*oot* you, Northbrook."

Northbrook. A character name from *The Prince and the Showgirl.* Only Beckett wouldn't know that since he wasn't a movie buff like Arch and me. Still, he didn't flinch.

"Just doing my job," he said, and I remembered that Mom had referred to him as the baron's personal aide. Either the man was quick on his feet or he'd planned this with Arch ahead of time, although how could that be when I'd presented him with my family crisis last-minute?

"Mr. Northbrook," Mom said as if suddenly aware of his presence. "You must be fatigued from the drive. Would you like some water? Tea? Coffee? What about lunch? You must know the baron's likes and dislikes. Join me in the kitchen while these two lovebirds say a proper hello. Tell me," she said at a lower volume as she ushered him into the dining room, "is *personal aide* code for bodyguard? The baron mentioned you're former military."

Number one: I've never known Mom to be so animated and gossipy. Two: I've never heard her utter the term *lovebirds*. And three: *proper hello* intimated intimacy. I'm positive she's never championed displays of affection. She didn't even hug me at the front door, for crying out loud! Yet here she was encouraging whoopee between me and a man she didn't know. Although he was—*cough*—nobility. Why did I get the sinking feeling that she was doing an internal happy dance, thinking, after years of struggling in the fickle, unstable entertainment world, I'd finally wised up and secured my future by landing an aristocrat.

As soon as they were out of the room, I wiggled out of Arch's arms. "What are you doing here?"

"Keeping my partner from ruining his career."

It wasn't the answer I'd expected. I wanted him to be here for me. The disappointment was crushing. "I assume you're speaking of the senator's case," I whispered.

"Aye."

"I didn't ask Beckett to do this."

"I know."

"How do you…?" I narrowed my eyes. "Someone on the team contacted you."

"Aye."

"But you were in London, weren't you? How did you get here before us? How long have you been here?" I paced to work off rising steam, fought to keep my voice to a frustrated whisper. "I came here because my family needs me."

"I know."

"I guess you heard that from Gina or Tabasco, too."

"I didn't hear it from you."

A sarcastic statement delivered without sarcasm. How

very Arch. I stopped in front of him, hands balled at my side. "Well, I *would* have told you if you would've answered the phone."

"You could've left a message, yeah?"

"Yes, well…"

"We *dinnae* have time for this, Sunshine." He nabbed my wrist and pulled me against his hunky body. "Listen and focus."

At times like this it was impossible to think of myself as six years his senior. He made me feel like a besotted teen, all hormones and giggles. I blinked up into those devastating gray-green eyes, my mind and limbs mush. The use of my pet name had been enough to burn off my temper, but it was the feel of his arms around me—strong and comforting—that unraveled the bulk of my anxiety knots.

"Do you want to reunite your parents? Do you want to appear successful in their eyes and in the eyes of your school chums?" He smoothed a hand down my back and I realized I was trembling. "Do you want to prove to Beckett and the rest of Chameleon that you've got the right stuff?"

I almost fell for it. Almost believed that he wanted to make my professional dream come true. Except I remembered his reaction—or lack thereof—when I'd told him Beckett had hired me and *then*…my blood boiled just thinking about it. "You don't want me to prove I've got the right stuff. You convinced Beckett to use me as a singer instead of an active player. And now you show up here and…what? What are you playing at, *Ace?*"

"Things have changed," is all he said. "Just know I'm here for the greater good."

Not a perfect explanation but one that appealed to my sense of decency. Which, of course, the manipulative bastard knew. "I thought you were here because of Beckett."

"I am. But I'm here for you, too."

My traitorous heart thumped.

"Friends in need, yeah?"

Friends. Right.

"We need to work this nobility angle, Sunshine."

My brain scrambled to break down his intent. Even though he said he wanted to keep his bogus title and our equally bogus relationship low-profile, surely he understood the power and speed of small-town gossip. Two days, tops, and the headline of the *Greenville Tribune* would read: European Nobility Romances Drama Queen. Mrs. Grable and my drama-club buddies would view me as a modern-day Grace Kelly. Who needs to perform when you've got a castle to keep? My family, specifically my Dad, would stop fretting that I was alone and floundering. He could give up the tavern and Mom could give up her shenanigans and all would be right in their world.

As for Beckett… My objective all along had been to dazzle him with my tap-dancing abilities, thereby earning my place in the field. If I could con an entire town—people who *knew* me—into thinking I was dating a noble, I could dupe a run-of-the-mill scum artist into believing anything.

Determination pumped through me, obliterating my concerns regarding Arch's motives. For now, anyway. "What's our story?"

He smiled. "That's my girl."

Only I wasn't his girl, not in reality. He didn't do relationships—his policy. I didn't mix business with pleasure—Beckett's policy. I'd puzzle on that later. One brain buster at a time.

A teakettle whistled, prompting him to launch into a succinct profile. "You're you."

"Whoopee."

"I'm Archibald Robert Duvall of Broxley, Baron of Broxley."

"Robert Duvall?"

"My ma took a fierce liking to the chap when she met him, yeah?"

"Are we talking about the same Robert Duvall? The American actor?"

"Aye. And, no, we're not blood. Last name's coincidence."

Forget the last name. I bounced back to the first. *"Archibald?"* It made sense, of course. Arch *would* be short for Archibald, but jeez. Who names their kid Archibald?

He raised a brow. "Time's ticking, Sunshine."

"All right. But wait. When word gets around—and it will—people are going to want the scoop on you. A titled Scot in Greenville? That's huge. They're going to Google the Baron of Broxley. Internet connection may be splotchy in these parts, but we are indeed connected to the cyber world."

"Then my Web site should garner several hits, yeah?"

I scrunched my brow. "You have a Web site?"

"The Baron of Broxley has a Web site. Mostly it's devoted to the town and people of Broxley. The history. Local events, you know?"

"You created a phony Web site?" What was I saying? He'd forged a passport. An official government document. Anyone with the software, a server and know-how could launch a Web site.

"Aside from occasional online tabloid mentions and brief interviews, I am now also, thanks to Woody, included in Wikipedia."

I smirked. "You mean, the baron."

He grinned. "The man is, like me, guarded about his life, but there's enough information out there to support his existence."

My mind cramped wondering what laws he'd broken or bent to bring the Baron of Broxley to life. "Hurry up and give me the rundown before my brain explodes. Mom and *Northbrook* will be back any minute."

"We met three weeks ago on a Caribbean cruise, fell into a heated affair and have been inseparable since."

I swallowed hard. "That's pretty much true." Except he'd left out the breaking-up-in-London part.

"In this instance, the closer we stick to the truth, the less room for error."

"Beckett said something similar."

"Taught him everything I know, yeah?"

He stroked my long bangs out of my eyes, and I flashed on all the times he'd performed a similar gesture in the midst of heated sex. Then my mind jumped to the vision of Beckett, first fresh out of the shower, half-naked, then later, when he'd lifted me into his arms and carried me to the sofa. "Everything?" I croaked.

"Professionally speaking."

My gaze slid to his mouth and the warning bells clanged. "I swore to Beckett that you and I...that this thing..."

"This is business, lass."

"Right."

I heard Mom's voice, knew she and *Northbrook* were rounding the corner. I felt the erotic pressure of Arch's hands on my backside as his face dropped closer to mine, and suddenly I was a blushing, hormonal teen cuddling in my parents' living room with the quintessential bad boy. "You're going to kiss me, aren't you?"

His devilish eyes twinkled. "Just a proper hello."

CHAPTER THIRTEEN

MILO CHECKED HIS temper as Arch said his goodbyes to Twinkie and her mom. He leaned back against the rental car, a blue midsize Ford, and mentally reviewed what would have been a clusterfuck if not for his extensive law-enforcement training and years of experience wading through grifter bullshit.

As for Evie—she'd played the scene perfectly, even though, like Milo, she'd had to play it cold. At this point he assumed she knew more than he did, as she'd been alone with Arch while he'd been trapped in the kitchen with her mother. He'd survived Mrs. Parish's interrogation by copping a client-confidentiality plea. *Privileged information* and *I'm not at liberty to discuss that* covered a lot of ground when fielding questions about a so-called person of title. He'd had to resort to double-talk when she'd asked the specific location of the man's barony and if he lived in a manor or a castle, because how the hell would *he* know? Although Arch—or, rather, the baron— had cleared that up over lunch.

The way he figured it, after overhearing Twinkie's looped talk about getting naked in his apartment, Arch had booked a flight from London to Philly ASAP. Didn't matter that Milo had called with a rational explanation. The man had been motivated by jealousy. That he was here in Indiana indicated he'd touched base with a team member while en route. Must have gone over big when he'd learned Milo was escorting Evie to her hometown under the guise of being her boyfriend. Details were murky, but the result was clear: the Scot had screwed Milo out of the role of Twinkie's knight in shining armor. Not to mention a kiss.

"Are you sure you don't want me to show you the way?" he heard Evie ask. No doubt she wanted extended privacy with Arch to grill him on his alias and intent. Milo related. Or maybe she just didn't want to be left alone with her mom. The tension between those two was tangible.

"I'm sure, lass. I'll be back to pick you up, as discussed, and you can give me a tour of this charming village, yeah?" Arch brushed his lips across her knuckles—nice touch—then nodded to Mrs. Parish. "Thank you again for extending the invitation to dine tomorrow evening and for humoring my peculiar request. I look forward to an authentic American cookout. Until then…."

The screen door closed and the suited Scot approached the car at an easy pace. Milo expected a cocksure grin as he neared, but instead Arch pulled a poker face. "I'll drive, mate," he said. "I know the way."

Milo tossed him the keys. "You're the boss."

"Someone had to take charge."

"Meaning?"

"Let's postpone this discussion until we're *oot* of view, yeah?"

Checking his annoyance, Milo climbed in the passenger side.

They buckled up and a few seconds later drove north

on Main, away from the center of town. Arch spoke first. "Are you mental? Questioning a direct assignment? What the fuck?"

"Not a direct assignment, an unofficial directive."

"A favor."

Milo grunted.

"Considering who the request came from and who it's for, same difference, yeah?"

Milo regarded his partner with a raised brow. "You flew all the way here to bust my hump about a case?"

"A case that could boost or break your career with the AIA."

"Since when do you care about my career?"

"Since you roped me into Chameleon. What affects you affects all of us, yeah?"

"Let me rephrase. Since when do you care about Chameleon? We both know the only reason you partnered with me was to keep your ass out of jail."

"I have other reasons now."

"That reason have anything to do with the blonde in the cartoon T-shirt?"

"It has to do with the likes of Simon the Fish."

Milo gave the man credit. If he had Evie on the brain, he wasn't letting on. "Simon's dead."

"World's crawling with his kind."

"Developing a conscience, are you?"

"Nothing so profound." Arch steered the car onto a back road, and just like that they were in the country, surrounded by sporadic green knolls, plowed fields and patches of dense woods. He didn't consult directions or a map. Wherever they were going, he'd been there before.

"So…what? This is an intervention? You're taking me to a safe house? Let me guess—Gina and Tabasco are waiting and they, along with you, will badger me until I see the error of my ways."

"Something like that."

"I knew they questioned my hesitation regarding this case, but I didn't think they'd come crying to you."

"Pops called me."

That stung. Samuel Vine was the one man he trusted without question. Wasn't like the old man to go behind his back. "Odd. He seemed sympathetic to Evie and her family crisis."

"He is. But he's also worried *aboot* you. He figured I could investigate Evie's troubles, allowing you to focus on the senator."

"I don't want to focus on powerhouses like Senator Clark. I don't want to recover the money his wife gambled away. He can afford to lose it, trust me. If he doesn't want to lose any more, he needs to have a talk with Mrs. Clark. Instead of courting Chameleon, he should be contacting Gamblers Anonymous."

"But you're going to look into it."

"I said I would."

Arch slid on his sunglasses as they swung around the bend and drove into the midmorning rays. "I spoke with the Kid. According to the file he typed up per your briefing, Mrs. Clark swears she was cheated."

"Lots of gamblers call foul when the cards don't go their way," Beckett said, shoving on his own mirrored aviators.

"An invitation-only poker game taking place in a private room of a new local hot spot owned by Frank 'Mad Dog' Turner, a former pro athlete turned restaurateur. Mrs. Clark learned *aboot* the exclusive game through a dealer at a nearby riverboat casino. Possible the dealer and Turner are in collusion, yeah? Possible the game's crooked."

"Possible." He slid Arch an annoyed look. "The only people invited to that game are hard-core players with deep pockets. The greedy who crave higher stakes. The arrogant who think they can beat the odds. The foolish who think they're too smart to be taken for a ride. The ideal sucker. Your mark of choice when you were still hustling. Wasn't it you who told me they got what they deserved?"

"Quite the speech."

"Chameleon's my baby, Arch. I wanted an elite group that would champion the poor schmucks who get taken for their life savings. People too intimidated or embarrassed to report the crime. Or the ones who do file a complaint and fall through the cracks because their local bunko squad is overworked or the con artist is too damn slick. Instead the Agency's been pressing me to investigate high-profile cases. Pyramid schemes, franchise frauds, managed-earning scams. Scams that target the rich or suggest corporate corruption. Now this. Since we're on suspension—"

"Thanks to me."

"—I chose to give priority to Mrs. Parish's potential mix-up in a fraud rather than win back the senator's wife's losses through deceit."

"Crowe wants more than that. He wants us to send Turner packing, preferably *oot* of the country. No cops. No press."

"No juicy fodder to muck up Clark's political career, present and future."

"I *dinnae* like this any more than you, yeah?"

"Then why are you pushing? Not long ago, you told me if I wanted to make a difference, go freelance."

"Aye. Still goes."

"So?"

"So wouldn't it be better to leave the AIA on fantastic terms? To have a politician in our pocket? Who knows when we might have need of the Agency or Clark's help—and they'd be more inclined were we in good favor, yeah?"

Milo didn't answer. Arch was right and they both knew it.

The Scot pulled into a long driveway that led to a sprawling two-story redbrick mansion with a Queen Anne porch. He recognized the architectural style as Second Empire, which dated the house to the mid to late 1800s. The exterior was in immaculate condition, as were the picturesque grounds. As safe houses went, it was high-class. Then again, Arch always arranged for the best. On the cruise ship he'd booked a suite, whereas Milo had ended up with an inside cabin with no view.

"Last time we worked together," he said, thinking back on Arch's obsession to fell a murdering hustler, "you were the one making knee-jerk decisions and I was the voice of reason."

"Figured I owe you."

"And Evie?"

"Definitely owe her."

That comment bothered Milo, though he couldn't say why. Nothing in Arch's tone or expression to suggest gratitude beyond the obvious. The man had roped her into a sting that had curdled. Milo hadn't witnessed the incident, but he'd certainly handled the fallout. In the chaos, Evie had been knocked around and eventually knocked out, while Simon the Fish's lights had gone out for good.

"Grateful because her bungle presented you with an opportunity to pay back Simon—eye for an eye? Or regretful that she got hurt in the struggle?"

"Told you before—I'm not a killer."

"But you did pull the trigger."

"Let sleeping fish lie, Beckett. The world's better off."

"No argument there." In addition to art fraud and land-investment fraud, Simon the Fish aka Simon Lamont aka David Krebs had been involved in heavy rackets. Violent. Deadly. Hell, yeah, the world was better off.

Milo pressed his fingers to his temples, pressed away the throbbing, pushed back the doubt. Better to believe the killing had been circumstantial and not premeditated. Bottom line: though not entirely reformed, over the past couple of years Arch had proven himself one of the good guys. His expertise had been invaluable in felling numerous unscrupulous scams. *Let it go,* he told himself, adding the team's motto, *for the greater good.*

Arch parked the compact rental in between two luxury sedans—a black Mercedes and a silver Audi. Tabasco would have arranged for the expensive wheels when he'd flown in the team. A beat-up Chevy wouldn't cut it for a hyped-up noble and his entourage.

Milo focused on the present ruse and regarded his partner with skepticism. "Northbrook, huh?"

"Ever see the movie *The Prince and the Showgirl?*"

"No."

"Then never mind."

"Northbrook got a first name?"

Arch's mouth quirked. "Not one you'd admit to."

Great. "You know, this scenario could have worked the other way. I could've posed as Twinkie's boyfriend and you could've been my aide. If I didn't know better—and

I don't—I'd think you had the Kid screw up my connecting flight so that Tabasco could get you here first. I'd think you didn't like the idea of me getting close to Evie even though it would be for show. Which implies jealousy, which implies you care about that woman seriously, which would be a first. As far as I know."

Arch unbuckled his seat belt, popped the trunk, then stepped out. By the time Milo rounded the car the man had hoisted his suitcase from the trunk. Milo nabbed his laptop satchel.

"Jealousy had nothing to do with it," Arch said as they walked toward the house. "It boils down to which one of us would make the more convincing baron. No offense, but your Scottish accent sucks."

"And why does Evie have to be mixed up with a Scottish baron?"

"Because it's going to be beneficial in getting us invited to that private poker game."

"Turner will do a background search, as will anyone who's interested in digging up dirt on the Baron of Broxley. I assume you backed up this guy's existence."

"He's the real deal."

"Sounds like you've got everything worked out."

Now came that cocksure grin. "*Dinnae* I always?"

CHAPTER FOURTEEN

I'VE BEEN IN TIGHT jams before, but this was ridiculous. I shimmied. I wiggled. But to no avail. I was stuck. I had more upper mobility than lower and, luckily, was able to reach around and snag my cell from the zippered pocket of the backpack I'd rooted out of my bedroom closet.

I checked the screen. Three-quarters charged but only two bars. I dialed Arch, praying that wherever he was, he had signal. If not, I'd call Beckett. Only I was still smarting from the Midol debacle. Exposing him to another one of my bonehead dilemmas didn't seem wise since I wanted to be taken seriously. Arch already considered me accident-prone. Besides, the sooner he got here, the sooner I could pick his brain about Mom's situation. "Please answer. Please answer."

"Yeah?"

"Thank God."

"You *dinnae* sound good, Sunshine."

"I feel worse."

"Are you sick?"

"Stuck."

"Your jaw?"

He knew about my TMJ. Had witnessed an episode. A mortifying memory with a sweet ending. His calm demeanor and sharp wit had worked better than Tylenol and an ice pack. "No, not my jaw."

"Did your ma press you on a point you're not sure of? I gave you plenty to work with when she grilled me on my background over lunch."

"She didn't press me on anything. She blew me off five minutes after you and Beckett left. I didn't get to talk to her about Dad or her new look or…*anything*. She said she had a dance lesson and she couldn't miss it or she'd fall behind. I asked if I could go with her. She said no. Said I'd make her nervous."

"That's understandable, yeah? You're a pro and she's just learning."

"I guess. But then I asked if I could meet up with her after and she said she had another engagement and wouldn't be finished before you came to pick me up."

"So?"

"So what if her engagement is with him?"

"Who?"

"*Him.* The man who's putting the spring in her step. The man who influenced her radical makeover and sweet-talked her into cashing in two war bonds. Didn't Beckett bring you up to speed?"

"He said your brother put an idea in your head *aboot* an affair and Tabasco flamed it with mention of a Sweetheart scam. I'm not saying it's impossible, yeah? But let's take it slow. Get the facts. If someone's taking advantage of your ma, we *dinnae* want to scare him off. There's a chance we could recoup her funds. Control your imagination and *dinnae* act rashly."

"Too late." I shimmied some more, and instead of improving my situation, I wedged myself tighter. Plus the strap of my backpack was snagged. Now I was really sweating. "I need help, Arch."

"I'm already en route to your house. Stay put and—"

"I'm not going anywhere. But I'm not at home."

"Where are you?"

"Up a tree without a paddle."

"What?"

"Don't ask. Just drive."

I rattled off detailed directions, calculated his arrival time at fifteen minutes—that's if he broke the speed limit, and he promised he would—and told him to look for the massive oak tree with a gazillion initials carved in the trunk and one pair of binoculars lying at its base.

I JERKED AWAKE AT THE sound of my cell phone. Not wanting to panic, I'd forced myself to relax by using a visualization technique taught to me by Jayne. Between the afternoon sun, the tranquil rustling of the leaves and exhaustion, I must've nodded off. "Arch?"

"No—Nic. I thought you broke up with Arch."

Fuzzy-headed, it took me a second to focus. "I did. I just…long story."

"I'm all ears."

"Not a good time."

"Why are you whispering? Is your cold worse?"

"I'm feeling much better, actually. I just don't want to be overheard."

"By who? Where are you?"

"Home."

"Then why aren't you answering the door? I've been knocking for five minutes."

"*Home,* home. Indiana."

Silence.

"There was a family crisis. Of sorts." *Crap.* I couldn't tell her my mom was possibly being swindled or, worse, having an affair. Well, I could. It's not as if I didn't trust her. I did. But I didn't know anything for sure. And I certainly couldn't tell her about Arch and Beckett being here. The why would involve mentioning Chameleon. *Double crap.*

Her tone softened. "Is it your mom? Your dad? Is one of them in the hospital or…worse?"

"No, no. Nothing like that. Physically, everyone's fine." Thank God. Well, except for me. But I wasn't about to explain my current predicament. "It's complicated," I went on. "I really can't talk about it right now. Humor me. Please."

"Evie? It's Jayne. What's wrong with your mom and dad?"

Obviously she was with Nic and had commandeered the phone. I repeated my explanation.

"Complicated, huh?" She blew out a breath. "How long will you be out there?"

"I have no idea."

"You'll call us if you need us, right?"

"Absolutely."

"All right," she said, but she didn't sound happy. "Your horoscope was a little on the bleak side this morning. Warned of a potential scandal."

I thought about the senator's wife, my mom and Fancy Feet, my infatuation with Arch and awareness of Beckett. Lots of potential. "Good thing I don't put stock in astrology."

"But I do," Jayne said.

"Give me the phone, Miss Doom and Gloom," I heard in the background, then a loud and clear, "Do you need us to do anything for you while you're away?"

Nic again.

"No, I don't think so." I swatted away a gnat. "Except maybe bring in my mail."

"Done." Pause. "Sure you're not the one having the crisis? This isn't some sort of delayed freak-out because of Michael and Sasha, is it?"

"I haven't given them a second thought," I said honestly. Which proved I really was over the man. Hallelujah. I heard another voice, distant but approaching the tree. "I have to go," I whispered.

"All right, but take care and call if—"

"I will." I disconnected and my stomach soured. For the past month I'd been lying to my two best friends. Well, not lying but certainly tap-dancing to beat the band. Or something like that. At some point soon I needed to have that talk with Beckett about what I could and couldn't reveal to Nic and Jayne. And ultimately, when this immediate crisis passed, to my family. "For the greater good," I told myself, because somehow that made the ruse feel less deceitful.

I angled my body as best I could to see who was coming. Arch! He was talking on his cell. "Just see what you can do, yeah? Thanks, mate." He disconnected and tucked away the palm-size mobile. I couldn't be sure, but it looked different from the phone he'd been using the last couple of weeks. Probably an upgrade. Men and gadgets. Jeez.

Three more steps and he was directly beneath me. Even from way up here and through the obstruction of leafy branches, I could see that he'd chucked the tie and opened his collar. I could see a hint of dark chest hair and that part of his neck where I liked to bury my face when we snuggled. *Sigh*. He picked up my dad's bird-watching binoculars, looked around.

"Up here," I called down in a stage whisper, which is louder than a real whisper but not loud enough to be heard across the lawn. "I'm right above you."

He pushed his sunglasses to the top of his head and peered up into the thick foliage. "You weren't kidding. You're up a tree. Are you mental?" he asked when he finally saw me. "Climb down before you have a tumble."

"I can't. I told you—I'm stuck. You're going to have to come up and help me out. But be discreet. I don't want anyone to know I'm up here." Not that I'd seen anybody walk by in the past hour. The oak was situated in the back side of the civic center. Most of the comings and goings were on the other side.

"Discreet," he mumbled, then laid aside the binoculars and shucked his jacket and shoes.

It didn't take him long to reach me. The branches were strong and plentiful, easy to climb. As a kid I'd hung out up here after school, singing songs to the birds and concocting whimsical stories. A place to hide away and be fanciful me. I knew this tree well. Now I knew it intimately as I swore one of it slimmer twigs had wedged down the back of my Wranglers.

"Are you all right?" he asked, skimming his hands over me.

"Keep touching me like that and I'll be over the moon."

He smirked. "You're fine."

"I'm stuck."

"So you said." He shifted and examined my predicament. "How'd you get wedged in this nook?"

"I was staked out on that branch." I pointed up. "Had a prime view, but then I bobbled the binoculars. I made a grab and lost my balance. Ended up here. Wasn't much of a drop—I mean, I caught myself, but I guess…" I trailed off, recognizing his controlled expression. Uh-oh.

"You could've broken your neck, for fuck's sake."

"You're not going to snap it, are you?" I asked with a teasing grin.

"I'm glad you think this is funny."

I indicated the two of us, the tree. "Well, come on."

He unsnagged my britches and the straps of my backpack, tugged and finessed my body and—ta-da!—freedom. Seems I should've been able to free myself, but I'd been wedged at an odd angle, unable to gain the right leverage—and, sure, I'm limber, but I have puny muscles. I, unlike Arch, did not work out every day. If I wanted to be a true member of Chameleon, I should probably be in top form. Mental note: take up jogging.

My muscles ached as I shifted to another branch. Rain check on the jogging. I didn't complain about my smarting hips or what suspiciously felt like a saucer-size bruise on my thigh. I didn't want Arch to think I was a baby, plus my relief was too immense. I was beginning to worry we might have to call the fire department. *Sex kitten treed. News at eleven.* Not that there was anything sexy about faded jeans and high-top sneakers, but I was wearing a Felix the Cat T-shirt. Any reporter worth his salt would spin that.

Arch settled on a fat, sturdy branch, his back against the trunk as he rolled up his shirtsleeves.

I hunkered down across from him, gaze riveted on his sinewy arms. I thought about the Celtic tattoo banded around his bicep, tamped down an erotic shiver and focused on his gorgeous profile. The man was definitely peeved—or anxious or bored. Hard to tell with Arch. "Why are you breathing hard? You do fifty push-ups without breaking a sweat. Don't tell me you're tuckered from climbing a tree."

"Waiting for my temper to settle, yeah?" He cast me a fiery glare. "Why the bloody hell were you up here with binoculars?"

He was worried about me? My heart fluttered. I told it to stop. "That's the civic center. The dance studio is on the second floor."

"You were spying on your ma?"

"Don't look at me that way. She's not herself and I'm worried someone's taking advantage. My brother thinks it's the dance instructor. Possible he's right. The man's fortyish, handsome. Reminds me of a young George Hamilton. Dark tan, bright teeth. Slick."

"His hair?"

"His personality. I'm talking *smooooth*. A real ladies' man. In fact, women accounted for seventy-five percent of his class. Probably why he focused more on the Cotton-Eyed Joe than the two-step. Group dance as opposed to couple dance," I clarified. "Some of the men appeared to be having fun. The others looked leery. I'm thinking it's because their wives are crushing on the instructor."

"You surmised all that through binoculars."

I shrugged. "Years of studying human nature when researching character roles, not to mention all of the crazy stuff I witnessed while performing on stage, sharpened my observation skills. What can I say? I'm good."

The left side of his mouth kicked up and he studied me in a way that made my hoo-ha ache for his wa-hoo. "You're cute when you're cheeky, Sunshine."

He'd made that observation in the past, once or twice, and each time it had led to a kiss—or more. Uh-oh. I squeezed my thighs together and mentally listed my turnoffs. Intolerance. Litterbugs. Know-it-alls. Women who squat in public toilets and end up tinkling on the seat and *not* wiping it clean.

"Anyway," I said, satisfied I'd cooled my horny jets, "Mom was partnered with some man for the two-step—a man closer to her age, mind you. She was doing pretty well, actually. A little stiff, maybe. But then things took a suspicious turn." I leaned forward, eyes narrowed, voice low. "The instructor kept cutting in, using her to demonstrate certain moves. With him she was loose, fluid. A regular Ginger Rogers."

"Maybe it's because the instructor was a brilliant lead, more confident, more skilled than her assigned partner."

I didn't want to see the logic in that. I knew how dancing worked, but my gut told me dance dude was a hustler—and I'm not talking the seventies disco-dancing kind.

"It's like making love," Arch said. "In the hands of a master, even a nervous bird can soar."

I wasn't sure when, how or why we'd gotten off track, but I was relatively certain neither one of us was thinking of my mom. "Are you referring to the first time we…you know…did it?"

"I am."

I crossed my arms over my chest, set my chin. Never mind that I had indeed been nervous and had, at his masterful touch, *soared.* "We did not make love."

"No?"

"No. We boinked like bunnies. Well, not bunnies, because it wasn't cute. It was—"

"Passionate? Erotic? The earth quaked? Stars shattered?"

"We had great sex. We did *not* make love."

He considered, nodded. "You're right. We haven't made love."

An unspoken *yet* hung in the air.

I blew my bangs off my damp forehead, certain the backs of my knees were sweating. Panic bubbled in my chest. I'd been diligent about maintaining emotional distance whenever we…boinked. Never in bed…well, not never, but never in missionary style while in bed. Resisting eye contact had been vital. The *L* word was never uttered, not once, on either side, no matter the intensity of the moment. If we *made love,* I'd fall in love. The realist in me knew I was already teetering on the edge. The realist also knew the danger should I jump.

"Yes, well," I said, scrambling to make my way down the tree, "that's history, because we're history. The romantic us, anyway."

"Just friends," Arch said with a damnable smile in his voice.

"I'm serious," I said as I lowered myself to the ground. Granted, I wasn't having an easy time with the transition, but it was absolutely for the best. "No hanky-panky."

"Except for business purposes."

"When we're *on,* you mean. Spinning the European nobility/drama queen romance." I fluttered a hand. "No problem." Although it would have been a heck of lot easier if I was, like on the cruise, playing someone other than *me.*

I dried my sweaty palms on my jeans and caught a glimpse of someone exiting the back door with a stuffed garbage bag. I'd know that broomstick-up-the-butt posture and abnormally jet-black mane anywhere. Monica Rhodes. The director of the Greenville Civic Theater. The woman

I'd lied to about not being able to attend the benefit because of a prior engagement. The woman I'd neglected to call or e-mail regarding that donation, even after packing my bags for home.

Oops.

Arch touched down beside me just as she looked our way. I grabbed two fistfuls of his shirt and yanked him against me. "Kiss me."

"But—"

Hard for him to argue with my tongue down his throat. Not that he seemed averse to kissing once I got the action started. *Ooh,* no. I think I maintained control for half a second, then he took over and—yeah, baby, yeah—kissed me stupid. Crushed between a hard trunk and a hard man. Life is good.

In idiot mode, I contemplated tackling him for a roll in the grass. His fingers skimmed beneath my T-shirt, igniting, of all things, sanity. "Public. Hometown," I rasped after breaking the kiss.

"You started it," he said in a husky voice.

"Yes, well, I needed to do something to keep Monica from seeing my face."

"Who?"

I peeked around his shoulder to make sure she was gone. She was. "I'll explain later. We should go. Mom already left, although I don't know with whom or where they went. Maybe if we cruised town…"

"Ravishing me doesn't strike me as discreet, yeah?"

"Are you still on that?" I nudged him to move aside. When he didn't budge, I huffed a breath. "It was perfectly rational. You want this town to believe we're an item, right? Besides, kids make out here all the time. See?" I wiggled around to point out the carvings in the oak's ancient trunk. "Countless initials. Inscriptions. *Kirk loves Kelly. J&T Forever.* You know how I named my suitcase Big Red? This tree is known throughout Greenville as Big Love."

One hand on the trunk, he leaned in, crowding me, studying the carvings. "Where are your initials, Sunshine?"

I flushed. "No initials."

"That's right," he said with a smile. "You're a good girl. Good girls don't snog under trees."

"*Was* a good girl." I'd live down that label or die. Good girls finished last. "And even then I was human. Of course I *snogged* under this tree." I scraped my teeth over my lower lip, feeling all kinds of uncomfortable. "It's just that none of my high-school boyfriends—" *all two of them* "—ever felt that way about me. Like I was their Big Love."

"Huh."

"We really should go." Here I was, a forty-one-year-old woman, talking about high-school nonsense. The hell of it was, Arch made me feel like a moony-eyed teen. Young at heart and full of hope. I swung away, picked up my dad's binoculars and stuffed them in my backpack. "Where's the car?"

"This way." He slipped on his shoes and jacket and guided me across the manicured lawn. "Where next? Your da's pub?"

"No. Daddy's sharp. I don't want to face him until I know what cards you have up your sleeve, *Ace.* I want to know why you're pretending to be a Scottish baron, of all things. I understand that you don't want to confess to being a con artist—"

"Former con artist."

"—or a member of a covert agency, but couldn't you have been a shoe salesman or a blackjack dealer or an oil jockey, for goodness' sake?"

"Had my reasons, yeah?"

"And I want to know them in detail, including what happened between you and Beckett after you left Mom's house. Where is he? What's the plan? How are you going to help the senator *and* me?"

"Okay." He steered me to a sleek Mercedes, opened the passenger door.

"Seriously? You're going to confide in me?" I was stunned. The last case we'd worked, he'd kept me in the dark for days. This suggested he trusted me or at least believed I could handle whatever he'd cooked up.

"We need to talk somewhere private. Where'd you used to go when you wanted to be alone?"

I jerked a thumb over my shoulder. "That tree."

He grunted. "Anywhere else?"

Probably wasn't smart to take him there, given the mushy feelings he inspired. On the other hand, I couldn't resist. I snagged the keys from his hand. "I'll drive."

CHAPTER FIFTEEN

As DAYS WENT, IT WAS a gorgeous one. Come summer, the humidity would be unbearable—leastwise for wimps like me who don't like the sweltering, sticky heat. I could imagine the weatherman touting today as spring, glorious spring. The temperature hovered in the midsixties. Plenty of sunshine. A soft breeze carried the fragrance of budding flowers and fertile fields.

Climbing out of the car, I noted the picturesque landscape and remembered instantly why I used to come here to ponder, sometimes to pout, but mostly to dream. There was something magical about Little Turtle Rock.

"Fantastic," Arch noted as we picked our way through bushes and trees to the river's edge.

The historical society had invested in stone benches sporadically placed along the bank. There were also a few picnic tables, although few came here to eat. If people came here at all during the day it was to gander at the locally famous rock formation across the river or to wade in the cool waters while breaking from a nature hike through the woods. It was mostly a hangout for teenagers, who parked on the opposing higher bank at night. You can guess why.

I plopped down on a shaded stone bench. Arch settled beside me, looking around before saying, "Private indeed."

"Most of the time." I pointed across the narrow, shallow river. "See that rock?"

"I see a lengthy wall of rock."

"Home in on the part directly across from us. It's like one of those puzzles where you have to stare and then it comes into focus."

"What am I looking for?"

"A man's face."

I watched him while he stared at the rock. Having Arch in my hometown, climbing my favorite tree, sitting in my special place, felt weird and wonderful and totally screwed with my efforts to retain emotional distance. The connection I feared he'd so easily severed still sparked between us. It wasn't just the atomic kisses—although they blew me away—it was the indefinable chemistry of kindred souls. Sure, the term was overused and romanticized, but I swear, it applied and it was scary as hell. But according to the list in my diary, he wasn't the smartest pick for a life partner.

"Ah," he said, derailing my thoughts. "I see it now. Nose, eyes, ears. Damn, he's got a high forehead, yeah?"

I smiled. "This place is named after that formation, Little Turtle Rock."

He squinted harder. "I *dinnae* see a turtle."

I laughed. "There is no turtle. That's his name. Little Turtle. He was a famous Miami Indian chief. His given name was Michikinikwca, but that's a mouthful for us white folk. Easier to refer to him by the meaning of the name." I scrunched my brow. "This is boring."

"Not at all."

Relieved—becaúse I truly did adore the legend—I went on. "His father, also a chief, was Miami. His mother was Mahican. So he wasn't exactly pure in the eyes of his people. He was a bit of an outcast, a black sheep, but he achieved great things regardless. He stood up for the oppressed and, when the time was right, championed peace. He was an optimist, I think, a dreamer. And determined."

"As a young girl, you related."

My heart swelled at his sensitivity. "Yeah. I did."

I caught him looking at me and suppressed an erotic tingle. "Anyway, there's this legend that when he died and crossed over, the stars rained down and carved his face in that wall of rock. There's probably a rational explanation. Natural erosion. Late-1800s pranksters. There's a sucker born every minute, right? But I believed. I still do," I realized aloud, the air humming with wonder and optimism. "Guess that makes me a sap, huh?"

"No," Arch said, voice low. "It makes you special."

I didn't dare look at him. Eye contact at this particular moment could be hazardous to my health. Surely I'd jump him, knocking us both from the bench into a patch of poison ivy or into the chilly river. I gripped the bench and hardened my will.

"Evie."

"Yes?"

"*Aboot* your ma…."

A little out of left field but safe ground. "Yes?"

"I'm not convinced she's being hustled. But if she is, we'll handle it."

"Without embarrassing her or my dad?"

"Goes unsaid."

Tears stung my eyes. "I really appreciate this."

He reached over and laid his hand on top of mine, squeezed. "The baron ploy works twofold," he said, gazing at the river. "Most would assume those with a title must be rich, yeah? If there's an operator in town, chances are he'll sniff around you in an effort to get to me—or rather, my cash. Or he may try to ascertain my weakness through your ma. If you can get her to confide in you, we *willnae* have to wait for him to come after us. We'll take the initiative. Although, as I said, we could be pissing in the wind. Your ma could have cashed in those bonds for something innocent, yeah?"

"Maybe."

"*Dinnae* suppose you could ask her *oot*right."

"No. My brother told me on the sly. She threatened to never speak to him again if he told my dad, so I'm guessing that includes telling me. Even though Christopher and I aren't close, I'd hate to cause a rift. Plus, I'm pretty sure if I asked her, she'd tell me what she told him, which was to essentially buzz off."

"Things have been tense between you and your ma since your parents' split?"

"Things have been tense between us since forever." I swallowed, shifted. "I proved a disappointment early on."

He stroked his thumb over my knuckles. "I'm sure that's not true."

Unfortunately, it was. "I'm too liberal, too free-spirited, too much of a dreamer. Too…everything she's not. All through my youth she reasoned with me, lectured me, threatened me, tried to mold me into who she thought I should be—a responsible, motivated career woman. Her goal was to send me to college. My goal was to follow my heart. She washed her hands of me the day I told her I was going on the road with a band. We talk, but we don't. Not about anything meaningful. Although that's pretty much the norm for the Parishes. Noncommunicative. Emotionally repressed. Yep. That's us."

"That's not you."

"Well, not lately, no. But for most of my life I followed my parents' lead. *Squash down your feelings. Keep it inside. Don't air your dirty laundry,* and all that jazz. That's what my diary's for." I realized suddenly that I'd never expressed my angst over my rocky relationship with my mom out loud. Yet I'd just sliced open my heart for Arch.

Making eye contact was stupid. The tenderness shining in those gray-green orbs liquefied my bones.

Dangerously close to an intimate moment, I slipped his grasp and walked to the river's edge. When I was certain my knees wouldn't buckle or my voice wouldn't crack, I glanced over my shoulder. "You said the baron hoax would work twofold. How?"

"What do you know about the senator?"

"Only that his wife's a gambling addict and he wants Chameleon to win back her losses."

He joined me and we walked slowly along the bank. "Mrs. Clark swears she was cheated."

Clark. Cripes. Not a state senator, then, but a U.S. senator. I blew out a breath. "How's that possible? Casinos employ security guards to patrol the floor and a surveillance department to operate CCTV cameras. Looking for cheaters is three-quarters of their job. If she's hooked on slots, then she's just—to be nice about it—unlucky, because the odds are plain against you."

"Casinos get taken all the time, love. Card mechanics, hand muckers, systems players, collusion. A hustler at the top of his game can pocket thousands, sometimes tens of thousands of dollars, before being barred for suspicion of cheating."

Again I felt like a wide-eyed rube, a grifter's prime mark. I'd been performing in casinos for twenty years.

Granted, I didn't spend much time on the floor. I'd rather invest in a sure thing, like new clothes or cosmetics, rather than dropping money in the slots on the off chance I'd win a jackpot. But how could I be so naive?

"Casinos try to keep those kinds of losses quiet for obvious reasons," he said as if reading my thoughts. "In this instance, I believe the mark was roped at a riverboat casino this side of Chicago, and the actual fleecing took place in a private poker game."

"The riverboat in Hammond?" I stopped in my tracks, shook my head. "What are the chances? Seriously. Two crises in my home state. At the same time. Both involving Chameleon."

"Fate does at times deal a boggling hand, yeah?"

"I'll say. This thing with my mom—it's huge to me, to my family. But this thing with Senator Clark..." I whistled. "He has his eyes on the presidency, you know."

"I've heard."

"He's wealthy."

"Aye."

"And powerful."

"Absolutely."

"And Beckett chose to help me over him?"

Pregnant pause. "Beckett's not thinking clearly just now, yeah?"

"Why? What's wrong?" I thought about the man's insomnia. Wondered what kept him glued like a zombie to Nick at Nite. Loneliness? Depression? Finances?

"Bit of a career crisis."

I snorted. "I know all about that." One more thing I had in common with the agent, aside from a retro-sitcom addiction. I thought about all of the kindnesses he'd shown me. I tried not to think about the unsettling *snap*. I reached out and gripped the lapels of Arch's jacket. "We have to convince Beckett to help Senator Clark. I hate to side with Gina, but she's right. If he turns his back on this case, he can kiss his career goodbye. We can't let that happen. His work is too important."

He looked away for a second, then nodded. "Gina and Tabasco are here. They're at the Appleseed B and B, fielding information sent over by the Kid. Beckett drove out to interview Mrs. Clark."

"I want to help."

"Why?"

It wasn't the question that threw me as much as the tone. I released him and shrugged. "Because he's nice."

"Nice."

"I like him."

"You barely know him."

"I barely know you and I…"

"What?"

My heart hammered in my ears, drowning out the word that almost escaped my lips. Holy cripes. I didn't want it and he wouldn't welcome it, so why give in to it? "Like you. I like you." I focused on Little Turtle, who seemed to be frowning now as if offended by my forked tongue. Gads.

"Just friends," Arch said.

"Exactly," I said, realizing I was scratching my neck, avoiding eye contact, blushing. He had once told me I was easy to read. *Your body language betrays your feelings.* I needed to work on my poker face—my poker body, for crying out loud. Only I couldn't lock down just now, this was too flipping *huge,* so I pivoted and marched into the woods, toward the car. "We should go."

"Friends who shag," he said, coming up on my heels.

"We're not shagging anymore."

"Not officially, but professionally…"

I tripped on an exposed root. Arch nabbed me by the waist before I took a header. Breathless, I turned in his arms. "What's that supposed to mean?"

"It means, you can help Beckett by convincing this town you're shagging a profoundly rich baron. You *dinnae* have to do it for real."

"Oh."

His lip twitched. "Disappointed?"

"Your ego's amazing."

"Your restraint's impressive."

I rolled my eyes.

"Your mission, should you decide to accept it—"

"Oh, brother."

"—is to give this town something to talk about. I want the local newspaper to hound the Baron of Broxley for an interview."

"Why?"

"So that I can divulge my many hobbies, including a fondness for cards."

I quirked a brow. "Wouldn't that kind of information be on the baron's Web site or one of those online tabloids?"

"Aye. But Turner *willnae* look into my background unless he considers me a mark. And he *willnae* do that until he gets wind that a titled foreigner with a weakness for gambling is in his immediate area. "

"Who's Turner?"

"The man who possibly bilked Mrs. Clark. Once that article hits, news will spread to subsequent media. Turner will know I'm in the state and will have already done a preliminary background check by the time we visit that riverboat casino, yeah?"

"So you're laying groundwork. You're going to weasel your way into that private poker game."

"Barons *dinnae* weasel. That's why they have personal aides."

"So Beckett's going to weasel your way into that game?"

"Actually, Gina and Tabasco are going in first."

"I'm confused."

"You're cute when you're confused."

"I thought I was cute when cheeky."

"That, too."

"You're going to kiss me, aren't you?"

"Consider it practice for when we have to put on a show in town."

I gasped when he yanked me against his body. *Bad idea,* my mind whispered, but I couldn't say why. He obliterated sane thought with an explosive kiss. Passionate. Overwhelming. He conquered. I clung. His hands moved over my face, through my hair, down my back. He grabbed my butt and lifted me and I felt the world tilt. No, *me* tilt. Falling. Floating on a wave of ecstasy as he kissed me into oblivion. Pressure. On my back, front. Squished between Arch and…something. Picnic table, I thought hazily.

Standing—at least one of us was still grounded—he'd wedged himself between my dangling legs, his upper body bent over and pressed against mine. Crazy with need, I reached between us and unbuttoned his shirt. I had it down to an art, this undressing-in-the-heat-of-a-spontaneous-moment thing. Seconds later my hands moved over his ripped abs, skimmed his sides and splayed over his strong back. Primal desires prompted monosyllabic thoughts. *Me. Want. You.*

My body burned and hummed as he suckled my tongue, my lips, nipped my jaw and sucked my earlobe. Cool air washed over my hot skin as he pushed up my T-shirt, my bra.

"What if someone—"

"I'll hear them."

Really? My heart pounded so loud even his voice, so close, sounded distant and muffled. Then he tongued my nipple and I no longer cared about voyeurs. He savored and I arched. *Me. Want.* "More," I demanded, even as he tugged down my zipper. White-hot sensations danced through me.

Broad daylight, good girl warned.

Afternoon delight, bad girl crooned.

He slid his hand down my panties, touched me…there.

Drunk on lust, inhibitions blew apart. I squirmed and, knowing this dance well, he took the lead, stroking, urging.

Coming, coming.

"Oh, my god. Oh. My. God." *Breathe.* Release *that* way only primed me for the bigger O. I gripped his waistband, thumbed open the clasp.

"Bollocks."

My heart skipped because generally that curse signaled he was turned on, only he grasped my wrist and said, "No condom."

"Oh." And not the I-see-stars kind. "Well, that's…"

"For the best." He rested his forehead against mine.

I'd yet to open my eyes. My safety mechanism. The feel of his bare torso against mine was so familiar I could easily imagine us in the shower of his suite on the ship or on the carpet of his grandfather's flat or in the closet at…well, lots of places. But then he eased away, setting my bra and shirt back to rights and my senses returned. Eyes wide-open, I stared up at the blue sky obstructed with leafy green and absorbed what had just happened, what almost happened. "We've groped and…"

"Shagged."

"…in some unusual places, but this takes the…"

"Cake?"

I willed my brain to kick in. Full sentences, please. "A public area in broad daylight, for crying out." I swung off the table and fastened my jeans. "Teenagers show more restraint."

"I *dinnae* know *aboot* that," he said, buttoning his shirt.

"Let me rephrase. Around here, teens don't have sex out in the open." I pointed across the river. "They do it over there. On the high bank. In their cars. They say they're going stargazing, but it really means parking, which, at least here in the Midwest, means they're going to make out and get busy in the backseat."

He studied the opposite bank while tucking in his shirttails. "Huh."

He looked so damned sexy—rebellious yet sophisticated. The urge to jump him welled all over again. Disgusted with myself, I marched for the car. "I'm not saying I didn't enjoy what just happened, but we're not supposed to be having sex."

"That was foreplay, love."

"Same thing."

"Not where I come from."

"I'm serious," I said, stopping at the Mercedes. "We have a real problem if we can't make it one day together without breaking our resolve. I mean, what does that say about us?"

"That we're attracted to one another?"

"Why are you making light of this?"

"Because you're making too much of it, yeah?"

He had no idea. My heart soared to the moon and back and I figured now was a good time to start practicing my poker face. "You're right. No big deal. No harm done." I was cool, calm and in control of this awkward relationship. Yes, sir, I could control my amorous feelings. I could hold my own with sexy bad boy. I quirked a sympathetic, blatantly insincere smile. "At least I got an orgasm out of it."

His mouth twitched as he slid on his sunglasses. "I got something *oot* of it, too, Sunshine."

I blinked, stymied by his cocky grin. "What?"

"Let's just say I'm not disappointed." He nabbed the keys out of my hand. "I'll drive."

So much for being in control.

CHAPTER SIXTEEN

THE CORNER TAVERN WAS just as I remembered it. Yellow. Banana-yellow, actually, with contrasting dark green shutters. A cracked and peeling eyesore, it had been in need of refurbishing for the last twenty years. I'm surprised Dad hadn't already hired a crew to strip and paint it white or some other nonoffensive shade. An afternoon hangout for retired farmers, railroad workers and between-gig truck drivers, the Corner Tavern sat on the corner—go figure—of Main and Fifth Street. The nighttime crowd was younger, rowdier and prone to drunk-and-disorderly behavior.

"I still can't believe he bought this place," I muttered as Arch parallel parked curbside.

"Bet he got it cheap."

"God, I hope so. I've only been inside once. I recall the inside being just as run-down, although the color scheme was less gaudy. It made the Chameleon Club look like an upscale martini bar."

Arch whistled low.

"Yeah." I glanced over, noted his expensive suit. "Even without a tie you are way overdressed."

"Guess I'll draw attention then, yeah?"

"Oh, right. You want to be noticed." He looked dashing and European and emitted the expected arrogance of a person of title. I looked like a funky artist—retro sixties. All I needed was a flower in my hair. There was also our age difference, which wouldn't matter as much to me if only Arch were the senior. Sighing, I flipped down the sun visor and checked my makeup in the mirror. I frowned at the faint wrinkles etching my eyes, then told myself to *stop* frowning because it only intensified the creases. "Why is it that on men crow's-feet look like laugh lines and on women they look like wrinkles?"

"You *dinnae* have wrinkles."

"What do you call these?"

"Character lines."

"I guess I have a lot of character," I said drily.

"An admirable quality, Sunshine."

I could feel his eyes on me, only this time I didn't give in to their hypnotic pull. "No one's going to buy that you are interested in me," I said while reapplying my frosty-pink lipstick. Amazing how I could talk and apply lipstick—expertly, mind you—at the same time. Multi-talented, that's me.

"They'll buy it," he said. "Got our story straight?"

"There's not much to it." Mostly everything was based on truth, except the baron part. Oh, and the part about us being a serious item. I felt uncomfortable lying to my dad, but I wasn't about to verbalize that. In the grand scheme of things, I wanted to prove I could fool even those close to me, aid a U.S. senator, dupe a swindler or two *and* mend my parents' frayed marriage. Bending the truth seemed reasonable. *For the greater good,* I mentally chanted as I unbuckled my seat belt.

Taking that as his cue, Arch rounded the car and opened my door, handing me out and onto the sidewalk. Con artist or titled nobility, he was always a gentleman.

He fed the parking meter, then clasped my hand. "Nervous?" he asked.

"No."

"Your palm is clammy."

Crap.

I imagined what we looked like, the baron and the hippie, striding up a small-town sidewalk.

"We make an interesting pair, yeah?"

Scary how he could read my mind. "Yeah," I said. In real life *and* undercover.

Arch opened the front door of the tavern, allowing me to enter first. I stopped short, eyes wide. The clientele was exactly what I'd expected: six to eight older men clad in faded jeans, plaid shirts or T-shirts, most wearing John Deere or Harley-Davidson caps. All sitting at the bar. All nursing bottles of domestic beer.

It was the tavern itself that took me by surprise. The interior had been tastefully redecorated into a country-and-western theme. Polished hardwood floor, gleaming oak bar, matching tables and chairs. The newly painted muted red walls boasted pictures and memorabilia from movies ranging from *High Noon* to *The Magnificent Seven* to *Urban Cowboy*. Movies I'd watched growing up. Movies I'd yammered about at the kitchen table, only I'd thought no one had paid attention.

Then I saw the stage.

Choked up, I whirled and smacked into Arch.

"Easy, love." He steadied me, frowning when he saw tears in my eyes. "What's wrong?"

"He bought this place for me. Redecorated for me. I can't believe…" I massaged a fierce ache in my chest, trying hard not to sob. "I can't believe it. I can't…face him until I settle down. He doesn't like scenes."

"Is he a stocky man? Average height? White hair, full beard?"

I nodded.

"Then suck it up, love. Here he comes."

"Evelyn? Is that you?"

I wiped away the tears, took a bracing breath, smiled and turned. "Hi, Dad." But as soon as I saw his face, a hundred kind gestures exploded in my memory. The diary had been the biggest kindness. Other considerations had been subtler, so much so I'd forgotten them. Maybe he'd never understood my artistic temperament, but he'd never condemned it, and now it seemed he was encouraging it. And at a time when I'd reconciled to retire from performing.

After a moment he patted me awkwardly on the shoulder. "Now, now. What's the fuss?"

Embarrassed, I gestured to the room.

"You don't like it?"

"I believe she's overwhelmed, yeah? Speechless, in fact." Arch stepped forward and extended a hand. "Allow me to introduce myself, Mr. Parish. I'm—"

"Archibald Robert Duvall, Baron of Broxley." Dad clasped his hand, a firm businessman's shake. "My son called," he explained. "Marilyn, my wife, phoned him with the news. I understand you're anxious to keep your title quiet, but we're family."

"I understand."

"It goes no further."

Not that I didn't believe Dad, but I knew it was only the beginning. Christopher would tell his wife (technically family) and, being the pompous person Sandy was, she'd call everyone in whatever snooty club she belonged to, and word of nobility in Greenville would spread like wildfire. By tomorrow afternoon the *Tribune* would be dogging Arch for that interview. He winked at me and I knew he was thinking the same thing. Tell someone to keep something hush-hush and, boy, they can't wait to blab.

"Join me for a drink?" Dad asked, glancing from Arch to me. "I think we could all use a stiff one."

I blushed, the picnic-table incident fresh in my mind. Gads.

Arch grinned. "Delighted," he said while handing me a folded handkerchief.

I blew my nose—loudly—and rasped. "Chablis, please." Maybe, hopefully, it would take off the edge.

"What's your poison, Bar—Mr. Duvall?"

"Call me Arch, please. I believe I'll have a scotch, thank you. Neat."

"J&B okay?"

"Perfect."

Dad smiled and nodded. "Swell. Oh, and my first name's George. Feel free to use it." Clearly he was convinced and pleased that the baron, though peerage, was not a snob. His manner was easy and genuine when he told us to take a seat. "I'll get those drinks."

I led Arch to a table far from the stage and I sat with my back to it, too. I didn't want to think about the time, money and effort Dad had put into a place he hoped I'd call home. So different from the cramped area Pops had carved out for me at the Chameleon Club. A raised stage. A lighting system. A quality sound system that had assuredly been purchased, not appropriated. And if my brother was to be believed, Dad had hired a full rhythm section, honest-to-gosh musicians, not a location scout who happened to diddle on acoustic guitar.

I should have been thrilled. I felt sick.

"You okay?" Arch asked.

"Peachy."

"I almost believe you, Sunshine." He squeezed my hand. "Try to get your da to talk *aboot* your ma and why they split."

I snorted. "Haven't you been listening? My family doesn't talk about private stuff, not even with family."

"Try."

"Here we go." Dad set our drinks on the table. After sitting, he said, "To life's surprises."

We toasted and I choked out, "To the Corner Tavern."

"Got it for a song," Dad said. "Figured I could increase business if I spiffed up the place. Invested in a decorator and attacked the inside first. Told her I wanted a Western theme. Nashville meets Hollywood." He sipped his beer, eyed me over the rim of the frosty mug. "What do you think?"

I think it's the nicest thing anyone's ever done for me. "I love it."

He smiled. "I'm glad." Unspoken sentiments danced in his eyes.

Hug me, the little girl in me implored.

He cleared his throat and focused on Arch. "Used to be in banking. Now I'm in hospitality and entertainment. Beats the hell out of retirement."

"Idleness promotes a lazy mind, yeah?"

"Bird-watching gets boring after a while and reality shows have ruined television. Never been much of a sportsman, so that left solitaire and jigsaw puzzles. After a month of relaxation, my brain and butt felt like Jell-O. Not to mention that twenty-four hours of togetherness was hell on the marriage."

Knowing how rigid and opinionated Mom could be, I could imagine. "So you bought this place," I said.

He sipped, shrugged. "I like making money. Like keeping busy. Like socializing. Plus, I thought…well, let's say I looked at it as an investment for the future."

Your future or mine? I wanted to ask but didn't. I sensed his unease. Frankly I was surprised he'd said as much as he had. I didn't want to push too hard too fast.

He drummed his fingers, visibly weighing his words. "This thing between your mother and me, this disagreement, I don't want you to fret, little one. She'll come around. Eventually."

So he thought she was in the wrong and I'm sure she thought the opposite. Great. "Have you seen her lately?"

"Ran into her a couple of days ago at the supermarket."

"How'd she look to you?"

"Miffed."

"No, I mean, how'd she *look?* You know, her appearance?"

"Same as always." He frowned. "Why?"

"No reason." So the makeover was recent and he hadn't seen it. My mind chugged down a few different tracks.

Arch met my gaze and raised a brow. His mind chugged, too.

Dad slapped a palm to the veneered tabletop. "So… just how serious is this thing between you two?"

"Dad."

"Fair question," said Arch. "Granted, Evie and I have only been acquainted for a month, but there's a special bond between us. Rest assured this relationship is more than a passing fancy, sir."

I sipped more wine, trying to sift truth from lies. A real chore given I was listening to a master of deceit. People believed Arch because he told them what they wanted to hear. My dad wanted to believe his daughter was dating an upstanding, moral and caring man. Only the latter applied, but Dad didn't know that and I wasn't about to squeal. Known for his honesty, he'd have a fit if he knew the man currently shoveling him a load of bull was a former confidence man.

"Trust me when I say," he heaped on, "that I have Evie's best interest at heart."

Never kid a kidder. Never trust a grifter. But Dad did and—dang it—so did I. He was *that* convincing.

Dad drank his beer, considered. "It's plain that you're sweet on my daughter." He turned to me. "I assume since you brought this man home to meet your family, your feelings must run deep."

I was insanely glad that he assumed and didn't ask. It meant I didn't have to lie—or, rather, admit to the truth. Yes, my feelings for Arch ran deep. Bad news for me. *He doesn't do relationships. No matter what he says, don't believe him. That's Baron Archibald Robert Duvall talking, not Arch Duvall.*

Right.

I gulped more wine.

"Don't suppose you'd be willing to give up a manor in Scotland for a ranch in Greenville," Dad said, focusing back on Arch.

"Actually, it's a stone cottage, but—"

"Cottage." He winked. "Sure. Well," he said on a long sigh, "at least my little girl won't have to kill herself trying to make a living in the casinos. I imagine you can open a whole lot of doors for a talented girl like Evelyn." He glanced toward the stage. "Doors beyond my reach."

A big fat lump clogged my throat. "Dad, I know what you had in mind, but—"

"Bah." He waved off another emotional scene. "Like I said, life's full of surprises. Just know that if this—" he indicated Arch and I "—fizzles, this—" he indicated the stage "—is here."

I wanted to throw my arms around him, to hug him for his supreme gesture, but I knew it would only embarrass him. Instead I blinked back tears and drank more wine.

Thirty minutes and another round later, Arch and I exited the tavern after striking a bargain with Dad. I'd sit in with the house band tomorrow night, just for fun, if he joined us at home for dinner beforehand. Inviting him without asking Mom was going to earn me an ear blistering, but I didn't care. Especially not after two glasses of wine.

My head spun, and not just because of the alcohol. Arch had hit it off with my dad as Michael never had. Actually, in all the years we were married, Michael only came home with me once. For him, once was enough. He hadn't said directly, but I knew he considered Greenville the boonies and its populace yahoos. Which, of course, made me a transplanted yahoo. Maybe that's why he'd lost interest in me…well, aside from the fact that I was no longer twenty. Maybe he thought I was unworldly. I knew for sure he considered me predictable and conventional.

I smirked. *If he could see me now.* A member of a specialized branch of a government agency. Evie Parish: Crime Buster. Heh.

We were two feet from the car, both lost in our thoughts, when I heard my name.

"Your mother told me you were in Greenville. Imagine my surprise."

Monica Rhodes.

From the shopping bag looped over her arm, I could see she'd come from the one store in town that carried lingerie similar to that of Victoria's Secret. The thought crossed my mind that that's where she'd run into Mom, although I couldn't and didn't want to imagine the woman who'd given me birth in anything but flannel.

"Thought you had a booking," she added in a condescending tone.

"That particular engagement has been postponed." Since it seemed Mom hadn't spilled the beans, I did. I looped my arm through Arch's and poured on the calculated charm. "I came home to introduce my boyfriend to my family."

"Boyfriend? Oh, that's right," she said with a smug smile, "your husband divorced you."

"It was mutual, actually."

"Really," she said, devouring Arch with her eyes.

"Archibald Duvall," he said, offering his hand in greeting. "And you are?"

"Monica Rhodes." She squeezed his hand, wet her lips. "You're not from around here."

Well, duh.

"Very astute," he said with a killer smile. "From Scotland, actually."

"What are you doing here in Indiana?"

"Meeting Evie's parents."

I smiled. "Like I said."

"Stunning suit," she said, ignoring me. "What business are you in, Mr. Duvall?"

Obviously she thought he was out of my league. "He

specializes in charity work," I answered. "He tries to keep it quiet—so modest—but he doesn't actually have to *do* anything." I leaned forward and whispered. "Old money." Just in case the black dye she'd been using since she was a teen had seeped through her scalp to her brain, I clarified, "*Lots* of money."

Arch squeezed my arm gently, signaling not to overplay it. No problem. Monica was already hooked.

"Really?" she said, hand pressed over her heart.

"My parents' fault. Inheritance and what have you," he said with a wink. "Comes with the bloody title." He motioned to the car then. "We should go, love. Your mum—"

"Right. About that donation…" I said to Monica as Arch opened the passenger door. "If you don't mind, I'd like to make a monetary one. I'll call you tomorrow. Toodles."

"Toodles?" Arch said after he buckled in, and steered away from the tavern.

"I can't stand her," I said, shoving on my sunglasses.

"I gathered. Care to fill me in?"

"Later. So what did you think of my dad?"

"What's not to like? He's a good man, Evie."

"I know. So why did Mom kick him out? Presumably it's because he bought the tavern against her wishes. But he bought it for *me*. He knew my divorce shook me emotionally and financially. He knew I was struggling to find work in AC. My insecurities and worries slipped out at my brother's wedding reception when Dad asked, 'So how's it going?' Normally I would have answered, 'Fine,' but I'd had a few glasses of champagne."

Arch smiled knowingly. Liquor, even in small doses, unleashed my restrained thoughts and emotions.

"The point is, he bought the Corner Tavern and refurbished it so I'd have a place to do what I thought I was born to do. Was Mom angry because he was encouraging a profession she despised? Or because he was encouraging me to move home?"

"You're making this *aboot* you, Sunshine. I think it has more to do with them."

I flushed. It's not as though I think the world revolves around me. Jeez. Although artistic types *do* tend to be self-involved. Hmm…. "Did he say something to you when I went to the ladies' room?"

"A comment was made *aboot* conflicting interests, as well as an argument over relocating. Apparently your ma had visions of flying south. Something *aboot* a snowbird."

I blinked at that. "She wanted to retire to Florida?"

"She did. He *didnae*. Then he bought the tavern. I think she resents the result rather than the intent, yeah?"

I smirked. "You got all of that personal info out of my painfully private dad in the four minutes I was away?"

He grinned. "It's a gift."

I snorted. "Maybe I should turn you loose on my mom."

"Or you could give it a go yourself." He pulled into my parents' driveway and cut the engine.

"Maybe." I eyed my native abode—home of the repressed, land of the realist. "We'll be alone tonight, Mom and me, all night." My stomach knotted at the thought. "Meanwhile *you* get to plan and connive with Chameleon. I wish I could be in on that."

"You're needed more here," he said gently.

Okay, that was sweet. Perceptive and kind. It was also another one of Arch's gifts. Recognizing a person's hunger and feeding it. He knew I craved acceptance and a more intimate relationship with Mom. He offered hope and a shot at a dream. The grand manipulator. Only in this instance I didn't feel manipulated. I felt…

Oh, no.

"I should go." Skin burning, heart racing, I pushed out of the car before he had a chance to unbuckle his seat belt.

He caught up to me on the cracked sidewalk. "I'll walk you to the door." He sounded concerned, which only heightened my anxiety. When he reached for my elbow, I dodged his grasp. Just now I couldn't withstand a physical zap. I was operating on emotional overload. I blamed the scene with my dad, the confrontation with Monica. The wine.

This time I walked in without knocking. I almost tripped over Big Red. "What the heck?" Earlier, Beckett had carried my suitcase upstairs to my bedroom. "Mom?" I called out.

She came from the direction of the kitchen, fluffing her new do.

I heard the back door creak shut and my imagination soared.

"I just knew you'd see her inside," she said to Arch, cheeks flushed. "A true gentleman. How did you find Greenville, Baron?"

"No need for formalities," he said with an easy smile. "Arch suits fine. As for your town, in a way it reminds me of the village of Broxley. Charming."

"How nice. And I suppose Evelyn introduced you to Mr. Parish."

He nodded. "Also charming."

"Most people think so."

"Mom," I broke in, trying not to obsess on who'd just made a hasty retreat. Must've been someone strong. No way had she muscled Big Red down a flight of stairs. "What's my suitcase doing here?"

"It's my way of showing you I'm not a prude, Evelyn."

The knot in my stomach gnarled tighter.

"I think you should stay with your boyfriend."

CHAPTER SEVENTEEN

TABASCO AND GINA were sitting at the dining-room table, playing cards when Arch escorted me into the Appleseed Bed-and-Breakfast.

The house vibrated with the sounds of classic rock. Doobie Brothers.

"You're second dealing," Gina said over the chorus of "Long Train Runnin'." "It took a couple of hands, but I see it now." She leaned forward, intent on the deck of cards in Tabasco's long-fingered hands. "What I can't tell is whether you're striking the second card or pushing off."

"Pushing off," he said with a cocky grin.

"You're a damn good card mechanic, Tabasco."

"You're a damn scary poker player."

She laughed. I'd never heard Gina laugh. "We need to rub off on each other. Let's go another hand," she said. "Five-card draw. Jacks to open."

Tabasco looked our way, muttered something to Gina.

She shifted, noted me, the suitcase and frowned. "What the—"

"Change of plans," Arch said.

Gina polished off a Heineken. "I need another beer."

Tabasco boxed the cards. Game over. "The pink bedroom's unclaimed. Probably called the Rose Room, now that I think of it. Roses all over the place. The wall-paper, the curtains, the bedspread. Real girlie. Not that I have anything against flowers…or girls, but—"

"You're babbling," Gina said, pushing out of her chair to shut off the radio.

The silence made me itch.

"I'll rustle up supper." Tabasco stood and pulled his shoulder-length hair into a ponytail. "You like steak, Twinkie?"

"I'm not hungry, thank you."

"Gotta eat."

"Maybe later." I clasped my throat, coughed. "Think I'm having a relapse."

I glanced at the carpeted stairs, desperate to escape. I was in no mood to socialize with the boys or to make nice with Gina. I wasn't even compelled to explore the reno-vated mansion, a property that had seen more owners than a pirated movie.

My mom had booted me out. The height of rejection, even though she swore her intentions were positive. Dur-ing the twenty-minute ride to the B and B Arch had asked three times if I was okay. Three times I'd answered, "Fine," even though it felt like Frankenstein had a mon-ster grip on my heart. I kept telling myself that everything happens for a reason and that somehow I'd spin this dis-appointing turn to my advantage. Since then, I'd come up with two sound motives for Mom showing me the door.

One: she wanted to marry me off to an aristocrat— and fast. If I couldn't have a sound career, a financially stable—and noble—husband would do. Or…

Two: she didn't want me pestering her about Dad and poking my nose into her…shenanigans.

Logically it was probably a little of both, and I was

trying very hard to be logical. Trying hard not to make it about me, as Arch had pointed out I tend to do. Still, it hurt. We saw each other for a few days every three years. How could she not want to spend every second with me?

"The Rose Room?" I asked in a distracted voice.

Unlike Gina, Tabasco looked concerned. "I'll show you the way, hon."

"I've got it," Arch said.

Although Big Red weighed a ton, he carried the suitcase up the stairs with ease. I followed him down the second-floor hallway, again obsessing on who'd been in the house with Mom. That someone had left via the back door, implying they didn't want to be seen. My stomach cramped thinking that *someone* was a no good womanizer or a conniving hustler. Maybe both.

Arch opened a door and waved me ahead of him. Tabasco hadn't been kidding. Roses everywhere. The curtains, the wallpaper, the quilt on the four-poster bed. He'd called it girlie. I called it Victorian. No denying the dominant color was pink. "Lovely," I said, because it was. This one room had more personality than my entire apartment. Again my stomach cramped. "So where are the owners?"

"Florida. Second home." Arch placed Big Red on the padded window seat. "Woody said they only open the Appleseed for business during the summer, yeah?"

"Makes sense." I tossed my purse and *Lucy* tote on the bed. "Who vacations in Greenville, Indiana, anyway?" Although some might enjoy the county fairs and state parks. "So…what? You rented the entire place? Must be costing Chameleon a fortune."

"Chameleon's not footing the bill."

That left the AIA or the senator. Or maybe Tabasco had somehow *appropriated* the property. I didn't ask. If it was the latter, I didn't want to know. "I guess Beckett's still with the senator and his wife."

"Probably on his way back by now." He slid his hands in his pants pockets and I fidgeted under his intense regard. "Sure you *dinnae* want to join us for dinner?"

"Will you be discussing the senator's case?"

"At some point."

Okay, that was vague. That was Arch circling around the subject. He knew I'd jump at sitting in on an actual team meeting, actively participating in the plotting, yet he didn't invite me. Apparently he only intended to feed me tidbits of information as he saw fit. Back to that need-to-know-basis-only bunk. Again I wrestled with the feeling that he wasn't keen on my being an active Chameleon.

If I were in better spirits and up to arguing my motivation and qualifications, I'd challenge his skepticism. The new and improved me wanted to talk my way into that meeting. The depressed and exhausted me lacked the gumption. I knew that, even if I did sit in, my opinions and suggestions, should I have any, wouldn't be welcome. What did I know about coordinating stings? What experience did I have with poker and card mechanics?

Except I *did* have experience. Not from working in their world but mine. I knew magicians who excelled at sleight of hand, which sometimes extended to picking pockets as part of the show. I knew about such things firsthand, as I'd worked a short stint as a magician's assistant.

Then there was *acting*. Making people believe you're someone else. A form of deception. Only the audience, known in grifterspeak as *the mark,* got something for their money—a night's entertainment—as opposed to getting taken for a ride. The lingo, the attitude and certain techniques were different. The smoke-and-mirrors objective the same.

Distancing myself, I understood why Chameleon didn't enthusiastically welcome me into the fold. It was the same in my entertainment circle. Say an outsider shows up for a gig cast with "regulars." Even if the newbie was talented, he or she still had to earn our respect.

I hadn't proven myself to Gina or Tabasco. Certainly not to Beckett. I didn't know what to think about Arch. As always, he had my head spinning.

He raised a brow and I remembered he'd asked about dinner.

"Thanks, but I've lost my appetite." Mom didn't want me around. Gina didn't want me around. And when it came to nitty-gritty sensitive grifter matters, Arch preferred to keep me at arm's length. I sat on the edge of the mattress, bristled at his assessing silence. "Please don't ask if I'm okay. I just need some downtime. It's been a long and eventful day." As action-packed and ludicrous as any episode of *24*.

"If you change your mind—"

"I won't. But…thanks."

He lingered on the threshold, those light-colored eyes studying me with an intensity that quickened my pulse.

Even though he'd disappointed me, the pull to move into his arms for a comforting hug was powerful. I sat tight.

"Good night, Sunshine."

"Good night."

He left and closed the door behind him.

I sat on the four-poster bed staring around the absurdly cheery room, thinking I'd felt more miserable. Just not recently.

MILO WALKED IN AT the end of dinner. From the looks of the remnants, the team had feasted on steak, baked potatoes and mixed vegetables. A hearty Midwestern meal.

"Saved you a plate," Tabasco said. "It's in the oven. I'll get it."

"Thanks." Exhausted, he smiled a little, thinking that when Pops wasn't playing caretaker, there was always Jimmy Tabasco.

Arch studied him, then rose. "I'll grab a round of beers. *Dinnae* start the fun with*oot* us, yeah?"

His tone was light, but Milo sensed concern. He tossed the car keys on a small table, moved into the dining area and sat next to Gina. "I must look like shit."

"You look tired, Jazzman."

"Long day." A day of disappointment and realization. Easier to write off Mrs. Clark when she'd merely been a name. Meeting her face-to-face only drove home Gina's observation that even the privileged suffer shame and remorse. Although he suspected Mrs. Clark's anxiety stemmed more from the fact that she'd introduced potential scandal into her husband's life rather than from the squandered money. Milo had assessed her regret and panic as genuine. She'd been scolded, all right, maybe threatened. By her husband, his advisors. She didn't care about the money, but her husband did. They all wanted to avoid a scandal.

Milo wanted to avoid pissing off Crowe. A conclusion he'd come to on the long, boring drive. Just because he was considering leaving the AIA, didn't mean he had the right to make that choice for the entire team. Everyone, including Arch, wanted to tackle this case. Fine. They'd tackle it. Then he'd make his decision.

He reached in his pocket for a hit of Tylenol.

Gina passed him the last of her beer.

"Thanks," he said.

"Sure."

He chased the caplets with Heineken, then picked at the label, deep in thought. "You were right about Mrs. Clark. The woman's an emotional basket case."

"And the senator?"

"Away on business."

"If you would have called ahead—"

"I did. Under an alias. I considered it a bonus that he was out of town. I wanted Mrs. Clark's story, not her husband's spin."

"And her story had merit."

"It did."

"Still have that bad feeling?"

"I do."

Winning back her losses wasn't the sticking point. If Turner was a cheat, he deserved tit for tat. It was the intimidation and cover-up aspect that left Milo cold. Made him feel like a hired thug. Making Turner go away. He still hadn't decided how to handle that part of Crowe's directive without completely obliterating his ability to sleep.

Tabasco and Arch returned, bearing food and drinks. Tabasco spoke first. "How'd the interview go?"

"After speaking with Mrs. Clark, I think there's a strong possibility she was, in fact, fleeced."

Arch smoothed a hand over his goatee. "So we're taking the case."

"We'll proceed as discussed earlier." Milo refused to admit he was actually looking forward to the challenge. Between determining whether or not Mrs. Parish was being scammed and playing a long con on a big cheat, it would leave little time to dwell on his Twinkie fixation.

He couldn't help remembering the way she'd melted at the sight of his partner. He'd remembered over and over on the ride to Hammond and back. The envy that had pumped through him, the disappointment. He couldn't help wishing she'd look at him with the same heart-pounding affection.

An Ellington classic taunted his brain. *I got it bad and that ain't good.* Then a phantom Evie kicked up his misery, singing Peggy Lee's "Fever." In a wet T-shirt.

Shit.

He traded the empty beer bottle for a full one, tipped the longneck toward the rotten apple of Evie's eye. "You and I will stay in Greenville, playing up the nobility angle, garnering publicity and credibility."

"I'll allude to my great wealth and leak my fondness for gambling to the press," Arch said. "By the time we're ready to rope Turner he'll be champing at the bit to rope the Baron of Broxley. But in order to beat the man at his crooked game, I need to know what I'm up against, yeah?"

Gina tucked her long, dark hair behind her ears. "Which is why Tabasco and I are going in first."

"There's no poker room on that riverboat, so you'll have to hit the tables," Milo said.

"Caribbean stud?" Gina asked.

He nodded. "You'll be playing against the house. No bluffing. They also offer four-card poker."

Tabasco grunted. "Serious players don't consider those games real poker."

"You can use that to your advantage," said Arch. "Make mention a time or two, yeah?"

"Sure."

"According to Crowe, Senator Clark will cover expenses," Milo said, "so you can both make a significant financial impression."

"Show your greedy side," Arch said. "Bitch about the stakes."

"Not high enough," Gina said. "Got it."

"I don't have the name of the dealer who steered Mrs. Clark to Turner's game, but I have a description. I called Woody on the drive back. Maybe he can narrow it down." Milo sawed the juicy steak. He wasn't hungry, but Tabasco was a gifted cook. "One of you needs to get roped into that exclusive game. We need a better description of the layout than what Mrs. Clark provided. And if Turner's cheating, we need to know how."

"Done," they said simultaneously.

"With pleasure," Gina added with a smirk.

"Meaning?" Milo asked while forking meat into his mouth.

"Meaning," she said, flashing a look at Arch, "this place is crowded. I'm happy for the night out."

Milo waited.

"Twinkie," said Tabasco.

"What about her?"

"She's here. Speaking of, I want to run her up a PB&J and a glass of milk. Maybe she'll give in to comfort food. Gotta eat something."

Milo watched the man go, then focused back on Arch. "I thought she was staying with her mother."

"So did she."

"What happened?"

Arch glanced at the stairway, then replayed the afternoon in a low voice.

Milo shook his head at the tree-climbing incident. He couldn't decide if she had a screw loose or initiative and balls. As for her parents… "You think her mom had another man in the house?"

"I *dinnae* know what to think."

"Must've hurt," Gina said, surprising them both. "Her mom pushing her away like that."

"She pretended it *didnae*. Told her ma she appreciated her new liberal *oot*look. If I *didnae* know…" Arch shrugged, swigged his beer. "She's getting better at snowing me. Not sure how I feel *aboot* that."

"I'd think you'd be ecstatic." Gina angled her head. "Unless you're not keen about her being an active operator. It is, after all, what we do—*lie*."

Milo eyed Gina and Arch, who were eyeing each other, and not in a good way. "Since I've got you two together, now seems a good time—"

"Water under the bridge," Gina said.

"We're fine," Arch said.

Milo frowned. "Right."

Gina leveled him with a look. "I don't care that Ace and Twinkie are carrying on, if that's what you're thinking."

"*Were* carrying on," Arch said. "Past tense."

Whether she believed him or not, Milo couldn't tell. He sure as hell wasn't convinced. "Then what's the problem?" he asked Gina.

"She doesn't have a background in law enforcement or grifting. She's not one of us."

"I didn't hire her to grift," Milo said. "I hired her to sing."

"What the hell did you need a singer for? You've got a jukebox, a CD audio system. Live entertainment might lure in new customers, and as I recall, the club's a cover, not a moneymaker, so the fewer patrons the better."

Milo didn't comment. She was right. He'd hired Evie because she'd suckered him with her passion, her determination and those big blue eyes. She was genuine and sweet, a rarity in his line of work. The optimist in him had viewed her as a ray of sunshine in his bleak world. The pessimist had viewed her as a way to control Arch—the man studying him just now with unnerving calm. Trouble was, the more he got to know her, the more he wanted to *know* her. Intimately.

Gina rolled over his thoughts. "You allowed Pops to bring her into the Cave. The heart of our operation. Team members only. You're not treating her like a freelance singer, Jazzman. You're treating her like one of us. You, too," she said with a quick glance at Arch. "You're both thinking with your peckers. It's dangerous. And more than a little insulting. She's a piece of fluff, for chrissake."

"There's more to Evie than meets the eye," Arch said. "As to my *willy*...Chameleon's juggling two potential swindles. Mind's on other things, yeah?"

Gina polished off her beer.

Milo started to say he didn't fraternize with team members, except he'd just told Gina he'd hired Evie as a singer, not an operator. So technically that made her fair game for both Arch *and* Milo without compromising his unwritten policy. Hadn't thought of that before. Well, hell.

Just then, Tabasco loped down the stairs. "Think I should make a run into town. Pick up some cold medicine for Twinkie. Want anything from the quick-mart?"

Everyone stared.

"What?"

Gina smirked. "You fell for that relapse line? She's not sick, you idiot. That cough was as fake as Ace's numerous passports."

Tabasco shifted his weight. "Her voice was hoarse and her eyes were watery."

Arch glanced at Milo. "Told you, mate. Honing her deception skills."

CHAPTER EIGHTEEN

MARK: A VICTIM OR intended victim.

Outsideman: the member of the con mob who locates the mark, brings him to the store and assists in fleecing him. Also lugger, roper.

Insideman: the member of a con mob who stays near the big store and receives the mark whom the roper brings. Insidemen are highly specialized workers....

The glossary of *The Big Con: The Story of the Confidence Man* by David W. Maurer was extensive and probably somewhat dated, as the original copyright was 1940, but it had been reprinted at least twice, and I'd heard Arch use many of the terms. I read with great interest, committing the basics to memory. I'd wussed out tonight, but I *would* finesse my way into an official meeting at some point, and when I did, I wanted to blow the team away with my knowledge of their profession. The lingo was colorful, the concepts fascinating. Each definition spurred me to look up a new word like...

The Big Store: an establishment against which big-con men play their victims.

Big Con: any big-time confidence game in which a mark is put on the send for his money, as contrasted to a short con, where the touch is limited to the amount the mark has with him.

Since I was in the dark about developments concerning the senator's case, I focused on my mom's. Applying these notions to her scenario and assuming she was being hustled, I surmised she'd fallen victim to a *big con*. She'd gone to the bank for a large sum, so she'd been *put on the send*. Was the dance studio the *big store?* Was the dance instructor the *roper* or the *insideman?* Was she, as Tabasco had suggested, a victim of a Sweetheart scam?

I swapped Maurer's book for a more recent release and snuggled deeper beneath the rose quilt as I consulted the table of contents. I read the chapter on Sweetheart scams twice. Lothario cons were on the rise, it said, due to Internet dating services. These days a con artist could swindle his mark without even meeting her in person. Seduction by way of numerous amorous e-mails. Once roped, he could utilize any number of scenarios to persuade her to send him money—a business opportunity, a plane ticket, a personal loan. In the end he'd break her bank account *and* her heart.

The whole thing made me sick and angry. Lonely people fell for these scams. Mostly the victims were older, divorced or widowed. When I got to the part where it described how some scum artists cruise the newspaper obits looking for premium marks, I decided I'd had enough for the night. "Slimeball rat bastards." I didn't want to believe Mom could fall victim to any of those scenarios. But then I thought of the bonds, the makeover and that dashing middle-aged dance instructor. She wasn't divorced or widowed, but she was surely disillusioned with Dad.

Needing to know there were some good things in this world, like hope and true love, I chucked the manual and dug out the romance paperback I'd packed in Big Red.

I glanced at the door, surprised that no one aside from

Tabasco had checked in on me. Although I'd made it clear I wasn't feeling well and wanted to be left alone. Which was true. Sort of. I settled under the sheets, trying not to think about Arch.

Two chapters into Lord Geoffrey and Lady Victoria's adventure, I drifted off with visions of star-crossed lovers going at it on a picnic table. Soon after, the whimsical dream about a dashing hero and a klutzy heroine turned sinister. The Lord and the Lady morphed into the Baron and the showgirl. She crippled a touchy-feely dance instructor. He hooked a slimy, smooth-talking shark. Slot machines and blueprints. Henchmen and G-men. Tripping. Tussling. Gun aimed at Arch. *No!*

I jerked awake—heart pounding, shirt damp with sweat. I set aside the novel, glanced at the bedside clock.

Eleven-thirty.

I'd conked out for three hours. It felt like seconds.

I listened.

Silence.

In-the-middle-of-nowhere silence. Scary Freddy Krueger silence.

Sure, I'd grown up in these parts, but we lived in town. Houses on either side, a stone's throw away. An entire neighborhood to run to for help. The Appleseed B and B was twenty minutes from civilization, the nearest farmhouse a good mile down the road. Assuming a crazed serial killer offed the other team members, saving me for last, no one would hear me scream, and if I had to run a mile…can you say *dead meat?* If Freddy didn't kill me, the sprint would.

"Get a grip," I whispered, releasing my white-knuckle hold on the quilt. "The others aren't dead, they're asleep." Probably.

My imagination was in overdrive due to the chaotic

nightmare. I massaged my temples, plagued by convoluted fragments of the Simon the Fish fiasco. Amazingly, I'd been spared similar nightmares. My subconscious, I suppose, was in denial, not wanting to dredge up that awful moment. Because I'd blown our cover, a man had died. A bad man, yeah. But dead is dead.

I'd broached the subject a couple of times with Arch. Every time I tried to recall the exact details, I remembered them a little differently. It made me nuts.

Let it go, he'd said. *You banged your head hard, twice. Blacked out. Suffered a concussion. No wonder you're unclear, yeah?*

Yeah. But it still bothered me, so I'd pressed, and he'd told me what he'd told Beckett, the facts supposedly backed up on tape.

"Let it go," I told myself, then I remembered what Marvin the janitor said. *We knew you'd see justice done.*

My brain threatened to explode. I grabbed my journal and pen and scribbled midthought.

Letting your imagination run wild. Arch is a lot of things, but he is not a premeditated killer. He only meant to con Simon, setting him up for a fall that would land him in prison. Locked away for his crimes. Justice done. So it ended differently. Not his fault. Mine. I botched things. Not Arch. Simon pulled the gun. Not Arch. I was trying to protect him. He was trying to protect me. Struggle and—bang! Self-defense. An accident. Not premeditated.

End of story. I set aside the pen, breathing easier now. I blamed the nightmare and my subsequent freak-out on my reading material. I shouldn't have crammed so hard on grifts, not in my exhausted and depressed state. All the lingo and definitions reminded me of my first sting gone bad, a troubling memory I'd yet to put to rest.

Now that I'd spewed on paper, I felt better. About that issue, anyway.

I ventured into the connecting bathroom, washed up and changed into paisley lounge pants and a white tee. My stomach grumbled and I kicked myself for blowing off that darn peanut-butter-and-jelly sandwich. Nearly midnight. No way was I going to traipse downstairs in this big old house. Alone. In the scary Freddy Krueger silence. And no chance of falling back to sleep, either. Not with slasher films on the brain.

I went back to my journal, sat at the antique desk— lovely—and turned to a fresh page.

I blocked thoughts of Simon the Fish. Of Arch. I focused on family. Dad's generosity made mincemeat of my heart, but it was Mom's new liberal attitude that vexed my brain. All these years I'd mourned her conservative nature, wishing she'd live and let live. Now she was doing just that and all I felt was resentful. At least I knew the old Marilyn Parish. The new version was a frustrating mystery. Who had been with her in the house? Why was she willing to distance me and Dad in order to stay close to that mysterious someone? *Dear Diary, What's the deal with my mom? Why can't she love me for who I am? A hug now and then would be nice. Same goes with Dad. A show of affection, please. I understand that saying "I love you" is hard. For some people, anyway. If you really mean it, that is. Although, why would you say it if you didn't mean it? And if you feel it, why wouldn't you say it?*

I looked up from the pages. "Because it's big. And scary. And if the other person doesn't say it back, you'll feel foolish."

No one wants to be the first one on the dance floor.

The heavens opened and angels sang. Not literally, of course. But epiphanies always struck me that way. I had to stop looking to others to get the party started. For approval. For fulfillment. Instead of worrying about who people wanted me to be, I just needed to be...*me.*

I doodled purple hearts, deep in thought. I swallowed a gasp when I heard someone moving around in the connecting bathroom. Not Freddy, I assured myself. Probably Gina. Although she was kind of scary. I refocused on my writing, adding...

Life's too short. I'm gonna boogie.

A knock on the connecting door prompted me to hide my journal. No way did I want Gina to know I kept a diary. I'm sure she'd view it as juvenile. She was one of those women who spoke her mind. Kind of like Nic. Only Nic was nice.

I padded to the door and eased it open. Not Gina. *Arch.* And just like that, the only thing on my mind was sex. My heart thudded and my mouth went dry. He looked much as he had the first time I'd seen him half-naked, except this time he was wearing gray sweatpants instead of a hotel towel. He smelled of Irish Spring and tobacco, and I couldn't decide which was sexier, his goatee or the Celtic tattoo. Both summoned primal urges.

I took a step back.

"Heard you moving around in here. Thought I'd check in before turning in." He eyed me hard. "You okay?"

I thought about the nightmare, my scribbled logic. I looked into Arch's eyes and all I saw was kindness. Still, Marvin's statement niggled. "I've never asked and I need to know."

"Aye?"

"Did you set out to kill Simon the Fish?"

"No."

"Because if you did—"

"I didn't"

"He killed your grandfather."

"I wanted revenge, aye. But I wanted The Fish to suffer. Life in prison would've been more satisfying."

That made sense. It also jibed with my scribbled logic.

He skimmed a thumb over my cheek. *Zing.* "I need you to let this go."

"Why?"

"Because it reminds me that I'll never see my grandfather again."

"And that makes you angry."

"Aye, but mostly sad."

I felt a twinge of guilt. I also felt manipulated. He knew I wouldn't press him on a subject that caused him pain. My head spun. Whether from his gentle touch or hypnotic gaze, I didn't know. The result was the same. Noodle limbs and mush brain. "Okay. Letting it go." *For now.*

"Good." He smiled. *Zap.* "Feel better?"

"A little." I smiled back like a mesmerized idiot. Then I shrugged. "Except, you know, this thing with my mom."

"Things will look up tomorrow."

"You think?"

"Mmm."

We stood there, hovering on either side of the threshold, inches apart. The air sizzled. *Arch* sizzled. The backs of my knees prickled with sweat.

"Hope you *dinnae* mind sharing a bathroom," he said at last.

"I don't mind." My voice pitched higher and cracked

a little. I sounded like the ditz in that old Steve Martin flick. The one where he invented screw-top zip-lock brain surgery.

Apparently Arch had the same thought. We laughed at the same time, obliterating any lingering somberness.

"Bang-on impression. Helluva funny movie," he said, flooring me once again with his astounding knowledge of movie trivia.

"Curious. When and why did you develop this fascination with film?"

He shrugged. "Chalk it up to a family quirk. A way to study costumes, facial expressions, body language, professions, languages, accents, various scenarios. As a wee lad I got a charge *oot* of watching my ma imitating the actresses on screen. Dazzling her with my own efforts was a way of bonding, you know?"

Since he rarely shared details of his past, I didn't confess my shock that a woman had trained her son for a life of crime. "Well, at least you bonded with your mom."

He angled his head. "*Dinnae* look so glum, Sunshine. There's still time."

Sorry I'd even brought her up, I looked around his sculpted torso, eyed the other door. "So that's your bedroom?"

His gaze locked with mine. "As luck would have it."

"Bad luck or good luck?"

"Yet to be determined, lass."

Previous reservations—his questionable ethics, his inability to commit—melted under his molten-hot regard. I could deny it until the cows came home, but I'd fallen head over heels for Arch Duvall.

Acceptance inspired wonder. More heavenly choirs, but with heralding trumpets and a harp to boot. Big-band angels for a big-time epiphany. Had I ever felt this over the moon for Michael? For any man?

I gripped the doorjamb instead of moving into his arms. The magnetic pull was fierce and exhilarating.

If you feel it, why wouldn't you say it?

Taunted by my own purple-inked scribbles.

Tell him how you feel.

Except blurting my feelings didn't feel natural.

Of course not, you dope, that's because you naturally internalize. Dredge up some moxie. Practice what you journal. Say the words.

They wouldn't come. Too big. Too scary. I frowned, imagining a big, honkin' *L* on my forehead. Strike that. A big-ass *W. Wuss!*

"What's wrong?"

"Just tired." And over the moon, tongue-tied, crazy in love. "So is everyone turning in?"

He braced his hands on the jamb, as well. The action emphasized the muscles in his arms, drew attention to that tribal tattoo. *Yowza.* My stomach quivered in anticipation as he leaned in, expression unreadable. "Gina and Tabasco left for Hammond. They'll be spending tonight at the riverboat casino and an exclusive hotel. Phase one of the gambling sting."

I swallowed. "Beckett?"

"Still downstairs. He's coordinating phase two with Woody via the Internet. His room's across the hall and two doors down, in case you're wondering."

"Why would I wonder?"

"Did you pack your dancing shoes?"

I stared because that was too weird. He couldn't possibly know what I'd just written in my journal. Maybe it was a European sexual innuendo?

"I booked a private lesson with that ballroom instructor," he said.

I blinked. "For both of us?"

"*Cannae* have Beckett showing me up, yeah?"

It took me a minute, but then I realized he was referring to the time I, as my alter ego Sugar, had danced with Beckett—or, rather, Tex Aloha—on the cruise. To my chagrin, I wasn't immune to the man's finesse. Afterward, Arch, as his alter ego Charles, had wowed me with a possessive kiss. At the time I'd wondered if he was jealous of Beckett. I wondered the same thing now.

"Phase one of the Sweetheart sting," he said as if reading my mind and steering it back to business. "Might as well cut to the chase, investigate your number one suspect. If that instructor's shoveling *shite,* I'll smell it."

"Pretty sure of yourself."

"When it comes to grifting, I'm bold-faced arrogant, yeah?"

"You're arrogant, period. Normally an off-putting quality."

"Abnormally?"

"You wear it well."

He quirked a grin.

Zing. Zap. I focused on my mom's shenanigans instead of Arch's sexy mouth. "Although I am stuck on that dance instructor, I've been reading up, and Mom *could* have fallen prey to any number of scams."

"Or none at all. Maybe she made a sound investment. Maybe she's celebrating her golden years by experimenting. New hairstyle, new hobbies. Maybe she's trying to compete with the tavern for your da's interest." He dropped a kiss to my forehead. "*Dinnae* let that imagination of yours run amok, love. Sleep well, yeah?"

As always, he'd addressed my worries with sensible alternatives. My heart thumped in gratitude. And admiration. The man was grounded. I, on the other hand, currently floated on a sensual cloud. *I'm in love.* I stood there transfixed and terrified as he moved into his bedroom. Okay. His butt—spectacular even in sweats—captured my attention, but so did the fact that he left his door ajar. I retreated to my room, wondering if we'd be able to resist temptation and, if not, who would crumble first.

CHAPTER NINETEEN

MY WILL DISINTEGRATED around 1:55 a.m. It wasn't sex I wanted as much as Arch. In our short time together he'd become a dangerous and delicious habit. Sleeping in his arms felt as natural as breathing. Just now my lungs burned for air.

I could list a dozen reasons explaining the wisdom in riding out this vexing need as opposed to crawling into bed with the man next door. But—darn it all—the man next door struck me stupid.

Fog-brained, I pushed out of bed and tiptoed across the room, praying the floorboards didn't creak. Praying Beckett had conked out. Praying I'd have the nerve to act on my epiphany. *If you feel it, say it.* Response—or lack thereof—be damned.

Dance, woman, dance.

I boogied into the adjoining bedroom, grateful for a pale wash of moonlight. Goody Two-shoes like me usually trip or knock stuff over when trying to sneak about. I made it to his bedside without incident. Now, if I could just find my voice. "Are you asleep?" I finally whispered.

"Not anymore."

"I'm sorry, I…"

He threw back the quilt and tugged me into bed.

Sighing, I snuggled against six feet of warm sinew. "You're naked."

"You're not."

Between the two of us we had my clothes off in three seconds flat.

Arch smoothed his hands over my bare flesh. My lungs blossomed in my chest. Every nerve ending sparked to life. Every brain cell glitched. The kiss, hungry and hot, promised a deep, hard shag. Bending me over the dresser or taking me on the floor wouldn't do—too noisy. By doing it at all we were both breaking our word to Beckett, only I hadn't actually *promised* anything, had I? Hard to think straight with Arch's skilled fingers stroking me to a breathless orgasm.

My taut muscles quivered, the pleasure intense and overwhelming. I struggled to endure rapture in silence. Sensitive to my dilemma, he smothered my throaty release with a lusty kiss.

Slick with want, I trembled as he maneuvered my body, preparing to take me from behind. An exciting position that we'd enjoyed before, an enviable position, as it allowed me to avoid eye contact. Only I no longer wanted that disconnection.

"I don't want sex," I whispered over my shoulder.

His body tensed, but his tone was unperturbed. "Okay." He fell back against his pillow, his hand on my hip. "We'll just spoon, yeah?"

I reached over and flicked on a reading lamp.

No more hiding.

I rolled over and squirmed beneath him, finessing our bodies into the missionary position, a banned position, a position I'd formerly declared *too intimate*.

"Mixed signals, lass."

I met his gaze and held it. "I don't want to *boink*."

After an intense heartbeat, he said, "Ah." His gaze was unreadable, but then he reached for a condom and kissed me dizzy. Safe to assume I hadn't scared him off, even if I couldn't presume to know his heart.

I locked my arms around his neck, pulling him into a deeper kiss, locked my ankles about his thighs. I silently urged him to take me, *take me now.* Only he took his time, treating me to the longest, sweetest, hottest kiss of my life. It was delicious, confounding…and infuriating. How could a kiss stoke so much desire?

In the hands of a master, even a nervous bird can soar.

Holy crow.

Suddenly I was aware of how tense I'd been. He was easing my fears by holding back yet giving more than he'd ever given. Emotions clogged my throat, damming up the words I wanted to say. I framed his face and broke the kiss. I gave in and let go. I gazed into his eyes and showed him my heart.

The air crackled with intensity. Two live wires connecting and melding.

He plunged deep and seduced my soul.

Together we made earth-quaking, star-shattering love.

Together we soared.

I WOKE UP TANGLED IN Arch's arms and legs, marveling that we'd survived what felt like a merging of souls. Being a man, I doubted he'd think of the coupling in those poetic terms, but I know he'd experienced a like rush. I'd sensed it in his touch. Seen it in his eyes. For a brief moment the closed-off con man had been an open book. The *L* word, though unspoken, had circled in our universe.

The weight of his thigh across mine had caused my foot to fall asleep, but I didn't care. *I could stay like this forever,* I thought sleepily. Except if we didn't show for breakfast, Beckett would come looking and, finding us in a naked human knot, would put two and two together.

I didn't know him well enough to anticipate his reaction. And it's not as though I'd been issued a company handbook. Was the penalty for mixing business and pleasure a stern-faced lecture? A warning? Suspension? Was it grounds for termination? I wondered if it would matter if I admitted I was in love.

My luck, it would make things worse. He'd worry that we'd let our personal relationship interfere with the job— not that I'd been approved for fieldwork. As such, was I even technically a team member? Did that policy truly apply?

I mulled over the consequences of the night's actions. Even more than risking my job, I'd risked my heart. Making intimate love had been the ultimate leap of faith. I kept waiting for fear and regret to seep into my bones, but all I felt was joy.

I took that as a sign and refused to second-guess my decision to boogie. If things…fizzled, I'd still have the Corner Tavern.

Thinking about my dad's thoughtfulness made me smile. It also reminded me that I still needed to address my parents' relationship, as well as my relationship with my parents. There was also the senator's case and Beckett's career to consider.

Considering, Arch and I needed to keep our on-again real-life romance a secret. At least for now.

I squinted at the bedside clock. Four in the morning. As much as I didn't want to return to my own bed, it was the smart thing to do. Better now while the house—or, rather, Beckett—slept. I tried to ease out of Arch's arms, but he clung.

"*Dinnae* go."

His groggy request made my heart dance with glee. "I'm thirsty," I whispered.

"I'll get you a glass of water."

"Thank you, but I'll get it myself." I sat up and pulled on my T-shirt, groped in the dark for my pants.

Arch propped himself up on an elbow. "Are you coming back?"

"I can't." I tightened the drawstring of my paisley drawers, steeled my spotty will.

"Are we going to pretend this *didnae* happen?"

"I'm not sorry it happened, if that's what you mean." He didn't respond.

"It's just that it's against Chameleon policy—"

"Beckett *dinnae* hire you for fieldwork. He hired you to sing."

"A temporary position until I earn my scales."

"What?"

"Pay my dues. Anyway, I told him we were kaput romantically, so at the very least I lied."

"There are all kinds of lies, Sunshine."

"Maybe, but that doesn't make them right."

"Depends, yeah?"

Typical response coming from a man who'd lived his life perfecting deception. "Point is," I said before he talked me in circles, "this isn't the time to make waves. There's the thing with Senator Clark…Beckett's career crisis…"

"Fuck Beckett. Strike that." He reached out and pulled me down on top of him. "Fuck me."

I grinned at the playfulness in his tone and touch. "How romantic."

He rolled over, trapping me between his hard body and the soft mattress. "You want romance, lass?"

"Am I a red-blooded female?"

"You're a bewitching female."

"Is that good or bad?"

"It's interesting."

"Hmm." Hard to analyze that observation when he was distracting me with his hands and mouth. "I really should go," I whispered, my eyes rolling back in my head as he nibbled my earlobe.

He smiled against my neck. "Okay." Then he kissed his way south.

CHAPTER TWENTY

AT FIVE O'CLOCK I slipped away and into the shower, too restless to sleep. The euphoria I'd experienced in Arch's arms swirled down the drain as I stood under the hot, pelting water—thinking, wondering, worrying. We'd taken our relationship to another level, sexually and emotionally. Only Arch didn't do relationships. It's not as if I needed a formal commitment *now*. We'd known each other less than a month. I wasn't dying to cohabit. I wasn't expecting a marriage proposal. But I needed to know that if our feelings continued to evolve there was hope for a you-and-no-other declaration. Otherwise, why was I spinning on the dance floor with my heart on my sleeve? Life is short. Especially when you're over forty.

Okay, that was melodramatic. That was…insecure. I wrapped my wet body in a thick towel and approached the steamy mirror. "You're panicking," I said to my hazy reflection. Arch knew what making love, intimate love, meant to me. He'd accepted my heart and given something of himself, as well. I've got a wicked imagination, true, but I didn't imagine that meld. Maybe, just maybe, he'd changed his mind about the relationship thing. At some point we'd have to discuss our future. Until then, I'd cling to hope. "Breathe and boogie."

Right. I didn't know this dance, so I'd just go with it.

And see where Arch led.

At six o'clock, dressed in loose black pants with flared bottoms and a bright pink tailored blouse, I crept downstairs, craving a big breakfast and a cup of coffee. Not necessarily in that order. Skipping supper had earned me a flat but grumbling belly. No way was I waiting for Arch and Beckett to rise before raiding the kitchen. I could eat a horse, but I'd settle for eggs and toast.

I nosed my way through a sitting room, a library and a dining area, admiring the eclectic period furnishings as I searched for the kitchen. Just as I tripped upon my destination, Beckett entered the modernized kitchen via a back door.

My heart thumped, not only because he'd surprised me but because it was the first I'd seem him since Arch had arrived uninvited and revised his original plan. "You startled me," I squeaked, flashing back to when he'd comforted me in the backseat of the taxi. The unsettling *snap*. Gads.

"Sorry." He shut the door, pushed his sunglasses on top of his head. "What are you doing up so early?"

Play it cool, Parish. No blushing. No scratching. No tell. I shrugged. "Went to bed early. Woke up early. Came down for breakfast. You?"

"Went to bed late. Tossed and turned. Went out for an early jog."

Jogging. Right. Hence the running shoes, gym shorts and T-shirt damp with sweat. Thunk to the forehead. "Not very observant before my first cup of coffee," I said with a smile.

His own smile was humorless.

I thought about his insomnia, his career crisis. I wondered if he was as lonely as I used to be, and my heart commiserated and warmed. Crap. "Want to talk about it?"

He dragged his forearm across his moist brow. "About what?"

"Whatever's troubling you."

"No. Thank you."

"I didn't mean to be nosy. It's just that you flew all the way out here to help me and that was really nice and I thought if I could help you…" If Gina were here, she'd say I was babbling. I couldn't help it. His bold scrutiny made me nervous. As if he knew what Arch and I had been up to this morning. I suppose it was possible. He *did* mention his pesky insomnia and the bedsprings *had* squeaked. Depending on how late he'd gone to bed or how early he'd gone out…definitely possible. I could feel my cheeks heating, so I stuck my head in the fridge. "Did you guys buy coffee?"

I heard a cabinet creak open, turned and saw Beckett taking down a bag of ground java and a box of filters. "Tabasco's thorough. There's a coffeemaker in the pantry," he said, setting aside the goods. "I'll get it."

"Thanks."

"Where's Arch?"

"Sleeping. I guess," I added. "I mean, it is awfully early." Back into the fridge I went. *Relax. He can't know anything for sure unless you tell him or he catches you in the act.*

Right.

I grabbed a carton of eggs, a roll of sausage and a pop-open can of biscuits. We were in the country. Might as well indulge in a Jimmy Dean breakfast.

"Would you care to join me?" I asked as he plugged in the automatic coffeemaker.

"You go ahead. I need a shower."

"I can wait." It was polite to say so, at least. I cursed

my growling stomach, searched a drawer for a coffee
scoop and settled for a tablespoon. "Besides, I should
inhale at least one cup of caffeine before attempting to
cook."

"Didn't get much sleep, huh?"

Avoiding eye contact, I spooned grounds and filled the
reservoir with water. "Things on my mind."

"Arch updated me on the family situation."

"He updated me on the senator situation."

"So we're both up to date."

Could things get any more tense?

"So what did you have in mind?" he asked.

"What do you mean?"

"When you said you could help me. How?"

I pushed the brew button and turned.

Beckett leaned against the wall, muscled arms crossed,
sunglasses perched on top of his salt-and-pepper buzz cut.
Former military. Former cop. Current secret agent.

Okay. He was attractive. He was…hot. But I was in
love with Arch, so I was immune. Sort of. "I know what
you're thinking."

He raised a brow. "Enlighten me."

"You're wondering what a girl like me could do for a
guy like you."

"You got me there, Twinkie."

"I'm an expert on career crisis. Been there. Still there."

He worked his jaw. "Who says I'm having a career
crisis?"

"Arch."

"He spoke out of turn."

"He spoke out of friendship."

He grunted, and I had to wonder about the dynamic
between Arch Duvall and Milo Beckett. How did they

meet? What prompted them to work together? What was the story with the rest of the team? I wanted to ask a dozen questions but didn't. Beckett, unlike Arch, did not mask his feelings 24-7. "Don't get bent," I said, driven by my new mission to speak my mind. "He's worried about you."

Silence crackled with tension. Colombian java wasn't the only thing brewing.

He pushed off the wall, moved into my personal space. It took some big honkin' restraint not to back away.

"Here's the thing, Twinkie. Friendship—any relationship, for that matter—is tricky with Arch."

"Why's that?" I asked even though I dreaded the answer.

"He comes from a family of grifters. Both sides. Did you know that?"

I nodded. He'd told me.

"Spent his entire life operating in the gray. Never been prosecuted. Know why?"

"Because he's good?"

"Because he never attaches himself to anyone he can't walk away from in a split second."

My stomach flipped. Arch's personal code. He'd told me that, too. I hadn't forgotten. I just kept hoping that one day I'd be the one he'd want to attach to.

The lists I'd jotted in my journal niggled my brain. Arch's cons. Beckett's pros. I cursed the awareness sizzling under my skin when the wiser choice stroked a thumb over my heated cheeks.

"Food for thought," he said, handing me a spatula and leaving me alone to stew.

EVEN THOUGH I'M A fairly optimistic person, it doesn't take much to send me into a spiraling dive of self-obsessed worry. Mom used to call me moody. Michael, too. I prefer *sensitive*. Arch would say, *You're making this aboot you.* To which I'd have to reply, *Ya think!*

Beckett had just warned me not to get too close or expect too much from Arch. He'd said nothing of company policy. There'd been no threat or ultimatum should I mix business and pleasure, just a gentle warning. If the going got tough, Arch would get going.

I'm thinking Beckett knows we're involved and doesn't want me to get hurt. Which is sweet, but I also think he has an ulterior motive. I think he's attracted to me. I'd have to be an idiot not to see the signs. He hadn't spoken to me as boss to employee, or even as friend to friend. Affection had sparked in his gaze and touch— *desire*. Criminy. I pictured myself in a hokey infomercial hawking a collection of Motown's greatest hits. *Seven CDs for just $24.99!* A Marvin Gaye classic grooving in the background… "Let's get it on."

Oh, man.

Stupid of me to be surprised. I'd caught him checking me out a few times on the cruise. But I'd chalked that up to being in character. Tex Aloha was a womanizer. And, okay, maybe I'd sensed interest here and there from Beckett himself, but I thought he was just curious about Evie the entertainer, not attracted to Evie the woman.

Never in my wildest fantasy… Okay, that's a lie. What woman hasn't fantasized about being the center of two men's adoration? But *come on*. A bad-boy grifter and a good-guy operative? That kind of thing happened to women like Nic or Gina, sultry beauties. Not Ivory-soap girls like me. Something was screwy with this picture. I imagined an overanimated TV personality jumping out of the pantry, shouting, *You're on* Candid Camera! or *You've been Punk'd!*

Yeah. That would be my luck.

I peeked over my shoulder. No cameraman. No wacky emcee. Just wacky me.

You're making too much of this, I could hear Arch say.

Maybe he was right. I wanted him to be right. Beckett's interest was flattering but unwanted. I'm a one-man kind of woman, and Arch was all the man I could handle.

I placed sausage patties in the skillet and focused on cooking up something other than trouble.

Unfortunately I was distracted by the sound of footsteps overhead. Water pipes groaning—or was that me? Beckett in the shower. Or Arch. Or both. Two handsome men. Two hot bodies. Naked. Wet.

Erotic images exploded in my brain along with another Motown classic. *When I get feeling, I want sexual healing.*

The doorbell rang, startling me out of a racy fantasy. Cheeks burning, I hurried toward the insistent chimes. UPS delivering a package? Girl Scouts selling cookies? I opened the door.

Nic sporting a frown.

"What gives, Evie? I book a red-eye flight thinking you're in some sort of personal hell. Thinking Michael and Sasha's elopement freaked you out more than you admitted. Or that something horrific happened to someone in your family but you were in denial. Several scenarios played in my mind. Except the one where I pull up to your house and your mother greets me at the door, saying, 'She's staying at the Appleseed Bed-and-Breakfast with her boyfriend. But of course, you know about Archibald. Can you believe Evelyn's dating a baron?'

"*As in, a person of title?* I wanted to ask, but I couldn't because, as your best friend, I was supposed to know all about *Archibald*."

First, I marveled that Nic was here. Second, I marveled how she'd nailed my mom's Midwestern twang. Then again, she was a gifted actress. She was also pissed off. I didn't blame her for being upset with me, but I also didn't know how to fix it. "I…I…"

"Save it." She shouldered her way inside, parked her suitcase by the blue medallion sofa. "So where is he?"

"Who?"

"Your *boyfriend*."

An obnoxious noise screeched, long and loud.

We both covered our ears. "What the hell?"

"Oh, my God." My nostrils twitched at an acrid smell. "The sausage!" I sprinted for the kitchen. My pounding heart stopped when I saw the flaming skillet. I bolted for the sink and nabbed an empty glass.

"Not water," Nic shouted over the wailing alarm. "It's a grease fire. Flour. Or salt," she said, banging open cabinets.

Meanwhile the alarm screeched, the fire raged and the haze choked. I squinted at the back door, thinking I needed to get the skillet outside before I burned down the house. But just as I reached for the handle, someone yanked me away—Arch. And someone smothered the fire—Beckett.

"You okay?" Arch asked.

I coughed into a pot holder and nodded, cursing myself because I didn't think of dousing the fire with a lid.

Beckett opened the back door.

Arch opened a window.

Nic stared.

As the smoke cleared, I saw what she saw, only I'd seen

it before. Beckett wet and naked except for the towel around his waist. Arch wet and naked, his towel upstairs or on the stairs or in the living room…but not around his waist.

It reminded me of the times Nic, Jayne and I had flipped through *Playgirl* magazine, only this was the real deal with live models—one my lover, one my boss—both hoo-ha-tingling gorgeous.

Okay, this was awkward.

"Where's the fucking alarm?" Beckett bellowed over the deafening screech.

"Up there, mate."

Both men were in adrenaline-charged savior mode. Probably why neither one had commented on Arch's naked state or the tall, gawking brunette.

I couldn't blame Nic for staring. Arch had an incredible body, not to mention an impressive—*ahem*—appendage. Except, *hello,* her focus was on Beckett, who was balanced on the stool Arch had slid across the room. The towel shifted when he reached up and disconnected the alarm.

Silence reigned just as I squealed and covered my eyes.

"Flashing your package, mate," Arch said with a smile in his voice.

"Look who's talking," Beckett said.

"Fuck sake. Where's my bloody towel?"

Snap. The third in less than a month. This one spurred by adrenaline and absurdity. A chaotic, uncomfortable moment. Nervous laughter bubbled. I smothered the inappropriate response with a pot holder, my eyes tearing—and it wasn't from the smoke.

Nic ripped the pot holder out of my white-knuckle grasp, handed it to Arch. "Here."

He looked at the pot holder, at her, at the pot holder.

I held my stomach and gasped out, "Too hot to handle," between stifled giggles.

She glanced over her shoulder at me and mouthed, "Lucky you."

Beckett nabbed an apron from a hook on the wall and passed that to Arch. "Here."

Arch tied the frilly thing around his waist and I collapsed into a chair. The harder I tried not to laugh out loud, the more my stomach hurt.

"*Dinnae* think we've met," he said.

"Nicole Sparks."

"Evie's friend."

"She told you about me?"

"Aye."

"She told me about you, too. Sort of. Didn't tell me about *you*," she said, glancing at the government agent.

He secured the towel. "Milo Beckett."

She eyed them both up and down. Lots of glistening skin and toned muscles. "Evie mentioned she was getting more adventurous, but hell."

"Oh, my God," I squealed, following her racy train of thought. "No!"

"Just happened to be showering at the same time," Beckett said.

"Separate bathrooms," Arch said.

"If you'll excuse us…"

"We'll get dressed."

They walked out all confident and guylike, Beckett in his towel, Arch in the apron. I swiveled, caught a rear view and, noting he'd tied the sash in a bow, broke into hiccuping laughter.

CHAPTER TWENTY-ONE

DRESSED IN PLEATED khakis and a green polo shirt, Milo stepped across the hall and knocked on Arch's door.

"Yeah?"

Invitation enough. He walked in and shut the door.

Wearing pin-striped trousers and a crisp white oxford, Arch stood in front of the dresser mirror knotting a Windsor tie. "Hell of a way to start the morning, yeah?"

Milo glanced at the man's rumpled bed. He suspected his morning had started with bigger fireworks but held his tongue. He gestured to Arch's getup. "Think Nicole's going to buy this baron bullshit?"

"Think we should be as honest as possible with*oot* compromising any trade or Agency secrets, yeah? *Dinnae* see that we have a choice. She lives in Atlantic City. She's Evie's closest mate aside from a bird named Jayne. You hired Evie to sing at the club. You can bet her mates will come round. Which means they'll see you—owner of a run-down bar, not keeper of a European noble."

He'd come to that conclusion on his own. Not to mention, they'd probably run into Arch, if not at the club then at Evie's apartment. If their affair was over, he was the Pope. No need to complicate matters beyond the existing clusterfuck. He blamed himself. He'd hired Evie. He'd complicated what was once a streamlined, tight-knit operation. He took responsibility, but he couldn't say he was sorry. "Keep it simple."

"Need to know."

"So what do you know about Nicole Sparks?" Milo asked as Arch nabbed a matching suit jacket from the closet.

"Actress, model. Outgoing and outspoken. Since she showed up thinking Evie was in need, I'd venture profoundly loyal to those she loves."

"Not easily shocked," Milo added, remembering how she'd reacted to their state of undress. Unlike Twinkie, she hadn't averted her eyes or blushed. She'd enjoyed the show. "She reminds me of Gina."

"In demeanor *and* appearance, yeah? Tall, dark, built. Only her eyes are green and her skin tone…" He paused, looking for the right word.

"Café mocha."

"Exotic combination." He slipped a pack of cigarettes into his inner jacket pocket. "She's thirty-eight and single, in case you were wondering."

"I wasn't." He was considering how best to handle the woman, what to reveal and what to withhold. He walked to the door, digesting that last bit of info. "You're telling me a dish like that isn't hooked up."

Arch shrugged. "According to Evie."

He stepped into the hall, thinking she must be a ball-buster. Why else hadn't a guy snatched her up?

"Interested?" Arch asked as they descended the stairs.

"No."

"Because I thought I sensed interest—"

"No."

"—from her."

AFTER RECOVERING from my giggling fit, I'd had to contend with Nic's odd silence as she took over the preparation of breakfast. At first I was relieved. If she didn't ask details about Arch and Beckett, I wouldn't have to lie. As it was, I was busted. What about when we returned home and I sang at the Chameleon Club? What if I lucked out and Arch shucked his personal code and committed to a serious relationship? He couldn't pretend to be nobility forever, and surely Nic and Jayne would visit the club and see Beckett.

Busted.

After setting the table for four, I returned to the kitchen for a second cup of coffee. Nic spooned scrambled eggs and green peppers onto a serving platter. She didn't speak. Didn't even look my way. I couldn't take it anymore. "Aren't you going to ask me about Arch and Beckett?"

"No. I'm going to ask them. Maybe they'll be considerate enough to tell me the truth."

Ouch.

Guilt-ridden, I followed her into the dining room carrying a basket of hot biscuits and a tub of low-fat margarine.

The men entered, looking relaxed and handsome and impressed with the food. "Peppers and eggs," Beckett said. "Great."

"Bagels would have been better than biscuits," Nic said.

"Tabasco said the only bagels he could find at the local supermarket were in the frozen-food section."

"Sacrilege," Nic said, then raised an expertly tweezed brow. "Who's Tabasco?"

"I'll get the coffee," I said.

"I'll help you," Arch said.

Once in the kitchen, I whirled, wide-eyed, hands spread.

"*Dinnae* worry," he said in a hushed voice. "We're going to tell her the truth."

"Everything?"

"Need-to-know basis."

"I've been on the end of that stick."

Arch winked. "Love it when you talk dirty, love."

Men. "What I mean is, when you only told me what you thought I needed to know about the last case, it only heightened my curiosity. I'm a pussycat compared to Nic. She won't take your guff like I did."

"Guff?"

"Nonsense."

"I know what it means. Just never known someone to use it, yeah? Kind of like *toodles* and *kaput.*"

"Are you making fun of me?"

Smiling, he backed me around the corner toward the pantry.

"Oh, no, you don't," I whispered, scowling but happy dancing on the inside. I dodged his embrace and nabbed the pot of coffee. "You bring the creamer and sugar."

When we reentered the dining room, Nic was inspecting a business card. "Fraud investigators, huh?"

"We investigate hard-to-solve scams and turn the tables on the scammers."

"Beat them at their own game, so to speak."

"So to speak."

Nic pursed her killer red lips. "Sounds smarmy."

"Smarmy?"

"Yeah. Sleazy. Tricky. Crafty. Suspici—"

"I get the point." Beckett shook his head. "You're a skeptical one."

"Learned the hard way," she said.

"Not easily fooled," Arch said as we both settled in our chairs. "Brilliant."

Except that it had made her cynical and distrustful of men and long-term relationships. I wondered suddenly about Beckett's broken marriage. Had he stomped on his wife's heart the way my husband had stomped on mine? My gut said no. Then again, as proven with Michael, my gut was not infallible. Still, for a man in the deception game, Beckett was surprisingly square with Nic. He said nothing of the AIA, nor did he admit to being a government agent, but he did mention that he was an ex-cop with years of experience dealing with grifters. He admitted to running the club and explained it doubled as a cover. He mentioned Arch's previous occupation—*Who better to partner with?*—and the fact that Chameleon operated at a low-profile status.

I poured coffee for everyone, soaking in the conversation, separating whole truth from need-to-know and committing it to memory so I wouldn't screw up later on. Mostly I was grateful for a day of revelations. The fewer secrets, the better. Now Arch knew how I felt about him— sort of. Nic knew about Chameleon—mostly. I knew something sparked between Beckett and me, more on his side than mine—I think. I decided to ignore it, trusting that the pesky awareness would fade as my relationship with Arch strengthened. All part and parcel of adjusting to a new job and the dynamics of several new relationships. I told myself I was up to the challenge. The new and improved Evie. Now, if I could just get my mom to clear up the mystery of the bonds.

"So…" Nic said, passing the platter of eggs, "the cruise ship. The acting gig. These guys hired you to work a sting, didn't they?"

"Yes." The admission lightened my heart consider-

ably. "Although I didn't know that going in." Lest she
think I'd been lying to her from the get-go.

She turned on the men. "What's wrong with you?
Suckering an untrained woman into a dangerous situation."

Beckett bristled. "We didn't—"

"She came home with a fricking bandage on her head."

"That wasn't their fault," I said. "I cracked out of turn."

"What does that mean?"

"Missed my cue. Made a mistake. The roper directed
us to the insideman. We were in the big store, but before
he could put us on the send, I cracked out of turn. The reverse con curdled, I faked a swoon and bonked my head."

Nic gawked. "Everything before *faked a swoon and
bonked my head* was Greek to me, Evie."

Arch sipped coffee, smiled. "You've been reading up
on the lingo, yeah?"

"Had her nose stuck in Maurer's *The Big Con* on the
flight from Philly to Cleveland," Beckett said. "Informa-
tive but outdated. If you want to learn—"

"She doesn't," Nic said.

"Yes, I do. This is my chance to do something important."

"When you perform, you make people happy, Evie.
That's important."

"Except the casinos aren't hiring me anymore."

"You know how it works in town. Cycles. This is a
phase."

"But not one I can weather. It's not about what's hot
musically, it's about what's hot physically. It's about age."
I laid my hand on hers, squeezed. "And you know it."
They weren't hiring her all that much, either. She kept
afloat by filming commercials and modeling at trade

shows. Two markets I'd never broken into, and at this late date, forget it. "Performers and con artists have a lot in common, Nic."

"I'll try not to take that as an insult."

I smiled. "I'll explain later. Eat your eggs. They're getting cold." The men had already cleaned their plates.

"Not so fast," she said. "Are you singing in that club for real?"

"Yes," Beckett answered for me. "I'm not putting her in the field."

"Yet," I said. "I have to pay my dues."

"I can only hope they're high," she said drily. "Second, did you break up with Too Hot To Handle over there or not?"

Arch's eyes danced with humor, but his expression and tone were stone sober. "She did."

I seconded that. I didn't blush. I didn't scratch. It wasn't a lie. I'd broken off with him in London.

"That's something, I guess. Trusting your heart to a con artist wouldn't be smart." She eyed Arch. "No offense."

He smiled at her over the rim of his coffee up. "*Cannae* argue with logic, yeah?"

His lame comeback revived previous reservations. Damn him. "He no longer grifts for personal gain," I felt compelled to say.

Nic smirked. "Let me put it another way. Trusting a man who's in the business of deceiving seems iffy at best."

Arch chuckled and winked at me. "No guff."

"Guff makes me gag," Nic said. "Tell it to me straight or tell it to the King."

Beckett's lip twitched. "Elvis or Larry?"

"Larry, of course. Who talks to dead people?"

"Jayne's psychic," I said. "Madame Helene."

"You know what I think of her." She focused back on Arch. "So why are you here? Why are *you* here?" she asked Beckett.

"What did you say to Mrs. Parish when she mentioned Arch and the baron angle?" he asked by way of an answer.

"What could I say? Since I didn't want to look like a fool, I played dumb. Said I misunderstood and thought they were staying with her."

"Brilliant," Arch said.

"Fortunate," Milo said, then added, "I don't suppose there's a chance you'll fly back home tonight, Ms. Sparks."

"Get real, Slick. I'm not leaving until Evie does or until one of you explains why you're all here."

He looked to me. "Want to tell her about your mom?"

Boy, did I ever. "I think she's being swindled."

Nic blinked. "I'm all ears."

I relaxed a little as she picked at her breakfast, grateful for a chance to come clean, at least in part, with my friend. I was also happy for the chance to impress Arch and Beckett with my newly acquired knowledge of the Sweetheart scam.

When I finished, the only one who looked dazzled— or maybe I should say dazed—was Nic.

"I'll drive you to the airport," Beckett said, to which she replied, "Like hell."

CHAPTER TWENTY-TWO

MIDMORNING, DRESSED, fed and primed for action, Arch and I headed into town. I didn't argue when he took the wheel; I needed to make a call, and reception was stronger closer to Greenville. A mile down the road I dug my cell out of my *Lucy* tote and powered on. Only… "Darn it."

"What's wrong?"

"I forgot to charge my cell and I need to touch base with my brother."

Instead of razzing me, like Michael, Arch simply reached around to his left side and produced his cell.

"Thanks." I held it in my hand, perplexed.

"Just press in the numbers, then hit the green button, yeah?"

"It's not that. I just…didn't you get a new phone?"

"No."

"I could've sworn…" Yesterday, on his way to rescue me from the tree, he'd been ending a phone conversation. I could've sworn the cell looked smaller, sleeker. Then again, I'd been several feet above him with leafy branches partially obstructing my view. "Never mind."

Noting several bars, indicating we'd hit a hot spot, I pressed in the number, hoping the signal held strong. Arch navigated the bumpy rural road. I handled Christopher.

"So you didn't learn anything yet?" my brother asked.

"It's not like Mom and I are best buds." I adjusted my seat belt, a subtle excuse to massage the ache in my chest. "I'm working on it."

"Maybe if you hadn't brought your boyfriend…"

"Actually, she's more forthcoming with Arch than she is with me." The ache intensified.

"So let him sweet-talk the information out of her. I heard the guy's smooth."

"From whom?"

"He impressed Dad, and Dad's not easily impressed. Also Sandy heard it from someone who heard it from Monica Rhodes."

"Monica is a self-absorbed, spiteful…witch."

"When are you two going to bury the hatchet?"

"She's the one holding the grudge. She didn't even offer me a part in the production the theater's putting on for Mrs. Grable. The other drama-club alumni are participating in some way. Me, she just invites to watch. Oh, and to make a donation."

Arch glanced over.

I waved off his concern. "Whatever," I said to Christopher. "Mom hasn't withdrawn any more money, has she?"

"No."

"Good. Listen, we're on our way into town. We could swing by the bank and—"

"I'll see you tonight. Mom invited us to the barbecue."

"Are you bringing the kids?"

"Of course."

Oh, goody. The snooty wife *and* her demon offspring. "Excellent. A chance to get to know them better."

"Sandy's looking forward to meeting…your friend."

European nobility. But of course she was.

Christopher made a queer sound in the back of his throat. "How in God's name did you hook up with a Scottish baron, Evelyn?"

As if I wasn't sophisticated or smart enough to mix with nobility. Evie the lowly entertainer. "I'm sure you didn't intend that like it sounded," I gritted out, wanting to give him the benefit of the doubt.

"What do you mean?"

"Never mind. See you tonight." I disconnected and banged my head against the car's luxurious headrest. Why did our exchanges have to be so cold? Why hadn't I followed through with my vow to be the first one on the floor? I could have ended the discussion with *I love you*—which I did. Or *I can't wait to see you.* Something, anything, to indicate sisterly affection. But as soon as he'd pushed me away, I'd taken offense and distanced myself even further. A habit I wanted to break.

Must. Boogie.

I passed Arch his phone, wondering suddenly if I'd at least remembered to toss my charger cord in my tote. More than once I'd needed to charge while on the road. I rooted in the jam-packed bag—wallet, address book, checkbook, sunglasses, hand cream...

Arch veered off the gravel road onto the paved road leading into town. "I take it we're not stopping by the bank, yeah?"

"No." Breath mints, three lip liners, two lipsticks, tampon...bingo! I yanked out the coiled cord and wired it from my cell to the car's cigarette lighter.

Arch just grinned. "But I'll meet your brother tonight."

"Yes."

"And his wife and kids."

"Stepkids. Yes. You've been warned."

"*Cannae* be that bad."

I copied my brother's throaty grunt.

"You *dinnae* fancy kids?"

"I adore kids." I slid him a look. "You?"

"Kids are great, yeah?"

"Yeah." My stomach lurched with a new and sickening thought. Not new to me but new in my thoughts regarding Arch and a long-term relationship. "I'm too old to have children. Safely, anyway. Not that you asked, but…"

"Not a factor, Sunshine."

"Because you don't want any?"

He peered over the rims of his sunglasses, a brief but soulful glance. "Just because."

Okay, that was…cryptic. Suddenly I wasn't so keen on being the first one on the dance floor where Arch was concerned. Sure, I'd implied I trusted him with my heart when we made love and I knew deep down I'd taken the plunge, but I hadn't out-and-out *said* the *L* word. The old me, the insecure me, had made a cameo appearance. I wanted him to say it first or to at least suggest his heart was up for grabs. Then Beckett's food-for-thought speech echoed in my head, doubling my trepidation. "Arch."

"Aye?"

"About this morning…the making-love part."

"Regrets?"

"No. You?"

"How can I regret something so profoundly fantastic, yeah?"

The romantic me melted. I wanted to believe him, but I didn't. Not completely. Damn him for once telling me not to trust him. Then I thought about his unconventional upbringing. His personal code. Maybe he was holding back because he worried he'd hurt me. Emotional attachments compromise a grifter's judgment—his words, not mine—and even though he no longer hustled for personal gain, he was still very much in the business. If he did love me, then he had to be wrestling with some powerful conflict. Maybe I needed to slow down, give him a chance to catch up.

Yeah, that was it.

"Nic wasn't keen about lying to my family." She'd doubled the guilt I'd already felt. "You know, the baron thing. I'm not all that keen on it, either. I know it's for the greater good, but when the truth comes out…" I trailed off because, even with my boffo imagination, I couldn't imagine.

He didn't respond. A second ticked by. Three. Five. The prolonged silence made me squirm. Then I realized I knew that look—or, rather, *non*look. It was the weighty pause that gave him away rather than his expression. Something I'd experienced a few times before. He was deciding how little or how much, if anything, he was going to reveal or admit about whatever.

My senses buzzed in anticipation.

"It's not a lie."

Buzz. Buzz. "What's not a lie?"

"I am the Baron of Broxley."

"For the time being, you mean. For show."

"For real and until I die or ditch it, you know?"

"No, I don't know." I struggled against the seat belt to face him as full-on as possible. The buzzing intensified. White-hot zaps of adrenaline. "What do you mean? No guff or so help me…"

He smiled, easing up on the accelerator when he

spotted the hood of a police cruiser poking out from behind a billboard hawking John Deere tractors. "In Scotland, it's possible to acquire a feudal barony if one possesses the required funds."

Buzzzz-zzzit! "You *bought* a title?"

"*Willnae* bore you with legalities, but any person who holds a barony with the land title recorded with the proper sources in Scotland is entitled to the name and dignity of a baron."

I narrowed my eyes. "Is this some sort of a test? Are you conning me? Trying to prove I'll fall for anything? Next you'll tell me William Wallace once slept in your bed and hid a sword under your floorboards, a sword that can be mine for the bargain price of fifty thousand dollars."

He laughed. "I'll have to remember that one."

I scrunched my brow. "You're serious about this barony thing?"

"Aye."

"Broxley's a real place?"

"Charming village."

"You own land?"

"Significant acreage."

"A castle?"

"A cottage. Although it is made of stone, and a man's home is his castle, yeah?"

My body burned and I consciously avoided looking over at the cruiser as we drove by. Surely my red face was freckled with the word *guilty*. Guilty of riding shotgun with a professional, sort-of-retired con artist. A man who frequently broke the law or at least frolicked in the gray. Guilty of sort of being turned on by the fact that I was shagging an honest-to-gosh *noble*. Yeah, boy, talk about your Cinderella fantasy.

I shook off my shock and shallowness and hurried on before he shut me down. The man was only so forthcoming. "You called the cottage home, but you only just bought it, right? To back up this sting? Talk about going above and beyond. That's a little anal, don't you think?"

Another smile—part amused, part thoughtful. "I purchased the barony four years ago."

I blinked. "Why?"

"To perpetuate a fantasy."

Must've been another big con. A mother of a con. "Must've cost a fortune."

"Worth every pence."

I mentally flipped through the pages of Maurer's book, trying to figure out what type of con would have justified that kind of initial investment. It was beyond my grasp. Then I wondered where Arch had gotten the money to pay for the barony in the first place. Was he like one of those superthieves in the movies who kept his wealth stashed in various foreign banks? What's more, who did he bilk over the years? For how much and why them specifically?

"I can hear your wheels turning, Sunshine."

"You've given me a lot to think about."

"I wanted to ease your mind, not vex it, yeah?"

I smiled—a stupid smile, I'm sure, because I was stunned and confused, but I wanted him to know I appreciated his honesty.

If he was being honest.

Crap.

Always the doubt.

I tell people what they want to hear. Perpetuate fantasies. Smoke and mirrors, love.

Double crap.

"Funny," I said, feeling my way. "I could swear Beckett was totally blindsided by the baron angle."

"He was," Arch said, flexing his fingers on the wheel. "He thinks I made it up to serve immediate purposes." He glanced over. "For now, I'd prefer to keep the truth of the matter between you and me, yeah?"

My chest constricted. "Why?"

"The more people know *aboot* me, the more vulnerable I am."

He'd told me that before. "But Beckett's not people, he's your friend."

"Our relationship is complicated."

"More than ours?"

"More than ours."

Okay. But… "I can't imagine why it would matter if Beckett knew. Purchasing a title, if I understood you correctly, is legal."

"I have my reasons for keeping portions of my life private."

"You don't trust him?"

"I *dinnae* trust anyone." He reached over and squeezed my knee, as if he knew I'd find that statement cynical and sad. "Nature of my profession."

"Fine," I heard myself say. "I just feel funny lying to your partner—*my* boss."

"You're not lying. You're just not offering information."

I quirked a brow. "You have a warped way of looking at things."

Another squeeze. "Perspective, yeah?"

Yeah.

"Take Nicole, for instance."

Okay, that wasn't a *too* obvious change of subject.

"She *didnae* fuss overly much *aboot* the profile you concocted for her. If pretending to be Beckett's girlfriend isn't a lie…"

"That's because she's my friend and she wants to help. Besides, it made sense. We're friends. Beckett's the baron's personal assistant. If he travels with you, then he was with you on your trips to Atlantic City. If she was with me when you and I met, then he was there, too, and there is such a thing as love at first sight."

Arch stroked his goatee, hid a smile. "Amazingly, I followed that cockeyed line of reasoning."

"Also reasonable was the scenario that her gig fell through last-minute, affording her time to join Beckett for a holiday at the B and B."

"Absolutely."

"Beckett could have been more gracious about it."

"He doesn't fancy complications. Though we've employed extras on occasion, in general he's not fond of working with unsanctioned players."

I bristled on my friend's behalf. "Nic's an excellent actress."

"As good as you?"

Knowing he considered me talented did wonders for my self-esteem. "Actually," I said in all honesty, "she's better."

"Then she must be amazing, yeah?"

I love you. I love you. I love you.

"Speaking of acting…" he said. "Why weren't you offered a part in the theater benefit?"

My heart settled back in my chest. "Doesn't matter." I shrugged. "It's not like I even want to be in the musical. I don't have it anymore."

"Have what?"

"The eye of the tiger."

"Theme song from *Rocky III*."

"I can't believe you got that reference. I can't believe you've seen *Rocky III*."

"Sly? Boxing? Adrenaline-charged drama? Come on." He turned the Mercedes onto Main Street. "So you've lost your killer instinct, yeah?"

"For performing. Yeah." The numbness was both startling and welcome. "I just…I don't burn to be on stage anymore. Not in the sense I know. I burn to make a difference. To prevent scum artists from preying on the vulnerable. I want to do what you do." *I want to be with you in every sense.* I swallowed hard. "We have to convince Beckett that I'm capable of maintaining—" I bit back the word *relationship,* not wanting to scare him off "—an affair with you without compromising my work in the field."

"You're not officially working in the field."

"Yet."

"What if we *cannae?*"

"You're a master manipulator. Of course we can."

"Appreciate your confidence, Sunshine, but Beckett is no easy mark. What if you have to choose?"

"I don't want to choose. I want it all."

He shook his head. "I love your enthusiasm, lass."

What about me? I wanted to ask but didn't.

We pulled into the civic center parking lot. Arch killed the engine, regarded me over the rims of his sunglasses—bad-boy baron in a badass suit and tie. "Ready to dance?"

More than you know. "Let's boogie."

CHAPTER TWENTY-THREE

RANDOLPH GISH WAS an accomplished dancer.

Arch was not.

In the first fifteen minutes of our private dance lesson he stepped on my toes five times. I was stunned. The man loved music. He listened to his MP3 player while exercising and primping after a shower. How could he not have rhythm? Then again, I knew some musicians who smoked melodically but had questionable timing. Talk about disappointing.

Unless he was faking—like me.

It took concentrated effort to botch steps I could perform in my sleep. Due to my work as a party motivator, in which I generally worked with a professional male dancer, I was pretty adept at the fox-trot, the waltz, the swing and the hustle. Not that you'd know it by my current two-left-feet performance.

"Bloody hell," Arch said when I mashed his instep. "This is hopeless."

"This is a challenge we shall overcome," Randolph said in his enthusiastic, semieffeminate voice. He clapped his hands twice. "They call me the miracle worker. How long did you say you'd be in town?"

"One, maybe two weeks."

The dance instructor palmed his hand over his

slicked-back hair. "Perhaps if we double up on the lessons…"

"Whatever it takes," Arch said, loosening his tie. "Money's no object. We're attending a prestigious charity ball at the end of this month. We'll be expected to dance, and I'd prefer we *didnae* make spectacles of ourselves, yeah?"

"It wouldn't be so bad," I added, "if at least one of us was confident. Maybe we could concentrate on one dance—say—I don't know…the waltz. We could dance the slow songs and sit out the fast ones, right?"

"Aye," Arch said. "I suppose that would work."

"Except not all songs are in three-quarter time," Randolph said.

"Does it matter?" Arch asked.

I knew that it did but shrugged.

"The waltz is danced to a triple beat. One-two-three, one-two-three," Randolph demonstrated in a singsong voice. "It calls for a certain amount of grace."

Arch raised a brow.

Randolph acquiesced with a slight bow. "The waltz it is." He moved over to his CD player and, not for the first time, I noted a slight swish of his hips. I knew better than to stereotype, but I had a pretty keen gaydar, and it blipped. I told myself I was imagining things, because that didn't mesh with my Sweetheart-scam theory. If he wasn't the hustler, I didn't have a clue as to who was.

Randolph pushed a button and the sultry sounds of Anne Murray filled the air. "Can I Have This Dance": a pop song in three-quarter time. "Let me show you individually before you attempt the steps together." He held open his arms. "Evie?"

I was distracted by a ringing phone. My phone.

Charged and working. "I'm sorry. Just let me see…" It was Mom. "I need to take this. I'll step into the hall. Maybe you can start with Arch."

I skittered out of the room, my slick-soled, funky Mary Janes sliding over the polished hardwood floor. Once in the hall, I connected. "Hi, Mom."

"Did your friend Nicole find her way to the Apple-seed?"

"She did. Thanks for giving her directions. Sorry I didn't tell you she was coming. Her gig got canceled and she thought she'd join us and…" I took a deep breath and out-and-out lied to my mom. *For the greater good.* "As fate would have it, she's actually dating Northbrook. Can you believe it?" I relayed the concocted story, thinking I could always submit scripts for soap operas if my job with Chameleon tanked.

"They make a handsome couple," Mom simply said. "Be sure to invite them to the barbecue. Speaking of…do you think Archibald would prefer German potato salad or egg potato salad?"

Obviously she was obsessing on dinner. "I don't think it matters." I honestly didn't know.

"It's all in the details, Evelyn. He said he wanted to experience an authentic American barbecue."

"I think he wants to experience a casual meal with the Parish family. We always have egg. Make egg."

"I've never operated your dad's new propane grill. I hope Christopher knows how to use it."

"I'm sure he does. Not that Dad will entrust his burger to Christopher. He always complains he overcooks the meat."

"I didn't invite George."

"I did."

Long silence. Strained silence.

Dance, Evie, dance. I had her ear, her attention *now*. Later tonight she'd have a house full of guests. Later she'd have a dozen reasons to avoid me. I rocked on my heels, weaved side to side like a fighter preparing for a bout.

Dance.

"Mom, I think I understand why you and Daddy split up. When he bought the tavern instead of a vacation home, you felt betrayed, cheated. Believe me, I know the feeling. It sucks."

"Language, Evelyn."

"But it's been a month. I can't fathom why you haven't made up by now. Surely you can strike a compromise. You love each other."

"This isn't about love. It's about respect. Compatibility. Trust."

I stopped in my tracks, reeling at her strained confession. Maybe it was easier for her to express her feelings over the phone rather than one-on-one. It was worth a shot. "Maybe it's about meeting halfway."

"It's more complicated than that."

"Have you told Daddy—"

"He wouldn't listen."

"How do you know if—"

"I really don't want to talk about this, Evelyn."

"Please don't shut me out." *I love you.* "I want to help."

"You have worries of your own."

"No worries. My life's on track."

"Thanks to Archibald."

"No. Thanks to me." Granted, Arch was a huge part of my newfound personal joy ride, but I'd landed the job with Chameleon on my own. Beckett was the one who'd agreed to give me a shot at a new profession. Not Arch. Arch was wishy-washy about me working with Chameleon. If I were the ultimate cynic, I'd think he was sabotaging my chances. *What if you have to choose?* I pushed the unpleasant thought aside.

"You've changed."

I swallowed. "So have you."

"Sometimes change is good. I'm glad you're learning that early."

"Mom—"

"I hear music."

"I'm at the civic center. I'm taking a dance lesson."

"With Randolph? Why? You know how to dance."

"But Arch doesn't. He has this charity ball coming up and…" God, I hated lying to my family.

"I understand. The paparazzi. They snap shots at the most inopportune times. Heaven forbid they catch the baron looking like a buffoon on the dance floor."

"Yes, well, that may happen anyway. The man has no rhythm."

"I must say, I'm surprised he didn't take lessons as a boy. Surely his parents knew he'd be obligated to attend various social functions, given his title."

"His mother paid for lessons, but he skipped them. He was a bit of a rebel." At least the rebel part was true. Oh, and the baron part, although he didn't *inherit* the title. My mind scrambled to keep fact and fiction straight. "As for social functions, believe it or not, until now he's easily avoided the dance floor. The man can talk his way out of anything." *Fact.* "But he knows I love to dance, so he's learning for me." *Fiction.*

"How sweet," she said. "Well, even if he does have two left feet, Randolph can help."

"He did call himself the miracle worker."

"He certainly worked miracles with me."

"Mom—"

"Did you tell him you're my daughter?"

"Not yet." My suspicions nettled. "Any reason I shouldn't?"

"No. Just wondering. I have to run now, Evelyn. So much to do."

"Mom—"

"See you tonight."

She disconnected and I stared at my cell. Had I just had a heart-to-heart with my repressive mother? Okay, there were still unanswered questions, but still. I practically floated back into the dance studio. Once there, I paused and cocked my head at the sight of two men in a loose embrace waltzing—sort of—across the room. My gaydar blipped.

"One-two-three, one-two-three," Randolph recited, emphasis on the *one*. "Ow," he said when Arch stepped on his foot, then, "Do not be deterred by small mistakes. I already sense improvement."

Anne crooned, *"Will you be my partner every night?"*

Randolph smiled—though to me it seemed forced— and squeezed Arch's hand. "Let's have another go."

Blip. Blip.

A phone rang. Not mine. "Be back in a second," Arch said. "Maybe Evie will do better."

He left the room and I stepped into Randolph's embrace, brain stuttering. Maybe he wasn't swindling Mom. Maybe she'd donated the money to a scholarship fund. She had a thing about scholarships. Or maybe she'd loaned the money to a friend. "Here's the thing," I said as Randolph assumed the lead position. "I know how to waltz. I pretended I didn't because I don't want Arch to feel bad." All part of the ruse, and it tumbled off my lips with ease. Gish wasn't family. I wasn't lying. I was improvising lines per my character: American girlfriend of a Scottish noble.

"I understand," he said without hesitation. "Your secret's safe with me."

That last part rekindled my suspicions, though I couldn't say why. Just gut. "It's just that Arch is a prominent man and…"

"Excuse me, Mr. Gish."

We stopped midwaltz and focused on the receptionist Arch and I had passed on the way in.

"There's a man here, a reporter from the *Tribune,*" she said. "Very insistent."

"Go ahead," I told him, hoping this had something to do with a hot scoop. *European Baron Waltzes into Local Singer's Life.*

"I'll be right back," he said to Arch on his way out. "Hit the replay-track button and practice. Remember— loose grip, elbow bent."

Arch crossed the floor and took me in his arms. "Where's he headed?"

"To deal with a pushy reporter."

He grinned. "That *didnae* take long."

"You're big news in a small town. Gossip travels fast."

"I'm aware."

"All part of your plan."

His eyes twinkled with equal parts mischief and arrogance.

"You're like a puppet master. Pulling people's strings, manipulating their actions."

"A necessary skill given my line of work, yeah?"

"If you hadn't blown your savings acquiring a title," I whispered, fishing for more info, "you wouldn't *need* to work."

He smiled down at me. "I *didnae* blow my savings."

I pressed my body against his, wrapped my arms around his neck. Swaying in place to the music, instead of waltzing, would save my toes and allow us to converse in hushed tones. Plus, I ached to be in his arms. "You could be living in your homeland, enjoying the lifestyle of a baron."

"I spend a bit of time there, but my heart is here."

I blinked up at him, touched and confused by the out-of-character sentiment. "Wow. For you that was down-right mushy."

"What was I thinking?" He winked and grinned, but the smile failed to reach his eyes.

"You weren't," I guessed. "Freudian slip. Suggests you're not as detached as you like people to believe."

"Thank you, Dr. Evie."

"So, should I be flattered? Or were you referring to Chameleon?"

"Let's just say the United States offers some interesting perks."

"In other words, no comment."

He responded by leaning in and nipping my earlobe. "*Dinnae* you want to know who called me?"

Evasion. Typical. Although I couldn't argue with his means of distraction. The ear nipping was hot. "All right, Puppet Master. Who was on the phone?"

"Beckett. He heard from Hot Legs and Tabasco. No luck scoring the invitation to that private game. But they did ID the roper. One more night at the tables should do it."

Just like that, my mind was back in the current game. My skin tingled with the thrill of the hunt. Or maybe it was because one of Arch's hands had drifted possessively to my butt. *Zing.* "We're off and running."

He narrowed his eyes. "When you say *we...*"

"I made some progress, too."

"Randolph?"

"Mom. She called to ask if you prefer German potato salad or egg potato salad. I said it didn't matter, but when pressed I went with egg."

"And this is progress how?"

"That's just how the conversation started."

"Ah."

"She talked about Dad. A little. I know she loves him and I know he hurt her. I suspect she's rebelling, hence the new, hipper Marilyn Parish."

"So she's acting out of spite?"

"Or maybe to get attention. Dad's attention. One thing's for sure—if she's being hustled, it's not by Randolph."

"What makes you so sure?"

"He's gay."

"He's good."

"What do you mean?"

"He's faking."

"Faking being gay?"

"Aye."

"What makes *you* so sure?"

"He has a tell." He dipped his chin, winked. "He's good. I'm better."

I rolled my eyes at his cocky tone, not that I wasn't intrigued. "Why would a heterosexual man pretend otherwise?"

"Have you any gay friends or acquaintances?"

"Lots. Men *and* women."

"The men—you like shopping with them, dishing with them, scoping out other men with them, aye?"

"Well, yeah. It's like being with one of the girls only…"

"There's a bit of sexual tension."

"Not always. But if I find the guy attractive, yes. You can flirt and show affection, but it's…safe." Throughout the conversation I'd been mindful of Arch's tone and body language. I didn't get any homophobe vibes, which was a turn-on. Plus, where sway dancing was concerned, his rhythm was dead-on, sexy even. Like I needed more reasons to be attracted to the man. *Zing.* "How do you know so much about the straight girl/gay guy buddy bond?"

"Understanding the human psyche. Basic equipment in a con artist's toolbox, yeah?"

"Along with control, observation, articulation and detachment," I said, frowning at the latter.

His mouth quirked. "When you study something you go all *oot,* yeah?"

"If my heart is in it, yeah." I looked around his shoulder, confirming we were still alone. "So…what? You think instead of a Sweetheart scam, Randolph's pulling a *Will and Grace* to earn Mom's confidence?"

"Will and Grace?"

"It's a TV show." Right. Beckett watched sitcoms. Arch movies. My mind drifted to my awareness of Beckett. Was there such a thing as a straight girl/straight guy buddy bond? "The point is, if you're right about him faking his sexual orientation, then he's not who he seems." I tugged at his tie, halting our seductive grind.

"I've got it. When Randolph comes back, I want you to misstep so I can trip over your feet."

"Why?

"So I can plow into him."

"So you can nick his wallet?"

I'd pulled that stunt—successfully—on the cruise. What was with the skeptical tone? "It's in his front pocket—" I'd verified that, subtly, while we'd danced "—which will make it trickier, but—"

"No."

"But it'll contain ID."

He disengaged my fingers from his tie, kissed my palm. "Bogus ID."

"Maybe. Maybe not. Either way, we could get a better bead on him. Maybe a clue that would help Woody trace his background."

"Maybe. Maybe not. It's not worth the risk, yeah? There are other ways."

I snatched my hand out of his grasp. Hard to think straight when he seductively stroked my inner wrist. "What risk? Remember when I picked the tour guy's pocket? He never suspected a thing."

"He wasn't a pro."

"We're not one hundred percent sure Randolph is, either."

"But if he is, he'll be savvy to the dip." His expression was relaxed, but I sensed irritation. "*Dinnae* counter me on this, Sunshine."

I bristled. Was that an order? A threat? A comment on my dipping proficiency? Steam built between my ears, but before I could explode, Randolph swept back into the room along with a wiry man wearing dark trousers and a wrinkled golf shirt. "I apologize for the disruption," the dance instructor said to Arch, "but Mr. Smith simply will not be deterred. He insists that you are European royalty. I've explained that you're a foreign businessman, but he insisted on questioning you himself."

"I'm not royalty," Arch said, straightening the tie I'd mussed.

"I have it on good authority," Smith said, producing a small spiral notebook, "that you're the Baron of Broxley."

"I am. But it is not a royal title, simply a title of nobility, yeah?"

The reporter beamed all the same.

Randolph touched his fingertips to his heart. "Good heavens. I'm teaching a baron to waltz." I could almost see dollar signs in his eyes.

"I apologize for not being up front," Arch said, affecting a lofty but congenial air. "I prefer to keep my title low-key. I'm here on holiday."

"To meet your girlfriend's parents," Smith said, pen to pad. "Since this is Ms. Parish's hometown, you see why the local newspaper is interested to scoop the news first."

"News?"

"The wedding."

I caught myself before I could blurt, *What wedding?* This wasn't about the real me, the wannabe Chameleon in love with a slippery devil. This was about the embellished me, the Atlantic City performer in love with a Scottish noble. Playing an over-the-top character like ditzy Vegas girl Sugar Dupont had been a cinch compared to this. Playing any role aside from this would be a cinch. This ruse was too close to home—literally.

I did what I always did when Arch sprung something on me. I followed his lead. He skirted the wedding issue and expertly fed the reporter information intended to

advance Senator Clark's sting. Though I pretended interest, my attention was on Randolph Gish. His enthusiasm seemed natural, but I had the distinct impression
he was sizing up a mark.

What a coincidence. So was I.

CHAPTER TWENTY-FOUR

ARCH AND EVIE WERE tripping the light fantastic in Greenville. Gina and Tabasco were holed up in Chicago in a luxury hotel. Both teams were actively engaging marks.

Meanwhile Milo was stuck in the fricking country, juggling calls from Pops, the Kid and the pain-in-the-ass director of the AIA. Preferring not to use the landline for business purposes, he'd strolled the grounds in search of signal for his cell. Frustrating, but not as frustrating as prepping the she-cat currently curled on the front-porch swing.

He breathed in the fresh spring air hoping for a dose of tranquility. Instead he got a whiff of her bold perfume, a spicy scent that revved his pulse. Clearly this career crisis had triggered a self-destructive gene. He backed away and settled in a wicker rocker. "Let's go over it one more time."

"Let's not. Ever heard of rehearsing something to death, Slick? If you're worried I'll—what did Evie call it?—crack out of turn, don't. Because I won't."

After one afternoon in Nicole Sparks's company, Milo understood why the woman was unattached. "Anyone ever told you you have a bad attitude, Nicole?"

"Anyone ever told you you're an uptight control freak, Milo?"

He rolled a kink out of his neck, thinking a man would have to be a saint, a masochist or a mama's boy to put up with her shit day in, day out. He didn't care how beautiful she was or what those glossed full lips could do to a man. She was stubborn and opinionated. Not as cynical as him, but close. She also smoked and cussed like a dockworker. She was a dark, stormy night compared to bright, sunshiny day Evie.

"I still don't understand why we have to lie at all. Wouldn't it be easier to tell Mrs. Parish the truth? *We think you're being swindled, ma'am,*" she said, dropping her voice an octave and mimicking Milo's mannerisms. *"Possibly by your dance instructor, who we believe has won your confidence through nefarious measures."*

"Ever been duped by someone you trusted, Nicole?" She averted her face, but not before he saw her cheeks flush. "Someone who took advantage, made you feel foolish? I'm guessing you didn't feel comfortable sharing what you perceived as poor judgment with friends, let alone strangers. Grifters typically go free because the victims are too embarrassed to report the crime."

"Thank you for the lesson in Scams 101," she said without looking at him. "I'll file away the knowledge."

"I'm just saying, if we can make this go away without embarrassing Mrs. Parish—"

"Yeah, yeah. I get it." She lit up her third cigarette in one hour.

"Those things will kill you."

She grunted. "That's original."

"It's your life."

"Yes, it is." Composed now, she met his gaze. "So how'd you meet Arch?"

"We were adversaries for several years."

She smirked. "Cat and mouse, huh? Wily mouse kept slipping through the claws of the law? That must've been hell on your ego."

"He kept me on my toes."

"And now he's working with you."

"He is."

She swept her long hair over one shoulder, perked up for a story. "How'd that happen?"

Milo stretched out his legs and crossed them at the ankle. "Classified."

"This Tabasco guy and what's-her-name, Gina. They were here, now they're not. What gives?"

"Classified."

"Why'd you hire Evie?"

His brain stumbled, but he responded automatically. "Need-to-know basis."

She held his gaze, blew out a stream of smoke. "I need to know."

He figured he owed her something. She was asking out of concern and loyalty to a friend. Had to respect that. "She caught me off guard."

"Not much of an answer."

"It'll have to do."

"Huh."

"What?"

"Just digesting." Her gaze slid south. "What's with the mismatched socks?"

He glanced down. One brown, one black. Hell.

She smiled. "So…ready to lie your ass off at that barbecue?"

He dragged his hands over his face. "Pretending to adore you is going to be a real stretch, Nicole."

"Ditto, Milo."

BY THE END OF THE afternoon Mr. Smith had his scoop, Randolph Gish had payment for several private lessons and I had a bone to pick with Arch. Strike that. An entire skeleton to pick with Arch.

In spite of last night's personal vow to speak my mind, I internalized. As long as we were in town, we were *on.* As a professional, I was committed to playing the part Arch had assigned me—a moony-eyed woman head over heels in love…with him. Similar to the role he'd assigned me on the cruise. My directive had been to fawn over him and follow his lead. Similar to this gig, only I got to wear my own funky clothes as opposed to dressing like a bimbo.

I understood, given the circumstances, that I had to play *me.* We were dealing with my family, after all, not strangers. I understood why the baron thing might help with the senator's case. Given his wealth and supposed weakness for cards, the Baron of Broxley made a prime mark. But why did we have to be a couple? He could've concocted a dozen other scenarios. Scenarios that wouldn't have flamed our physical attraction. Now I was officially in love with the man and flirting with disaster. Loving Arch—a man with more secrets than an international spy—complicated things in ways I didn't want to imagine.

But I did.

The entire time he schmoozed that reporter and baited Randolph. And after, when we grabbed lunch at a local shake-and-burger joint. Arch knew I had a weakness for happy-tummy food. Even that felt like a manipulation of some kind. But we were in public and we had to play our parts. I fawned like a pro and let him lead the way.

Until we were in the car and driving back to the Appleseed.

What if you have to choose?

"We need to talk."

"You're pissed because I asked you not to pinch Randolph's wallet, yeah?"

"You didn't ask. You ordered me not to defy you."

"I *didnae* order." He flexed his fingers on the steering wheel, reconsidered. "I apologize if I sounded harsh."

"Apology accepted, but…" I tried to think of a delicate way to put it but couldn't. "Stop manipulating me, Arch."

"I prefer to think of it as protecting, yeah?"

Okay, that was sweet and it did cool my jets a little. Good intentions and all that. Still… "I don't want to be protected. I don't want to sit on the sidelines. I want to live and learn and grow—and I can't do that if you're being a mother hen."

He smiled at that. "No one has ever accused me of being a mother hen."

"Yes, well, if the beak fits…"

He laughed.

His good humor was annoyingly sexy. I could feel my anger fizzling. Sometimes, like now, I really hated that he could so easily derail my runaway thoughts. Speaking my mind came easier when I was pumped up, so I locked down. I ignored his bone-melting grin and my fluttering heart. I focused on the dashboard and stated my gripe. "I feel like you're relegating me to the backseat. I know I'm a greenhorn in the confidence game, but I do have relevant skills. I also have a personal stake in this case."

"I'm aware."

"I appreciate your help in this matter but resent the way you flew in and took over. At least Beckett…"

He glanced over. "Aye?"

Something in his tone told me to choose my words carefully, except I was too revved to think of a way to wrap a pretty bow around the ugly truth. "At least Beckett's motivations for coming here were pure."

The car picked up speed, eating up the country miles as Arch took an unexpected detour. I checked my seat belt, angled the air vents so that they blew directly on me as I battled a bout of flop sweat. I wanted to ask where he was going. I wanted to demand he slow down. Call me tongue-tied.

"What was that supposed to mean?" he finally asked.

He didn't glare. He didn't shout. Too bad for me, because that would've triggered a red haze. Instead I struggled to state the ugly truth as I saw it. "Beckett was genuinely worried about my mom. He came here to help, to lend his expertise, not to show off. We discussed the situation. We came up with a plan. *We can do this,* he said. Costars, not the leading man and the starlet extra." Tears pricked my eyes as my heart bumped its way further up my throat.

"*Dinnae* stop now, Sunshine. You're on a roll."

I balled my fists in my lap so as not to sock him in the arm. I'm not a violent person. Usually. The things this man brought out in me… "You said you came here to keep your partner from botching his career. As if he's incapable of functioning without you—but that's another matter. Then you said you were here to help me, too. Like I was an afterthought. I think you're too much of a coward to admit what really propelled you across the ocean to Greenville, Indiana."

"Yeah?"

"Yeah. Want me to say it for you?"

"Do I have a choice?"

"Jealousy."

He jammed on the brakes and I knew I'd gone too far. Not that I cared. He was right—I was on a roll. Ensconced in the red haze, patriotic music blaring in my ears, I unbuckled my seat belt and faced him. "You're jealous of Beckett."

He left the car and slammed the door behind him.

I did the same. I rounded the Mercedes, hopped up on tearing down Arch's walls.

He loosened his tie, worked his jaw. "Sometimes I just want to…" He mimicked strangling me.

"Right back at you." I understood his anger was born of frustration and fear. More than once he'd commented he was slipping. If I thought I was losing my singing chops, I'd be freaked out, too. He'd taught Beckett everything he knew and now Beckett was having some sort of career crisis. Was the government agent looking to fly solo? Did Arch view him as competition? Circulating in the entertainment industry, where artists, including myself, often measured self-worth by degree of talent, I knew the pitfalls of envy. Professional jealousy could be toxic. "Why can't you just admit it?"

"Fine. Have it your way." He came toe to toe, stared me down. "The thought of you naked in Beckett's apartment drove me insane, yeah?"

My righteous tirade keyed down a notch. *What?*

"And what *aboot* the skimpy nurse's uniform? What the hell?"

My mind scrambled.

The Midol/whiskey debacle.

I faintly remembered Beckett being on the phone a

couple times. Arch must've been on the other end of the line. He'd overheard snippets of my slurred speech. My cheeks flushed hot. Surely he didn't think… "Are you accusing me of sleeping with Beckett? Do you think I want to work for Chameleon so badly that I'd seduce the man in charge?"

"You seduced me into sharing industry secrets, yeah?"

I swung out, but he caught my hand before it connected with his face.

"Sorry. Fuck." He blew out a breath. "I *didnae* mean that."

Furious, I tried to wrench my wrist from his grip, but he held tight, tugged me closer.

"You're right. I'm jealous. Christ." He dropped his forehead to mine. "I *dinnae* think you shagged him, but the possibility got under my skin, caused me to book the first flight to Philadelphia. Pops phoned as the jet touched down, brought me up to date. I *didnae* want Beckett to be your champion. It had to be me, yeah?"

My heart pounded in my ears. "Why?"

He cradled my face and kissed me. A tender meeting of the lips. A romantic gesture filled with promise. I burned as I'd never burned. Body—melting. Mind—ash. Maybe this was as close as he could get to admitting he'd fallen in love, too. This man who lived his life shunning emotional attachments.

"Gee," I said as he eased away, "you make it hard for a girl to be mad."

He brushed my flyaway hair out of my eyes. "I've been wanting to snog since we danced."

My lip twitched. "Toe mashing turns you on?"

"Not the waltzing, the grinding."

"Ah, yes." I smiled. "That was nice."

"Nice?" He smoothed his hands down my arms. "How romantic," he said, turning my own words on me.

I unknotted his tie. "You want romance, Ace?"

"That's why I brought you here, yeah? Sure as hell wasn't to fight."

I looked around, noted our location. He'd parked the Mercedes under a large elm, on the edge of a grassy bank. Below us, the river and Little Turtle Rock. "Oh, my God."

"*Stargazing* you called it."

"But it's the middle of the day."

"Planned on showing you the stars in my own way, lass."

Zing. Zap. "In broad daylight?"

"Turning conventional on me?"

As far as I could see, the only ones around, aside from us, were the birds and the bees. *Snort.* I whipped off his tie, pushed off his suit jacket and tossed them in the car through the lowered front window.

He opened the rear door and gave me a playful shove inside.

I stifled a giggle. "What are you doing?"

"Relegating you to the backseat."

"Smart-ass."

He kissed me. Hard.

I was all over that. All over him. Our tongues dueled as we fought to unbutton each other's shirts. Could a person expire from dire want? I smoothed my hands over his bare chest, his strong shoulders. Leaned into him as he reached around to unhook my bra. All the while we kissed and kissed.

He tasted of peanut-butter pie and chocolate milkshake—decadent. I breathed in his spicy aftershave—*zing*. Reveled in the feel of his hands on my bare skin—*zap*. His fingers trailed lightly down my spine, inciting erotic shivers. Heaven. No. *Sin City*. I broke away, dropping my head back to allow him access to my throat, my shoulders, my breasts… "Wait!"

"What?"

"There has to be music. You can't stargaze without music." I wormed out of his arms and leaned over the front seat. I keyed the ignition, switched on the radio and scanned for a station, any station with no static.

Arch grabbed my hips. The heat of his touch seared through the fabric of my pants.

He bit my butt and I giggled.

He bit my other cheek and I screamed.

"Sorry, love."

"Not you! Him!" I covered my bare breasts with one arm, used my free hand to point at a man with a camera, not more than ten feet away and snapping pictures through a telephoto lens.

Arch flew out of the car just as the photographer sprinted for a copse of trees. He must've parked down the road.

I grabbed a shirt, shoving my arms in the sleeves as I scrambled out of the Mercedes.

"Screw the *Tribune*," I heard the man shout. "The tabloids will start a bidding war over these babies!"

Could a person die of embarrassment? The bastard had my breasts, Arch kissing my breasts and biting my butt, on. film! This was worse than the casino incident. I shouted a victory cry when Arch tackled the man to the ground. "Pervert!" The photographer, not Arch.

Buttoning the shirt—Arch's shirt, I realized as I struggled with the too-long cuffs—I raced forward, meaning to bash that camera to smithereens if I had to. As I dived into the tussling match, I heard the *whoop-whoop* of a cruiser siren.

Somewhere in the back of my brain Beckett groaned. *Only you.*

CHAPTER TWENTY-FIVE

DEPUTY LEECH WAS bored out of his skull, I decided. Disturbing the peace? He had to be kidding. I'm pretty sure the birds and the bees weren't disturbed by three bone-headed humans wrestling for possession of a camera.

The photographer, Joe Kitt, worsened matters by accusing us of assault.

Arch countered with invasion of privacy, only we were in public, Deputy Leech said. He even tossed indecent exposure into the brewing pot after Kitt treated him to digital images of Arch and me stargazing.

At this point I was seriously considering posing for *Playboy*. It seemed the entire world was destined to see my perky 32Bs. Might as well cash in on my fate. And, of course, when I thought things couldn't get worse, they did. Deputy Leech hauled us down to the station. Arch had to call Beckett to intervene, and I had to call my Mom to explain why we'd be late for the barbecue.

My life was fast becoming a screwball comedy. Had I landed a part on a reality show and forgotten? I glanced around my surroundings, equating the police headquarters to the jailhouse featured on *The Andy Griffith Show*. Comparing Deputy Leech to Barney Fife and the silver-haired receptionist—the only other employee in the room—to Aunt Bea. I fidgeted under her grandmotherly appraisal.

"Just sit tight and behave yourselves," Leech said, "while I take Mr. Kitt's statement."

He settled behind a dinged metal desk across the room and motioned the bloody-nosed reporter into an adjacent seat.

Frowning, I scooted my chair closer to Arch. "What's he think, we're going to go at it in front of an audience?" I asked in a low voice. "It's not like we're exhibitionists." Although I couldn't deny the naughty thrill of going at it with Arch in the middle of the day in the backseat of a car. Especially after he'd bared his heart—sort of.

"Tell me Leech is going to come up with credible data if he runs Archibald Robert Duvall, Baron of Broxley, in the computer. I'm not sure a Web site and Wikipedia would do it for the law."

"Relax, Sunshine." He smiled and squeezed my hand. "If he researches, he'll find proper documentation supporting my claim."

Oh, right. The land title was registered somewhere. Being a pro, he'd probably covered his cute butt in several ways. Some legal, some…creative. Again I reflected on the phony passports and bogus credit cards he'd created for the cruise sting. No doubt he had several extensive methods for creating and substantiating aliases. Which ignited a scary thought. What if *Arch Duvall* was an alias? What if everything he'd told me about this past—not that he'd revealed much—was a lie?

Cripes.

Don't go there, Parish. Not now. You've got enough to worry about. Like Joe Kitt. "If that rat-bastard photographer insists on pressing charges—"

"He won't. Beckett will see to it, yeah?"

On cue, the government agent strode in. He didn't

look angry exactly, but he didn't look pleased. Wearing my own shirt now, I glanced down to make sure I'd buttoned up, then tucked my hair behind my ears in an attempt to look prim and proper.

Unfortunately, sans jacket and tie, cuffs rolled to mid-forearm, Arch looked as rumpled as me. Plus, since I'd worn his shirt during the tussle, it was smudged with dirt and grass stains.

Beckett looked our way and I read his thoughts.

Busted.

I clenched my teeth and felt a twinge of pain. *Chill, Evie, Chill.* The last thing I needed was for my TMJ to flare. *So Beckett knows you and Arch were screwing around. Not in town, not for show, but for your own personal pleasure. At least it's out in the open. Maybe it won't be so bad. Maybe he'll take this in stride.*

He braced his hands on the desk, exchanged hushed words with Aunt Bea, then glanced over and caught my gaze.

Or not. The man was ticked. But I sensed something else. Disappointment? Jealousy?

What if you have to choose? Arch's question echoed in my ears, taking on broader meaning, exacerbating my jaw clenching. Between what? Arch and Chameleon? Arch and Beckett? Happily ever after or happy for now?

"Deputy Leech," Aunt Bea called across the room. "Someone to see you."

The cop glanced over his shoulder. "Take a seat, mister. I'll be with you when—"

"This is a matter of international diplomacy," Beckett said, forgoing a chair and approaching Leech and Kitt.

"Who are you? Part of the baron's entourage?" The deputy stood. "We don't give special treatment to royalty in this town. Law's the law, and I've got a complaint to sort out, Mr...."

"Northbrook." He gripped the officer's hand in greeting, eyed the smirking photographer, who'd stuffed tissues up his nostrils to stem the bleeding. "The Baron of Broxley is a title of nobility, not royalty," he said. "Nevertheless, Duvall is a foreign dignitary who works closely with specific nonprofit charities. You can see why he'd want to protect his and his lady's reputations."

Kitt rubbed his hands together like the maniacal Snidely Whiplash. I half expected him to twist the tissues he had stuffed up his nose into a handlebar moustache. "I'm thinking the *National Enquirer.*"

My stomach turned. I'd always wanted to be famous. But not like this. "Tie me to the railroad tracks, why don't you?" I mumbled. Talk about a train wreck.

"Don't you work for the *Greenville Tribune?*" Leech asked the guy.

Kitt patted the camera sitting on the desk. "*Tribune* can't pay me enough for these babies."

Arch, who'd been listening quietly until now, leaned forward in his seat. "How much?"

"Forget it, *Baron.*"

"I'm sure we can come to an understanding," said Beckett.

Just then, my mom burst in. "I want to see my daughter this instant. I—Evelyn!"

I stood and braced myself for a lecture. *Good girls don't go parking. Nice girls don't strip in public. You're over forty. What were you thinking?* I was prepared for anything.

Except the hug.

She rushed forward and grabbed me up in a rib-crushing embrace.

Arms locked at my sides, I stood stiff, shocked.

"Are you all right?" she asked.

At a loss for words, I nodded.

She stepped back, scrunched her brow. "What were you thinking?"

That was more like it, only the question had lacked bite. *Who are you and what have you done with my mother?*

She turned on Arch. "What were *you* thinking? A gentleman of good breeding, for goodness' sake. The least you could do is put a ring on her finger first."

My skin heated—a full-body blush.

"I admit to poor judgment," Arch said, looking suitably contrite. "I tend to lose my head when I'm around your daughter, yeah?"

"Of course, no one would have been the wiser if not for the paparazzi," she said reasonably, then narrowed her steely blue eyes. "Where is he?"

Arch and I pointed to Joe Kitt.

Red-faced, Mom steamrolled across the room.

Deputy Leech staved her off with a halting hand. "Listen here, Mrs. Parish."

"Don't you speak to me in that tone, Ronnie Leech."

I knew that voice. Her teacher voice. *Ronnie* had to be one of her former Math students. She'd only been retired a few years, and he looked to be in his late twenties. It added up.

While I calculated and they faced off, the door slammed open and Dad strode in with Sheriff Jaffe. I didn't know Deputy Ronnie Leech. But I knew Ben Jaffe. He'd been policing Greenville for thirty years. He and Dad were tight.

"What in the blue blazes is going on, Deputy?" Jaffe

bellowed. "I take a day off and you spark an international incident."

Leech sputtered and Jaffe extended a hand to Arch. "Sheriff Ben Jaffe. Welcome to Greenville, sir. I'm sure we can work this out."

Before Arch could say boo, Jaffe spun off and stalked toward Leech. Mom stood next to the pinch-faced deputy, giving Joe Kitt hell.

Dad squeezed my shoulder. "You okay, little one?"

The entertainment industry might consider me over the hill, but I was still Daddy's little girl. Call me touched. Call me two seconds from a good cry. "I'm sorry for the scene. Sorry I embarrassed you."

He waved off the apology. "Bah."

"How did you know we were here?" Arch asked.

"Marilyn called me, up in arms about our daughter being arrested for indecent exposure."

I groaned.

"Not arrested," Arch said. "And your daughter's the most decent person I know."

"You're a good man, Archibald. Need to control your urges, but a good man." He rapped Arch on the shoulder, then focused on me. "Thought your mother would be here by now."

"She's over there, Dad."

"Where?"

"Lecturing that reporter. You're looking right at her." I realized he didn't recognize her right off because he had a rear view and her hair was short and blond and she was wearing jeans and pink running shoes. Not her typical style. Also she was yelling. Mom rarely expressed her anger in words; mostly she gave you the silent treatment. But when she did speak up, she never yelled. Amazing how hurtful a person could be with calm, well-chosen words. This moment, there was nothing calm about Marilyn Parish. She wanted Joe Kitt to give up those pictures, *now!*

Kitt yelled back and Dad marched toward the action. "That's my wife you're bellowing at and that's my daughter you violated, you weasel!"

"Slander!" Kitt yelled. Then he rattled off something about freedom of the press.

Mom countered with freedom of speech, in Dad's defense, and Dad cited freedom to protect one's kin.

I stared because, hey, this was just too weird. What happened to all the squashing down your feelings and not airing dirty laundry? Not that I cared. Air away!

Jaffe and Leech got in on the argument, as did Beckett, although Beckett didn't raise his voice. Once or twice he glanced our way and I felt the intensity of his displeasure. Yikes.

Arch stood beside me as cool as Danny Ocean or any one of his fictional grifting cohorts. Only Arch was the real deal. His ability to stay as loose as a goose in abnormally tense situations was astonishing. It made the moments he did lose control—like when he'd admitted he was jealous of Beckett—all the more powerful. My heart fluttered when I thought about his unspoken confession. *He loves me.* A smart woman would run for the hills. I reached out and clasped his hand.

He gave it a squeeze and smiled down at me. "We could slip out just now and no one would notice, yeah?"

"I'm not leaving without those pictures."

"'Course not, Sunshine. Just pointing *oot* that though we are the topic of discussion we are not the center of attention."

I, too, saw the absurdity of the situation and smiled. Six people stood across the room engaged in a shouting match. Aunt Bea watched from her reception desk as she gabbed into the phone—no doubt igniting a firestorm of gossip. Meanwhile my heart swelled and thumped. Though the room surged with frustration, I was feelin' the love. From Arch. And most surprisingly from my parents. They'd not only rushed to my rescue, they were also fighting for my honor. Me, Evie Parish, the black sheep of the family.

I choked back tears. This was a first. This whole day was a first, stocked with surprises. I barely flinched when Smith, the reporter who'd interviewed Arch at the dance studio, and another man—rotund and chomping on a cigar—charged through the front door.

"Those pictures are the property of the *Tribune!*" Cigar Man shouted as he jumped into the angry swarm.

"Our chief editor," Smith explained as he approached, pad and pen in hand. He zeroed in on me. "This seems to be a running theme with you, Ms. Parish."

I blinked.

"I understand you've been banned from performing on the casino stages because you flashed your, uh, bosoms during an audition. Care to elaborate?"

"She does not." Arch grasped the man by the elbow and steered him away from me, and suddenly there were two heated discussions in progress.

I stood away from the action, dazed. One episode of righteous insanity almost a month ago had turned my world inside out and led me to this bizarre moment. Though I really didn't want to see seminude photos of me on the cover of a tabloid, I couldn't dredge up an iota of regret.

"Guess a nudie shot is big news in Greenville."

I jumped at the sound of Nic's voice. "Where'd you come from?"

"Milo told me to stay in the car, but then half the town rushed in here, and I thought, *Screw you, Slick, I'm going in.*" She eyed the chaotic sideshow. "Looks like Arch gave the shutterbug a bloody nose. Is that it? I expected worse, given the charge of assault."

"Actually, I'm the one who socked Kitt. Didn't mean to. Clipped him with my elbow when we tussled."

Nic snorted. "Priceless." She pushed her big black sunglasses on top of her head and eyed me with concern. "You okay?"

"I'm mortified. We have to get that camera, Nic."

"Or the compact flash card. I dated a photographer with a camera like that. The pics you're worried about are stored on a digital memory card. If I could get close without drawing attention, I could pop and pocket that disc. If the camera goes missing, they'll notice right away. The card…" She shrugged.

I flashed on the change-raising scam I'd pulled in that London pub and recalled the key to escaping with something that didn't belong to me. "I have an idea."

She knotted her long hair into a low bun. "I'm all ears."

CHAPTER TWENTY-SIX

EVEN THOUGH HE WAS in the midst of an infuriating argument, Milo sensed the moment Nicole walked into the jailhouse. He should've known she'd ignore his request. Frankly he was surprised she'd remained in the car as long as she had. Then he saw Twinkie and her friend eyeing the reporter, the camera, and whispering.

Don't do it, he mentally ordered. A wasted effort. Even if they had telepathic abilities, they'd ignore him because they were both obstinate.

They launched into action before he could extricate himself from the verbal free-for-all. When he saw Twinkie drifting toward the media circus and Nicole fading into the fringes, he had no choice but to be sensitive to whatever they were about to pull. He just happened to catch Arch's eye and directed his attention toward the potential disaster.

The Scot ratcheted up the level of hostility geared toward the reporter and his boss. "If you print those pictures, I will bloody well sue!"

Milo lost his temper on purpose with the by-the-books, I-despise-foreigners deputy. "Was that a slur against the Scottish people, son? I know people in Washington and I *will* have your ass!"

"Simmer down, everyone!" the sheriff bellowed.

"I'm sure she didn't hit you on purpose," Mrs. Parish told the photographer. "Don't be such a baby! It's just a nosebleed."

"Give me those pictures," Mr. Parish said, shaking his fist, "or, by God, I'll do worse."

"Take your best shot, old geezer."

Evie got in the photographer's face. "Stop harassing my parents, you rat-bastard rat!"

She shoved and—Sweet Jesus—the idiot shoved back.

Milo and Arch spun to her aid, but Mrs. Parish beat them to the punch. She swung her pocketbook and connected with his nose.

The rat-bastard rat shrieked. Blood spurted and Evie swooned. Toppling forward into the scumbag photographer, they both crashed to the floor, and everyone flocked to them like magnets to steel.

"Millie!" the sheriff shouted to his receptionist. "Get the first-aid kit."

The photographer wiggled out from under Evie, shouting his pain to the world. "Crazy bitch broke my nose!"

Evie lay on the floor, seemingly unconscious.

"*Cannae* stand the sight of blood," Arch explained as he and Milo dropped their faces close to hers.

Milo assessed her limp body with dread. "You okay?" he whispered over the ruckus.

"My boobs are in safe hands," she whispered.

Arch grinned. "Brilliant."

Milo looked up, looked around. The camera was there, but Nicole was gone. He assessed and bit back a grin. Fucking brilliant.

I'VE ALWAYS CONSIDERED myself pretty decent at improvisational theater. There's a certain thrill that comes with not knowing what's going to happen next. Relying on one's wit and imagination instead of scripted lines. Reacting to another actor's words or actions off the cuff. If there's chemistry, there's energy, and let me tell you, the jailhouse rocked.

Nic exited off stage unnoticed, returning a scant minute later with a bottle of water from the car and the excuse that she was worried I was dehydrated. Arch, Beckett and I cued off her ad-libs and played the room beautifully. Fifteen minutes later—thanks to some diplomatic double-talking on Beckett's part and the sheriff who just wanted this to go away—everyone left the jailhouse grudgingly satisfied. The *Tribune* had tomorrow's front-page story, plus Beckett had promised the baron's *publicist* would e-mail them candid photos to accompany the piece. Joe Kitt had been overcompensated for medical bills and the memory card that had mysteriously vanished.

Refraining from performing my victory dance after we exited onto Main Street took enormous energy. My body vibrated like a wound-up toy. The air crackled with excitement and tension. I sensed everyone had something to say to someone, just not in front of the entire group.

A few feet away from the jailhouse Dad broke the ice. "I hope one of you pocketed that disc. I'd hate to think it was Millie or even Deputy Leech."

"You don't think they'd sell those pictures, do you?" Mom asked, aghast.

"You never know," Dad said. "Could wind up on the Internet."

"They won't," Nic said with a knowing smile.

Dad scratched his beard, then grinned full out. "Enough said."

Mom nodded in agreement, and I thanked my lucky

stars they were willing to drop the discussion on the pit-falls of stargazing. I had a feeling it wasn't a dead topic with Beckett, but I'd cross that bridge later. In private.

"There goes my barbecue," Mom said out of the blue.

It took a second to realize she was lamenting the weather, not the *incident*. The sky had turned dark and angry and thunder rumbled in the distance.

"No reason to forfeit the night," Dad said. "Why don't you bring the fixings over to the tavern. I'll close down for a private shindig. We'll fire up the grill in the kitchen. Drinks on the house."

"But you'll lose a night's business," Mom said reasonably, skeptically.

"Don't give a flip, Marilyn."

Because I was used to their crappy communication skills, I read between the lines and took control before they botched what smacked of a possible truce. "I think it's an excellent idea." I elbowed Arch.

"Brilliant," he said, draping an arm over my shoulders. "*Dinnae* know *aboot* the rest of you, but I could use a pint, yeah?"

Nic tucked her sunglasses into her designer purse. "I'll second that."

Beckett eyed her, then addressed Mom. "I'll be happy to help you transport the groceries, Mrs. Parish."

As Arch's supposed aide, it made sense that he would offer, but I wanted private words with Mom and this seemed the perfect opportunity. "That's okay," I said brightly. "I'll do it."

"I'll come with you," Nic said. "We'll meet you men at the bar."

I hadn't planned on Nic's company, but I couldn't exclude her and, besides, I got the feeling she didn't want to be alone with Beckett. Though I'd initially sensed an attraction on Nic's part, all they seemed to do was knock heads. Looking at my smart and beautiful friend, I couldn't imagine why Beckett would prefer me over her. For that matter, what did Arch see in me? He could have any woman. Heck, according to his janitor buddy, Marvin, he routinely enjoyed a smorgasbord of pretty birds. Was I a passing fancy? For that matter, was *he* a passing fancy? That would explain my awareness of Beckett. Had I mistaken fantasy love for true love? Technically, I suppose, Arch and I were in the giddy, obsessive first stage of falling in love. What if we didn't weather the second stage? What if this was a simple case of sexual chemistry?

I massaged my throbbing temples.

Without a word, Beckett produced one of those painreliever travel packs from his pocket and passed it to me.

"Thanks," I said.

"Sure," he said.

I washed down Tylenol with the water given to me by Nic, cheeks heating under the calm stare of Arch. *Uh-oh.*

Nic grunted and spun away. "I need to get something out of the car."

"You okay?" Dad asked.

"Just a tension headache," I said, letting my parents assume it was because of the boobs-on-film fiasco.

"All the more reason to get dinner started and some food in your stomach. We'll take my car," Mom said, smoothing a self-conscious hand over her hair.

It was an invitation for Dad to comment on her new do, but he didn't. Cripes. "What do you think of Mom's new hairstyle and color, Dad?" *Please say something nice.*

"I like it," he said simply. "Very pretty. Very—" he cleared his throat "—flattering."

Mom blushed and looked away. "It was time for a change."

Nic rushed back, obliterating the awkwardness. "I'm ready."

"Tavern's a couple blocks up. No need to drive separately." Dad motioned to his four-door. "Hop in."

Arch brushed my bangs from my eyes. "Cheers, Sunshine." But I knew he meant *Good luck with your ma.* He took off with my Dad.

"Be right there," said Beckett.

"My car's across the street, girls," Mom said, making a dash as she looked toward the boomer clouds. "Hurry."

I stepped to the curb, glancing over my shoulder to see Nic perform her role as Beckett's girlfriend. She leaned in and kissed him sweetly on the cheek. "See you in a while, honey." But as she walked away, he snagged her hand and pulled her against his body.

Rubbernecking without looking obvious was impossible, so—to hell with it—I gawked straight out.

Beckett kissed Nic on the mouth, then whispered something in her ear before allowing her to catch up to me. My imagination soared. I wondered about that kiss. Sweet? Hot? Not that I was jealous, just curious. And what did he whisper? Did he demand she give him the memory card? He'd paid handsomely for it, after all. Did he blast her for taking it in the first place? Tell her to tell me I'm fired? Once we started across the street, I asked. "What did he say?"

"It doesn't matter."

"Tell me."

She shoved on her sunglasses—weird, given the overcast skies. Stranger still, she blushed. "He said, 'Well done.'"

MILO HADN'T INTENDED to encourage Nicole and Evie's reckless behavior. The compliment had slipped out in the aftermath of a disquieting stir. He'd kissed Nicole for appearance' sake. A chaste kiss, yet he'd felt a brief pulse of lust. Goes to show how lame his sex life had been of late. Sure, she was gorgeous, but that's where the attraction stopped. She was also cynical and rude. If he experienced a stir kissing someone he didn't even like, what would happen if he kissed Evie?

Curiosity stoked the attraction, and it would only get worse. One kiss would solve the mystery. If he felt nothing, no chemistry, the infatuation would die a quick death. On the other hand…

Shake it off, Beckett.

He blamed his wayward thoughts on the residual adrenaline coursing through his system after an inspired performance. Two men trained in the confidence game. Two professional actresses. They'd clicked like an experienced team. He couldn't deny the rush. Couldn't deny the women's talent. His ability to think in terms of black and white had been compromised. Lack of sleep didn't help.

By the time they reached the Corner Tavern and settled in at the bar his mood had turned as frosty as the mug of Bud served up by Mr. Parish. His mind churned as the man shooed everyone out, patrons *and* employees. Next he called and canceled the band for the night, with pay. *Generous,* Milo thought. *Honest. Like father like daughter.*

He waited until the elder man disappeared into the kitchen and turned to Arch. "If you tell me you planned that episode just so you could land a front-page story in order to advance the senator's sting, I won't be believe it. Not even you are that good."

Arch opened a fresh pack of Marlboros. "Let's cut through the *shite,* Jazzman."

"Think you're capable?"

"Evie and I are involved, yeah?"

"The truth. Huh. Sounds odd coming from you."

"Sarcasm. Sounds natural coming from you."

Longtime adversaries before they'd partnered, Milo was used to this verbal sparring. All part of their complicated dance, although it suddenly felt as if they'd lost their rhythm. Probably because someone now stood between them.

Milo drank his beer, cursed the jealousy stabbing his gut. Arch's admission hadn't come as a surprise, but it sure as hell worsened his mood.

The Scot lit a cigarette, tossed the match in a boot-shaped ashtray. Unlike the Chameleon Club, the Corner Tavern was themed and dressed for success. Milo could imagine Twinkie on that stage. He could hear her whiskey voice paying homage to Patsy Cline. But he couldn't imagine her moving back to Greenville, as he knew her Dad hoped. Though she'd retained certain small-town sensibilities, she'd outgrown the low-key lifestyle.

She doesn't want to go back.

Convenient. Milo didn't want to leave her behind. She made him smile during this joyless period of his life. She kept him connected to innocence and the pursuit of dreams. She reminded him of the good in people, inspired him to stick to his guns, thumb his nose at the naysayers and make a difference. She wanted to do something important. So did he.

Arch blew smoke in the opposite direction, then caught Milo's eye. "I need to make something clear, yeah? Regarding Evie's integrity. She did break off with me in London. She wasn't lying *aboot* that. She respects your stand on team members screwing around."

"But you don't."

"She's not an active player."

"Not the point."

He shrugged. "Things happen, mate."

"Yeah. You and Gina. You and Evie."

"This is different."

"Why?"

"Because Evie is different."

"You mentioned that before. She's not like us, you said. I agree. She's wounded and bitter about certain aspects of her life, but she's not jaded. She hasn't developed skin as tough as a rhino's. She won't bounce back like Gina when you get bored and cast her aside."

"It's not like that."

"What's it like?"

"With Gina it was *aboot* sex. Just sex."

"And with Evie?"

He didn't answer and Milo's gut kicked. This was bad all around. Knowing Arch—as well as one could—he couldn't imagine him committing to a long-term relationship. "Are you prepared to marry this woman? That's what she'll expect if you keep heading down this path. In case you haven't noticed, she's in love with you."

"I noticed."

Milo waited. Part of him reveled when Arch didn't profess the same. Part of him cursed the detached bastard. "This complicates matters."

"Because you've got eyes for Evie yourself, yeah?"

There was that. But he was also thinking about the overall dynamics of the team. And Evie. Instead of denying or confirming Arch's allegation, he said, "I don't want to see her hurt."

"Neither do I."

"You've put your all into Chameleon, I'll give you that, but you're hardly reformed. Over the years you've gone renegade more than once. Jetted off to bumfuck wherever to engage in activities known only to you."

"I'm entitled to a personal life, yeah?"

"Not when it entails criminal activity. I put my neck on the block for you, Arch. Played loose with the law to keep your crooked ass out of prison."

"So you're fond of reminding me."

"Point is, you've got another life, a secret life. I've maintained a less-I-know-the-better attitude because I needed your expertise to obliterate the worst of your kind. Evie's interest in you is genuine. If you continue to deceive her, then you're nothing but a stupid, selfish prick."

"*Dinnae* sugarcoat it," Arch said, gaze level as he sucked on that Marlboro.

"If you truly care for Evie, you'll come clean with her. No secrets. Otherwise any lasting relationship—if you're capable of such a thing—is doomed."

"You speak, of course, from experience."

A prick *and* an asshole. Milo didn't need to be reminded of his own failed marriage. The disconnection and disillusion. The secrets and betrayals. He'd like to think he'd learned from the fucked-up experience. God forbid he share that wisdom with a friend. Not that Arch was a friend in a traditional sense. But there was—and had always been—a mutual admiration and warped camaraderie between them.

"Lecture over?" Arch asked.

"Go to hell."

"Probably." The Scot crushed out the cigarette while seemingly weighing his words. "Evie has her heart set on being an active member of Chameleon, you know?"

Milo nodded. "I think she's got potential."

"Aye. She's a natural. But I *dinnae* want to subject her to our world. Not on a regular basis. She's sensitive and good and…"

"Not like the people we tangle with on a routine basis." He knew what Arch was trying to say because he felt the same way. As though they were tainting something pure. Still, she deserved an honest shot at a job she badly wanted. He checked to make sure they were still alone. Even so, he lowered his voice further. "If she proves she's a capable shill, I'm not going back on my word, Arch. I'm not going to manipulate her."

"I sense an unspoken *like you*."

"You claim you flew in to keep me from ruining my career. I think you're here because you didn't want me to act as Evie's savior. What if I busted the man scamming her mom? What if Evie's gratitude grew into something more intimate? What if we seriously bonded? What if *you* turned out to be nothing more than a dangerous thrill?"

Arch betrayed nothing in words or expression, but Milo knew he'd hit the mark. He barreled on, wanting to make the amoral man think, feel. "Even though you and I have worked together for almost three years, you still operate as though we're competitors. You second-guess me, you counter me, you constantly take the lead. I think your need to be top dog is at work here. I'm less sure of your motive. Do you honestly want Evie? Or is it that you don't want me to have her?"

"Are you saying you're going to make a play?"

Milo heard Mr. Parish coming their way. He polished off his beer, mentally ticking off all the reasons Twinkie would be better off with him than Arch. "If she makes the first move."

CHAPTER TWENTY-SEVEN

"WHERE'S NICOLE?"

"She ran up to the bathroom to freshen up." I wrung my hands as Mom located three paper bags and set them on the counter. I glanced down at my pink shirt, frowning at a few specks of Kitt's dried blood. "I also asked her to search my bedroom for a fresh shirt. Must be something in there that still fits. And I hope you don't mind, but I asked her to raid Christopher's room for a clean shirt for Arch. His is stained."

"Why don't you run up and help her look?"

"She'll do okay. Besides, I wanted a few minutes alone with you." On the ride home I'd decided to be as truthful as possible with Mom in hopes that she'd do the same.

"Why?"

"We need to talk."

"No, we don't. I was young once, Evelyn, and stargazing was around before you were born."

Okay, I'm not sure I wanted to know my mom used to make out in the backseat with boys. Then again, it did make her human…and truthful. "Actually," I said, stopping her as she reached for the fridge handle, "I was hoping to talk about you and Dad."

She tensed and I saw a glimpse of the repressive woman I'd grown up with. "It's private," she said in her no-nonsense teacher voice.

"Yes, I know. I respect that, but…" *Start the party. Be the first one on the dance floor.* "I love you, Mom." When she didn't respond, I boogied on. "I want you to be happy. I know whatever's going on between you and Dad is private, but we're family, and if you can't confide in me…" I clasped her hand. "I know I made a mess of my own marriage. I know you don't think—"

"Hold on, Evelyn. You don't know what I think."

My back went up. "You told me if I had paid more attention to my husband and less to my career—"

"I was angry. Not at you but at Michael and the situation. I don't express myself well." She sighed. "It's something I'm trying to change. Please—" she squeezed my hand, nodded toward the kitchen chairs "—sit down."

My heart pounded anticipating news that the world was coming to an end because, *hello,* Mom and I were talking. About stuff that *matters.* I sat, stiff-backed and poised on the edge of the seat.

She eased into a chair, placed her hands on the table and fixed her gaze on the napkin holder. She was quiet for so long I wondered if this was a new bizarre silent treatment, but then she lifted her chin and looked me in the eyes. "You didn't fail your marriage, Michael did."

My shoulders sagged with relief. My friends had uttered similar words, but I'd still felt guilty. Until now. Mom's support worked like an elixir.

"I was distraught at the thought of you being alone in your early forties, angry because the profession you'd chosen was turning its back on you at such a young age."

"Forty-anything isn't young in the entertainment industry, Mom."

"That's my point, Evelyn. Please listen. This isn't easy for me."

I suppressed a smile. We were talking, and nothing, not even a small reversion to her former snippy self, could dampen my elation.

"Everything in your life went down the commode at the same time."

"Yes, I know," I said with ironic humor. "I was there."

She quirked a fleeting smile. "If you'd gone to college, if you had a diploma to fall back on, you could've gone into teaching dramatics or music, even at this late date. You would've had stability. No mother wants to see their child flail, living paycheck to paycheck or, worse, sinking into deep debt. When I brought up getting a respectable, reliable nine-to-five, you balked. I blamed you for being foolhardy and stubborn, just as I did all those years ago when you joined a band instead of enrolling in a university. That was wrong of me. I see that now. You are who you are because of the choices you make. You are a beautiful person, Evelyn."

The lump in my throat was easily the size of an orange. Vision blurry, I clasped my hands in my lap.

"Don't cry, dear. Otherwise I won't be able to continue."

I nodded and squeezed back tears.

"I don't think like you do, Evelyn. I'm logical, grounded. I never understood your artistic spirit. When your life fell apart, I didn't know how to help. I was convinced, given our history, that you wouldn't be open to any of my suggestions, so rather than risk rejection, I barely tried. Instead I focused on my own life, my own marriage, thinking nothing would make me happier than spending my golden years living in Florida with your father.

"As you know, we did not see eye to eye on that score.

I wanted to relocate, instead he bought the tavern. I kicked George out because I was hurt. He preferred work and his cronies to me."

"That's not true, Mom."

"It's a little true. I've realized since then that I am opinionated and rigid. But I don't want to get into that. The point is, I soon learned that he intended to refurbish the tavern so that you would have a place to earn a living doing what you love to do. I thought it was thoughtful and generous and I resented not being a part of that. It made me feel selfish and small."

I massaged a dull throbbing at my temples. So much to take in. "I don't understand why he didn't tell you up front. About his reasons for buying the tavern, I mean."

"Because I had always been opposed to your creative pursuits, he anticipated a fight, and you know how your father hates scenes. Also, at the time we weren't getting along. Being around each other seven days a week, twenty-four hours a day is…difficult."

"I suspect that would be the case for most couples, Mom."

"Maybe. Still, living alone for a week gave me a lot of time to think. I decided to make some changes. I wanted to make an effort to understand you better, so I decided to try something creative. That's when I met the man who showed me the light."

I fidgeted in my seat, unsure if I was ready for this next part.

"You met him," she said, lighting up with a smile that cramped my stomach. "Randolph Gish."

"The dance instructor."

She nodded. "I signed up for his class thinking I was going to get dance lessons."

I arched a brow. "And?"

"I got life lessons. I can't believe how fast and well we hit it off. He's charming, don't you think?"

I shrugged. "He's okay."

She pursed her lips. "You say that because you only have eyes for Archibald."

"Are you saying you have eyes for Randolph?"

"In a romantic sense? Heavens, no. First of all, I'm married. Second of all, he's much too young for me. Third, he's…"

"Gay?"

"You noticed." She leaned forward, voice low. "He's in the closet. Said he's suffered discrimination and that's why he moves around a lot. Said his classes thrive more if he pretends to be heterosexual."

A straight man pretending to be a gay man pretending to be straight. If I were less imaginative, that would have given me a brain cramp. "So…what? You're friends?"

"Good friends."

Straight girl/gay guy buddies. "Did he talk you into this makeover?"

"He did. And I'm not sorry. I love it and, just as Randolph predicted, George approved." Her cheeks flushed. "Did you see the way he looked at me?"

"Who? Daddy?" My heart fluttered. "Yes, I saw. I think he's quite smitten with your sexy new look."

"Sexy?" She gave a nervous laugh. "It's been a long time since George looked at me the way Archibald looks at you. I have to confess, I like it."

I smiled. "You want to reunite with Dad."

"I do. But not as the old us. I'm working hard on becoming a more tolerant, sociable person, but he needs to make an effort to change, too. A good relationship involves sacrifice and compromise, respect and trust. Meanwhile, I'm investing in our future."

Warning bells clanged in my head. "Investing?"

She bit her lower lip. "I promised Randolph I wouldn't tell anyone. The project's in the preliminary stages. A once-in-a-lifetime opportunity, and I'm getting in on the ground floor."

Common buzz words and phrases used in a come-on. I'd heard them, read them. Gish had hooked and reeled Mom in, pitched an irresistible deal. He'd probably cough up a small return—the *convincer*—then soak her for an additional investment. I wondered if he'd played any other women in his dance class, swearing them all to secrecy. My blood burned, but I played it cool. "So what is it? Stock? Land?"

Her face lit up. "A multiplex entertainment center for seniors in Boca Raton, Florida. It's going to make a mint. I will easily make back five times what I invested. I'm going to reinvest my earnings into a second home in a nearby housing development. That way your father and I can divide our time between here and Florida. The best of both worlds. Compromise."

I was clenching my teeth so tight I feared a bout of lockjaw. *Chill, Evie, Chill.* "How is it that Randolph is privy to this awesome investment opportunity?

Mom leaned forward and whispered, "His partner. You know, his…"

"Lover?"

She nodded. "He's the head architect. I spoke to him on the phone. Lovely man. He even e-mailed floor plans for me to look at."

Phony floor plans, no doubt. But how would she know that? And Mom was no fool. According to my reading and conversations with Arch, con artists intent on bigger scores often target professionals. Politicians, doctors, bankers, teachers—the college-educated were as susceptible to scams as the blue-collar workforce. It boiled down to the grifter ascertaining the mark's weakness, winning their confidence and telling them what they wanted to hear. Something Arch had down pat, a troublesome skill that kept me on my toes.

How can I trust you?

You can't.

The stairs creaked, signaling Nic's return. It reminded me of another creak, a hasty retreat. "Last night when I came in, I thought I heard someone leave through the back door. Was it Randolph?"

"He dropped by to discuss the investment," Mom said, the picture of innocence. "He snuck out because our meeting was confidential." She hurried to the fridge, retrieving several pounds of hamburger meat and a huge bowl filled with potato salad. "Don't tell your dad about Boca Raton. It's a surprise."

I bagged the chips and buns, mulling over a course of action. "Don't worry, Mom. Dad won't hear it from me." I spotted a box of chocolate cupcakes, a favorite childhood snack, and tossed those in, too.

"And Evelyn?"

"Yes?"

"I love you, too."

CHAPTER TWENTY-EIGHT

BY THE TIME WE PARKED in front of the Corner Tavern I was ready to claw out of my skin. Again I wondered if I was on *Candid Camera*. This day had been too bizarre to be real, and it wasn't over yet.

In the back of my jam-packed brain my mom's declaration of love played over and over, but it was hard to enjoy the moment knowing a bastard like Randolph Gish was on the loose in Greenville. I hated that he'd wormed his sleazy way into her life. Hated that he'd made a mockery of my gay friends. I despised him for fleecing Mom and women like her. Trusting. Needy. I wanted him gone and I knew just the man to do it.

The rain and thunder mirrored my stormy mood as the three of us moved inside under the protection of two umbrellas. "Now, remember, Mom. If the opportunity arises, come clean with Dad about what you told me."

"Except the investment part. Remember your promise," she whispered.

I crossed my heart.

Beckett moved toward us. "Let me take those bags."

Mom held tight to hers. "Is George in the kitchen?"

"No. He's in the game room with Arch and your son."

I swallowed, anxious about seeing my brother. Just

thinking about dealing with another awkward relationship was exhausting. "Christopher's here?"

"Showed up a few minutes ago. We paired up for a game of pool. I just came out to use the men's room and saw you come in."

"Did he bring Sandy and the kids?" I asked.

He shook his head. "Something about an inappropriate influence."

"That would be the bar." Mom rolled her eyes. "I'm going to start supper."

She took off and I passed my barbecue booty to Nic. "Could you...I need to speak to Beckett."

"Sure." She flashed a fake smile at the man, then zipped after Mom.

Beckett watched her go, then addressed me. "If this is about the photographer incident—"

"It's about another slimeball."

He must've detected the hostility in my voice. He moved in close. "What's wrong?"

"I need to talk to you in private. *Now.*"

"Follow me."

As soon as we were locked away in Dad's small office, I spewed. Everything Arch and I had learned via our private dance lesson. Everything Mom had revealed about Gish. Now and then Beckett nodded to indicate he was following, otherwise he held silent. I worked hard to keep my voice down to an enraged whisper. "I wanted to drive over there. I concocted a story in my head, a reverse con. I know I could rope him into roping me."

"To what end?" Beckett said.

"Verification. Confirmation. Proof that he's a scum artist. But then I thought, what if I blow it? Not that I think I would, but what if? And what if it trickled over and compromised the senator's sting? I've done enough damage today."

"I'm glad you practiced restraint, Evie. Emotions have no place in this business."

"I know, I know. It's just that this is so personal."

He perched on the corner of the desk, folded his arms. "Can I ask you a question?"

I nodded as I paced by. "Shoot."

"Why are you confiding in me right now and not Arch?"

"Because you're my boss, plus you have the badge and the clout."

"You lost me, Twinkie."

I stopped in front of him, fists clenched at my sides. "I want you to run Randolph Gish out of town."

"Excuse me?"

"Call Woody. Tell him what I told you. He can run a background check on Gish, look into that building project. You said he's a whiz at acquiring information. I'm betting he'll dig up something you can use against the rat bastard."

"You want me to threaten the man."

"I want him gone."

"Let me get this straight. You're asking me to use my badge, my government position to—"

"Get creative. That's what Chameleon calls it when they bend rules, right?" I wrapped my arms around my middle, hugging away the hurt. The stomach cramp signaled I wasn't totally okay with what I was asking, but I ignored my gut in favor of what I saw as the greater good. "I don't want to risk Gish mucking up my parents' reconciliation. I don't want to waste time roping him into an elaborate sting." I moved in and placed my hands on his forearms. "I know I've been a pain in the butt. I know

I misled you regarding Arch and our on-off-on…
whatever. It's just that so much has happened so fast. I
just need—I want—this Gish to go away."

"Okay."

"You'll do it?"

"You can kiss your mom's six thousand goodbye."

My heart pounded. "That's all right. I have that part
figured out."

"Should've known."

Humor, admiration and frustration mingled and
danced in his pointed gaze. My pounding heart skipped
with…what? Gratitude? Hero worship? Affection? I realized suddenly that I had a death grip on his arms and
that I was standing close, too close. Unhinged, I backed
away and resumed my pacing. "I'll dip into my savings.
My brother can help with the banking aspect. All I need
is a sample of Gish's handwriting. If I root through his
trash at the studio or his apartment—"

"I see where you're headed." He pushed off the desk
and stepped in my path. "I'll save you the trouble and get
him to pen a letter. An explanation and apology for the
cancellation of the building project. *Sorry. Here's your
money back.* Something like that, right?"

"You can do that?"

"Apparently I can work wonders with my badge and
clout." He stuffed his hands in his pockets and looked
down at me, a somber gaze that streaked through my
body, causing my skin to prickle with unease. "Let me
ask you something. What about the other women Gish
might be fleecing in this town? What about their lost
funds? Or suppose your mom is his sole mark here. What
about when I run him out of town? He's going to land
somewhere and start anew. What about those women?"

Like Arch, Beckett had stayed calm throughout one of my emotional tirades. He'd put a rational spin on my narrow view, citing a bigger picture. My skin flushed as his words sunk in. I hadn't been thinking of the greater good, I'd been thinking selfishly. About how Randolph Gish's treachery affected me and my family, not beyond. Home front versus homeland. I wanted to be a Chameleon. Trouble was, I didn't think like one.

A hundred thoughts and fears swirled in my brain, twisting my vitals into knots. I couldn't voice them and my diary wasn't around. The events of the day took their toll and I imploded—or exploded, I'm not sure which. Hard to think straight when you're sobbing uncontrollably.

"Oh, Christ," I heard Beckett say under his breath.

"I'm sorry," I squeaked while crying into my hands.

Next thing I knew I was in his arms and blubbering against his chest.

He stroked a calming hand up and down my back. "Easy, Twinkie. We'll work this out."

We. I sensed the same connection I'd felt the day we'd arrived in Greenville. I felt the support of a new and special friend. I felt safe. The tears increased with a sickening realization. Though I loved Arch, I didn't trust him.

I trusted Milo Beckett.

Unlike Arch, he generally shot straight from the hip. He wasn't willing to put me in the field right off, but he offered hope should I prove myself capable.

A good relationship involves sacrifice and compromise, respect and trust, I could hear Mom say.

But then a smooth voice with a thick accent intruded. *I didnae want Beckett to be your champion. It had to be me, yeah?*

It was too much.

I pushed out of Beckett's arms, sleeved away tears. "I can't…whatever this—" I indicated "us" with a nervous flick of my hand "—is…I can't. My heart… Not smart, I know. But…"

"Can't choose who we love." Compassion swam in his eyes. "I understand."

I grabbed a tissue from a box on my dad's desk, blew my nose, hoping my brains didn't leak out in the process. I felt all kinds of weird. "I'm sorry."

"No apology needed."

"So am I, you know, fired?"

He frowned. "For what?"

"Complicating things." I shoved my hair off my heated cheeks. "I've heard you don't like complications."

His mouth curved into a soft smile. "Not generally."

"Normally I'm a simple person, I mean, easygoing, I mean–"

"I know what you mean."

"It's been a rough year and then I met Arch and you and now this thing with my mom. I'm a little off balance."

He walked me to the door. "Understandable."

"I don't tend to cause waves. I'm not a troublemaker. I'm a team player. You don't have to worry about my personal life interfering with my professional life because I'm—"

"You're not fired."

I blew my nose one more time, then pocketed the wadded tissue. Relief flooded through my system, making me weak in the knees. He was willing to ignore whatever simmered between us and accept what sizzled between Arch and me. I think. One thing for certain—I still had a place with Chameleon.

"You okay now, Twinkie?"

I nodded and forced a watery smile as he opened the door. "This would be a lot easier if you weren't so darned nice."

"Oh, I can be a real bastard at times." He glanced over my shoulder. "Just ask Arch."

I closed my eyes briefly, thinking, *Oh, no.* But then I opened them and, oh, yes, there he stood, alongside a wide-eyed Nic.

She cleared her throat. "We've been looking for you. Your mom…she wanted…help."

"In the kitchen," Arch added, his mood unreadable as he studied my puffy, tear-streaked, no doubt crimson face. He glanced at Beckett and my stomach churned. He'd admitted to being jealous of the man. Now I'd unwittingly given him reason. Not that I'd done anything wrong. Although I guess confiding in a man other than the one I'm sleeping with might be construed as disloyal. Any way you cut it, this was an awkward moment.

He glanced back down at me. "You okay, Sunshine?"

My heart pumped at the concern in his eyes. "I had a minimeltdown." Might as well come clean with the obvious. "This thing with Mom…" I trailed off, looking to Nic for help.

"Speaking of," she said, "she's waiting. We should go, stop by the ladies' room first and freshen up." She tugged me away.

"Be right there," Arch said, calm as you please.

Uh-oh. I glanced over my shoulder, saw them both watching after me.

I felt a little guilty leaving Beckett behind in the wake of a storm. But they'd known each other a long time. Surely they'd weathered worse.

CHAPTER TWENTY-NINE

"WHAT'S GOING ON, EVIE?"

"Nothing. Things. Life. It's just…complicated at the moment." I was really beginning to detest that word.

"Well, there's a big frickin' news bulletin." Nic leaned back against the sparkling tile of the ladies' bathroom while I splashed my face with cool water. "You're neck-deep in lies and playing with fire. This isn't like you."

I patted my face dry with a coarse paper towel, suppressing a frustrated scream. "I told you—I've changed."

"No, you haven't. Not deep down. That's the problem. You're still sweet, kind and honest to your core. Duvall and Beckett are dangerous. They deal in deception. A con artist and a burned-out cop, for chrissake. Their worlds are far and away from yours, and you should stay far and away from them. This has *disaster* written all over it."

I resisted the childish urge to cover my ears. Instead I pulled a compact from my tote and powdered my face. "I know what I'm doing."

"So do I. You're running away."

"From what?"

"Your life." She pushed off the wall and stood behind me while I freshened my lipstick. "You were crushed when Michael divorced you. You wallowed for more than a year. Yet you claim that you don't give a shit that he got

Sasha pregnant, eloped, then honeymooned in your dream city? I don't believe it. You feel something, Evie. Hurt, resentment, anger. You just don't *want* to feel it."

I caught her gaze in the reflection in the mirror. "Do you have any mascara?"

She worked her jaw, rooted around in her sleek black purse. "Here."

"Thanks." I focused on working magic to disguise my meltdown. Meanwhile I imagined myself in a pretty pink bubble, a bubble that deflected Nic's well-meant but irritating words.

"On top of the Michael/Sasha issue, you're struggling with age insecurities and a flagging career in entertainment, which I understand, but there are ways other than performing in casinos to capitalize on your talent."

"I know. Utilizing my acting skills to dupe scum artists."

"I was thinking more along the lines of relocating to New York City or Los Angeles. Exploring Broadway or film."

"No, thanks."

"But if the opportunity came along—"

"It won't. And even if it did…" I turned and returned her mascara. "It's gone, Nic."

"What?"

"The passion to perform on stage. I don't feel it anymore—and I need to burn for something, otherwise I'll shrivel up and blow away. Right now I burn for Chameleon."

"And Arch?"

I peered up at her through newly plumped lashes. "I burn for him, too."

"Beckett?"

"Just friends."

"Mmm."

I squeezed her hand. "Please support me on this, Nic. Or at least don't fight me."

"I just want you to be happy, Evie."

"I'm working on it."

"Okay." She shook her head. "Fine. Doesn't mean I won't watch your back."

For Nic, that was downright sappy. I smiled and hugged her. "I should catch up with Mom before she sends out a search party."

"I'll be along in a minute. I need to step outside, make a call. I promised Jayne an update."

"What are you going to tell her?"

"As little as possible," she said as we exited the bathroom. "At least until you've duped your mom's swindler."

I PASSED THE GAME ROOM on my way to the kitchen, caught a glimpse of Arch and Beckett shooting pool with my brother. Couldn't hear what they were saying, but the mood seemed jovial enough. Whatever words Arch and Beckett traded in the office must've been brief. I couldn't help wondering what was said. Did Arch warn Beckett to keep his distance? Did Beckett tell Arch that I'd asked him to run off Gish? I pressed a palm to my flushed cheeks, wondering if my brother had grilled Arch—or, rather, the baron—on his investments. Christopher was all about high finance.

Mind racing, I pushed through the kitchen door…and caught Mom and Dad in a lip-lock.

Oh. My. God.

I silently whisked sideways into the open pantry, skulked behind the partially closed door. Why didn't I back out the way I came in? Head thunk. Now I was stuck with the canned cocktail fruit and jars of dill pickles, the image of my parents making out forever burned on my corneas. The fact that they were kissing was good. It meant they'd made up, right? It's just that I'd never seen them *kiss* like *that,* all grabby-feely. *Criminy.*

"George, dear," I heard Mom say in a breathless voice. "We must get hold of ourselves. What if someone walks in?"

I dropped my forehead into my hands.

"So what if they do?" he said. "No crime against kissing my wife. I've been wanting to get my hands on you ever since we left the jailhouse."

Okay. That was hot. But that was my *dad!*

"Because of the makeover?"

"No, because you gave that photographer hell."

"I made a scene," she said. "You weren't embarrassed?"

"Are you kidding? That rascal threatened to scandalize our daughter. You gave him what for."

"I gave him a bloody nose."

"Belted him good."

"*Pursed* him good, you mean."

They both laughed. I blinked. Did Mom just make a joke?

"Seeing you stand up for our daughter like that made me proud," Dad said on a more serious note.

"I love Evelyn, too, George."

I bit my lip. *Don't cry. Don't cry.*

"I know you do, Marilyn."

"Then why didn't you tell me why you wanted to buy this place?"

"Didn't think you'd be happy about me encouraging her

musical aspirations. Also…I was going through a bit of a crisis, I guess. I needed to feel like the man of the house again. The caretaker. Guess you'd call that chauvinistic."

"Are you saying retirement made you feel less of a man?"

"Guess I am."

Oh, Dad.

"Oh, George."

He cleared his throat. "I should've been more open about the purchase of this place."

Mom sighed. "I should've been more sensitive to your's and Evelyn's needs."

"We should talk more," he said.

"So much to say."

Tell him about the savings bonds!

"What about later tonight?"

"Your place or mine?" Mom purred.

Purred, for crying out loud.

"Sorry I'm late. How can I help?" Nic pushed through the kitchen door, then stopped in her tracks. "Oops. Sorry."

From her reaction, Mom and Dad must've been going for another smooch.

"Quite all right, Nicole," Mom said, sounding more like herself. "Grab a spatula. You can help me with the burgers. George, you go play pool with the boys. Go on now. Leave the cooking to us girls."

I watched through the crack, saw my dad saunter out the door, noted his cocky smile. Jeez.

"Where's Evie?" Nic asked.

"I was wondering the same," said Mom.

I peeked around the pantry door, caught Nic's eye and mouthed, "Help!"

She shook her head as if to say, *Only you.*

"What is it, dear?" Mom asked.

"Nothing, I just…" Nic palmed her forehead. "I think I feel a migraine coming on."

"Goodness. You girls really need to eat better."

"I'd kill for an aspirin."

"I have some in my purse," Mom said. "You watch the burgers. I'll be right back."

As soon as she left, I zipped out of the pantry. "Thanks, Nic."

"What the hell?"

"I'll tell you later." I grabbed a hamburger patty and slapped it on the grill. I asked Nic about her last commercial shoot.

In the midst of her lamenting the idiosyncrasies of the director, Mom returned with a glass of water and a bottle of pills. "Evelyn, where have you been?"

"Bathroom. That time," I said, knowing she wouldn't press about something as intimate as my monthly.

"Ah." She tapped two aspirin into Nic's hands, casting me a look. "I guess you're feeling a little under the weather then, too."

"A little." Not wholly a lie. The scene with Beckett had left me shaken.

Her lips twitched. "Would it make you feel better to know that your Dad and I are on the mend?"

I smiled while we flipped burgers in tandem. "It would."

CHAPTER THIRTY

GETTING THROUGH THE rest of the night was a trial. Although I was thrilled about Mom and Dad's good humor, I couldn't help dwelling on Randolph Gish. As long as he was in the picture, my parents' reunion was on shaky ground. No telling how Dad would react if he learned Mom had been bilked for six grand. What if he went after Gish himself? Then there were Mom's feelings to consider. She thought of Gish as a friend.

The more I thought on it, the more I wanted to keep the truth from being revealed. Better to let Chameleon handle Fancy Feet. Better to get the six thousand back in Mom's hands my way. I really needed to talk to Christopher. So far, our conversation had been limited to superficial table talk.

"You all right, Evelyn?" Dad asked as he spooned Neapolitan ice cream into everyone's dish.

"I'm just drained," I said honestly. I'd been in town for two days and it had been one emotional moment or physical fiasco after another. The only reason I didn't beg off dinner sooner was because I enjoyed seeing Mom and Dad together. They were talking and laughing, and whatever was happening between them was real. Every other relationship in the room felt strained or false.

Secrets and lies weighed heavily on my heart, making

me thoughtful and abnormally quiet. Plus, I hadn't been alone with Arch since he'd caught me coming out of the office with Beckett. The fact that he was playing the besotted baron only made me feel worse. What was he feeling on the inside? For real?

A phone rang. My brother's. "Be right back," he said.

Meanwhile Mom grilled Arch on the history of Broxley. Fascinating, although I had to wonder how much was fact and how much fiction.

I am the Baron of Broxley.

Was he really?

Christopher returned. "That was Sandy. Small crisis."

"Are the kids okay?" Mom asked.

"They're fine. But I need to go." He said quick goodbyes, no hugs or kisses, though he did shake hands with Arch and Beckett.

When he got to me, I stood. "I'll walk you to the door." I registered his surprise, bit back a sad smile. Brother and sister yet strangers.

"Your friends," he said as we walked, "they're nice."

I looked over my shoulder and caught all three eyeballing me. Their concern was tangible. "Yes, they are."

"Duvall seems…attentive."

"Yes, he is. Surprising, I know, considering younger men typically don't find older women attractive."

"Obviously I was unaware or I wouldn't have said that, Evelyn."

I flushed, feeling contrite. He'd made the comment days ago in passing, but the hurt lingered. "I know. It just…struck a nerve."

"You're very attractive."

I cleared my throat, uncomfortable with the compliment. "Thanks."

"And persuasive. I've never seen Mom and Dad so... clingy. What did you say to get them back together?"

"Nothing specific. We just talked."

"Talked."

"Had a conversation. Dad and me. Mom and me. We should try it sometime."

He leaned against the doorjamb, brow quirked. "You and me."

I shrugged. "Yeah."

He pursed his lips in thought. "So... Did you find out what she spent the money on?"

"Yeah." I frowned, wondering what to reveal. If I told him about Gish, he'd want to go to Sheriff Jaffe. "I think I know how to get the money back into Mom's hands without embarrassing her and without Dad ever knowing what went down."

Christopher frowned. "Sounds fishy."

"It sort of is."

"Illegal?"

"I—we—won't be breaking the law, no. But it would involve a certain degree of deception."

"In other words, we—you and I—would be lying to Mom and Dad."

Think like Arch. Be a Chameleon. I tucked my hair behind my ears, shrugged. "There are all kinds of lies."

"Like the kind that spare people's feelings. White lies."

In that moment I felt a bizarre click with my brother. Did he actually on occasion fib to be kind? If so, it definitely put him in a new, softer light. "I don't think Mom and Dad are officially back together," I said. "They have issues to work through. But they are on the mend and I don't want this bond snafu to muck things up. I can come up with three thousand dollars. I was hoping you might be willing to fork in the other half."

"Why not ask your baron? I'm sure he could afford—"

"I think it should come from family."

He narrowed his eyes. "You're determined to fix this."

"I am."

He looked at me differently, too, with something akin to respect. "When you're ready, come and see me at the bank." He pushed off the doorjamb with a small smile. "We'll talk."

I returned to the table more shaken than before, though I adopted my best poker face.

Arch leaned into me. "You okay?"

So much for my poker face. "I think I just bonded with my brother," I whispered.

"You look exhausted, Evelyn," Dad said.

"She's under the weather," Mom said. "Archibald, maybe you should…"

"Brilliant idea." He pressed a hand to the small of my back. "Let's call it a night, lass."

I hedged at first, then acquiesced when Nic and Beckett volunteered to help Mom and Dad clean up. "Promise I'll be in a better mood tomorrow. I just need a good night's sleep."

Arch drove us back to the Appleseed. It was dark and the roads were slick with rain. Thankfully he proceeded at a cautious speed, unlike earlier today when he'd zipped along this route in anger. Was it only this afternoon that I'd accused him of jealousy and he'd intimated he loved me? Just now, I was grateful for his silence, although I did wonder what was going on in that complicated brain.

By the time we reached the B and B I was more anxious than curious. I recognized his silence for what it was: the calm before the storm. I couldn't weather another confrontation, not tonight. Plus, I'd sort of bonded with my family and I wanted to fall asleep enveloped in that warm, fuzzy feeling. "I'm really tired," I said the moment we stepped inside.

"Meaning you want to go straight to bed."

I nodded.

"Alone?"

I didn't meet his gaze. "Well, Nic is here and—"

"She'll be sleeping in the room across the hall."

"That's Gina's room."

"Gina and Tabasco are spending another night at the hotel."

"Still, Beckett—"

"Knows we're hooked up. No need to pretend anymore, Sunshine." He stroked my cheek. "Just say it, yeah?"

I tensed with dread. "What?"

"You *dinnae* want to sleep with me tonight."

I bit my lower lip, looked anywhere but at him. "It's just…"

"It's been an emotional day and you need some time alone, yeah?"

"Yeah." He knew me so well and I didn't know him at all. Or at least didn't trust what I *thought* I knew. I blinked back tears, hoping a good night's sleep would revitalize my inner bad girl. She'd rocked in London. My happy place. With Arch.

Just the two of us.

He took my hand and led me up the stairs. He vibrated with restrained…something. Anger? Frustration? Disappointment? I didn't ask. I didn't want to know. Not tonight.

I expected him to leave me at my bedroom door, but he followed me inside. I tossed my *Lucy* tote on the rocker, toed off my Mary Janes and turned down the quilt.

He didn't take the hint.

He leaned against the doorjamb, arms folded. My brother's faded Indy 500 T-shirt stretched tight across his chest. The short sleeves rode up, exposing the monochrome tattoo that generally reduced me to a drooling sex monkey. Mom had commented on that tattoo—curious as to why a titled man would indulge in such a thing. He'd admitted to being a rebel in his younger days with a fascination for Celtic mythology and art. He'd said his grandfather, an artist, had sketched the design, standing alongside him as the tattoo artist made it permanent. Knowing how much Arch loved Bernard Duvall, the story had been especially poignant to me. I wondered if it was true. The line between fact and fiction with Arch was forever blurred.

"This afternoon, when you went back to your house— what happened between you and your ma, Sunshine?"

The question caught me by surprise. I'd expected him to ask about Beckett. Either the G-man had kept my ramblings in confidence or Arch wanted to hear it from me. His quiet regard intensified my guilt.

I should've gone to him first.

I sat on the end of my bed. A nervous rash prickled. Unsettled, I spilled everything about my dad, the purchase of the tavern, Mom's feelings about me and her friendship with Randolph Gish.

Throughout the recounted tale we both held our ground. Me sitting on the bed. Him standing in the doorway. It felt…ominous.

"I'm glad you and your ma are talking," he said when I finished on an exhausted sigh. "And it seems your parents are on the road to reconciliation. As far as Gish… leave it to me, yeah?"

Him. Not us. Not *we*. Red-faced, I met his gaze.

He arched one brow. "Or is it already being handled?"

My stomach dropped.

"You already spoke to Beckett *aboot* this, yeah?"

"Is that what he told you?"

"He told me you were exhausted and overwhelmed. Said he just happened to be there when you cracked and steered you into the office so you could have a cry in private."

Yeah. That sounded good. I was insanely relieved to know Beckett left out the part where I'd asked him to run Gish out of town. Oh, and the bit where I'd acknowledged a mutual physical awareness. And no way was I going to admit I'd assessed Beckett the wiser choice. It's not as though I planned to play it safe.

"Other than that," Arch said, "he was tight-lipped."

"That's because there's nothing to tell." I wasn't lying, I told myself. I was sparing his feelings.

He dragged a hand over that sexy goatee and studied me with those devastating eyes.

I realized, with a mental curse, that I was scratching my prickly skin. A surefire indication that I was uncomfortable. My nervous tell. He knew it and he knew I knew it. I eased my hand to my lap. But too late.

Busted.

"Private stuff, yeah?" He pushed off the door frame and walked to the desk.

I watched, heart in throat, as he opened the drawer and took out my purple pen and diary. The one he'd bought

me, the one he'd signed. He passed me the book, para-
phrased the words my dad had uttered to me as a girl. "For
when your heart and mind's jammed up." He kissed my
forehead and left the room. "Good night, Sunshine."

CHAPTER THIRTY-ONE

"NICE TO SEE MR. AND MRS. Parish getting along," Milo said ten minutes into the drive home.

"Yes, it was."

"Christopher seemed like a decent guy."

"If by *decent* you mean he has a broomstick up his ass," Nic said, "then, yeah. He's decent."

Milo smiled in the dark. She was right. Evie's brother was wired tight. But he didn't get a bad vibe off the man. As for Evie's parents, though they weren't as repressed as he'd expected, they were perhaps reserved and old-fashioned, and he had to wonder how Evie had become, well, Evie.

His chest constricted when he thought about the way she'd come to him and begged for his help. He'd been ready to follow through with her wishes even though he didn't fully agree with her method, but then he'd thought about what Arch had said about tainting that purity. He was certain if she detached and looked at the bigger picture, she wouldn't want to dispense with Gish so rashly. He'd been right. But then she'd broken down and he'd felt like shit.

He still felt like shit.

He'd wanted to kiss away those tears. But she hadn't moved into his arms, he'd pulled her against his body. His initiative, not hers. He'd settled for comforting her, but then—god*damn*—she'd vocalized the chemistry between them. It made it worse. Mainly because she wanted to ignore it. Which meant he had to ignore it.

Unless she changed her mind.

His exchange with Arch had been brief. *Nothing happened. Wish I could say different. She was upset and I just happened to be the convenient shoulder.*

You sound suitably disappointed. Warms my heart, yeah?

Fuck you.

Bugger off.

The dance.

In truth, nothing *had* happened. Except she'd made it clear her heart was with Arch.

Milo flexed his fingers on the wheel. He needed to get his head out of his pants and back in the game. He needed a distraction. Just now, the best he could do was Nicole.

He turned onto the gravel road, glanced at the woman in the passenger seat. Moonlight accentuated her exotic beauty. This was a woman who got recognized for her looks first and everything else, like her talent and wit, after. Ten to one she'd been used and abused more than once. *I learned the hard way.* That accounted for her tough outer shell. Maybe if he softened toward her, she'd soften toward him. A truce, at least, would be nice. "What'd you do with that memory card?" he blurted for lack of something to say. In truth, he was curious.

"Destroyed it."

"Smart."

"I thought so."

"How long have you been an actress?"

"A long time."

"You're good."

"Thanks."

"When Mrs. Parish asked how we met, you had me believing in love at first sight."

"Like you said, I'm good."

"So you don't actually believe in love at first sight."

She rolled her eyes, then looked out the side window. As if there was anything to see except rain-drenched plowed fields.

Milo wasn't big on small talk, but her silence irritated him, especially after she'd been so sociable with the Parishes. Mostly he didn't want to be alone with his thoughts. "Your other friend, Jayne—is she a realist like you? Or a dreamer like Evie?"

"Jayne is like no one you've ever met." She shifted in her seat. "Is there something on your mind, Slick?"

The moniker grated, but only because it sounded like an insult coming from her. Was that how Evie felt when he called her Twinkie? "Why do you ask?"

"Because you suck at chitchat. Tells me it's not something you normally engage in. So why now?"

Because he didn't want to think about Evie. Evie and Arch. Evie and Arch in bed.

She blew out a breath. "Does she know?"

"Does who know what?"

"Does Evie know you're in love with her?"

He tightened his grip on the steering wheel, schooled his expression. "If that's what you think—"

"It's in your eyes, Slick. I know that look. Subtle but present. The look of *lerve*," she teased. "I caught it this morning at breakfast, then at the jailhouse when you passed her the aspirin, then later, coming out of the office." She whistled low. "*L-O-V-E* or something damn close."

"I can't decide if you're full of shit, a pain in the ass or both." Milo could feel his blood pressure rising, but he played it cool. "What I do know is that you're off base."

"I'm not the only one who noticed," she said, blowing over his denial. "Arch sees it. He's just better at hiding his jealousy than most men. Listen, I get it," she rushed on, and Milo cursed himself for opening the floodgates. "Everybody loves Evie. She's sweet and funny, kind and generous, smart and talented, a little on the whimsical side. Hell, *I* love Evie. Jayne loves Evie. The kid who delivers her Chinese food loves Evie. The only one who doesn't is that bastard ex of hers who eloped with his pregnant girlfriend."

Milo glommed on to that last part as he pulled into the drive of the Appleseed B and B and parked beside the Mercedes. "Stone eloped?"

"He didn't even have the courtesy to tell Evie. Didn't tell her about knocking up Sasha, either. I got the honor on both counts. Lucky me."

He keyed off the ignition, processed.

She blew out a breath. "Look, Evie's been through a lot these past couple of years. She's trying to find new direction, happiness, and she thinks those things lie with Chameleon. I'm not happy about that, in case you haven't noticed, but it's her life. Unfortunately she's fallen in love with rebel boy—hope that doesn't come as a shock to you—and I'm not sure he's the best man for her. Not sure you're that man, either," she said as she opened the car door, "but, of the two, you are certainly the most trustworthy."

She swung her long legs out of the car. Before he could rebut, she got in the last word. "Hurt her, Milo, and I will become your worst nightmare."

She slammed shut the door and he sat there, stunned.

"Well, hell." He wasn't sure what to make of her observation. Wasn't sure what to make of *her.* He'd flown out here hoping to clear his head, to make some decisions, except he was more confused now than when he'd left Atlantic City.

One thing was certain—he didn't want to stay here any longer than he had to. No good could come from being cooped up under the same roof with Miss Tell It Like It Is and Arch and Evie, who were probably in bed together. His life had turned into a frickin' soap opera. It smacked of the triangle debacle he'd gone through with his ex-wife. Only, instead of the injured party, this time he felt like the fucking "other man"—and he hadn't even done anything. "Fuck!"

He pushed out of the car, sloshing around the muddy fricking yard, holding out his cell phone and looking for a goddamn fricking signal. At last, two bars. He phoned Woody for the second time in three hours. "What'd you get on Randolph Gish?"

Five minutes later he entered the house, surprised to find Arch sitting in the dark on the living-room sofa, nursing a glass of scotch and watching a black-and-white movie on the nineteen-inch TV. "Where's Evie?" he asked while shucking his muddy shoes.

"In her room."

"Nicole?"

"Marched straight upstairs, yeah? Not sure if she's in her room or Evie's." He polished off his drink. "You two have words?"

"She certainly spoke her mind." Milo slipped into the dining room and grabbed his stashed laptop. He came back, placed the computer on the coffee table and sat next to Arch. "Woody e-mailed something you're going to want to see."

"Something on the senator or Turner?"

"Something on Gish."

Just like that it was no longer personal but professional. United purpose. The warped camaraderie. He motioned to the liquor bottle. "Grab another glass, will you?"

By the time Arch came back from the kitchen he'd fired up the computer and was signing on to the Internet. "Goddamn dial-up," he complained as the other man poured and handed him a glass of scotch—two fingers, neat. He pointed to the TV. "What are you watching?"

All About Eve."

"Are you serious?"

"Ever seen it?"

"Don't think so." Milo squinted at the actress on screen. "Who's that?"

"Fucking Anne Baxter. How can you not know Anne Baxter?"

He glanced from the TV to the laptop—still connecting—and back. "Is that a young Marilyn Monroe?"

Arch grunted. "Her you know."

Milo took a hit off his scotch. "What's it about?"

"An aging actress and her theater friends."

"You're kidding."

"Lot of memorable quotes in this flick, yeah?"

"Hit me."

"'We're a breed apart. We're the original displaced persons.'"

"Huh. Don't recognize it, but I like it. Could apply to our kind, as well as Evie's." He sipped more scotch, keyed in his password when the screen popped up. "Let's hear another."

"'Fasten your seat belts, it's going to be a bumpy night.'"

"That one I've heard. Hold that thought." He typed in another password, a site secured by Woody for Chameleon activity, clicked on the specified e-mail and downloaded a file.

"This could take all night," Arch said, refilling his glass. "How do people deal with*oot* high-speed-modem access?"

"Almost there," Milo said.

"Almost where, Slick?"

He glanced up and saw Nicole standing to their left. He was surprised to see her wearing glasses. Which meant she wore contact lenses during the day. Just now, it was too dark and she was standing too far away for him to tell if the contacts had augmented the color of her eyes. The vibrancy of their green had almost been unnatural. Meanwhile the glasses with the oval black-rimmed frames did little to detract from her sexy aura. She'd changed into a black lounging suit and had plaited her hair into two long braids. Face scrubbed of makeup, glasses and all, she still looked exotic as hell. At least he noticed. Hello, distraction. "We're doing some late-night work."

"Looks like you're watching TV." She moved into the room. *All About Eve?*

"Aye," said Arch.

"Priceless." She smirked at Milo. "Ever seen it?"

"No."

"Story about ambition and betrayal."

"Nice." Milo minimized the computer screen.

"What are you drinking?"

"Scotch," said Arch.

"Mind if I join you?"

"Yes," both men said.

She scooted into the kitchen, presumably to get a glass.

"Pain in the ass," Milo muttered, pulling up the file.

"Relax, mate. Anything classified in here?"

"Don't think so." Milo pointed at the mug shot. "That our guy?"

"That's him. Quite a few aliases, yeah?" He leaned in next to Milo, skimmed the text. "Transient grifter. Lengthy arrest record. Made a lot of mistakes. Sloppy."

"Who?" Nicole settled next to Milo and helped herself to the liquor.

Up close and personal now, he could see that her eyes were indeed jade-green. Unique. He frowned. "I'm asking nicely, Pocahontas. Take your drink and make yourself scarce."

"That wasn't a question, Slick. But here's one." She peeked at the file. "Is this about Evie?"

Arch kept reading. "Aye."

"Then I'm staying."

"Fine," Milo said, nudging her away. He pointed to a chaise lounge. "Would you mind sitting over there?"

"View's better here."

He muttered under his breath.

"I've been called worse," she said, then curled her feet beneath her and sipped her drink.

"No convictions," Arch said. "But look here."

Nicole leaned in and again Milo nudged her away. "That's the part of the Kid's report that caught my interest."

"We could play it a couple of ways, you know?"

"Agreed. I say we let Evie make the call."

Arch rubbed his hands over his face—conflicted, perturbed—but holding his thoughts close to his chest. "Agreed," he finally said. "But she's wiped *oot*. Maybe this could wait until morning."

Nicole stirred. "She'll sleep better if something's settled tonight."

"In that case," Milo said, "would you mind asking your friend to come downstairs?"

She set aside her drink, muttered under her breath.

He cocked his head. "I've been called worse."

"Wait," Arch said. "I'll go up and explain the situation, lay *oot* the alternatives."

Milo summed up a lecture in one sentence. "Let her decide."

Arch saluted, then rose. He may as well have given him the finger.

Milo watched as he climbed the stairs. In all the times they'd argued they'd never thrown punches, but something told him that day was near.

"What do you want to bet we don't learn the outcome until tomorrow morning?" Nicole noted, picking up the liquor bottle and topping off both glasses.

Milo didn't answer. He was too busy warding off images of Arch seducing Evie into submission. If the Scot had his way, they'd take down Gish without her.

"Don't know about you, but I couldn't sleep now if I tried," Nicole plowed on. "What are the alternatives? Glad you asked. You could let me read that file and fill me in on Evie's choices."

"Or?"

"I could fill you in on what's transpired in this movie so far and we could watch the rest while polishing off this bottle."

Milo shut down the laptop, snatched up his drink in one hand, the TV remote in the other, and hiked the volume. "So what's Bette Davis's problem?"

CHAPTER THIRTY-TWO

I VENTED IN MY DIARY until my fingers cramped. My heart and mind were still jammed. I took a hot shower, hoping to ease my tense muscles and rinse away the icky feeling of betraying the man I love. Which is sort of what I did when I asked Beckett to solve my problem instead of Arch. At least I'm sure that's how he viewed it. In all honesty, I couldn't blame him for being bent. Especially after he'd admitted his desire to be my champion. A man's ego, I'd decided, was as fragile as, if not more than, a woman's.

The more I obsessed on the day, the more my stomach hurt. I regretted not driving over as I'd first intended and handling Randolph Gish in my own way. I'd second-guessed my abilities. If I didn't believe in me, why should anyone else?

I glanced at the clock—11:00 p.m. Even though I'd been in bed for half an hour, even though my mind and body were drained, I was still wide-awake. I actually welcomed the knock on the door. "Come in," I said, switching on the nightstand lamp.

The door opened and closed and suddenly Arch was standing next to my bed. He'd changed into gray sweat-pants and a loose-fitting black tee. Nothing sexy about the ensemble, yet he took my breath away.

"I expected Nic," I said, cursing the hitch in my voice.

"I need to speak with you, lass."

My mouth went dry and my stomach flipped. "Are you breaking up with me?" Hello. What was I, sixteen?

"Do you want me to?"

"No."

"Good. Scoot over."

He climbed into bed, on top of the covers, and crossed his legs at the ankles. Repositioning a pillow, he relaxed against the headboard and pulled me into his arms. "You smell good, yeah? Like soap."

"I took a shower."

"Sorry I missed it."

Zing. Zap. No matter our conflicts, the physical attraction sparked like white lightning. I ignored the tingling between my thighs, braced myself for our talk. "What's on your mind?"

"Randolph Gish."

Not Beckett. My heart settled in my chest as I rested my cheek on his shoulder. "What about him?"

"Woody sent over a report. A criminal-arrest report."

"So he *is* a con artist." I tried to sit up, but he pressed my head back to his shoulder.

"Just listen. Gish isn't in the league of the grifters Chameleon normally cracks. Still, he easily falls into your rat-bastard-rat category. Though he's been arrested on various short cons, he specializes in Sweetheart scams. Nurturing relationships through Internet dating services and business ventures."

"Like his dance lessons."

"Aye."

Pain zinged up the side of my face. I relaxed and massaged my jaw, skin sizzling when Arch took over the task. Gentle yet strong, his touch worked miracles. "If he's been arrested, why isn't he in jail?" I asked.

"Several arrests," he said, "but no convictions. Gish is sloppy, but he keeps slipping through the justice system for dozens of reasons. Not important now. What *is* important is that there's an *oot*standing warrant, a victim willing to testify and enough evidence to put him away for a good bit."

"What did he do?"

"Short story—he embezzled the savings of a seventy-year-old widow by taking and cashing blank checks over a one-year period."

"How much?"

"Fifty-two thousand."

My head and heart throbbed. "I suppose he pretended to love her, earned her confidence."

"That's the way of it, yeah?"

"Where is she now?"

He didn't say anything, and this time I did push away so I could look into his eyes. "Where is she, Arch?"

"She's a ward of the state. No family. No funds."

My blood pumped. "Rat bastard."

"Aye."

"We have to turn him in right away."

"That's one choice."

I wiggled around to face him and perched on my knees. "What do you mean *choice?* He has to pay for what he did to that poor woman. We have to inform Sheriff Jaffe or call whatever police department or agency that issued the warrant."

"Blow the whistle now, make a scene, and your ma will know she was bilked."

"Her money's history anyway, right? Spent or stashed

in an overseas bank account. Along with any other booty he might've scored while in town." That's why I'd approached Christopher about replacing the funds ourselves.

"He's not stashing his score in a cookie jar, I can tell you that."

"And the fact that he's still here signals he intends to soak Mom for more. Shooting for another fifty grand, maybe?" I curled my fingers into fists. "I could wring that thief's neck!"

Arch angled his head. "Remember, lass—he *didnae* steal your ma's money. This was a crime of persuasion."

"That's why those crimes are hard to convict."

"One of the reasons, aye."

"I don't care about the money. I talked to Christopher and we're going to cover the loss. It's only six thousand," I said, although that was a lot of money to me. "It could be worse." Like *fifty-six* thousand. "At least Mom has Dad and Christopher and me. She's not destitute. She's not alone." My heart broke for that fleeced widow.

Arch interlaced his fingers with mine. "You're a good soul, Evie Parish."

I'd given my friends the runaround, entangled my family in a web of lies, run to Beckett instead of Arch… My cheeks flushed. "Not so good."

"Matter of perspective," he said, studying me at length. "Remember when I said there are all kinds of lies?"

I moistened my lips. "Yes."

"There's more at stake here than your ma's money. There's her pride. Remember how you felt when you were scammed in the islands?"

Like it was yesterday. "Stupid. Humiliated. Violated. Angry."

"Multiply the intensity of those feelings by ten, Sunshine. That was a street hustle. A hit-and-run. Gish has been working your ma for weeks."

"She thinks they're friends." I felt ill. "Good friends."

"We could finesse this so your ma never knows that Gish took her for a ride, yeah? Lead her to believe the project went belly-up. Like playing the market, she risked and lost her investment. Advise Gish to claim he's moving on to be with his lover. The money's gone, but her pride is intact."

Essentially what Beckett and I had discussed earlier this evening. Only I'd planned to insert the cash, supplied by Christopher and me, in an envelope along with a letter from Gish. A letter Beckett would type and coerce the rat bastard into signing. *An explanation and apology for the cancellation of the building project.*

Again I felt a pang of guilt. Either Beckett had shared the details of our talk after all or he and Arch thought an awful lot alike. *Taught him everything I know.* I decided on the latter because it made me feel better. "You're suggesting we lie to save Mom's feelings."

"I'm suggesting it as a choice."

"By *moving on* to be with his lover, I assume you really mean Beckett would turn Gish in to the appropriate authorities."

"Bang-on."

"If Gish's case makes the news, there's a chance Mom will find out anyway."

"He's wanted on the West Coast, and though what he did is despicable, it's not big news, love. Not to mention he played that game under another assumed name. Randolph Gish is just one of many. *Dinnae* see how she'd make the connection."

I chewed my thumbnail, considered Arch's scenario. "Handling Gish and my mom's situation as you mentioned would take time. By finessing, you mean manipulating Gish, some sort of turnaround confidence. Meanwhile that widow has no satisfaction, no closure. And who's to say the slick menace won't take off on a whim. He is on the run, after all. Greenville's just a stopover, a small town where he can lie low, pull a short con or two. And, call me cynical, but who's to say my mom won't fall prey to a future scam. A telescammer? An inheritance swindle?"

Arch noted the fraud and swindle books stacked on the night table. He scratched his forehead and frowned. "*Dinnae* know *aboot* you and this research, Sunshine."

"You're the one who said I needed to open my eyes to the real world."

"Aye. What was I thinking?"

"You were thinking you wanted to protect me because you…care. You didn't want me to get suckered and hurt in the future. You opened my eyes, and I learned and I won't make the same mistake twice because now I'm educated. Mom is all about education. Part of me thinks I should show her the courtesy you showed me."

His lips curved into a small smile. "Like I said—a good soul."

My heart slammed against my ribs. Lately I'd been thinking good girls finish last. Now I wasn't so sure. "What's my other choice?" I asked, trying not to think about the way he made my body sing with that sexy mouth.

"Beckett makes use of that badge straightaway tomorrow and Gish is gone. No fuss. No reasons. Just gone. Your ma is a smart woman. If you *dinnae* tell her she was fleeced, she'll figure it *oot* on her own. How she'll handle it, I *cannae* say."

My head spun. "Let me get this straight. Either way, Beckett's going to turn Gish over to the authorities. What I need to decide is, do I want my mom to know she was fleeced or do I want to shelter her from the ugly truth?"

"Also, do you want her to eat the loss or spin it so that she gets *her* money back?"

Realist and dreamer warred within. "Part of me wants to come clean with Mom. *You were duped and here's how I know.* A wake-up call to the real world, my new world. *I know you're humiliated—been there—but now you'll be sensitive to other scams.* Except she's lived most of her life in the real world, a grounded woman with narrow views. Finally, after all these years, she's thrown caution to the wind, indulged in something artistic, indulged in herself, took a chance on the unknown, invested in a dream."

I dragged my hands through my damp hair, wanting to rip it out by the darkening roots. "This Sweetheart scam could turn her off to ever going out on a limb again. What if she reverts to her old self—closed, wary? Not sure how Dad would feel about that. And how would their marriage fare? How would *she* fare? She's happier now than I have ever seen her, Arch. She's moved on." Instead of pacing, I hugged my knees to my chest and rocked. "I don't want Mom to go back. I want her to escape this mess with her pride *and* her money. I want to deliver Gish's head on a plate to that poor widow."

Humor and admiration sparked in his gaze. "You want it all."

"Call me a dreamer."

"I was thinking more along the lines of a crusader."

I scrunched my brow. "Really?"

"A quality that seduces and frustrates me simultaneously."

That coaxed a smile out of me.

He reached out and took my hands, stroked his thumbs over my knuckles. "So instead of a white lie or a lie by omission, we move up to a whopper, yeah?"

"Meaning?"

"You get it all, but not with*oot* sacrifice."

"Define *sacrifice*."

"Keeping your family in the dark *aboot* Chameleon. Continuing status quo at least until we've handled things for Senator Clark."

"Secrets and lies."

"Smoke and mirrors."

"For the greater good."

He kissed my palm, infusing me with passion and purpose.

The connection. The bond. So implausible. So real.

"Does Beckett know about Woody's report?" I asked.

"He's the one who filled me in."

"What does he think we should do about Gish?"

"He said it's your call."

A muscle jumped under his eye, and I realized that once again it seemed like I was deferring to Beckett's judgment instead of trusting Arch's experience. A Freudian slip that I scrambled to cover. "What do you think?"

"It's your call."

My heart pounded with resolve. "I want it all."

"You're sure?"

"Positive." The tension in my body eased and I knew, heart and soul, it was the right thing to do. The dreamer in me made way for the crusader, a champion of noble causes, a person of action. A warrior and peacemaker rolled into one. Chief Little Turtle, with a spin. "So what's the plan?"

"We'll hash it *oot* with Beckett in the morning, yeah?" He paused, a thoughtful pause that caused my neck to itch. "Evie...I need to ask you something."

Don't scratch. "Yes?"

"Back at the pub...I understand that you were upset. But why did you go to Beckett? Why not me?"

Breathe, Evie, breathe. "His badge."

"Come again?"

"Mom had just told me about Gish and the investment. I was angry. Call it a bad case of tunnel vision. I wanted Beckett to bully Gish with his badge. To run him out of town."

His eyebrows rose. "That's it?"

Initially, on the surface, yes, it was. "Isn't that enough? Essentially asking a government agent to behave like a thug? I'm pretty sure I insulted Beckett."

He smiled at that.

Sensing he was willing to live and let live, relief whooshed through my body. "I'm sorry."

"No need to apologize." He shook his head, laughed. "I seem to be having champion issues. Bloody unsettling."

Okay, I had trust issues with this man, but knowing he wanted to be my champion blew my reservations to smithereens. At least for this pulse-tripping moment.

"It's been a wild day, lass. Get some sleep."

I clasped his arm when he tried to roll away. "Stay. Please."

He waggled his eyebrows and adopted a Humphrey Bogart lisp. "You're the boss, Applesauce."

Amazing that he could make me laugh after a day like this. My body hummed with equal parts elation and exhaustion. I didn't know what had transpired between Arch and Beckett, but something had inspired Arch to offer me an active role in this matter even if it was simply allowing me to choose the course of action. I felt empowered. It did wonders for my spirits. Earlier I'd obsessed on problems, now solutions percolated in my brain.

He switched off the lamp, and together we snuggled under the covers, fully clothed.

I melted against his warm, hard body, wrapping my arm around his torso, throwing a leg over his thighs. I sighed when his mouth found mine. I tasted liquor on his lips, his breath, his tongue—*sinful.* Yet it was the tenderness in his touch that went to my head. This relationship wasn't perfect, but it had wondrous possibilities. *This,* I thought, *is where I want to be.* This is where the party is. In this man's arms. In this man's life.

Dance, Evie, dance.

"Arch?" I whispered, drunk on his potent charisma.

"Yeah?"

"I love you."

He stroked a thumb over my cheek. "I know."

If it weren't for the smile in his voice, I would've been miffed or hurt by his arrogant, noncommittal reply. But I recognized the patter.

I love you.

I know.

A vision of an ambitious princess and a shifty pilot came to mind. "Princess Leia and Han Solo. *Star Wars— The Empire Strikes Back.*"

"I was hoping you'd get that reference." He distracted me with a kiss that rocketed me into a galaxy far, far away.

CHAPTER THIRTY-THREE

MILO WOKE UP WITH Nicole's head in his lap. *Hey, now.*

Not wanting to wake her, he resisted the urge to shift and stretch. He blinked away the cobwebs, trying to recall how they'd ended up like this. Ah, yes, the movie and a bottle of scotch.

He faintly remembered matching Nicole glass for glass. Recalled making it to the end of *All About Eve* and midway through a documentary on war. He remembered she was a liberal. Not a surprise. Aside from Arnold Schwarzenegger and a few random others, weren't all entertainers left-wing?

He didn't remember falling asleep—sitting up, no less. And the last he recalled, she'd been coiled at the opposite end of the couch like a bespectacled black cat. Now her glasses were on the coffee table and she was curled on her side…her head in his lap.

Huh.

The light from the TV illuminated the room in a soft haze. Moe, Larry and Curly yukked it up in muted silence. He squinted at his watch. Five in the morning. He studied Nicole's exquisite features. The little-girl braids and lack of makeup perpetuated an air of innocence. Of course, as soon as she woke and spoke, that illusion would be shot to hell. Nicole Sparks had issues. Considering he struggled with his own demons, they'd make a volatile match. Not that he was interested. Not that she'd flashed signals. They didn't like each other. If they did, even a little, last night would have ended differently.

Instead of getting busy between the sheets, they'd passed out on the couch. A blessing, really. He'd had enough personal drama, compliments of his ex. When it came to a mate, he wanted someone with a lighter spirit, someone like…Evie.

Damn.

Okay, then, why was Mr. Happy suddenly pulsing to life?

Well, Beckett, he thought reasonably, *maybe it's because a beautiful woman's luscious mouth is, at this moment, a scant two inches from your johnson. Oh, and you haven't been laid in four months.*

Right.

"Hell."

Nicole shifted, doubling his misery. His cock twitched and his thigh vibrated. The latter a result of his ringing cell. Signal in the house? This morning was full of surprises.

He eased out from under Sleeping Beauty, slipping a throw pillow under her head before slipping away and out the front door. He palmed his cell, glanced at the incoming number. Tabasco. "What's up?"

"Sorry to call so late, Jazzman."

"You mean, early."

"Haven't been to bed yet."

"You've been at the tables all night?"

"Mostly. Hot Legs, too. But it paid off. She's in. Our crooked dealer not only told her about Turner's private game, he invited her to breakfast."

He smiled at the envy in the other man's tone. "Don't take it too hard. She's prettier than you."

"Better card player, too."

"Surprised to hear you admit that."

"Blame it on the bourbon. A cutie-pie cocktail waitress kept them coming."

"Where are you now?"

"Sitting in my car in front of a Denny's, inhaling coffee."

"Why?"

"I told you—Gina's inside having breakfast with the roper."

A bonus, as far as Milo was concerned. A skilled flirt, if there was any inside information to glean about Turner's private high-stakes game, she'd know it by the time her idiot date paid the bill. "Tabasco."

"What?"

"Gina can take care of herself." An ex-cop expertly trained in self-defense. Milo often joked she could seduce and throat-punch a man with equal proficiency.

"I know. Just watching her back."

Standard procedure within Chameleon. His team. His family. Only the dynamics had shifted when Arch slept with Gina. And now Evie was in the mix. Damn. "I appreciate that, Jimmy." He padded across the damp porch in his socks, breathed in the rain-fresh country air. Again tranquility eluded him. "Did Gina tell you when the game's scheduled?"

"Tomorrow night. I mean, tonight. I really need some sleep. Anyway, I've been drilling her on cardsharp techniques. If Turner's cheating, she'll spot it."

"And we'll know how to spin that to our advantage. Fast work. Good work. Thanks. I'll let the senator and Crowe know we're making progress."

"We'll check in later this afternoon," Tabasco said. "After we get some shut-eye. How are things on your end?"

"ID'd the man scamming Mrs. Parish. Hope to clear this one up today."

"Talk about fast work. You've only been in town two days."

"Helped that Evie's brother was already suspicious of the bastard."

"Speaking of Twinkie, how's her cold?"

Smiling, Milo rolled back his shoulders. "You've been hanging around Pops too long. Later, Mama Bear." He disconnected and slipped back inside the house. No sign of Nicole. She must've woken and gone up to bed. He considered settling back on the couch—he'd slept sounder there than he had in weeks—then decided on a morning run to rev his mind and body. He had a feeling today was going to top yesterday in terms of controlling his emotions.

He wondered about Evie's decision regarding Gish. Wondered about her future with Arch. Hell, he wondered about his own damn future. At this point little was clear beyond one fact.

Change was in the air.

BREAKFAST WAS A SOMBER affair even though I was in a chipper mood. In fact, my chipper mood seemed to add to the tension. Especially where Nic was concerned. I didn't want to say anything in front of Arch and Beckett, but I was pretty sure she had a hangover. I didn't remember her drinking much during the indoor barbecue, so she must have tied one on afterward. Alone or with Beckett, I didn't know. I was dying to ask, but I didn't.

"Let's go over it one more time," Beckett said.

"Let's not," Nic said, "and say we did."

"I'm okay with running it again," I said. "I mean, I've got it, but to be on the safe side, I think Beckett's right. Fancy Feet stole a widow's savings and left her destitute. I want to do what's right for her *and* my mom and I don't want to screw it up. If Gish suspects we're onto him and runs—"

"I get it, Evie," Nic snapped, then shoved her glasses higher up her nose. No contacts. *Tinted* glasses. Bitchy mood.

Definite hangover.

"If you *dinnae* want to do this, Nic," Arch said, "say the word. We'll alter the come-on."

She wet her lips. "I want to do it." She reached over and squeezed my hand. "Of course I want to do it. Ignore me. Let's go through it again."

Heart full, I poured her another cup of coffee. "Thanks, Nic."

Beckett, who sat directly across the dining-room table, pushed away his oatmeal and spared her a glance. Again I wondered what had happened between them last night. Although maybe it was nothing more than a clash of personalities. Nic could be stubborn and Beckett was a control freak. After a private conversation with Arch, he'd spent the rest of the morning on the phone speaking with various authorities, hashing out details regarding Gish's arrest. I wasn't privy to those details, but I did know Beckett hated complications, and just now Nic was being difficult.

My tension eased a little when he focused back on me. No hint of desire. Just now, the man was all business and he exuded—hallelujah—confidence. "You and Arch have a scheduled dance lesson with Gish at eleven-thirty," he said. "Don't be surprised if people stop you on the sidewalk and want to make nice. Word's out. The Baron of Broxley is in Greenville, Indiana. Aside from word of mouth, we know you two made the front page of the *Tribune*."

"Thanks to Christopher, who called bright and early this morning," I said with a roll of my eyes. Who wakes up and reads the paper at five-freaking-thirty in the morning?

"It's a good thing," Arch said, "for multiple reasons, yeah?" He winked at me and nudged my foot under the table. The playful gesture reminded me of the tender bond we'd forged last night and the hot sex we'd had this morning.

Flustered, I fumbled my fork. I bent over to pick it up from the floor at the same time he said, "I'll get it." Our faces met beneath the tabletop and he stole a quick kiss before we both straightened. *Zing. Zap.*

Nic smirked. "Where's your fork?"

"Oh." Blushing, I bent back down and retrieved it.

"Naturally, interest in the European noble and the homegrown performer will spike," Beckett continued, looking annoyed. "Makes sense the baron would want his assistant-slash-bodyguard along. Wouldn't want another paparazzi episode."

"And since I'm your girlfriend," Nic said, blowing over yesterday's debacle, "and her best friend," she said with a nod toward me, "naturally, I'd tag along."

"We all four enter the dance studio," Arch said, "and play it by ear."

Nic stirred sweetener into her third cup of coffee. "Soon after, I excuse myself to go to the ladies' room."

"Soon after," I said, "my cell phone rings. It's Nic pretending to be my mom. We have a brief conversation and I put her on the phone with Gish."

"*Randolph,*" Nic said, affecting Mom's voice and Midwestern twang. *"I don't know how it happened, but George found out about the bonds I cashed. Either I'm going to have to tell him the truth or produce that money. What should I do?"*

Silence reigned as Arch, Beckett and I stared at Nic. She sounded *exactly* like Mom.

"Brilliant," said Arch.

"Amazing," said Beckett.

Nic shrugged. "It's a gift."

I smiled. "After Gish says whatever he says to Mom and signs off, I express my apologies. *I have to leave. Mom needs me.*"

Arch slathered strawberry jam on wheat toast. "I express concern *aboot* you running around town with*oot* me."

"Or me," Beckett put in.

"Whereafter I reenter," Nic said, "and offer to come along."

"We leave you men alone with Gish," I said, "and then…"

"They've got it down," Arch said to Beckett.

"Like there's a lot to remember," I cracked. "But then what? What are you guys going to do or say that will convince Gish to cough up my mom's money and write her that note before you whisk him away and turn him over to the proper authorities? How is that going to work?" Last night Arch had as good as said Gish wouldn't have that kind of cash on hand, yet this morning he'd told me not to bother pooling my funds with Christopher's. *Trust me,* he'd said. Tall order.

Beckett stirred sugar into his coffee.

Arch chewed his toast.

"They're not going to tell us," Nic said.

"That's not fair," I said.

"That's life," she said.

Arch caught my eye. "For the greater good."

CHAPTER THIRTY-FOUR

THE SCENE WITH Gish went down exactly as we'd rehearsed. It almost seemed too easy and it was over—my part, anyway—much too soon. Throughout the charade I'd been on an adrenaline high. The rush far greater than any I'd ever experienced on stage. Obviously because more was at stake. The goal wasn't to entertain an audience but to bamboozle a despicable human being. The reward for a flawless performance not a standing ovation but satisfaction in knowing I'd brought a scum artist to his knees. I could get used to this.

"I hate not knowing what's happening in there," I whispered as Nic and I made our way down the hall, leaving Arch and Beckett alone with Gish in the dance studio.

"You know what the end result will be. Maybe they feel the less you know, the better. What if they're doing something illegal?"

"They call it *creative*."

"Whatever."

I chewed my thumbnail as we descended a wide set of carpeted stairs. "At least I didn't crack out of turn this time and no one ended up dead."

"What?"

"Never mind." Even though I knew I should shut up,

adrenaline kept my mouth running. "I wonder what the come-on will be or if they plan a straight-out shakedown. How are they going to get him out of town and into the hands of the law without alerting Sheriff Jaffe? You don't think Beckett's going to escort him all the way to Washington state, do you?"

"I'm not sure what you're more enamored with," Nic said as we hit the first floor of the civic center, "Arch or his profession."

"What's that supposed to mean?"

"Just that you're starting to sound like one of those thrill-seeker junkies."

"I'm not—"

"Mrs. Parish, for the last time, I can't put Evie in the show. All of the parts are taken."

Nic and I stopped cold. She didn't know the irritated voice booming from somewhere down the hall, but I did. And unless Monica had business with my brother's wife, she was talking to my mom.

"I understand that. I just thought someone may have dropped out. It happens."

Mom.

Nic and I ducked around the corner, behind a potted palm. Yeah, boy, *that's* not conspicuous.

"I thought you said your mom was spending the afternoon with your dad," she whispered.

"That's what she told me when we spoke on the phone this morning. Said they had a heart-to-heart last night and that they were going to take the reconciliation slow. Said she was going to spend the afternoon lending a helping hand at the tavern. I hope she didn't stand him up."

"That's the least of our worries," Nic pointed out. "She knows you had a dance lesson scheduled. What if she pops upstairs to say hello? She could blow this whole thing."

"We have to get her out of here." I slapped a palm leaf out of my face and stepped into the open. "Follow my lead."

"Maybe Evelyn can be featured in some other capacity," Mom went on. "Maybe she could host the auction or sing a special song during the aftershow party."

"As I said before, everything is set, Mrs. Parish."

I walked down the hall, following the voices and looking for the door marked Civic Theater Director. I attributed my racing pulse to Mom acting as my champion for the second day in a row. I didn't give two figs that Monica was barring me from taking an artistic part in Mrs. Grable's benefit. Okay, that's a lie. Maybe I didn't have the eye of the tiger, but I had pride. Rejection sucked on any level, but in this case it was doubly unfair because it was vengeful.

Reaching our destination, I peeked through the partially open door and saw the back of Mom's new blond do. She sat ramrod straight in an orange vinyl chair, ready to do battle. Monica slouched in a high-back leather chair, looking bored. Between them, a desk boasting Playbills, scripts and a mock Tony statue. I could easily imagine Monica stroking the golden trophy and delivering a teary acceptance speech behind closed doors. How long was she going to cling to that dream? For a moment I actually sympathized with the woman.

"Hello?" I stepped inside uninvited. "Mom. It *is* you."

"We thought we heard your voice," Nic said.

"What are you doing here? I thought you were going to hang with Dad."

"I was," she said, rising from her seat and clutching her

purse in both hands. "I am. I just stopped here first. Thought I'd peek in to see how Archibald was faring with his lessons. Then I remembered Monica's office was here and…"

She trailed off, her cheeks flushing as she looked from my high-school rival to me.

Monica smirked and any empathy I felt vanished. "Really, Evie. If you wanted to be in the musical that badly, you could've talked to me yourself instead of sending your mother."

Wow. I'd never known someone to hold a grudge so fiercely for so long. And just because I'd beat her out for lead roles in the spring and fall productions of our junior and senior year. Talk about shallow. It's not as if I slept with her boyfriend. Or bribed Mrs. Grable with promises that Dad could lower her mortgage rate. I'd landed the parts fair and square. Well, except in Monica's eyes. Like I said, professional jealousy can be toxic.

Her petty dig bounced off me, but Mom looked ready to swing her potent pocketbook.

Nic interceded. "Pity Evie's not in the show. Talent aside, she also brings the Baron of Broxley to the table. Word of his visit to Greenville is spreading throughout the state thanks to that newspaper article. I'm thinking the TV news stations would be all over a small-town celebrity-studded benefit."

"I'm sure you're right, Nicole," Mom said with a take-that-Monica smile. "Ticket sales would probably double, and who knows what other advantages media coverage would provide."

"Yes, well…" Monica shuffled papers, visions of being *discovered* no doubt dancing in her head. "Carla Beck is a little iffy in her role. And a tribute song at the afterparty *might* be a nice touch," she said without looking at me.

I smiled. "I'll think about it." I looped my arm through Mom's and whisked her toward the door. "You don't mind if Nic and I join you and Daddy for lunch, do you? We're famished." We were headed for the tavern anyway. The designated rendezvous with Arch and Beckett.

I spared Monica a parting glance and a fake smile. "Have a nice day."

My smile turned genuine when Nic mumbled, "Bitch."

"Language, Nicole," Mom said, though her tone lacked real censure. "I'm sorry if I embarrassed you, Evelyn," she continued as we escorted her down the hall. "It's just that I haven't seen you perform in a long time and I know your dad would enjoy seeing you on stage, not to mention Connie Grable. She asks about you whenever I run into her. To this day she views you as a shining star."

My heart pounded with mixed emotions. I was shocked and flattered that Mom had asked Monica to include me in the show. Apparently it wasn't the first time. Knowing she genuinely wanted to see me on stage was also touching, considering how she'd looked down on that part of my life for so long. And I knew the extent of Dad's support. He'd bought the tavern so I'd have a place to sing, for crying out loud. But these days every time I thought about getting on stage and subjecting myself to people's opinions, I felt ill.

Her clothes aren't tight enough.

Her skirt isn't short enough.

She's not showing enough cleavage.

She doesn't have any cleavage.

Her hips are too big.

Her lips are too thin.

And those were just a few of the complaints I'd heard over the last few years. If not about me directly, about a fellow performer. The last time Mrs. Grable and my fellow high-school thespians had seen me perform I'd been eighteen. Now I was forty-one and far less successful in the business than they'd expected. Although I'd been more successful than Monica. I simply didn't feel the need or desire to compete.

I did, however, want to show off, just a little, for Mom and Dad. "How about if I sit in with the band at the tavern tonight?"

She patted my hand. "I'd like that, Evelyn." We'd almost reached her car when she dug in the heels of her pink track shoes. "Wait a minute. Where's Archibald?"

Drat! "He's still upstairs with Randolph."

"The man has two left feet," Nic said, not unkindly.

"He needs extra practice and I was making him nervous."

"I can understand that," Mom said. "It's not easy performing in front of people. I don't know how you girls do it."

"Call us crazy," I said as we piled in her car.

Mom smiled. "I've been calling you that for years, dear."

CHAPTER THIRTY-FIVE

MORE ADEPT WITH electronic gizmos than me, Nic text-messaged Beckett to let him know we'd caught a ride to the tavern. His car was still in the lot, the key hidden under the bumper. I obsessed on what was going on inside the dance studio. It reminded me of the Simon the Fish sting, when Arch had sent me off to shop with Gina while he and Beckett engaged in mysterious grifter activities. I realize that, as a team, every player has their part. I just wanted a bigger role. To hell with paying my dues.

My mood was anxious when we entered the Corner Tavern. I expected the next hour to drag, but that front-page article doubled Dad's afternoon business. At least thirty people, men and women, slipped into the tavern for a quick lunch or a lazy beer. Dad stepped in as a second bartender. Mom helped out in the kitchen. I fielded questions about the Baron of Broxley and my life in Atlantic City as a "specialty performer." Nic piqued interest, as well. The two of us worked the room like a special event party, drawing from real life, as well as our character profiles and improvising when necessary. It reminded me of old times—but fun times. Waiting for Arch and Beckett to show up was downright brutal, so I welcomed the distraction.

At one point Mom took a break and joined me for

lunch. I was sitting at a table dipping French fries in ketchup and telling her about the time I'd twirled a rifle in the Tropicana atrium dressed as Calamity Jane, when Arch came up behind me and kissed the back of my neck. "You missed the excitement, Sunshine."

My heart stuttered, partly from his sexy presence, partly because I was dying of curiosity. I braced myself for his tale. Since I didn't know specifics, I'd have to improvise. I revved up for the challenge. "What excitement?"

"In a minute, lass." He dropped into the seat next to me. "I'm in dire need of a drink."

"How did your lesson go, Archibald?" Mom asked. "Did you work up an appetite?"

"I could eat a wee bit, yeah?" He caught the passing waitress's attention, pointed to my burger and fries. "I'll have what she's having and a pint of whatever import you have on tap, please."

Mooney-eyed, Tina handed him a cocktail napkin and her pen. "Could I have your autograph, Baron?"

"Sure, lass." He scratched a message and sent her off with a smile.

"That must happen to you all the time," Mom said.

"Only in the States."

"Speaking of, will you be returning to Scotland anytime soon?"

"Depends," he said with a glance toward me.

"Evie loves to travel, don't you, dear?"

"Mom." I sipped my soda, trying to appear nonchalant. "So what did I miss? Did Joe Kitt burst in and snap shots of you and Mr. Gish midwaltz? I can imagine the spin he'd put on that one."

"Thankfully, no. And the lesson was going profoundly

well, Marilyn—thank you for asking—until the phone call."

"What phone call?" I asked, feeling as curious as Mom looked.

"Larry someone-or-other called from Florida."

"Larry Ruben," Mom said, "Randolph's…friend."

"Close friend, I gather, as he took the news quite hard."

"What news?" Mom and I asked at the same time.

"Not entirely sure. Some sort of crisis, yeah? Larry was distraught and Randolph was desperate to lend emotional support in person. In my estimation, the man was too shaken to get behind a wheel. After giving him a lift to his apartment, where he quickly packed a bag, I asked Northbrook to drive him to the airport."

Mom touched a hand to her heart. "Heavens, it must've been terribly serious for Randolph to pick up and leave like that."

"As I said, some sort of crisis. I wouldn't worry," he said, giving her other hand a quick squeeze. "Randolph insisted it wasn't of the medical nature, yeah?"

Mom relaxed against her chair. "Just like Randolph to want to be there for his…friend. Such a thoughtful man."

I choked on a fry.

Arch patted my back, then smoothed his palm up and down my spine. Though meant as a comforting gesture, my nerve endings sparked from the *zing-zap* connection. I actually felt light-headed. Maybe it was the adrenaline. I don't remember Michael ever rendering me dizzy with a simple touch. It made me sad because it meant something had been lacking in our intimate relationship. That realization steered me down a road I didn't want to travel just now. Must. Focus.

"Are you all right, dear?" Mom asked.

"Went down the wrong pipe." I sipped my soda. "I'm fine."

"I wish the same could be said for Randolph and his friend. I hope he sends word through the dance studio as to how Larry fares and when he'll return," Mom said.

"I'm sure you'll be hearing from Mr. Gish soon," I said.

Arch's food arrived and Mom turned the conversation toward his charity work. I knew in that instant she'd bought his story hook, line and sinker. *Jeez Louise.* But then, why shouldn't she? Arch had delivered the plausible tale with the utmost sincerity. The scenario played out in my mind like a Lifetime channel movie. In a few days she'd receive a letter or wire from Gish along with six thousand dollars. He'd explain how the building project had fallen through and that he wouldn't be returning because Larry was shattered and needed him. He'd wish her well and say something about how much he'd enjoyed their friendship. He'd promise to keep in touch, but, of course, he wouldn't.

In reality, Randolph Gish—or whatever the rat bastard's real name was—would be serving time in a Washington state jail.

It was over. We'd salvaged my mom's pride and money and bagged a scum artist to boot. On the inside I performed my signature victory dance. Only my dance was slightly subdued because I still didn't know specifics. Like how they'd gotten Gish to cough up the money. Who'd actually written the letter? How did they get Gish to leave with Beckett without making a scene? It shouldn't matter, but it did. Even though I'd played an active role in the sting, I still felt like an outsider. Talk about anticlimactic.

Time dragged as Arch finished his meal and chatted amiably with all who dropped by our table, including my dad. Again it occurred to me that Arch got along ten times better with my parents than Michael had. Unlike my ex, he seemed genuinely interested in my family and comfortable in Greenville. The warm fuzzies intensified when he mentioned heading back to the Appleseed to shower and change before coming back to the tavern tonight. He was as keen on watching me sing with the band as my parents. His enthusiasm warmed my heart. The twinkle in his eye heated other parts of my body. It made it difficult to determine my priorities. Interrogate him about Gish and then jump his bones? Or vice versa.

"Let's find a coat closet," I whispered in his ear, still unsure as to which would come first—questions or kissing.

Arch grinned. "I'm going to need more room than that."

Zowie. Not sure what that meant, but it zapped my libido like a live wire.

I located Nic, who was sitting in a booth sipping ginger ale and allowing a cute guy sporting a John Deere cap and a smitten grin to drool all over her. "We're leaving," I said.

"Where's Northbrook?"

"He gave Mr. Gish a ride to the airport. Some sort of personal crisis," I said, keeping up pretenses in front of the infatuated local.

She looked over my shoulder at Arch, then back at me. "Think I'll hang out here," she said, smiling at her new hunky friend. "I'll call you later."

"Um…" I leaned in and whispered in her ear. "Don't you think Northbrook would be a little jealous if he knew—"

"We had a fight," she said in a normal tone.

A real fight? Or a fake fight? "Did I miss something?"

"It was fun while it lasted, but his heart wasn't in it," she said with a fake pout and a glance toward her friend. "I'm calling it quits."

I didn't know what she was talking about. I hoped to hell Beckett did. "Does he know?"

She smiled. "He will."

Ooookay. I vamoosed, pondering her strange behavior.

Arch met me at the front door. "Where's Nic?"

"Back there, encouraging the interest of some beef-cake tractor guy." I frowned. "She said she's breaking up with Beckett. I mean, Northbrook. Do you know anything about that?"

"No."

"She's in a mood today."

"I noticed." He narrowed his eyes. "I can hear your wheels turning, Sunshine. *Dinnae* worry *aboot* how this affects the overall ruse. Whirlwind affair gone bad. Simple as that. Happens all the time, yeah?"

Not exactly the words I wanted to hear considering *we* were engaged in a whirlwind affair. "Yeah."

"Except where we're concerned," he said, clearly reading my mind. He quirked a knee-melting grin. "Look at it this way—for the time being, it's just you and me and the entire B and B, eh, Sunshine?"

Zing. "What are we waiting for?"

IF IT WEREN'T FOR fear of Joe Kitt tailing us with his tele-photo lens, I would've indulged in some racy inclinations while Arch drove. Instead I behaved like a good girl, tightening my seat belt so I couldn't ease over and palm Bad Boy's erection.

"Now that we're alone," I said, trying to sidetrack my naughty thoughts, "tell me what really went down with Gish."

He slid on his sunglasses as we left the shaded streets for the sunny countryside. "What matters is that you get it all, yeah? Your ma's money and pride and knowing Gish is going to pay for his crimes."

"Well, yeah. But I'm dying to know how you and Beckett pulled it off."

"We fucked with his head."

"Yes, but—"

"Evie."

"What?"

"You know the scenario in a movie where a soldier refuses to talk with his family *aboot* what he saw or did when he was at war?"

"Sure."

"What *aboot* the homicide cop who withholds the grim details of his job from his wife and kids?"

His expression was relaxed, his tone controlled. Uh-oh. "Are you saying you don't want to talk about your work?"

"I'm saying that I think you've glamorized what Chameleon does, yeah? It's not much different than what I used to do—and I know how you feel *aboot* that."

I opened my mouth and he cut me off with a raised hand. "I know. Now when I con, it's not for personal gain but the greater good. I'm beginning to regret the day I used that phrase on you."

"I don't understand why you're angry."

"Do I sound angry?"

"No. A dead giveaway that you're two seconds from blowing your cork."

He regarded me over the rims of his shades with a cocked brow. "My tell, yeah?"

"Now that you mention it."

"I promise I *willnae*...blow my cork. It's just lately... I'm not always proud of what I do, you know?" He focused back on the road and my stomach did a little flip. I'd never heard him talk like this. And apparently he wasn't done. "I may be working on the right side of the law, but the tricks of the trade are the same. I deal in deceit, something that goes against your nature. You're striving to be a bad girl, but it's the good girl I adore. That I admire, yeah?"

My heart jackhammered in my chest.

"I understand that you *dinnae* want to go back. I just *dinnae* want to see you lose touch with what makes you shine."

On the surface, that statement packed a heck of an "aw" factor. Truly it was a sweet sentiment, and I confess my heart fluttered like the wings of a hyper butterfly. But I also worried if I peeled away the pretty layers, I'd learn an ugly truth. "Are you saying you don't want me to be part of Chameleon? Are you asking me to choose?"

"I worry that subjecting you to deceit and manipulation on a regular basis will desensitize you. It's the way of things, yeah? But I also acknowledge that you are a skilled actress with brilliant improvisational skills, full of potential and surprises. Watching you work the jailhouse yesterday and Gish today...it gave me a bloody hard-on."

Sweet *and* sexy. Holy smoke.

He pulled into the driveway, parked and cut the engine.

My mouth went dry when he tossed his sunglasses on the dash and angled to look me in the eyes. "If I did ask you to choose—"

"Please don't."

"I just want to know you're in love with me and not my world."

The vulnerability in his tone undid me, along with the raw openness in his gaze. "I think that's the most honest you've ever been with me."

"A moment of weakness."

"A rarity."

"Aye."

"It was hot."

He cocked his head. "That so?"

"Really hot. The backs of my knees are sweating."

"Is that a good thing?"

"It means it's all about you." I launched across the seat, fired up and desperate to soothe his worries. Yes, I was fascinated with his world and a little obsessed with learning about his profession, but it was the man who'd won my heart. I tried to cram all of that sentiment into an impassioned kiss.

From his ardent reaction, I'm thinking he got the message. "Let's take this inside, lass."

I wouldn't let go, so he had to maneuver both of us out the driver's side. I locked my arms around his neck, my legs around his waist, and continued to ravage his mouth as he carried me inside the deserted B and B.

Once over the threshold, he slammed shut the door and set me to my feet. I unknotted his tie without breaking the kiss. God, could this man kiss.

A retro R & B groove welled in my head. George Michael serenaded my senses as Arch rendered me topless. *I want your sex. I want your love.*

Crazed with desire, I yanked open his shirtfront. Buttons flew and clattered to the hardwood floor. I ran my hands over his chest, shoulders and back, delighting in corded muscle, heated flesh.

He flipped me around, trapping me between the wall and his amazing body. I moaned my approval as he kissed a trail from my mouth to my cleavage. He nipped and sucked my breasts while sliding my jeans and panties to my ankles, then moved farther south to kiss away the ache between my legs.

I felt brazen and naughty, braced against the wall, half-naked, enjoying the hot flicks of Arch's tongue. The thought of being caught in the act mortified and excited me at the same time.

Delirious, I tensed and cried out my climax, too breathless to argue when he picked me up and threw me over his shoulder. Not sure how I would've navigated the stairs with my pants around my ankles anyway.

Seconds later we burst into his room and he tossed me on the bed. I scrambled to shuck my shoes and jeans while he stripped naked. He was faster. "My socks," I said as he pushed me back and pinned me down.

"Leave them." He glanced down, then nailed me with a wicked smile. "Kind of sexy, yeah?"

Bright yellow socks decorated with tiny green frogs? I laughed. "That so?"

He winked. "Definitely sexy." He captured my mouth in a ravenous kiss, pinned my wrists over my head with one hand while exploring my curves with the other.

The mood was so hot and playful I expected him to bend me into some exotic position. I was quite flexible and he was scary creative. While in London, we'd experimented plenty. Call me a pretzel. Not that I ever complained. Mostly I moaned and groaned and spoke in broken sentences. *Yes. Do it. Oh, God. More!*

But instead of flipping me over or turning me sideways or having me balance on one leg, he took me on the bed, on my back, him on top, missionary style. Just like the first time two nights ago. Except he gazed into my eyes the entire time we made love. The R & B groove gave way to angelic voices and Celtic melodies.

I'm pretty sure I stopped breathing. The moment was *that* beautiful. When we climaxed as one, I cried. What a ninny.

"I've never felt anything like this," I whispered as he kissed away my tears. "It's not just sex. I mean, the sex is great. It's the connection. You and me. We don't make sense, but…"

"I know." He kissed me, slow, deep.

Questions and reservations whirled in my brain. So much I wanted to ask about the future…only the longer he kissed me, the more my thoughts blurred.

Then suddenly he was inside me again, filling me, loving me, and all that mattered was this moment.

CHAPTER THIRTY-SIX

BUSTED.

*I scrambled to cover my tush but cracked out of turn.
Just us—Charlie and Sugar—the Fish and a squirrely thug.*

"Pat them down."

Panic.

Fainting. Falling.

My head!

Bleary-eyed. What's happening?

*"Get your hands off me, old boy. Allow me to help my
wife."*

Arch fighting.

Gun.

Must help.

Shoving.

Bang!

Falling.

Bang! Bang! Bang!

My eyes flew open. Heart pounding, I stared at the
ceiling. Gunshots echoed in my ears.

"What is it, Sunshine?"

I reconnected with the conscious world, naked and
disoriented but safe in Arch's arms.

He smoothed my hair from my damp face. "What's
wrong?"

"Nothing."

"Something."

"Bad dream." Suddenly it clicked. Dreams, Jayne had once told me, are rarely literal. Deep down, I worried that I wasn't up to Chameleon standards, that they'd never accept me as a full-fledged team member. I knew for certain Arch thought I was too soft to weather his world. My insecurities, my fear of failure, had crept into my subconscious. I blew out a breath, shook off the feeling of dread. An anxiety dream. "I'm okay now. Really."

Arch propped himself on one elbow, quirked a devilish grin. "What you need is a distraction." He brushed featherlight fingertips over my shoulders. I shivered with sensual delight as those fingers tickled my collarbone, the swell of my breasts, my ribs...

I didn't remember falling asleep, but I remembered quite vividly the exhausting lovemaking. It was the first time we'd been alone like this since London and we'd made the most of our privacy. One nice thing about shagging a younger man was his stamina. Then again, a man as potent and sexual as Arch would probably have stamina even at seventy-five. Of course, at that point I'd be eighty-one—or six feet under. *Don't go there, Parish.*

My head lolled to the side as his fingers circled my belly button. My stomach tightened and quivered as his touch skimmed my inner thighs.

The bedside clock jolted me like a bucket of ice water: 4:00 p.m.

Beckett would be back from Indianapolis soon. I thought about the clothes strewn in the foyer and the living room. An embarrassment I could forgo. I clasped Arch's hand. "Sad to say this will have to wait until later tonight."

He squinted at the clock. "Voice of reason, yeah?"

"Yeah." With regret, I rolled out of bed and shimmied into my jeans. "I'm going downstairs to get our clothes and a couple bottles of water."

"I'm going to hop in the shower." He grinned and slapped my butt. "Hurry and you can join me."

I pulled one of his T-shirts over my head. "I don't think I have the strength."

Buck naked, he strode toward the bathroom with a bad-boy smile. "Your loss."

No argument there. Suitably distracted, I skittered from the room, thinking if I hydrated, maybe I'd get a renewed burst of energy. Heh. Barefoot, I sailed down the stairs and picked up our shirts and my bra and started hunting down his buttons.

Then I remembered I left my purse in the car. I dropped our clothes in a pile and hurried outside. I turned my face to the clear blue sky and breathed deep. It helped to burn off the residual glum of that dream. I padded across the lush green lawn and focused on the good. Mom and Dad's reconciliation. Gish's incarceration. Bonding with my brother. The indefinable connection with Arch.

I nabbed my purse off the front seat. Saw Arch's suit jacket and grabbed that, too. Sophisticated cut. Expensive fabric. The man had great taste. Then again, he was portraying a baron.

"Strike that. He *is* a baron." Paying for the privilege didn't diminish the outcome. Arch possessed title and lands and a stone cottage—the size unknown, but did it matter? Images of the Scottish highlands burned bright in my head. Scenes from *Braveheart* and *Rob Roy*. How could he not want to live there year-round? "I would."

I pressed my face into his jacket and inhaled his sexy scent. Maybe Broxley could be my happy place.

Declaring myself a besotted idiot, I draped the jacket over my arm and traipsed back to the house. I felt a zap. No, a vibration. Curious, I investigated and found a slim silver phone tucked in his inner breast pocket. Definitely not the cell phone I'd used to call my brother. Closer to the one I'd spied from the tree. "Why would a man carry two phones?"

Another vibration.

I should let it roll over to voice mail. *But what if it's important?* Not nosy, I told myself, responsible. I flipped open the cell. I couldn't help but notice the displayed name of the caller before connecting. "Hello?"

Silence. Well, except for the background noise. Music. Culture Club? Then dead silence. Call over.

Hmm. I guess *Kate* wasn't expecting a woman to answer Arch's phone. His *secret* phone.

Instead of internalizing and letting my imagination run amok, I decided to ask him straight out. No sooner did I cross the threshold when I heard the personalized ring of my own phone. I dug the cell out of my purse and answered, thinking it was Nic, shocked that it was Michael.

"Hi, hon."

Hon. His pet name for *all* women. I sank down on the nearest chair, which happened to be a padded footstool. "Hi," I croaked. "Where are you?"

"If I told you, you'd hate me."

I frowned at his slurred speech. "I know you're in Paris, Michael. I meant, where specifically. It's the middle of the night over there, isn't it?"

"We had a fight."

I assumed he meant him and his new wife. "So you went out and got drunk?"

"She locked me out of the room."

"What did you do?"

"Brought up your name one too many times."

My stomach dropped. "You're on your honeymoon, Michael. Why in the world would you bring up your ex-wife?"

"Because we're in Paris."

"I know."

"The city of your dreams."

I gritted my teeth. "You don't want to go down this road, Michael. Trust me."

"It's just that I've been feeling guilty, hon."

That catapulted me to my feet. Furious, I paced the foyer. "What do you want from me, Michael? Forgiveness? For what? For cheating on me? For giving another woman a baby after telling me you didn't want children? For marrying her without telling me and whisking her off to *my* dream city?"

"For introducing you to Arch."

"What?"

"He's a—"

"I know what he is." Nic was right. I *did* feel something. It felt good to let the anger out. "What I want to know is how you know and the dynamic of your relationship."

"Long story. Point is, Evie, he's bad news. The work he does, the people he hangs out with...you're not like that."

"Don't tell me what I'm like. You don't know me, Michael. Not the new me, anyway."

"What's that mean? Oh, hell. Oh, *fuck*. You slept with him, didn't you?"

My cheeks heated and I fought to keep my voice low. "That's none of your business." Then, remembering I wanted to prove to him that I was not uptight and pre-dictable, I added, "And so what if I did?"

"Christ, Evie. Tell me you haven't fallen for him."

"So what if I have?"

"As long as I've known Duvall he's never been in a se-rious relationship. He hops from one woman to another, including the women he works with."

I was trembling now, furious with Michael for trying to sabotage my happiness, furious with myself for not hanging up on him.

"Remember the actress you replaced on the cruise ship gig?"

"Yes."

"He'd used Pam as a shill a few times, and according to her, they'd been intimate. Jesus, last I heard, he was doing the brunette on Beckett's team."

I stopped cold. I felt cold. Like a cadaver. *Beat, heart, beat.* "Gina?"

"I don't know her name, just that she's an ex-cop."

Oh, God. I sank back down on the footstool, massaged my chest. *Beat, dammit.* It explained her bitchy behavior. On the cruise and after. Was she in love with Arch? "I have to go."

"I just…I want you to be happy, hon."

"You've got a funny way of showing it. Sober up and go back to your wife. Goodbye, Michael." I signed off and dropped my head in my lap. *Don't cry. Don't cry.*

"Stone got remarried?"

I snapped up at the sound of Arch's voice. Fresh from the shower, he stood on the stairway dressed in a T-shirt and faded jeans. Handsome and sexy. I hated that I noticed. "He's honeymooning in Paris as we speak," I said past the lump in my throat.

"Why didn't you tell me?"

"Why didn't you tell me you had an affair with Gina?"

He dragged a hand through his wet hair. "Stone's a bloody bastard."

"Sometimes. But in this case I think he meant well. Why didn't you tell me?"

"Because it was over and done."

At least he didn't lie and deny it. But, damn, the truth hurt. I massaged my injured heart.

He sat on the bottom step, not far from where I sat on the footstool. He clasped his hands loosely between his knees. "There's nothing between Gina and me, Evie."

His words fell on deaf ears. I was numb with shock. Numb with anger. "Does she know that?"

"Aye. It shouldn't have happened, but it did. I ended it before she was ready and I didn't end it well. Bad form, I'm ashamed to say. She was pissed at me but she took it *oot* on you. I'm sorry for that, yeah?"

"I suppose you thought you were sparing my feelings by withholding the truth."

"Why would I tell you *aboot* a brief affair with another woman? It meant nothing. It happened before I met you. Over and done."

"But *Gina* knew. And you knew. And—" *cripes* "—Beckett?"

Arch nodded.

Unbelievable. My heart bumped to life, pounded against my ribs. I was on my feet again, pacing, venting. "I feel like such a fool. I thought I was special, but I'm just another *bird* in the flock. If Pam Jones hadn't wrecked her car on her way to the airport that day, you would have been boinking *her* on the cruise! For God's sake, *Ace,* do you seduce every woman you work with?"

"I'm not going to apologize for my past affairs, Evie. What matters is now."

He looked so calm, so flipping in control. I wanted to rattle him. I wanted to… "So I'm the only woman in your life? The only one you're seeing? The only one—"

"Aye."

I stooped and rifled through the jacket I'd piled with our discarded clothes. I snagged the spiffy slim cell and tossed it to him. "Who's Kate?"

He palmed the phone, stared daggers into the carpet.

"I wasn't snooping. The phone rang and I thought it might be important. Her name flashed on the screen."

"What did she say?"

"Nothing. Either she thought she had the wrong number or was shocked to hear a woman's voice and got frazzled. Or miffed. Who is she?"

"Someone from my past."

Great. Just as I'd thought. Another conquest. "So why is she calling now? Why is her number stored in your phone?"

His gaze flicked to mine. "It's not what you think."

"Then what is it?"

"We have a mutual interest."

"Aside from music?"

He raised a brow.

"Culture Club was playing in the background." His MP3 player was loaded with '80s classics. I had a sudden and intense dislike of a decade I used to love. Or at least for Boy George. "This mutual interest," I said when he said nothing, "is it grifting?"

"Yes and no."

The room buzzed with tension, and it wasn't coming wholly from me. I sat back down before my knees gave way. "You're not going to tell me, are you?"

He stroked a thumb over the silver flip-top. "There are some aspects of my life I'm not ready to share, Sunshine."

"*Some?* You're the most secretive person I know! Take that phone, for instance. I asked straight out if you had a new one and you said no."

"It's not new. I've had it for some time."

I grunted. "All right then. Why do you carry *two* phones?"

He pocketed his cell. "This one's for private stuff, yeah?"

I narrowed my eyes. "I get it. You're referring to my journal."

"Would you be comfortable allowing me to read the contents?"

I thought about my deep musings on Arch. Gushy stuff. Sexy stuff. Angry stuff. *Private stuff.* I'd scribbled my doubts regarding the Fish fiasco. And—*oh, God*—the list comparing Arch and Beckett. The pros and cons. "You've made your point." Let him speculate. Let him go mad with curiosity. "So. You have your secrets and I have mine. Only you have more."

"I'm a grifter, Sunshine. Secretive by nature whether I'm working for personal gain or for the greater good, yeah? You asked me to stop manipulating you. I'm asking you to accept me for who I am."

I wanted to claw my hair out. "But who *are* you?"

"A man who's trying to do the right thing, and I'm going *aboot* it the only way I know how."

"Cryptic but noble." I wrapped my arms around my stomach, willing away the hollow ache. I didn't expect a straight answer, but I had to try. "How do you know Michael?"

"Long story short—in the past, he occasionally supplied me with extras when a large cast was needed for a big con and experienced grifters were sparse. *Dinnae* worry. The actors were never in danger. Nor did they know they were involved in anything suspect."

"But Michael knew." How could I be so blind to such a critical dishonest streak? Married for fifteen years. Married to a stranger. I felt another snap. The snap of finality. Over and done. The truth had set me free.

I plowed on, wanting, *needing* to establish more essential realities. "Do you feel any remorse whatsoever for killing Simon the Fish?"

"I thought you were going to let that go."

"I've tried. I can't. *I* feel guilty. Because I screwed up, you have to live with the fact that you shot a man. Accidental or not, that's a heavy load."

"My conscience is clear, Sunshine."

"Really? Completely?"

"Aye."

"I find that troubling."

"I'm not surprised."

I blew out an impatient breath. "Please don't tell me I feel too deeply."

"All right."

"But that's what you're thinking."

He dragged a hand over his goatee. "I'm thinking Simon the Fish was an evil bastard who ruined countless innocent lives. I'm wishing you wouldn't agonize over his death. What's done is done and in the end the world's a better place, yeah?"

Hard to argue with that logic. Probably a true Chameleon wouldn't try. I backed off in search of more truths. "Are you really the Baron of Broxley?"

"Aye."

"Is your real name Archibald Robert Duvall?"

"Unfortunately."

I cocked my head. "So your mom really was a film fanatic."

"You've heard the term *rabid fan?*"

The twinkle in his eyes was playful but genuine. A bit of optimism filled the hollowness. "About Kate…"

"The only woman I'm interested in is sitting right in front of me, yeah?"

I wanted to believe him with all my fluttering heart, but his unwillingness to discuss Kate made my wary. "This connection, it's…"

"Exciting? Wondrous? Hot?"

"Baffling."

The corner of his mouth lifted. "Baffling but exciting." *Busted.*

I'd never been one for confrontations, and when I did overheat, my temper soon cooled. Especially when the person I blasted failed to blast back. No tinder to fuel my fire. Now that my blood wasn't roaring in my ears, his earlier words sank in. Holding past affairs against him *would* be petty. Plenty of single men bed-hopped, especially men who'd been ingrained with the notion that emotional attachments were dangerous. Still, knowing he'd recently bedded a succession of women, namely Gina, stung.

As for Kate…maybe a leap of faith was in order. Maybe their connection was purely business. Shady but professional. Just because he wasn't willing to share that aspect of his life now didn't mean he wouldn't open up as our bond strengthened. It's not as though we'd been together for years. It had barely been a month. A *month*. That essential reality put our relationship in a new light. I was expecting too much too soon. Spinning too fast on the dance floor.

I felt Arch's warmth and strength as he reached over and clasped my hand. "You're not the only one with reservations, Evie."

His honesty caught me off guard. A thousand scenarios assaulted my mind. All of them hinging on my shortcomings or physical flaws. And, yeah, boy, my age. "Such as?"

"My gut says you're dangerous."

Another unexpected revelation. Color me confused. Then I remembered he'd mentioned something to that effect on the cruise. *I've never met a more dangerous woman.* Except he'd also declared me cheeky, accident-prone, soft and—the mother of all monikers—a good girl. I smirked. "I thought I was nice."

"From my perspective, that's a potentially hazardous quality." He pulled me over onto his lap, wrapped me in his arms. "But it's a quality, in you specifically, that I'm attracted to."

"Nice is boring," I said, feeling unreasonably insulted.

"Nice is sweet. Admirable. Sexy."

Okay, that rocked me down to my frog socks.

"Guys like me *dinnae* typically get girls like you. Not for the long run."

I pushed off his chest so I could look up into his eyes. "What are you talking about?"

"What first attracted you to me?"

"Your charisma. Your sex appeal. No, wait. Your accent. We spoke on the phone first and I had visions of…" I blushed. "Never mind. And, okay, I'll admit it, your hot body."

He grinned at that. "Anything else?"

"Please don't make me say it."

Silence.

"You're going to make me say it."

Silence.

"All right, I'll say it." *Jeez.* "You're a rebel. The quintessential bad boy. Girls like me don't typically get boys like you." I fluttered a hand. "You know, except in our fantasies."

He nabbed my hand, kissed my knuckles. "Bang-on."

Now it was my turn to stare in silence.

"Bad boys are the fantasy. The joyride. Not the kind you take home to Mother. Not the kind you ride off with into the sunset. That honor is typically awarded to the nice guy."

I would have been insulted if I weren't hurting for him. "You think I'm taking you for a joyride?"

"Not consciously, no. I think your feelings for me are genuine. But I also think you're enamored with my mysterious side. Learning all my secrets could be a double-edged sword, yeah? The more you know me, the less you may like me. The more you'll be drawn to the safe guy, the nice guy, the guy you trust."

Beckett.

Heart full, I cradled his gorgeous face. "You're scared."

"Cautious."

"So we take it slow."

"Feel our way."

I looked into his eyes, listened to my heart. "We don't make sense, but we connect. We just have to find our rhythm."

His lip twitched. "You're killing me, Sunshine."

"Is that a good thing?"

He pressed his lips to mine—sweet, hot. "It means it's all about you."

CHAPTER THIRTY-SEVEN

GIVEN THE EMOTIONAL ups and downs of today and my current cynicism regarding the entertainment industry, I really didn't expect to have a blast that night when I stepped on stage at the Corner Tavern. Color me surprised.

I didn't dwell on not knowing how Gish's bust went down. I celebrated that Gish was busted. I didn't dwell on Arch's past. I embraced the present.

Take it slow. Feel our way.

I celebrated my parents' love and their love for me.

I'm not sure if it was the live band, the appreciative audience or the vodka and cranberry—I'm thinking a combination—but I was flying high. Of course, I got an additional rush every time my parents applauded like crazed fans and Arch flashed a proud smile. For tonight, at least, I had the eye of the tiger.

I'd intended to sing two songs and ended up performing throughout the night. I jumped on and off stage, singing lead on assorted tunes but mostly singing backup. I have a good ear for harmonies. Love listening for the missing part and filling in the gap. Working with the other vocalists to create a rich, euphonic sound. *Teamwork.* When we did it right, I got the chills. Kind of like Chameleon. Everyone had their specialty, and I was learning to blend.

Magic.

Once in a while I eyeballed Jazzman to make sure he hadn't slit his wrists. This band was all country all the time. I took it as an encouraging sign that he actually seemed to enjoy the music. Maybe that meant he'd allow me to stretch out into genres other than jazz when I started singing at the Chameleon Club. At least I assumed that would be my main job once we wrapped the case with the senator—not that I'd heard much on the status of that sting other than Gina had won an invitation to that private high-stakes game. The thought of facing her, knowing that she'd slept with Arch, twisted my insides. I knew I'd come around—everybody has a past, right?—and I believed him when he said it was over, but it still hurt. Mostly because of the way I'd found out.

I pushed Michael from my mind, wondering what I'd ever seen in him. Currently I moved onto the dance floor with Nic. Her mood seemed lighter so long as she kept her distance from Beckett. I still didn't know what had happened between them, but I'm pretty sure she'd gotten busy with Tractor Boy. I'm pretty sure Beckett suspected the same. Not that she'd been subtle. She'd spent most of the night drinking and dancing with the local man, and he'd been darn attentive. To my parents and the rest of Greenville, it looked exactly as Arch had said: an affair gone bad. And now Nic was kissing up to another guy in order to make "Northbrook" jealous or angry. No one knew, including me, but plenty of people speculated, including me. It felt weird and uncomfortable, like an unscripted soap opera.

Beckett, who sat at a nearby table sipping beer, looked our way now and then. Mostly he ignored Nic—for show or for real, again I didn't know. On the surface he appeared the ultimate professional, concentrating on his job as watchdog for *the baron*. That article had kicked up quite a bit of interest. Just now, Arch was at the bar speaking with my parents. I tried not to obsess on what they were talking about.

"I'm leaving tomorrow."

I blinked at Nic, danced closer. "What?"

"I said I'm leaving tomorrow," she shouted in my ear as the band wailed on a kick-butt song. "Now that Gish is gone and things are square with your mom and dad…" She shrugged. "I flew out here because I thought you needed me. You don't. You're doing fine, Evie. In fact, I haven't seen you this happy, this optimistic, in a long time. I'm happy for you. Just promise you'll be careful."

"Chamelcon's not dangerous."

"Maybe not. But juggling two men is."

"I'm not—"

Tractor Boy cut in and stole Nic away. I stood there feeling dazed. The band segued into a slow song and someone pulled me into his arms. Beckett.

Crap.

He smelled good, not that I noticed. Okay, that's a lie. I just tried not to enjoy the light, spicy scent. Ditto on being pressed against his hard body.

"You okay, Twinkie? Look like you've been hit by a truck."

"Nic's leaving tomorrow."

"It's for the best."

I narrowed my eyes, tried to read his mind and his body language—and failed. "How so?"

"She's not one of us."

Us? The word, the hope that he now thought of me as one of *them,* a Chameleon, stuck in my throat.

He swayed in perfect time with the music. The man was a natural on the dance floor. "I haven't had a chance to tell you, but you did a nice job earlier today," he said. "And yesterday, that bit with the memory card. I'm impressed."

"Thanks." I flushed, unsure as to whether I was uncomfortable with the compliment or the way his hands settled on my bare back. Of all nights to wear a halter top. His palms felt warm and strong. I remembered how I'd cried in his arms, the comfort he'd easily given. The safe guy, the nice guy, the guy I'd brought home to Mother.

My neck prickled with a nervous rash. "I haven't had two seconds with you since you returned from Indy. I'm dying to know—how did it go with your...cargo?"

His breath tickled my neck, intensified the rash. "Best have this discussion in private."

My heart pounded in double-time. Details? Yeah, baby, yeah! But I didn't want to disappear without a word. "I'll meet you in the alley in two minutes."

I breathed easier when he released me. Cripes, his touch was unnerving. Arch being sensitive to my *awareness* of Beckett only made it worse. He pushed through the crowd, making his way to the rear exit. I serpentined bodies and tables, heading for the bar. Several people stopped me, complimenting my singing and congratulating me on my regal hookup. The positive attention was a definite rush. It was tempting to bask in the celeb spotlight, but the promise of learning details regarding Gish won hands down.

I finally made it to the bar, but I didn't see Arch.

Mom breezed by carrying a tray of fries and wings. "They were swamped in the kitchen," she said. "Thought I'd lend a hand. Be right back. Oh—Dwight Miller wants to know if you know 'Freebird.'"

I rolled my eyes but smiled. I wondered if Mom even knew who Lynyrd Skynyrd was or that some wiseacre *always* requests that song. I remembered Dwight Miller from school. Definite wiseacre.

I shimmied between two patrons and flagged down Dad. My smile broadened. I was used to seeing him juggle papers and cash, not bottles of liquor. He leaned over the bar and shouted over the cacophony. "Can you believe this crowd?"

"After tonight, I bet you can expect more of the same. The renovations and the band are a hit, Dad."

"You're a hit! You rocked the house, Evelyn."

I laughed. "Where'd you hear talk like that?"

"The musicians."

Now a lump clogged my throat. All my life I'd felt like the black sheep. Now suddenly, at forty-one, I felt like an accepted member of the Parish flock. Even Christopher had shown up for support.

In the past few weeks the dynamics of the relationships in my life had altered drastically. Needless to say, I was overwhelmed and discombobulated. "Where's Arch?"

"He had a phone call. Too loud in here. I told him to take it in my office."

I ignored a flicker of jealousy, told myself he was talking to Woody or Tabasco, not the mysterious *Kate*. Not wanting to dwell, I pushed off the bar. "Gotta talk to someone, Dad. If Arch asks, I'll be in the alley." I sort of hoped he didn't ask, because I didn't want him to deter Beckett from giving me a play-by-play. At the same time, I didn't want him wondering where Beckett and I were and thinking the worst.

The tavern was loud, crowded and hot. I was flustered and sweaty by the time I stepped outside. I found Beckett leaning against the banana-yellow exterior, just out of the wash of a security lamp, looking cool and collected.

My ears welcomed the relative quiet. My body welcomed the cool evening air. A breeze ruffled my hair, lifting damp strands from my neck. I sighed. "Feels great out here. I don't know about you, but I'm hot."

"Definitely hot."

Something in his tone caused my cheeks to burn. Self-conscious, I smoothed my damp palms over the seat of my jeans. Surely he didn't mean… I'd traded my sneakers for wedge sandals, and instead of a T-shirt I'd worn a paisley red-and-yellow halter top, but I was still relatively dressed down. And sweaty. "About Gish—" I said, wanting to home in on business.

"He's in the hands of the proper authorities. By tomorrow morning he'll be in Washington state. With any luck, there'll be a speedy trial and his crooked ass will soon be in prison."

"That's good. That's great, but I was wondering… hoping you'd fill me in on the particulars. How did you get Gish to cooperate?"

"Manipulation. Intimidation. Didn't take much to convince him to pack a bag."

"Guess you and Arch can be pretty scary when you want to be."

"Let's just say we're good at what we do."

My pulse accelerated as I imagined Chameleon's brightest tangling with shady criminals. I'd seen Arch in action during the Fish fiasco. "Sorry I missed the excitement." The admission boomeranged and winged my sensibilities. What if Nic was right? Was I a thrill-seeking junkie?

"So are you."

I focused back on Beckett. "Sorry?"

"You're good, Evie. I know you wanted to play a bigger part in the takedown, but you played your part perfectly. You didn't let ambition get in the way."

I smiled a little, basking in his compliments. "I didn't crack out of turn."

"No, you didn't." He stepped away from the wall, into my personal space. "Heard from Gina a few minutes ago," he said in a low voice. "She's positive Turner's cheating but isn't sure how. We've got our work cut out for us. Means hanging around this area awhile longer, perpetuating the baron ruse. Right now you're part of that, and your role could get more intense. If you're uncomfortable in any way, we could alter—"

"I'm not uncomfortable." Okay, that's a lie. Personally and professionally, I felt like I was on the edge of something scary. But I didn't blush. I didn't scratch. "I'm up to this, Beckett."

He studied me hard. "I think you are."

"I just want you to know straight out, Arch and I…"

"I know. Complicates matters."

"You don't like complications."

"I'm a man of my word. You passed the audition, so to speak."

My heart danced in my chest. "I'm in?"

"Don't get too excited. I'm not sure about the future of Chameleon."

"But for now?"

"For now."

I squealed and hugged him tight. "Thank you." Overjoyed, I kissed him on the mouth. It was quick, innocent, but when I stepped away, he pulled me into his arms and…holy cow. There was nothing innocent about the way his mouth conquered mine.

I was stunned.

I was curious.

I needed to know that Arch was wrong. That Beckett wasn't a threat. I didn't encourage the kiss exactly, but I didn't refuse when his tongue teased open my lips. I waited for it. The white-hot *zing-zap*. No *zap* but definite *zing*.

Crap.

Panicked, I pushed out of his arms…and saw Arch.

Double crap.

Arms crossed over his chest, he raised one brow. "Feeling your way, yeah?"

"It's not what you think," I blurted.

He glanced at Beckett. "I'm thinking the better man made his play."

"He didn't…we didn't…I was excited."

"Just what I wanted to hear."

"I didn't mean it like that!" Flustered, my thoughts tripped over one another. I turned pleading eyes on Beckett. "Would you please explain? Tell him he's wrong. Tell him you didn't—"

"I can't."

"Why not?"

"Because I did."

I blinked, speechless.

"I knew this would happen sooner or later," Arch said in an eerily calm voice. "I was just hoping on later." He uncrossed his arms, clenched his fists.

"Go ahead," Beckett said. "Take your best shot. I would."

Instead Arch raised his hands in surrender. "Fuck it. It's as it should be, yeah?"

"Just like that you're giving up on me? On us?" My

words came out in a croaked whisper. Stunned and crushed, I went toe to toe with the man. "I can't believe you just passed me off to your best friend."

"Beckett isn't my—"

"Yes, he is. You don't want to admit it because friendship is an actual relationship. Now you're getting cold feet because *we're* in a relationship. At least I thought we were. Never attach yourself to anyone you can't walk away from. Wow. Beckett was right. When the going gets tough…" I choked back a sob.

Arch glared at me, hurt, angry. "I thought it was all about me, Evie."

"It *is*."

He got in my face. "Now who's being dishonest? You didn't look unwilling."

I sensed more than heard Beckett approach. "Arch."

"Shut up."

I felt Arch draw away from me. As the seconds ticked by, his heat disappeared before my eyes, cooled into something scary. Quiet. Resolved. And I understood it because—oh, God—he was right. I could've pushed Beckett away sooner, but I didn't. Guilt settled in my stomach like a ton of bricks. My heart and mind jammed. "I'm sorry."

"So am I."

I backed away, eyes tearing, heart cracking. I thought about what Dad had said. If Arch and I fizzled, I'd always have the Corner Tavern. It was a comfort, as were my parents, but it's not where I wanted to be. "I'm going to stay at my folks' house tonight. Don't worry—I won't blow our cover. I'll come up with some…lie. Smoke and mirrors, right? I'll be back on the job tomorrow."

I willed him to reach for me, but he didn't. He showed

only the coldness I'd always feared, the detachment that would allow him to walk away. I wouldn't let him do it to me. I knew I'd crumple into a heap. I couldn't let that happen twice in my life.

I turned and walked away first.

CHAPTER THIRTY-EIGHT

I WOKE UP IN MY childhood bed, exhausted and sad. What little sleep I'd managed had been fitful. I stared at the ceiling, replaying last night's fallout over and over. Arch haunted me. The hurt in his eyes. The disappointment in his voice. *I thought it was all about me.*

I ached for my journal, but it was at the B and B. I bolted upright. What if Arch read it? What if he wanted to know how I really felt about him? About Beckett? I cursed that damn list of pros and cons.

"He won't read it," I told myself. "He respects my privacy." Another pro. "Why didn't he fight for me?" Con.

Dammit.

Massaging the ache in my chest, I moved to the desk where I used to do my homework, where I journaled late at night. I searched the drawers and came up with a Scooby Doo notepad and a number-two pencil. Good enough.

Dear…Scooby Doo, Why didn't Arch fight for me? Because he thinks you're better off with Beckett. The safe guy, the nice guy. The better man. He told you the bad boy never gets the good girl. You told him it was all about him. Then you let the nice boy kiss you. Can you blame Arch for walking away? He's just giving in to what he thought would happen anyway.

"What should I do?"

He doesn't think he deserves you. Convince him otherwise. That's if you really want to be with him. If you honestly love him.

"I do."

I set aside the pencil, tore the page out of the notepad, then located my purse. I folded and stuffed my musings inside, then flopped down on the bed. Head lighter, I plotted my strategy, which basically consisted of the truth.

I heard a tentative knock. "Come in." I expected Mom, but it was Nic who pushed through the door. Dressed in sleek black pants and blood-red blouse, her dark hair combed into a sophisticated ponytail, she looked like a runway model. But instead of a designer purse, she carried a brown paper bag. I pointed, quirked a weak smile. "The latest trend?"

She rolled her eyes. "I stopped by the B and B this morning to grab my things and to say goodbye. Beckett told me you were here." She placed the bag on my vanity chair. "Couldn't manage that monster suitcase of yours, so I just chucked a change of clothes and a few essentials in here."

"Don't suppose my journal's in there."

"No. Why? Do you need it?"

"No. It's just… Never mind. I'm good."

"You sure?"

"Pretty sure."

She sat next to me on the bed. "Beckett didn't tell me why you were here, but I assume it's because you and Arch fought. And I'm thinking maybe Beckett was the cause."

I pushed myself into a sitting position, tucked my

tangled hair behind my ears. "Why would you think that?"

She smiled. "Because I have eyes. Because I've had more experience with men than you."

My cheeks heated. "I think Beckett likes me."

"I'm thinking it's a little more serious than like."

"He kissed me."

She arched a brow.

"I sort of kissed him first."

"Sort of?"

"An automatic response to great news."

"What news?"

I shrugged, the thrill dampened because of the fight. "Beckett offered me an official position with Chameleon. Fieldwork, Nic."

"Whoopee."

I tugged at the sleeve of her blouse. "Hey. You said you'd try to be happy for me."

"I am trying. It's just…Arch, Beckett, Chameleon—I can't see you thriving in that world."

"I'm tougher than you think."

"I don't want you to be tough. I want you to be you."

I frowned. "You sound like Arch. Speaking of…"

"I didn't see him."

My heart sank. "Oh."

Nic frowned. "You're in love with that guy, aren't you?"

"Yes."

"Beckett?"

"I'm a little confused about Beckett."

"Terrific."

"I don't love him. How can I? I love Arch."

"Christ, Evie. It's possible to be infatuated with two different people for entirely different reasons."

My stomach churned. "I don't like the sound of that."

She shrugged, a worldly been-there-done-that shrug. "It can be thrilling. It can be ugly. Depends on the personalities. With you, I predict ugly."

I frowned. "Terrific."

She squeezed my hand. "Fly home with me."

"I can't. I don't want to. Chameleon business."

"Are you sure—"

"No. But I want to try."

"Okay."

My heart swelled. "Really?"

"Of course. Just know Jayne and I are here for you if—"

"I know." I reached out and hugged her even though she wasn't the huggy type.

"I have to go," she said, but not before hugging me back. "My plane."

She was halfway to the door when a thought occurred. "Nic."

"Yeah?"

"I have to ask. When you first arrived, I thought I sensed...I thought you were interested in Beckett."

"Slick?" She grunted. "Please. No."

"You're sure?"

"The man's a control freak."

"I noticed."

"Do me a favor," she said, pausing on the threshold. "Don't keep us—Jayne and me—in the dark. We love you, Evie."

Tears burned my eyes. I was leaving one world and entering another, but I didn't want to lose past ties. "I love you, too."

In her wake, I scooted from beneath the covers,

dredging up my inner bad girl. The tough girl. The girl who'd know how to fix things with Arch.

Mom walked in.

"Of course I'm happy that Nicole secured a commercial shoot, but it's a shame she had to leave before she and Northbrook kissed and made up. Such a handsome couple."

I didn't know what to say, so I spoke a truth. "Nic's never been very lucky in love."

"They'll come around. In time," Mom said. "Mark my words."

"Spoken like a true romantic," I said, tongue in cheek. "When did that happen?"

She averted her gaze. "Don't be flip."

I smothered a smile.

"I have something to say, Evelyn."

I curled my fingers into the sheets, braced myself.

"You were wonderful last night. On stage. I'm ashamed I never encouraged that talent."

"You did what you thought was right." I could see that now and I didn't want her to feel guilty. "You wanted a secure future for your daughter. The entertainment industry is fickle."

"Still…I was impressed with your voice and presence. So much energy. Your dad and I, we're so proud. We understand that your home is in Atlantic City. That you want to stand on your own two feet. And, not that you need our approval, but we very much approve of Archibald. Perhaps you'll soon be calling Broxley home? Whatever happens, we just want you to know that you're welcome here anytime. For as long as you like."

Tears filled my eyes. "Arch and I had a fight."

She quirked a sympathetic smile. "I had a feeling."

"We'll work it out," I said, though I worried we wouldn't.

"I'm sure you will." She patted my leg. "Speaking of, Archibald called here a few minutes ago. Said he couldn't reach you on your cell."

I crossed my arms over my queasy middle. "I shut it off."

"He wants you to meet him behind the civic center in a half hour. He said you'd know the place."

I knew it, and the memory of our sweet moment in the tree made me hurt. What would he say? I only hoped he'd listen to my heart.

Thirty-five minutes later, dressed in the contents of the paper bag—gauzy red sundress and wedge sandals—I crossed the civic center grounds, determined to set things right.

Dressed in a suit, looking handsome and regal and dangerous as hell, Arch stood with his back against Big Love. My heart raced when I thought about the way he'd climbed to my rescue.

"'Morning, Sunshine."

"Good morning."

My pulse skipped and paused when he produced a bouquet of wild daisies. "The florist was closed," he said. Nicked these from the backyard of the B and B. Not as romantic as roses, but—"

"They're beautiful." I clutched the long stems and inhaled the petals' simple fragrance, willing my nerves steady. Were the flowers a preface for a kiss-and-make-up or goodbye?

"Last night…you were right. Cold feet. Actually, more like scared *shiteless*. Seeing you in Beckett's arms…I'm not keen on the way it made me feel."

I swallowed. "About me?"

"About myself. Beckett's a good man, Sunshine."

"So are you," I said. "I feel it in my heart, Arch. Otherwise I don't believe for one second I would've fallen in love with you."

His lips curved into a soft smile as he caressed my cheek. "Let me finish. I spent a sleepless night assessing my asinine behavior." His eyes glittered with sincerity, making me weak in the knees. "I worry I'm not the right man for you, but then I think I'm the only man for you."

My pulse raced, but I held my tongue, grounded my imagination.

"I've spent a lifetime walking away from people, detaching from relationships. That's the way of it in my world, yeah?"

"And now?"

"Now you're in my world and things are different."

Tears pricked my eyes. "I want to trust you, Arch."

"Then I guess I have to earn it."

"I want you to trust me, too. Beckett…I allowed him to kiss me because I wanted to prove to myself that I'm not attracted to him."

"And?"

I swallowed hard. *The truth will set me free.* "I felt a little something, but nothing near what I feel for you."

"I appreciate your honesty, Sunshine." He brushed my bangs from my eyes, smiled.

Zing. Zap.

"I've been staying a step ahead of Beckett for years. More than ever, I have a reason to *oot*maneuver him, yeah?"

Okay, that was sweet. That was…disconcerting. I hugged the daises close to my heart. "You're not going to turn this into some kind of competition, are you?"

"Sunshine, we've been competing for your affections since you bounced into our lives and I *dinnae* intend to lose. You've got a stranglehold on my heart. A first."

A smart woman would run away. I threw myself in his arms. "I want us to work, Arch. The bad boy and the good girl. I want you to prove your theory wrong. Fight for me. Woo me."

"Challenge accepted." He kissed me then, kissed me optimistic.

When he eased away, he angled me toward the tree and I burst into joyful tears. Carved in the ancient trunk for the world to see...

Arch loves Evie

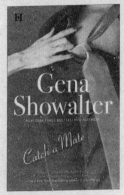

REQUEST YOUR FREE BOOKS!

2 FREE NOVELS
FROM THE ROMANCE/SUSPENSE
COLLECTION PLUS 2 FREE GIFTS!

YES! Please send me 2 FREE novels from the Romance/Suspense Collection and my 2 FREE gifts. After receiving them, if I don't wish to receive any more books, I can return the shipping statement marked "cancel." If I don't cancel, I will receive 4 brand-new novels every month and be billed just $5.49 per book in the U.S., or $5.99 per book in Canada, plus 25¢ shipping and handling per book plus applicable taxes, if any*. That's a savings of at least 20% off the cover price! I understand that accepting the 2 free books and gifts places me under no obligation to buy anything. I can always return a shipment and cancel at any time. Even if I never buy another book from the Reader Service, the two free books and gifts are mine to keep forever.

185 MDN EF5Y   385 MDN EF6C

Name	(PLEASE PRINT)
Address	Apt. #
City	State/Prov. Zip/Postal Code

Signature (if under 18, a parent or guardian must sign)

Mail to **The Reader Service:**
IN U.S.A.: P.O. Box 1867, Buffalo, NY 14240-1867
IN CANADA: P.O. Box 609, Fort Erie, Ontario L2A 5X3

Not valid to current subscribers to the Romance Collection,
the Suspense Collection or the Romance/Suspense Collection.

Want to try two free books from another line?
Call 1-800-873-8635 or visit www.morefreebooks.com.

* Terms and prices subject to change without notice. NY residents add applicable sales tax. Canadian residents will be charged applicable provincial taxes and GST. This offer is limited to one order per household. All orders subject to approval. Credit or debit balances in a customer's account(s) may be offset by any other outstanding balance owed by or to the customer. Please allow 4 to 6 weeks for delivery.

Your Privacy: Harlequin is committed to protecting your privacy. Our Privacy Policy is available online at www.eHarlequin.com or upon request from the Reader Service. From time to time we make our lists of customers available to reputable firms who may have a product or service of interest to you. If you would prefer we not share your name and address, please check here. ☐

BOB07

HARLEQUIN

More Than Words

"Changing lives stride by stride— I did it my way!"

—**Jeanne Greenberg,** real-life heroine

*Jeanne Greenberg is a Harlequin More Than Words award winner and the founder of **SARI Therapeutic Riding.***

Discover your inner heroine!

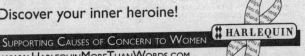

SUPPORTING CAUSES OF CONCERN TO WOMEN

HARLEQUIN

WWW.HARLEQUINMORETHANWORDS.COM

MTW07JG1

HARLEQUIN

More Than Words

"Jeanne proves that one woman can change the world, with vision, compassion and hard work."

—**Linda Lael Miller**, author

*Linda wrote "Queen of the Rodeo," inspired by Jeanne Greenberg, founder of **SARI Therapeutic Riding**. Since 1978 Jeanne has devoted her life to enriching the lives of disabled children and their families through innovative and exciting therapies on horseback.*

Look for "*Queen of the Rodeo*" in
More Than Words, Vol. 4,
available in April 2008 at eHarlequin.com
or wherever books are sold.

SUPPORTING CAUSES OF CONCERN TO WOMEN ❈ HARLEQUIN
WWW.HARLEQUINMORETHANWORDS.COM

MTW07JG2

Beth Ciotta

77207   ALL ABOUT EVIE   ___ $6.99 U.S. ___ $8.50 CAN.

(limited quantities available)

TOTAL AMOUNT $ _____
POSTAGE & HANDLING $ _____
($1.00 FOR 1 BOOK, 50¢ for each additional)
APPLICABLE TAXES* $ _____
TOTAL PAYABLE $ _____

(check or money order—please do not send cash)

To order, complete this form and send it, along with a check or money order for the total above, payable to HQN Books, to: **In the U.S.:** 3010 Walden Avenue, P.O. Box 9077, Buffalo, NY 14269-9077; **In Canada:** P.O. Box 636, Fort Erie, Ontario, L2A 5X3.

Name: _____
Address: _____ City: _____
State/Prov.: _____ Zip/Postal Code: _____
Account Number (if applicable): _____

075 CSAS

*New York residents remit applicable sales taxes.
*Canadian residents remit applicable GST and provincial taxes.

HQN™

We *are* romance™

www.HQNBooks.com